You are not alone.

Please call:
988
Suicide and Crisis Lifeline

THE SUICIDE MERCHANT

CHEYNE PECK

Archway Publishing books may be ordered through booksellers or by contacting:

Archway Publishing
1663 Liberty Drive
Bloomington, IN 47403
www.archwaypublishing.com
844-669-3957

Scripture taken from the King James Version of the Bible.

ISBN: 978-1-6657-3792-0 (sc)
ISBN: 978-1-6657-3793-7 (hc)
ISBN: 978-1-6657-3842-2 (e)

Library of Congress Control Number: 2023901996

Print information available on the last page.

Archway Publishing rev. date: 02/01/2023

What's worse than failing is giving up. It isn't life
that gave up on you, don't give up on life.
—Ben Weaver

PREFACE

"Oh! Make her a grave where the sunbeams rest, When they promise a glorious morrow; They'll shine o'er her sleep, like a smile from the west, From her own lov'd island of sorrow!"

Veronica stared, hollowed and perplexed, as the words called to her soul, as if the writer knew what spell would encourage that acute longing in her to end it all. She was just a girl. A girl, broken and destroyed by everything that hurt her and made her feel like less of a person, everything that had made her angry, sad, and alone. She meditated on the poem, drifting heavily into the plot where it would bury her, away from the environment that had made this life unbearable.

No other words had ever impacted her that way. It was as if the meaninglessness of her existence had survived only to see these few poetic lines. She couldn't hear the teacher's voice, not as if any of what was said mattered, or the whispered chatter behind her back that would torment her on any other day. It was all muffled and weak, losing its strength as the clock ticked on. Up front and centered high enough to glare tauntingly down on the class, the plain white face read three o'clock. Her eyes drifted from the whiteboard and loomed over its black pointy hands. Her sight blurred and then sharpened as a camera that couldn't stay focused. *Only ten more minutes to go*, she thought, then whispered under her breath, "It will all be over soon."

She had only to find repose in the last bit of time remaining. She wanted the last few moments of her existence to be just as peaceful as what she expected from her final rest. It would be clean and gentle, as easy as falling asleep. She had envisioned it for some time now, and her recent meditations gave her impetuous to see it through.

Veronica's gaze fell to the back of Keith Olson's head. *You will never close the door on me again*, she thought. Her eyes shifted to the right and focused on Bianca Lamberson's black ponytail. *And you will never ignore me.* Again, her eyes turned and found the sprawled-out jackass of the classroom, Dustin Tanner. He was the only student who found napping to be a better use of his time than anything Mrs. Rawling had to teach. Veronica could spit in the air at so close a range and watch as saliva and phlegm burst over his napping face. Most days, it was thoroughly tempting. *You will never make another fat joke. Neither will you, Kaylee, snickering behind my back. You knew I heard it. You always knew and didn't give two shits about how it made me feel.*

Her hand crawled into her pocket and began stirring her little cocktail of prescription and over-the-counter drugs collected from her parents' medicine cabinet. Most were the pills that helped her mother sleep through the nights when Veronica cried to the point of exhaustion. "Pills before parenting" had become the family motto. A few were the recently expired oxy pills from her mother's back surgery she'd started harboring a few months prior. And then there was a bundle she didn't recognize, but it looked like an excellent blend to finish the job. Now she had about twenty or so, sleeping pills and painkillers alike, a colored variety, all hidden in the drawer of her jewelry box until this very morning.

Her eyes climbed towards the clock again—eight past three. Two minutes left. Veronica glanced to the left of the room, where she knew she'd find a distraction to fan her hate even more. Heather Mansour, among all others, was the devil in the room. The thin, blond-haired monster who sat in her chair like a perfect angel, with a cruel vivacious smile, poised to fool everyone except those who felt the smolder of her fiery tongue. *How I hate you.* Veronica glared at her through the top layer of her eyelashes, noticing her smirky, blush-colored lips. *You will never call me a cow again. You will never say, "Veronica Dupree jumped into the sea. The sea jumped out, shouting, 'Don't sit on me!'"*

Even now, she could hear their echoes from endless days of taunting, still breaching the silence of the classroom in her head and their unrelenting laughter. Her glare floated over the sight of Heather's flower-print dress relaxing over her perfectly crossed legs. *You will never know what it feels like to be caged in by mocking crowds, shoved or yanked to the floor by your backpack. You, you devilish princess, will never know that shock of losing your footing as you fall back, the electric sting of your head and concrete colliding. And they laugh and gather to see what humor they can extract from your pain. Not one body standing there, willing to help, to stop them and save you. No. No one. You'll never be lying on the ground, listening to the words "stupid, fat bitch" linger in the air as you try not to give them the satisfaction of your tears.*

Her eyes shot back up. *Perfect little angel, my ass*, she thought with a sneer. She sniffled, letting out an accidental snort, and then choked it back in, hoping no one noticed. *I won't let them hurt me. Not ever again.*

Only one minute left. Veronica's legs started to twitch. Unexpected butterflies swarmed in her gut, looking for a way to escape. Her pencil was hot and dull in her fingers, "It will all be over soon," she whispered again. Her eyes roaming over the classroom, she began to say her final goodbyes. *Goodbye, classroom. Goodbye, shitty school. Goodbye, Heather Monsour, you bitch. I hope you and all your friends burn in hell one day.*

Suddenly, in almost perfect unison, she heard the deep whump of books shutting and the high screeching sound of metal chairs rubbing against the linoleum floor. This would be her grand farewell. Students rose around her; none she could call her friends. Not that she cared for friends anymore, but she couldn't ignore a latent desire for someone to notice her in the current moment. Embarrassed by that realization, heat gathered in her cheeks. She collected her belongings while grasping snippets of conversations around her. Talks about weekend plans and arrangements for some to hang out after school. Inside, she was screaming. Outside, she was as silent as a mouse, and just as discrete. Nobody asked if she was okay. Nobody cared.

* * *

Somewhere along Cherry Street, her legs became sluggish, practically sloth-like, as if hinting that they weren't ready to be laid to rest. However, she was determined not to falter. She reached deep into her pocket, jumbling and mixing the cocktail of pills. They were warm, sandwiched between a hot layer of denim and a sweat-ridden thigh. Curiously, she pulled one out and brought it to the tip of her tongue. It was hard, chalky, and tasteless. Growing numb to emotion, she closed her eyes and placed them back into her pocket. *"Oh! Make her a grave where the sunbeams rest, When they promise a glorious morrow"*; the words returned to her.

Determination forced every step. Her face paralleled the ground, eyes burning, unable to endure the brightness of sunlight. With each stride came more rationale as to why this was the only solution. School days were torture, and she hated every minute of them. At home, she was alone. Her parents were strangers, consumed by work hours more important than her and medicated sleep. It was apparent they didn't care. She had no siblings, thank God, but also no one to talk to, no one to say, "Please don't do this," and she used this reality to further digest her fate. Her pace quickened a bit more, now breathing out the rhythmic words, "It will be over soon," as she gasped what was sure to be her final cluster of breaths.

It wasn't long after that something made her choke on a dab of saliva and come to a jarring stop. Her face sprung up, following the trail of a shadow that surprisingly belonged to a child standing a few feet in front of her path. He stared at her with intention, as if he had expected to meet her at this place and time. His hands grasped a soccer ball just below his pudgy toddler gut.

Veronica's stride proceeded with an eerie caution. She did her best to pass by without his distraction, but every glimmer of her failure blushed the boy's face. She couldn't look away. Suddenly, a bold, high-pitched voice grabbed her ear. "Hello," was all he said, slightly winded yet holding an uncompromising grin. On his face, cheeks puffed out on both sides.

Immediately, Veronica went to glancing around for a parent or nanny or anyone. Somebody who would claim guardianship of the spirited child. It didn't take much observing to see that the boy was no older six. And that was being generous. He had big, beautiful brown eyes; she'd never seen eyes of such depth in a child before. They were void of childlike innocence, the kind that belonged to a man who had seen too much in his life. They seemed to hold a secret—one especially for her. His hair was soft brown and shaggy, falling just below his ears, and he was wearing a red-striped polo shirt and khaki shorts. He had a smudge of earth on his cheek that seemed to match the dirt pattern on his knee. She decided to try to ignore him. Besides, he didn't seem to be in any imminent danger.

"You wanna play with me?" she heard his sweet, raspy voice say.

"I don't have time for this," Veronica muttered, mainly to herself, as she skirted around the boy, heading for home.

He kept his eyes fixed on her as she passed by. "Why do you look so sad?"

Taken aback, Veronica halted. "Are you supposed to be out here alone? Where are your parents?"

The child shrugged, looking down. His little fingers began spinning the ball over the pudge of his belly.

"You be safe," she said, taking one step off the sidewalk to limp a few uncomfortable paces around him. She held certainty that she would never see his face again, and with that certainty came her final advice to such a young, spirited child. "There are bad people out here. People who want to hurt you. Stay far away from them."

The boy turned. "But you aren't one of them," he said.

His words stung Veronica in a way that froze her entire body. She couldn't feel the ground. She couldn't feel the breeze. She couldn't even feel the pills sweating in her pocket. If she was breathing, she had no way of telling.

"You should play with me," he went on saying.

Veronica mustered enough effort to turn and face him, thinking, *Who does this kid think he is?* As her eyes fell onto the boy, reluctantly, she asked, "Don't you have friends?"

"You are my friend," he said.

What he said punched Veronica in the gut and expelled every ounce of her breath. Her eyes widened. Her pupils went to the size of a pin tip. "Why would you think that?" she asked.

Without explanation, he tossed the ball toward her. It bounced twice before rolling to her feet. She looked down at the ball as if it were an extraterrestrial object that fell from the heavens. Veronica gathered all the strength she could muster and knelt to retrieve it. She took her time, reading the squiggly name marked on the ball in a red permanent marker and in all newly learned caps—BEN.

She then turned her attention to the child. This time, she felt he was speaking to her, not at her. "If you play with me, then maybe you'll wanna stay and not go to sleep for so long."

Her eyes burst. Her jaw tightened as fright draped over her face and left a sallow tone on her flesh. What he had said. How he had said it. It called her emotions to rise within her and take his side. The courage she thought she had to do what she felt had to be done unraveled with the few simple words of this … Ben.

"My daddy always said a new day will come. It doesn't have to be over. If you'd like, I can show you," he said. Stubby arms stretched wide toward her, calling out to her for a hug.

At first, she took a step back, only to withdraw it midair and settle it back in place. The last phrase came out with a hint of mystery. "What can you show me?" Veronica said.

"You're special," he said.

Veronica wanted to laugh, she wanted to cry, and she wanted to tell the kid to just let her be. However, the mixture of emotions took to her body like a drug, casting a hallucination more potent and real than anything her pocket pills could offer. They seemed to be producing a panic attack that lowered her to the ground. She knelt, trying to compose herself. Her eyes closed. Her breathing overtook her head, followed by the steps of tiny feet that crept closer.

At last, they stopped right in front of her. She opened her eyes, expecting to see an expression of curiosity, but there wasn't a hint of such a thing. What she did detect was a purpose. As she sat submerged in her own reverie, she could feel his arms string over her shoulders, wrap gently around her neck, and his tiny body pressed against her.

Suddenly, a firm squeeze crushed the shell that held all her pain and allowed years of torment to unfurl. The cold, lonely sadness she had endured for so many years felt as if it were melting under the embrace of this little boy. It was all vanishing, slipping away like dry leaves in an autumn wind. Relief was pouring over her. In the gentle care of that child, the whole direction of her heart was shattering.

At that moment, Veronica's head flipped back. Her mouth broke wide open to the sky. Her eyes were filmed over as white as the clouds. Her body shook, and her insides warmed with the tingles of several small bursts of electricity. It ran up from her toes, over her body, and out her fingertips. The child grasped her tighter as if he held on for dear life. Pictures began to flood into her head, ideas and visions birthing, too numerous to keep the old ones alive. The familiar feelings of pain, anger, loneliness, and regret no longer existed. There was no hopelessness. If anything, she felt reborn.

Just like that, it was over. Veronica lifted her hands to inspect them. They were the same hands, but everything felt different. It took her a moment to realize that the boy was no longer embracing her or standing before her. She spanned the yard, finally drifting her eyes down to where he was lying faceup next to the sidewalk. His body lay spread out as if he had lost consciousness before hitting the ground. His eyes were closed in a lifeless practice. The color had been drained from every part of his face and exchanged for perspiration glistening on his brow. The only part of him that showed movement was the foaming saliva that crawled out of his mouth.

She observed him for another few seconds, paying careful attention to his chest, begging it to rise and fall. At last, it answered her call. *Thank God*, she thought, but only for a breath as she reached out to touch him, hoping to nudge the poor child awake. Quickly, she drew back her fingers and cupped her mouth. He was breathing, but he was also cold—gravely cold.

"Help!" she cried out at the settled air. "Someone, please help!"

ONE

There was a war raging in the waiting room. A battle of patience, where the enemy's weapon of choice happened to be the small, rectangular screen that seemed to flash every number but the one that was theirs. Together, they sat, herded like cattle between rows of sweat-stained chairs, waiting for that one merciful number to blip up on the screen. The room had been overtaken by resounding noises of phones ringing, babies crying, pages shuffling, and loud personal banter. The raunchy stench of perspiration and old coffee tainted every sip of air, choked on like mustard gas by every poor soul who trotted into this free-willed prison, if only to bolster the essence of what hell was awaiting them.

From the moment he stepped through that door, the room was brimming with people looking for help, but no none ever seemed to make progress. Ben sat in the middle of this battlefield, serving his time crammed between a lady who looked as if she had slept in that seat all night and a man who smelled of aftershave and Cuban cigars. His fingers were intertwined, resting impatiently over his lap as he hunched forward, jawline set. At the same time, he squinted at the numbers on the wall, daring them to move. According to his watch, he had been there an hour and fifteen minutes. According to his head, he had been there since 2008.

At first, it had been amusing, watching the people scurry to get in line. Their lackluster bodies exploded to life as soon as they saw the one magical number that proved it was finally their turn, only to be told by a grumpy old hag with a disheveled face and a name tag that they had completed the wrong form or didn't have proper documentation. Pathetically and reluctantly, they'd turn around like a fool caught in a revolving door. Now, as it seemed like another decade slipped by him, Ben sat waiting in his piss-scented chair, realizing that he had become one of those fools. He, too, was stuck in that same revolving door of inconvenience—or more appropriately, he thought, a living hell.

The numbers flashed, moving up one more digit. Like that, every eye turned to the small green numbers on the rectangular screen. They feasted on it like visual meat, disregarding how far it was to the one printed on that scrap of paper clenched in their sweaty hand. However, for Ben, it was a meager two digits off. Two small, insignificant numbers away from getting out from under the fluorescent glow of this government-run madhouse and back to the sweet, sunlit world beyond the doors that read DMV.

He surveyed the room briefly, then leaned over to one side and reached deep into his back pocket to retrieve a shoddy piece of paper and a moist gathering of crumpled-up bills. Gripping them tightly, they looked more like a collection of trash blossoming out of his rifting hand. He looked around once more, noticing the woman sitting next to him in her nightgown-formed dress. She eyed the money with a distrusting sideways glance, gnawing at the corner of her plump bottom lip, feasting on the wad of cash with her glare. Ben glanced back at her while making an obnoxious, growl to clear his throat. The woman bolted up a brazen look, sneered, and quickly rolled her eyes. Reaching down, she picked up her bag, attempting to look discrete, and slipped casually away, letting her backside speak the vulgar cursing on her behalf.

Ben shook his head and sighed in disbelief before shifting his attention back to his money. He placed the folded-up paper under one of his legs and began to unrumple the wadded-up bills. Then he started to iron out each bill along the tight surface of his pants, sliding them back and forth and finally separating them into two distinct piles of unwrinkled cash—one to pay for his license and one for later that evening. He glimpsed the rectangular screen for a second as he worked, counting out fives and tens, with a few twenties popping up in the fold from time to time. He had two hundred fifty dollars' worth in one pile and a hundred in the other by the end. It was more than he'd typically carry on himself.

Consumed in his task, he jumped at the unexpected voice, uncomfortably too close to his left ear. "Going to be a long day eef it stays like this, wouldn't ju say?" A garrulous Hispanic man was now sitting where the woman had been. He'd somehow managed to sneak into the chair undetected. He was roughly twenty years Ben's senior, dressed in fatigued work attire. An old cap darkened the man's eyes. He looked at Ben with a pleasant, almost cheerful glare and carried the luminous tone of a spirited young man whose life had treated him well. "Ju be here long?"

"Longer than I wanted to be," Ben murmured, folding up the paper and cash and slipping it into his side pocket.

"Yeah. I just got here myself," the man said, obviously, as he still had that merry will to live. The man raised his hat just enough to show a contrasting tan line across his forehead. He offered his hand, saying, "*Me llamo* Hector, Hector Ortiz."

Ben investigated Hector's hand; a palm made of desert terrain. Hints of green stained the lighter hue around his fingers, trailing under the nails and up along the side of his wrist. He reached across and took the laboring man's hand. "I'm Ben ... Weaver."

Hector smiled, his eyes brightening to a hazel-brown tone under the transparency of the fluorescent lights. "So, what they got ju in for?" he inquired as Ben discretely pulled his hand away first.

"Suspended license," Ben replied, combing his fingers through his disheveled brown hair. He would avoid elaborating if possible.

Hector gave a dramatic grimace. "Ooh. Ouch," he hissed. "Me, I here to get my license." Then he quickly clarified, "California license. Yessir, I be here ... mmmm 'bout t'ree months now. Getting a feel for the land and all, ju know, that sort of thing. Of course, that's what I do, ju know?" He pointed to the logo patch sewn on the front of his cap. "Landscaping. Landscaping, landscaping. Been at it for twenty-nine years now. Started young, when I was just a *mijo* working for my papa." Hector leaned back, stretching his arms up and back into the air to release an airy grunt of pressure.

"Then I moved out to Arizona to make a life of my own. Work for me, right?" He turned to look over both of his shoulders, and then he leaned closer, invading personal space again. "Can I say some-ting? I hated Arizona. Hated it." His hand plummeted and smashed against his denim thigh, rustling up a small dust billow that rustled over his lap. "Too much dirt, not enough grass. Too many rocks and not enough flowers. I couldn't tell you how few trees there are. How's a man like me s'pose to make a living off that, ju know?" Ben shrugged. "I swear if I never see another piece of limestone in my life, I die a happy man," he stated as if it were a fact. "That's why I move to California. *Muchos* trees. Muchas flores. Mucha hierba … I mean, grass. And between ju me, lots of dinero to keep 'em." Out of his words came a light chuckle that ended with a sigh. "So whad'ju do?"

"What do I do?" Ben laughed at the thought. Such an easy question with a complex answer. That, and it was a question he never cared to answer. It never ceased to fashion a whirlpool spiraling him into some bottomless acknowledgment of his dismal purpose. He didn't want to be rude, but he was too vexed to handle such a burden under the present conditions. Unfortunately, his mind wasn't prepared to form a scapegoat answer either. "I, uh, guess you could say I work freelance. You might call me an independent contractor. You know … that sort of thing." His eyes grazed about the room, pretending to be distracted, but in reality, he was hunting for a savior to relieve him of this conversation.

Hector poised an impressed frown over his face. "Such ambition for a young hombre! An' work's good?" he persisted.

"Work's steady," Ben replied with a tinge of pain in recognizing the truthfulness of this response. He straightened up, unaware that this adjustment probably revealed some discomfort.

"Steady *es* good," Hector replied sanguinely.

Ben grinned a little awkwardly. His jaw clenched as he again leaned forward to allow his eyes to graze the floor, which was oddly heavy with the exchanges of all they had already seen.

Hector continued, "So tell me, gringo, how 'zactly d'ju get 'er license suspended?"

"I hit a neighbor's tree," Ben replied impassively.

Hector chuckled. "Wait." He paused, pointing at Ben. "Ju tell me that ju hit 'er neighbor's tree—*un árbol*—with no person, no cars other than jers, and dey suspended ju license for that? Ju drunk?"

A sincere chuckle took Ben's mouth. "Nope. I don't drink. And yep … for one agonizing month. Can you believe that?"

Hector's eyes furrowed while he slipped off his hat, wiped the sweat off his shimmering bald head, and placed it back slightly off-center. "Aya, *mijo*, seems little much for one accident. Sure ju didn't have a little nip—*quizas bebiste un poco*?"

Just as Ben was about to respond, his number flashed up on the screen. He pushed himself onto his feet and then tugged the bottom of his shirt down into its proper place. Hector looked up at him, patiently waiting for some reply.

"Don't know." Ben shrugged. "I guess it's because I hit the damn thing five times that month."

Hector fell speechless, allowing Ben plenty of time to offer a "good luck with all your plans" expression before strolling through the wayward crowd to find his place in line.

* * *

Skirting across the busy road, Ben felt reenergized. There was a pop in his stride, a spiritedness to his rush. Still, he did his best to compose his eagerness to be done with this pedestrian lifestyle and get back behind the wheel of a vehicle. He would cherish the walk home from the DMV for the moment, determined to make sure it would be his last. The weather had been perfect for a calm afternoon. Vessel clouds sailed across the vast sky, towing a breeze that pleasantly kissed his face. He gave no thought to where his feet were leading him, not until he found his eyes strolling over a reflection of his childhood on a street that had changed rapidly over the years. Old houses had been torn down and replaced. Yards of dust and debris had been tended to and were lush with well-tended gardens. Shops closed, and new shops opened, adding a fresh coat of paint to every storefront. The old video store was now a corner smoke shop. The Radio Shack had become a 7-Eleven. Even the timeless bookstore, where he would rush to get the latest issue of *Gamer Pro,* was now a quarter Laundromat with never more than a half dozen people inside at a time. Yet there was still a flavor of nostalgia he could taste as he passed by.

It wasn't long before Ben was on the last stretch of sidewalk passing by houses that had never changed. Out front of a yellow house with a traditional white picket fence knelt Mrs. Lucas in her sunhat, tending to the most spectacular rose garden anyone had ever seen on that block, her golden Lab Rosco basking faithfully at her side.

"Good afternoon, Mrs. Lucas," Ben chirped.

Mrs. Lucas turned, pruning shears held firm in her wrinkly little fingers. "Why hello there, Ben. Enjoying the weather?"

"Sure am," he said, reaching over the fence and calling to Rosco. Gray whiskers exposed the animal's age in a way that made him a suitable companion for a lady as old as Mrs. Lucas. He raised nothing more than his head at Ben's call, sniffed the air for a bit, and rested his head down.

"Oh, pish-posh, you lazy mutt," Mrs. Lucas hissed, slapping her dog on one of his thighs, hard enough to make a sound but not enough for Rosco to give thought to it. "And how is the Nelson clan? Are they treating you well? Are they feeding you? They better be feeding you," she said. "You know I have a room here for you. Cleveland's old office is clean and bare, and you know I like to cook."

Just then, Ben's stomach perked at the thought of food. With all he had planned that morning, he forgot about breakfast and coasted right passed lunch. With the turn of his gut, he gave up calling the dog and looked back at Mrs. Lucas. "Why, Mrs. Lucas, are you trying to seduce me?" he inquired playfully. "You know darn well they have been taking good care of me."

Mrs. Lucas turned back to her gardening. "Just checking," she said, snipping at the bush in front of her with her sheers. "Rosco can't be around forever, and it will sure be awfully boring 'round here once he's gone."

As Ben took a knee to retie his shoe, a pop and airy grunt came from his body. These days, it had become a common occurrence, especially when attempting certain tasks that any man of twenty-three should have no trouble accomplishing. But he was far from any man of twenty-three. And for that, he felt the aches and pains of someone Cleveland Lucas's age, had he still been alive.

Mrs. Lucas wiped her brows and peered up at the sun. "I think it's about time to call it a day," she said abruptly.

Ben grinned in agreement, fighting the sharp teeth of hunger chewing into the side of his abdomen. His heart began to pound heavier, making it hard to catch his breath. Large beads of sweat broke out over his face, drawing the moisture from his mouth and throat and holding back his swallow. The pain became more and more intolerable, beyond hunger, beyond anything he had felt since ...

"Are you okay, dear?" Mrs. Lucas asked, a pale shroud of concern draping over her face. "You don't look good at all."

Ben froze. Moisture pooled in his hands and dripped from his chest. He could feel his feet taking root in the ground beneath him. His muscles tensed. Hot blood pumped through his veins to the point of catching fire. His eyes widened, yet he saw nothing. There was no Mrs. Lucas. There was no dog or picket fence or yellow house. There was no clear blue sky or rose garden or sidewalk. It all went black.

Ben's body began to feel as if a weight was crushing him from all around, squeezing him with immense pressure. His entire body felt wet, his clothes sticking to his body like honey. Opened or closed, his eyes burned under this salty liquid. It burned his chest, filling his lungs with black water. Unfamiliar sounds swashed in his ears, progressing into screaming accusations and fist throwing that sent his head spiraling into a sense of vertigo. The clanking of bottles, the pouring of booze, the liveliness of a street—all sounds heard through the waxy ears of a homeless man. Ronald Miller—the name broke over him as if being called up on stage. One after another, they came, the visions of a tortured life, brimming in disappointment and failure, flashing faster and faster until that last still frame posed. Now he was there. Now he was Ronald Miller.

Gradually, the picture became alive, taking him in to see what he needed to see. It was night, starlit and empty. The hint of a cold, salty breeze swirled around him. The lingering fragrance of stale popcorn, salt water, garbage, and beer choked the atmosphere. "I can't do this anymore," he said with someone else's tongue. The cheap booze he could now taste saturating in his mouth. He looked down. Below, several violent waves crashed against the pillars under the dock, which were colored indigo by the glow of a stone-shaped moon. They roared and spat up at him, foaming like rabid beasts, waiting to devour him in their watery cage below. "Please, just let me fall. Let this all end." He was scared but not enough to step down. With his balance, held only by the support of the short wooden barrier he felt pressing against his knees, he teetered slightly over the edge, his chest protruding over the pounding surf.

Ben could feel his eyes close and his heart skipping that one vital beat that would tell him that this was not the answer. *It will probably only hurt for a minute. Just a little more pain.* He could feel the thought churning in his head. *And then never again.*

He teetered again, a little more and a bit farther, feeling the last few wisps of his breath being given away to the cool ocean air. He leaned over, allowing the wet atmosphere and the stability of intoxication to decide his fate. "Dennis, I'm sorry I wasn't a better father to you. I-I'm sorry I wasn't the man you needed me to be, the man your mother needed me to be. I'm so sorry."

There was weightlessness spiraling around him. It carried him down to where the fatal crack of hard water smashed his face. His head was on fire, scared and confused as the tide took the body of this man down, farther and farther, until there was nothing left for him but death, dressed in the obscure blackness of the ocean. And then, just as Ronald Miller realized how much he wanted to live, he drowned.

Ben awoke. He bent over and laid his hands on his knees, regurgitating the salt water that poured from his mouth and nose. Staring down at the pavement, he spat and snorted over and again, gasping for air until he could straighten up enough to get a sound dose of oxygen back in his lungs. A concerned, wide-eyed Mrs. Lucas was struck dumb by him, with a phone in her hand and the calls of an emergency operator playing like a broken record on the other end. Ben's face was cold and sweaty, bleached with a sudden rush of dread, but still held enough composure to let her know he was all right.

Mrs. Lucas hung up the call, just as Ben nonverbally instructed. "Why do I get the feeling this is not the first time this has happened?" she asked, not expecting a detailed answer but enough of one to keep her from the regret of hanging up the phone.

Ben felt the uneasy sense of bloating flood his gut and cheeks. His legs, arms, fingers, and toes still trembled from dread of the oceanic weight. His mind, no less rumpled than his body, fought eagerly against the dizziness that had swept over him as he returned. He stood there for a time, staring back at Mrs. Lucas, trying to ease her mind while at the same time composing himself.

"Uh, I'm, okay?" he finally uttered. Mrs. Lucas was even more baffled over the episode she had just witnessed.

"Hon, you're sweating harder than the devil at church." Her eyes shot to the phone in her hand, then back to him. "You sure you don't need an ambulance or something?"

Ben reached out and placed his hand against her upper arm. He could see that Mrs. Lucas was shocked at how cold and damp it felt to the touch. He straightened himself a bit more, enduring the torture for her peace of mind, and gave a firm, confirming squeeze. He then proceeded to hobble away from her, away from her concerned look and her dog and her house. His hands clenched into fists and drilled into his pockets as his shoes sloshed every step along the way.

Santa Monica Pier, he thought, not more than a hair after he turned the corner. He pulled out his phone and began to search for something on the web, urgently strolling through photos as he rounded the next corner. He knew that pier well. It was a stone's throw away from his Sunday spot, the place where he and Jeremy had been going for a couple of years and long enough that they had grown to expect them. However, it wasn't Sunday … it was Thursday, Westwood day, and he was expected to be there as well. He knew that Jeremy would show up. That wasn't a problem. However, it was his turn to buy. He had the hundred dollars drenched in his pocket, and that was a problem. For some, this was all they had, and this assignment could risk them going hungry for another week.

"C'mon." He sighed, discouraged as he scrolled through the strand of information, only glancing up occasionally to make sure he didn't run into a fence or some low-hanging branch … again.

Ben stopped to breathe and collect his thoughts. His brain was more scattered now than when he first slipped back into consciousness in front of Mrs. Lucas. Dropping his head back, he closed his eyes and began to pray. "Please, God, tell me what to do," he said earnestly. "There are a hundred people expecting me to bring them food and one man desperately needing my help."

Just then, something prophetic came to mind, a story he remembered from his years back in Sunday school about a shepherd who had left tending his flock of ninety-nine sheep in order to save just one, as if that one was worth more to him than anything else in the world. It came to him like an echoing cry, out from the depths of his very soul until it rang as clear as a bell. "This is your one sheep," it said. "Save him."

There was no time for food. Two right turns and a shortcut through a schoolyard, and he was on his way home with a stride faster than lightning. He headed down that final street and into a quietly discreet cul-de-sac.

Soon after, something popped up on his phone that sprouted a grin over his face. "I gotcha! Yes!" he said victoriously as he clicked save and slipped the device back into his back pocket.

On one side of the cul-de-sac, there was a slightly zigzagged, chain-link fence and moderately fractured unfinished sidewalk. A very different view of well-kept lawns was on the other. Near the end of the street and parked snuggly against the curb in front of a particular yard was a ghastly 1996 Ford pickup, forest green, rust colored, and beaten half to hell on the passenger side, and next to that, the tree that caused most of the damage—or vice versa. Determination fueled him as he sprinted up a long driveway toward the small guesthouse he had long been renting.

Without pause, he bombarded his way inside and grabbed the keys off a single nail, hammered crooked into the wall. Throwing the door closed behind him, he rushed back down, making his way to the truck, sweat faced and dizzy, praying once more that the old piece of crap would start. With a few forceful turns of the key, the lock popped, and the door squeaked open. Ben jumped into his seat and, as always, played a quick game of hide-and-go-seek with the ignition switch. "Oh, God, if you're there, please let this pile of trash start." The key slipped in. He turned it, and like the sound of a lawnmower, it puttered to life. Fumes and smoke spewed from the exhaust as he threw it into reverse and screeched urgently away, hoping he'd make it in time.

* * *

By the time Ben arrived at his destination, the sun had shone a molten hue, with bleeding ribbons of orange and red tinging the sky. Lights began to flicker while those studded around the outline of the pier illuminated in a surrounding constellation. Beachgoers started to thin, leaving not much more than a few scattered, dark silhouettes of surfers occupying the waters. Soon enough, they too would be gone. Reflections of the Ferris wheel and other attractions faintly appeared, dancing upon the waters. The bars and restaurants were active with crowds bustling inside and out, flashing pungent colors while outbursts of merriment cluttered the ozone up and down the eastern side of the pier.

Ben located an empty bench down at the west end, where the anglers sat waiting for their last catch of the day. He assumed as comfortable a lying position as he could muster while he waited. The air swelled in the cold from the ocean. The taste of salt filled his mouth with a bitter flavor, preparing him for the task at hand. A nervous sweat had long been accumulating over his forehead. Drowning was a first for him and happened to be one of his biggest fears. He had felt the poison of drugs rush into his bloodstream, choked on the exhausted fumes of a carburetor, and agonized over the instant pressure of falling several stories down, but never had he felt the scorch of drowning.

He bit down on his lip and began chewing. He tried to give his mind over to less frightening thoughts, but the heavenly view above coerced him to think of only one other thing, or more specifically, one person, and he couldn't go there either. It may have relieved him of fright, but it was exchanged for pain. He closed his eyes and began thinking of words to a song, which led to humming, followed by fingers tapping nervously on his leg to the melody. During this time, the sky grew dark. *How I wish I were back at the DMV,* he thought. *A cakewalk compared to this wait.* Ben pulled out his phone to check the time and be sure his last search was kept on hand. As he slipped it back into his other pocket, he heard a folded stack of paper crumpling under his phone. He realized he still had the hundred dollars he was going to spend on food for those down at Westwood. What to do with that, he already knew. Everything else was a worry left for another day.

The sun had long descended. The moon was floating indolently over the foothills, pulling the tide in and blanketing the shore for the night. Blackwaters glistened like polished silver. Waves crashed to the rhythm of nature's own song. A heavenly host of bodies and a city brazen with lights competed in a wonderful display from all around. It was all failed distractions, none of it worth glancing at for a second look.

His eyes began to weigh on him as he grew heavy with sleep, and this was only magnified by the stress of waiting for almost certain death. Halfway dozing, he heard a vague shuffle. He pried himself up slowly and gave his eyes a moment to adjust when suddenly a figure appeared in the distance. He was tall and scraggly, tripping over his feet and trampling bunglingly from side to side. As he came into the light, it was evident to Ben that this was the man he had been waiting for. Dressed in trash can clothes, a stained beard, and greasy black hair, he was a disheveled mess. Booze soaked and street ridden, he practically wore his hopelessness like a trench coat three sizes too big. This certainly was Ronald Miller.

Ben watched as the last bit of a cigarette flung from the tips of Ronald's fingers, launching embers of paper and tobacco up in the smoky haze, only to fall like a frat of withering stars. Ben stood and began to walk toward the man, pacing himself to make sure he wasn't just creeping on some random guy who had one too many drinks that night. Without reason, Ronald stopped. Ben stopped. Ronald turned, and Ben waited. Then Ronald began to scamper ardently toward the railing on the north side of the pier. *This is the guy, no doubt*, Ben thought as he began to rush toward him. Ronald stepped up on the lowest plank of the rail, his knees resting heavily against the top. His body swayed side to side with the ocean breeze, then back and forth, leaning more and more over the edge each time, ready to make that sloppy summersault off the pier and into the dark, frigid abyss.

Already, Ben could feel the sharp edges of the pier pressing into his kneecaps, just like in the vision. He grew dizzy for a spell, feeling an empty gut rummage through his intestines for something, anything to digest or spew out. For the first time, he was grateful his stomach was bare.

"Ronald!" Ben cried, choking down acidic saliva as he settled his throat and called again. "Ronald Miller!"

Head bobbing, Ronald looked over at Ben, his eyes watering with conviction, glowing by the lights of the pier.

"What are you doing?" Ben hollered.

In the same head-bobbing gesture, Ronald turned and looked down into the ocean. Ben suddenly began to see flashes in his mind of waves crashing into the beams.

"I, I don't know you," Ronald said, sullen, sluggish, and weary. A deep scar of southern twang was magnified by the effect of his intoxication.

"But I know you," Ben said. "I know all about you."

"Whaddaya know 'bout me?" he said, looking back to Ben with dark, beady eyes.

"I know that your name is Ronald Miller and that you were a good father at one point. I know that you still care about your family, especially your son. But you've made mistakes. You let your drinking get the best of you; let it take everything from you." Quickly he added, "But I also know that there are people out there who still love and care for you. Your family." He let the last word hang in the air. "They still love you."

"I have no family," Ronald murmured, his throat welling up, choking back tears.

"You do," Ben called, taking a gentle step forward. "And I can show you."

"You can't show me nuthin'. Not a goddamn thing," Ronald muttered, partly condescendingly and partly broken. His eyes were sunken and dull. His feet found themselves slipping down off the plank.

"I can, Ron. But you must let me." Ben reached out one open hand to him. "Please, take my hand. I have a gift for you."

A shade of sobriety washed over Ronald's face. "Look, kid, I-I don't know what this is or how you knew my name, but if you're try'n' to push your drugs, y-you just best be gettin' on!"

Ben shook his head, raising his hands to head high, palms facing the man. He took another gentle step forward, heal then toe, as if walking on ice. "No drugs," he said slowly. "What I have for you is hope."

Ronald drifted his sight across the sea of night sky and over Ben. An offering hand reached out close enough for him to touch it and then grasp it. He turned and looked once more over the railing. "I haven't seen hope in 'bout thirteen years. Not sure I would know it if I did ever see it again. Hell, I ain't even sure it still exists in this godforsaken world."

"I assure you, it does. And I can give it to you—right here, right now. But I need you to take that step down and trust me, if only for a minute. Can you trust me, Ron?" Ben said, reaching out his hand a little farther. The cold, salty water and air splayed around them.

Ronald turned back to Ben. Tears broke through the hardened exterior of a street-worn man to show the hurt that had been tormenting his insides.

"Ron, can you trust me?" Ben asked once more.

Without a word, Ronald reached out and took a step down. His fingers, ridden with grime and smoke, slid over Ben's palm and off its edge, wrapping around his wrist and trembling in pain.

Ben took one deep breath, held it, and then pulled him in tight, wrapping his arms around Ronald's brittle form. Ronald squealed, bursting out the tears that had been drowning him for so long. His arms latched around Ben as if an electric charge surged through Ben's body and connected with Ronald's nerves. All the pain, all the regrets, all the mistakes that led him to stand and drift over the edge of that pier began to dissolve within that hug. All the thoughts of his valueless life became less than a memory.

"Oh God, I don't want to die," Ronald cried. He felt the tears begin to wash all the hurtful things he did to himself and others away for good.

Ben coughed once, then again and again as steam developed over the two, exfoliating all the torment from Ronald's body. The old man could feel the hot slap of electricity running over each molecule of his skin. His head shot up. His mouth opened wide as a white film covered his eyes. Flashes of visions started to trickle into his head. The first was of him standing in front of a handsome young man, hugging him. The young man's eyes mirrored his own to a tee. He was smiling at him, like that of someone he once loved. Suddenly, he was on a porch, swaying back and forth in a comfortable wicker chair, homemade iced tea in his hand, and he was lightly sweating under the warmth of a Texas summer. At his feet, two girls were playing with their dolls, laughing and bouncing, asking him if he wanted to play. They called him grandpa. Another vision took its place with him lying in a warm bed. The man with similar eyes, only older now, was standing over him. His eyes were red rimmed and sad, but he had a smile on his face. Ronald turned his head to the other side of the bed to see three beautiful women, one of whom worked diligently to make their house his home. He was looking up at them all, his breathing becoming shallow, his eyes intermittently closing for longer and longer periods of time. His hand, which grasped another, was losing its strength. He was going away, but he was content. He was fulfilled.

Water began to gargle and spit out of Ben's mouth as he held on to Ronald. His throat swelled, gargling heavier amounts of salt water and dirty vapor. A deep crimson rushed over his face only to turn blue. His clothes dripped water around his feet, pooling under him. They were drenched in a deep oceanic stench. Soon the apnea would set in as he gasped for air, struggling to stay awake. *It's not over*, he thought as he continued to take in the years' worth of pain. Not yet. His body convulsed, spouting water from his mouth over his face and down his struggling body. He was losing his grip, losing strength, losing consciousness. His eyes fought to stay in place, using all that they had not to roll over. More water spouted over him, this time with a thread of blood. *Not yet.*

His hands slipped and dropped to his side. His knees bent. His stomach was bloated to the point of exploding. He could no longer see the stars or the neon rides or lights of the pier. He couldn't feel the wood planks under his feet or the embrace of Ronald as a new purpose reorchestrated his mind. He couldn't think. He couldn't move. As far as he could tell, he was dead.

* * *

Ben opened his eyes to see the soft glow of a crescent moon staring back at him. The wind felt artic on his body. He wasn't sure if he was alive or dead, nor was he certain the exchange held long enough. But he was still wet. That was for sure. And his chest was on fire. His head throbbed tremendously. He was ashen and woozy. In time, he realized he was breathing, which was more than he expected, but he still wasn't certain he had done enough. As he slid his hands over the damp boards of the pier and onto his chest, he felt the fast, steady beat, *thump-thump … thump-thump.* He was still alive indeed.

A newly familiar voice with a hint of surprise called out, "You're alive!" Ben's head fell off to the side, and he looked down to see Ronald Miller sitting cross-legged at his feet, a smile as wide as the coastline showing his relief. "You got something special 'bout you, don't you, boy? What the hell it is, you got me, but it's fantastic," the man said, passive and a bit cheerful. "You okay there?" he asked. "Kinda look worse than I do."

Ben looked back to the moon and ached out a sigh. "Yeah, no, I'm … good."

"Oh, well, good," Ronald said before pausing and scooting up to sit by his face. Ben sat up wearily. "'Cause I got questions. First off, what's your name, son?"

"Ben," Ben grunted, spitting the distaste of water out the side of his mouth. "Ben Weaver."

"It's a pleasure to meet you, Ben. Now that you're okay, and I'm more than okay, I'd like to know what exactly was that? I mean, my God! I haven't felt this sober since…" his eyes strayed with his thoughts before circling back to Ben. "And all that stuff you showed me when you did that …that," He pointed to his head and made a laser-type sound.

"Hope." Ben breathed deeply and coughed his lungs out all over the pier. "That was your life. The one you almost gave up on."

"Huh." Ronald took a minute to rake his beard, not exactly shocked the way most people were when he made an exchange. It was almost as if he supposed it. "Hope. I like it. An-and what about that man? Th-the one with the same eyes as me?"

"That's your son, Dennis. He's been looking for you." Ben sighed and closed his eyes.

"Dennis?" Ronald stood, shaking his head rampantly, wiping the water and dirt off his knees. "Nope. Nah-ugh. No way! It can't be. That boy hates me. He hates me!"

Ben began to try to stand up, his dank-fitted shirt stretching over his back as he maneuvered around to his hands and knees. "He doesn't hate you. He's never hated you. You hated you." He began to put one foot flat on the floor to push himself up and grunted. "And you let that get in the way."

Ronald fixed a wide, gleaming look. "So, wait. If that was Dennis, then that means that those girls are …"

Ben nodded. "Your granddaughters."

Ronald collapsed, hands covering his face. Deep, heavy breaths inflated his back as he cried for the life he almost gave up. Ben put an arm around him as tears glittered off the tip of his crooked nose and onto the wooden floor. Where?" Ronald asked. "Where would I look?"

Ben pulled out his phone, damp but still alive. "I …" He coughed, more water spitting off his cold lips. "I did a search of all the Dennis Millers in Texas and found one just outside of Dallas."

Ronald looked up and then sputtered. "One? You found one Dennis Miller in all of Texas?"

Ben crooked his face. "Well … one that matches the bill at least." He swiped open his phone and proffered it to Ronald. "Look. You see … daughters and all."

Ronald took the phone and drew it close to his face. His eyes glinted as he lightly touched the faces on the screen. "Well, look there," he said, pointing. "That's … the patio where I was drinking iced tea and watching them." Ben reached out and took back the phone as Ronald's eyes went blank. "How though? How will I ever get to them? I got no money. And as sure as hell, a bus ticket gonna set you back at least—"

"A hundred dollars," Ben interrupted, pulling out a wad of drenched cash from his pocket and handing it out to him. "These hundred dollars to be exact."

Ronald was dumbstruck. "I … can't … take that."

"Yes, you can," Ben objected. "It was meant for you." He grabbed Ronald's hand and slapped the cash down in it, sending trickles of salt water down Ronald's hand and along his wrist. Ronald looked down at the drenched money in his hand. Slowly, unbelievably he closed his fingers around it, giving Ben a look that said much more than thank you. "All I ask," Ben continued, suppressing a smile, "is that you promise me we will never try this again?"

Ronald turned his head slightly off-center, eyes gleaming with life, giving Ben a notching grin. That was all that needed to be said.

TWO

Lunch was over, and the students had started to gradually leak through the cafeteria doors in their everyday clusters of friends. They shoved and pushed in a disarranged line, insensible to anything other than the twenty minutes of freedom that awaited them just beyond the steel doorway. Then they scattered all over the asphalt and broad fields, greedily taking over the play yard, indulging their playful spirits before they were snatched away by a teacher with a whistle and another two hours of schoolwork. Along the outskirts of the field, the trees became animated by the Santa Ana winds. Shards of California gold beamed through the rifts of the branches, brushing patterns of sunlight over the yard's soft, carpeted grass. Up at the far north end, the pavement splayed bright and warm with tattooed designs of game courts, actively being used for friendly competition. Still others chose to lounge under the shade of trees, reading or gossiping about those who were the cutest, those who weren't, and those who were right or wrong for thinking so. Quickly the air filled with the good-humored banter of children enjoying one another's company.

Inside the cafeteria, where it was dim, the only sounds were the clean-up staff and the low, whooshing hum of the AC unit; Calvin sat alone. His brown paper sack was still balled up in front of him. His uneaten sandwich sat stamped with the imprint of Gabe Debarro's malicious fist. His chips, crushed into fine shards, sat wantonly atop his sandy blond head, leaving it to him to comb them out of his hair. The milk they had poured out in his lap while chanting, "Calvin Gardner pissed his pants," still drenched his trousers. By the time lunch was over, the liquid had spread out along his crotch and down his legs, creating a slow dripping pool that gathered beneath his seat to look as if he had indeed pissed his pants.

As he processed the embarrassing display that had become his constant existence, hunger ate at Calvin's stomach. He alone had been jeered at by those he should've been able to call his peers. Those who could have stopped it chose to disregard such embarrassment completely. His mind swam in the batter of lamenting anger, conflicted by the loathing he felt for the ones who taunted him and the others who decided to turn away. With the dining hall now empty, his face sank lifelessly over his lap, still traced with the blush of bitter rage. He sat alone. His heart ripped apart as another piece of humanity had been victimized at the amusement of a surly few.

The doors burst open, allotting a heavy amount of blinding sunlight to spread over the tiled floor, shining around the scraggly form of a boy named Travis Mason. From Calvin's point of view, Travis looked like nothing more than an upright shadow. As Travis called to him, he sat unmoved. Singing Calvin's name, Travis danced blithely over to his friend. His features developed as the door gradually closed behind him. His hair was left unkempt. His clothes were wrinkled and dingy. His wore an oversized black shirt with the word *Pantera* printed in red to look as if it were spray-painted on, cargo pants in military green, and shoes that looked like the hand-me-downs of a hand-me-down.

Calvin gazed dully at the boy who had been his friend from back when being anything didn't seem to mean anything. They met when Travis came to the school as a new student in the third grade. They realized fate brought them together during a PE session when both were taken out for questionable injuries during a softball game, one claiming to be the face and the other claiming the crotch. They spent the rest of the hour holding ice packs and discussing comic books and action figurines, those of the metahuman sort. That same day, Calvin went home to his dad, who protested that sports kept a boy social and taught one how to achieve victory and handle failure. He wanted to see Calvin apply himself to sports. Still, athleticism wasn't in his makeup, for which he gave credit to a genetic hiccup.

"What's up, butt munch?" Travis asked flippantly as he leaped onto the table and sat with his legs dangling off the side. "You going to sit here 'til the bell rings, or will you come hang with me?"

"Where were you?" Calvin asked, grizzled eyed, looking up so that Travis might see the abuse his friend had endured.

"Whoa! Crap. What happened to you?" Travis asked. His face showed a quick change of sincerity.

"Gabe." Calvin spat the name from his mouth like curdled milk, his eyes pink and swollen by a tragic number of dried-out tears. "Gabe happened. And you were nowhere to be found."

Travis threw his arms in the air, presenting himself. "Dude, I'm sorry. I was stuck in the nurse's office."

"For what?" Calvin snapped, his voice trembling, his hands shaking. "'Cause Lord knows you've had the flu like—what, nine times this year. Or, maybe it was something a little more intimidating this time?"

With eyes glazed over, Travis brooded down at his feet. "I don't know what you're talking about," he murmured.

"Oh, please. They push you around just like they do me," Calvin said, and Travis winced. "I'm not blind."

"Yeah, well … at least I don't go moping around like some kind of a wuss," Travis replied, overly defensive, as he leaned back and took a dramatic grab at his crotch. "I have balls."

Calvin raised a brow. "Really? And how did those balls work out for you when they threw your stuff out in the street last week?" he asked, snide and lowly. As soon as the words fired from his lips, he knew it was a low blow.

Travis twitched a smirking frown, fighting against the heavy amount of self-disgust he had for letting it happen, as if he could ever fight them all at once. "Let them try and do it again," he sneered. "I dare them."

Calvin straightened himself. He burnished the saline over his eyes, becoming fully engaged. "What are you talking about?" he probed, concerned with what deranged thoughts Travis had running through his brain. "They will try it again and do it again. And like always, you're just gonna sit back and let it happen because that's what we do, isn't it?"

Travis shook his head. "Nope. Not the next time. Next time, they're gonna get what's due them. That, I promise you."

Calvin stared at Travis, sharpening his sight as he watched his best friend work something out in his eyes, like the brilliant scheme of a madman. This was something big. Something more consequential than he might want to know, but he asked anyway. "Dude, what are you getting at?"

"Let's just say I have something in the works."

* * *

Ben grunted and moaned as he awakened in the driver's seat of the old truck that somehow managed to be parked halfway up the curb by his neighbor's house again. His neck ached and popped as he leveraged it away from the seat to peer behind him. He had to make sure the tree hadn't become the reoccurring casualty it usually was after his amnesic drives home. A bit bungled from the hard night, his sight was gradually clearing to see (for once) his neighbor's tree safe and sound and lacking any new contusions. The back of his shirt stuck to his body, still damp in places where it was sandwiched between him and the seat. His feet were sandy and pruned, riffling inside his crusty socks. His mouth had the bitter, salty taste of gargling seawater and fish guts. His hair was matted and encrusted with sand.

He turned back and laid his head against the rest, sighing with an uncommon relief. Looking up in the rearview mirror, he saw a debilitated version of himself. Half his face was worn pink with the intrusions of the cloth pattern of his seat. He was dehydrated, bloodshot, and worn out. However, he was alive, and so was Ronald, who was well on his way to Texas. He could only hope.

He pushed open the door with more aches and rolled his body out, his feet hitting the pavement as if he had fallen two stories straight down. The ground burned, even with his shoes on. Much like any other day, the temperature had already been set, blistering hot with just enough breeze in the air to piss someone off. It had that distinctive blend of spring and summer that had become increasingly common. His eyes seared from the reflection of the sun, which struck the fresh coat of asphalt, as black as midnight, as well as the driver's door, which reflected heat exactly where he stood. There was no escaping it, which made him frustrated and uncomfortable.

Tirelessly, he walked, grating his feet over the melting asphalt before scuffing them up the driveway. Looking ahead, he saw the homeowner's car backing toward him, reflecting the scorching brilliance of the day. Mrs. Nelson was in the driver's seat, accompanied by her two teenage children. She drove down slowly, rolling down her window and breaking just as Ben approached.

"Well, it seems you had one heck of a night," she said, her ever-cordial demeanor resonating out of her tone. "Didn't see you come in, so I sent you a text, but I never heard back. I wasn't sure if you were okay or not. Must have been a long line in Westwood."

"I wouldn't say that exactly," Ben croaked. "Truth be told, I never made it down there." He tried his best to fight the glare and look her in the eyes but couldn't quite keep them open. "Had a situation in Santa Monica I needed to resolve. And I'm pretty sure my phone is either broken or dead."

Mrs. Nelson looked exceedingly at him. "That explains all the voice mails from Jeremy on the house line." Her voice lowered to a hair above a whisper. "What was it this time?"

Looking deep in the car, he saw both teenagers consumed by whatever was on their phones, with lengthy earbuds ribboning down from their ears. "A jumper," he explained, "off the pier. He was going to drown himself."

"How did it feel?" she asked. "I mean … are you okay?"

"Fine, but the worst one yet, for sure," he replied, rubbing the bulge that seemed to be lodged in his throat. "I could have sworn this one was going to kill me."

Mrs. Nelson readjusted her grip on the steering wheel. Her arm twisted to expose a series of long, slender scars running from the center of her forearm down to her wrists. Even after all these years, he could still feel it. They never left him, the mementos of every exchange logged in his memory, though from time to time, hers seemed to flaunt itself more than the others.

"Good Lord," she gasped. "Did he have any kids?"

Ben nodded. "A young man, married, with two little girls of his own."

"Where is he now?" she asked.

Ben looked off in the distance. "On his way to Texas, I assume. That's where they live. That's where I saw him in his future."

"Thank heavens," she said, relieving herself with a long, drawn-out sigh as if she had known Ronald Miller personally. Ben guessed in some small way she had. "Well, you get inside and get some rest. After a night like that, you certainly need it." Before Ben could walk away, Mrs. Nelson quickly added, "Oh, and if you get a little hungry, there's a container of gluten-free lasagna in our fridge. I made it last night. Feel free to help yourself because the good Lord knows no one else will."

Ben mustered a weary smirk, hacked up salty phlegm, and continued his way up the long driveway, feet burning every step of the way.

As Ben turned the unlocked brass knob to the guesthouse, he recalled the day he met Mrs. Nelson for the first time. Back then, she held the name Peggy Tanner. He was at the cusp of being a teenager, and she happened to be a teacher's aide at the junior high school he was attending. She passed him a few times in the halls, but it didn't hold a significant spot in his memory, although he did remember their eyes meeting once or twice. Her rare, deep shade of red hair and hazel-green eyes would have captured anyone's attention for at least a moment. While he was tending to his studies and just trying to survive adolescence, she nurtured a dying marriage that she felt was worth her investment. All the while, she juggled a career she had long poured her heart into. Children had always been her passion, and she couldn't imagine a life without any of her own. This was her dream.

Peggy's husband, a well-known home builder around those parts at that time, worked tirelessly night and day to build a life of comfort. The more they planned and prepared, the heavier her inability to conceive pressed down upon her. "A future isn't worth a lick if there is no one to pass that future onto," her husband would remind her.

Unfortunately, time showed how thin the walls of their marriage really were. One day, those walls crumbled down in their final collapse when she stumbled upon her husband's other life. What started out as adultery had turned quickly into an affair, then a child and a new family. All this had been harbored under a façade of overtime in the office and obligatory travels.

Of course, when it all came out, he blamed her for the collapse by not giving him the one thing he expected of her. "This," he said, "was the wrecking ball that did the most damage." The bastard left her with nothing more than a thousand dollars in her account, a mind scrambled by the whisk of mental abuse, and a clear understanding that no man would ever want a woman so disappointing. These were the ingredients that distorted her sense of self-worth.

By the end of it all, he found a lovely new home concealed within the vineyards of Sacramento. In contrast, she found her life in the insect-ridden confines of a single-room apartment, left surrounded by the company of cockroaches, sleeping pills, razor blades, and suicidal depression. It was only natural for her demeanor to decline the way it had.

With that came days of calling in. To work was to voluntarily torture herself for hours a day. If she didn't show up, she was drinking and cutting. If she did show up, she was already drunk. Her passion became her curse. Parents dropping off kids, telling them they loved them from outside the passenger windows, gloating over their fortune with no consideration toward those who could never have. Hell, she probably spent more time with those kids than their parents did. She probably knew more about them too. And yet it was she who drove home alone each day to an empty apartment, not the hundred or so parents she had to pose a smile for each morning. "The hell with all that," she'd grumble as she poured another glass.

At that time, visions of her despair began to flood Ben's mind, particularly while he slept. He'd burst to wake in the middle of the night. At least that's what he thought. The first images interrupted his ridiculous, fuzzy dreams. Sadness dominated his feelings for unknown reasons, accompanied by a tinge of fear. As his world came into view, he gazed first upon his hands. They were the hands of a woman, clearly. Shortly after, her memories began to take over entirely. He saw things about her and felt things skulking inside her that no human should have to experience. This once spirited young woman had become a shattered persona of who she was. Broken into pieces by all her troubles, she sat on the brink of ending it all. He could feel her heartbreak, loneliness, hatred, and betrayal—for her husband and herself. She had let it fester and transform into a brooding monster like so many. He could see all of it, the past and the present. Then the bright hope of a future.

When Ben truly awoke, it was about four thirty that morning. The energy quickly began pumping through his body as he realized what he needed to do. He threw the covers off and promptly arose from bed. He dressed, pulling on the same jeans and simple gray shirt he wore the day before, as they were conveniently lying on the floor at his feet. He grasped and yanked on the black backpack wedged between the bed and the nightstand, slipping his arms through the straps to secure it against his back. Then he carefully slid open his bedroom window before crawling out swiftly. He made every effort to prevent waking his mom while avoiding the slightest delay. When his feet hit the ground, he immediately sprinted to the front of the garage and mounted his bike. Loose gravel spat from his wheels, cutting over the grassy corner of his neighbor's yard with every ounce of energy and leaping off the curb and onto the street. Ben took to the main road, riding over the corners of several other lawns and jumping his bike off several other curbs. Winded, he scoured through the dark morning, taking in large doses of the calm morning air, searching for the complex that would seem unreasonably familiar.

There it was. Its name still flickered, its tired glow bright enough for a young boy to find it in the darkness: La Casa en Emberwood. Such a worn, dingy sign, practically useless at such an unholy hour, had become Ben's greatest ally. He didn't slow down as he followed the chain-link fence that led to the back of the building, knowing his quickest chance of getting in was through the janitor's entrance. He threw his bike down, sprinted to the heavy metal door, and heaved a sigh of relief, fortunate to find it unlocked. He darted through the halls to where the office and main entrance met without slowing pace. He reasoned that it would soon be five o'clock from the distant thunder of garbage trucks rumbling down the street, meaning it was still too early for a staffer to see him breaking in. Just his luck.

Ben threw down his backpack to retrieve his lock picks and immediately got to work. He glanced intermittently from side to side with every other breath to ensure no one startled him. The door lock clicked, and he rushed inside, straight to the filing cabinets that lined the back wall. "Resident files, resident files, resident files," he repeated in a whisper. He trolled the metal cabinets, row by row, calling out the syllables written on every white label.

"Aha!" Grabbing a new pair of picks from his set, he surgically worked on opening the drawer. His fingers sifted through files as his mind recited the alphabet until he identified and grabbed the file he was there to retrieve. He slammed the drawer shut and sprinted out of the office, only briefly stopping to pick up his backpack, shove his lock pick kit in it, and slam the door shut behind him. As he scurried around the corner, he nearly toppled over the trash can on wheels as the janitor dodged out of the way. "Sorry, sir!" he shouted as he ran, thinking he might have to do some significant damage control later.

It was after five, about the time the sun began to peek over the horizon to shine a golden glow upon the front of the apartment complex. Ben knew just by this effect that he was hitting his deadline. Peggy lived on the first floor, and her front door lined the block. She was only a few steps from a sidewalk that Ben and his mother strolled down regularly, just never at that time of day. While he worked, using his skill to break in, he already knew where she was—and worse, what she was about to do.

Peggy soaked her despair in the hot tranquility of her bathtub like a pool of social Novocain, making herself numb to the world. She hadn't slept all night. Being that she decided this to be her last day on earth, she figured that time was more beneficial for downing bottles of courage and that there would be plenty of rest soon enough. An orange haze shone through the window above her as loneliness and heavy currents of privation coursed through her veins. Already accustomed to the procedure, it was simple. She would slowly pick up the razor and press it into her flesh. From there, she would get cold and tired. And that would be that.

However, she couldn't predict how heavy that razor felt in her fingers. Her ability to hold it steady as she pressed it tightly against her skin proved to be an unexpected challenge as well. But why? It played out so effortlessly in her mind—intoxicated or sober. Tears trickled as she clenched her eyes shut and pressed down. She could hear the flesh pop in her head as it split between a thin metal sheet. Weeping profusely, she dragged the blade down to her wrist. With pain came release. With the release came darkness that plagued her thoughts and grew at every attempt to slice away the harsh words her husband left behind as a farewell gift. Swearing to herself, she repeated over and again, "Never again will he make you cry. Never again will he hurt you. Never again ..." each time taking the blade to her arm and plowing another line of tragedy into her skin. Already, the water was swirling with the pink tinge of her bitter life. It was tragic and beautiful. It no longer hurt her body and mind as they drifted equally from this life. *This is how they will find me*, she thought. At last, her eyes became somnolent, the pain nearly absent and her mind still perceiving her never wanting to see this wretched world again.

As she faded, she heard the loud and sudden bang of the bathroom door, as if death were attempting to break it down. She tried to lift her head to see her intruder but lacked the strength. Water was coming up over her chin and seeping into her mouth, warm and pink. Suddenly, with a violent crack, the door burst open. To Peggy, death was a blur in the shape of a young man rushing toward her. She felt his body over hers, dressed and warm, heaving her up and out of the water. Even in her state, she found it odd that she couldn't feel her fingers or toes, yet she could feel every fraction of his embrace. It was the last thing of which she was consciously aware. Then came the light.

It wasn't long after Ben made the exchange that Peggy Nelson met her second saving grace. He was a widower going on three years with two children of his own. He was looking for that person to love and call his wife. His heart was open for someone who could tenderly adore him and his young ones as if they were her own. Indeed, it was a rare trait, but one Peggy had been blessed with for reasons she couldn't grasp until then. He crossed her path in aisle three in the grocery store, an unexpected meeting that followed with coffee, dinner, and an inseparable connection. That following year, they were married in a beautiful garden ceremony, small but lovely, dressed in ivy and flowers with a white gazebo opened to the kisses of a spring sun. At last, Peggy found her home.

Ben never saw the loveliness of their wedding. In that same year, Ben's mother became terminal with cancer. This unforeseen tumor fed off her pancreas for several years unknown. His days were spent watching over her lie in that cold hospital room as she held his hand, as faint and frail as a withering flower.

"It's all right, my love," she whispered, seeing his head hung and tears descending to the floor. "You have a gift I don't understand. But you are strong like your father, and I know this—it will not break you." Her translucent neck strained as she grappled for more air. Ben wiped his eyes with his sleeve and cupped her fingers with his other hand as well. She looked at him, life purging from the elegant colors that once painted her eyes. "You are so strong, my son. And God never gives us more than we can handle, whether we know it or not."

Ben watched as those few words took the last supply of strength away from her. Her eyelids flittered a spell. It took all he had to lean over the bed and press his head against her temple while listening to her shallow breathing. This was the last time he would hear that angelic voice in his ears. "I love you, Mom," Ben gently whispered into her pale, drooping ear. With that, she fell asleep to never awake again.

For the first time since he could remember, Benjamin Weaver had learned the pain of losing, the most brutal way a young man could, alone. There was no vision from which he could wake up. There was no exchange awaiting to be dissolved. He was a forlorn youth who found himself without a family or a home in the blink of an eye. Not growing up with a father and existing in the disarranged life he now inherited, he was the one in need of saving for the first time in his life. He could recall an aunt on his father's side, who was last known living somewhere in Hollywood. However, over a decade, to be more precise, that was years ago, and the last memory he had of her or her husband involved a brutal falling out between family. He could recall that as well.

It wasn't long before Peggy Nelson got wind of Ben's loss. Rumors of the aunt circulated among staff. Some were out of concern. Others were for the sheer sake of meaty gossip. For Peggy, it was a calling that tugged at the motherly desire she had harbored for so long. She yearned to take up that mantel left void by his mother. With each failed attempt to contact the aunt, her heart had become more set on obtaining some amount of custody for the boy. She knew his secret and its worth. More importantly, she knew what he would need to keep going. There would be an atmosphere no foster parent or government-run housing could fathom, let alone offer the boy.

* * *

Calvin and Travis walked home together, a trend that had become more common over the school year. The walk gave ample time to shake the dust of another school day off their feet. Well, ample enough time. In addition, something could be said about the boys being safer in pairs. Maybe it was because bullies like Gabe didn't care much about having to put any real effort into making other people's lives a living hell. At least that was the case when his goons weren't there to back him up. Thank the Lord for parents who picked their kids up after school. Sure, he could probably get a cheap lick in as he passed by them if he wanted to. That one last affront for Calvin and Travis to take home, like a punch to the gut or a more subtle trip or slap to the back of the head. But with Travis's fractious temperament, any actual assault would be no less different for Gabe than for a bobcat fighting a porcupine. He was likely to get his victim if he really tried but not without a few quills in his paw. Gabe was the sort of miscreant who hated to be pricked.

They strolled wistfully down the sidewalk, backpacks leaping from side to side, peaking nosily over their shoulders as Travis kicked along an old plastic bottle. At the same time, Calvin's fingers strummed across a chain-link fence while tinkering nervously with the hand-crafted necklace around his neck. The strap was made of leather string with a three-fold knot in the back, making it look like a small brown tail. The charm consisted of two small fragments of wood. One tied over the other, crossing each other slightly above the middle to make a type of symbol that had a meaning of a higher power.

What's more, this power also suffered on this earth but willfully. He had made it some time ago at a spiritual boys' camp. This was the only thing he took back home with him when his parents weren't sure if "this" was working for them anymore. His dad had become closely acquainted with the bottle, especially on days off. He wasn't a mean drunk, quite the opposite, but was still a drunk. He began missing shifts or showing up buzzed, not a good habit for a police officer. When Calvin came home from camp, his dad had already attended three consecutive AA meetings and hadn't taken a drink since.

Calvin found it more than ironic that the meetings began the same day he made the necklace. He had seen the symbol several times before but never considered it. Most days, the charm held nothing more than a bit of superstitious luck. On other days, it was powerful enough to keep his parents together and his dad sober through all these years. If only it was enough to keep him from coming home with bruises every day. Nonetheless, it had never left his neck for fear of what might happen if it ever felt he had forsaken it.

Hardly a word had been spoken between Travis and Calvin as they continued dragging the toes of their shoes across faulted pavement. There were a few sighs, a few unintentional nudges on the shoulders, collisions of scrawny arms when one wasn't paying enough attention to where they were going. But for the most part, Calvin seemed to care more about rolling the small wooden cross between his fingers and less about the company of friendly banter. Travis seemed willing to accommodate him, at least for a while.

"So … hey." Travis broke the silence while holding his attention to the bottle on the ground. "You wanna come over to my place and play a little Xbox or what?"

Calvin sighed, thinking it over for half a second. "Nah. I think I'll just go home, change my pants, and read or something."

Travis nodded palely. "That's cool." He paused and then turned to face Calvin. "Hey, you, uh, you ever talk to your dad about what's going on … like at school and stuff?"

Calvin returned eye contact, solicitous about where this was going. "Not really. Why?"

Travis shrugged. "I dunno. I was just kinda wondering if maybe he'd be interested in taking a crack at Gabe and his goons. You know what I mean … scare the piss outta them a little bit. Being a cop and all. He could do that, right?"

Calvin tittered. A dash of bemusement dressed his face. "I don't think so. Maybe lecture them a little, but what's he gonna say that won't make it a billion times worse for us? That bullying his son could lead to hard times in the state penitentiary? Please," He huffed. "Could you imagine how hard school would be after a scolding like that?"

Travis shrugged, raising an eyebrow and giving Calvin a sidelong look. "Yeah, I guess. But he does have a gun."

Calvin stopped, causing Travis to lose control of the bottle and look back at him. "Dude, my dad's a cop, not a friggin' hitman," Calvin said.

"I'm not say'n' shoot the creeps," Travis said. Then he mumbled under his breath, "I'm not say'n' not to. You know, just take it outta the holster, point it around a little bit, so they know it's there. Besides, he's practically the self-proclaimed god of the police force," Travis rebutted. He jeered as he placed his hand against his chest and articulated every syllable with an overly regal tone, "Judge, jury, and executioner. Am I right?"

"Not since he sobered up," Calvin said and then rolled his eyes. "And he's never been that bad."

"Not that bad?" Travis cackled in disbelief. "Dude, come on. The guy practically read you your Miranda rights every time you showed up to dinner a few minutes late, if he could remember the words."

"He did not," Calvin objected, then murmured, "not always. But trust me, he's about as passive as they come these days."

"Well, then get him drink'n' again." Travis snickered.

Calvin stopped. His head tilted. His eyes narrowed. A flimsy fist was sent out and struck Travis on the shoulder. "Dude, that's not funny!"

Travis stood there and took the blow as if it were a gust of wind. "That's it?" He chuckled. "That's all you got. Man, we need to muscle you up."

"Screw you," Calvin said as he went on and left Travis behind to dust off the punch.

"Hang on, hang on," Travis called, quick to catch up and be at Calvin's shady side. I swear I didn't mean any harm. It was a joke, a bad joke but only a joke. All I was getting at was that it would be nice if we could get the upper hand on Gabe and his band of thugs. That's all. I just thought that your dad might be able to help."

"He can't!" Calvin replied, sharp, quick, and clenching his necklace. "We'll have to find some other way."

As they approached Calvin's weed-infused driveway, Travis asked, "So whatchu got going tomorrow?"

Calvin looked around with a waddling gaze. "I dunno," he said. "Chores, I guess." He shrugged. "Why?"

"Well, I was thinking of hitting up that pawnshop in the old town," Travis said, his eyes tightening, his mouth flicking a twitch. "I figured you might wanna come too?"

Calvin gave a furrowed expression. A pawnshop? They'd never gone to a pawnshop before, at least not together. Based on all the movies and TV shows he'd seen, he figured pawnshops were the ATMs for petty criminals. Their own JP Morgan Chase was a convenient place to get cash for some hot goods. "Why would you figure I'd want to go to a pawnshop?" he asked.

Travis let his eyes drift to the ground, where the toes of his shoes began pushing around a few migrating stones. "I dunno." He shrugged. "My brother always finds some pretty cool things there, ya know. I thought we might be able to find some cool things too."

Knowing Travis's brother as a criminal only confirmed Calvin's regard for such places. His head leaned sideways in thought for a minute, mulling over his options. It could be dangerous, possibly, but it could also be fun. What else would he do other than yard work all afternoon? Pulling one hell-spawned weed after another, blistering hands, cut fingers, and a sore, crooked back—with minimal impact to show for all the hard work he put in. Then, probably, he'd go into his room and suck out a few brain cells while playing video games. Or he could watch his Facebook blow up with crude and hate-filled comments, all the while feeling isolated by his own parents. If he went, at least he'd be with someone who wanted him around, even if they were hanging out in a dingy, old place filled with garbage and stolen goods, which seemed eerily familiar to hanging out at Travis's house.

"Yeah. Okay," Calvin said, leaning more toward the possibility. "We could do that."

"Really?" Travis grinned, unexpectedly surprised. "Well, cool. I guess I'll see you tomorrow then." Just as Travis was about to walk away, he turned to Calvin with one last thing that came to mind. "Real quick before I go," he said. "I have a question to ask you."

"Shoot," said Calvin, not realizing how ironic his choice of phrasing had been.

"Well, I was thinking about it on our way home, and I was wondering. Has your dad ever shown you how to use one of his guns?"

* * *

Grunting, Ben woke up late that Saturday morning. He could still feel aches and sores in various muscles, but he knew he needed to get moving. Besides, the most prominent pain penetrated from the pit of his stomach, and only a refrigerator could ease that. He remembered the last thing he ate was the sandwich before the incident with Ronald. Not caring what he digested, he sloshed his way to the main house and pulled the gluten-free lasagna from the fridge. As far as breakfast went, he could've done much worse. The microwave seemed to desire to test his patience that afternoon, somehow managing to stretch two minutes out to what felt like ten. But he waited, still not lucid enough to do anything else. The youngest of the Nelson family clan, Daniel, slunk into the kitchen and poured out a jumbo-sized bowl of sugary cereal, eating it dry and with his fingers. Waking up in the afternoon was common for him when not in school. Those days, he'd teeter around the house like a zombie in boxers and an old gym shirt. He found a seat across from Ben, where Ben would watch him for a brief second. No "good morning" nod, nothing. The boy showed signs of teenage fatigue, the side effects of too much sleep, marked by red and droopy eyes. His hair was half-styled, half-smashed, and flattened against his scalp. Daniel eventually raised his head, dazed after staring at the floor for several minutes. Finally acknowledging Ben, he threw up his head to communicate.

Ben smiled. "You awake?" he asked while setting his plate down to eat.

Daniel scooped up a handful of stale cereal to place it in his mouth. Still, the handicap of drowsy coordination only allowed 60 percent of it to make its mark. Still, with multicolored marshmallows and rice cereal spilling from his mouth, he grunted (quite impressively) the word "Unfortunately."

"Hey, man, you, uh, want any of this?" Ben asked, sliding the plate closer to the center of the table.

Daniel grimaced, trying to choke down a mouth full of food without spewing it on the table. "No thanks. I'm still regurgitating the piece I had the night it was made. But you enjoy," he sarcastically said.

"Come on, it's not that bad. Besides, isn't this the type of stuff you kids eat nowadays?"

"Ha!" Daniel quickly retaliated. "My mom made it, and you're eating it voluntarily. So yeah, no current observable evidence is in your favor. Also, I'm pretty sure all that gluten-free crap started with your generation, man. And—"

"All right, all right!" Ben chuckled. "You've made your point. I'll own it. Good Lord." After a few minutes of chewing his food, he added, "I thought you were tired."

"What made you think that?"

Ben stared back at him in disbelief.

Daniel changed the subject without skipping a beat. "Have you ever thought about getting a motorcycle?" He shoved more cereal in his mouth while waiting for Ben's reply.

"Why?" Ben replied.

Daniel shrugged. "I don't know. I just …" He paused, considering the conversation's direction. "I've never seen you with a girl, which is kinda weird, being how old you are and whatnot. So I was thinking that maybe if you got rid of that crappy truck and bought something sweet, like a bike or something, it might make you more, you know … appealing."

Ben took another bite of the lasagna. "Actually—"

Without warning, the fork slipped out of his fingers as if he had suddenly become paralyzed. Lasagna caught just below his throat. His eyes widened, causing Daniel's to match. His eardrums exploded, melting under the pressure of a high-pitched sound that by all measures appeared to derive from the bouncing silverware. His sight turned obscure, filling with dread as he could barely make out Daniel jumping up from the table and calling out something that sounded like, "Dad!" His head began to swell. His mind went blank, tightening like an overfilled balloon ready to pop. A hot blast of pain seared throughout his chest and arms, crushing his chest and ripping every puff of breath out of his lungs. Below the skin, he felt an agonizing stab of his ribs being pressed until they shattered, organs exploding, filling up inside with heavy amounts of liquid. He had been shot.

Ben leaned back in the chair, trying to bring air back into his lungs without choking on the mangled-up food still residing in his mouth. As Daniel rushed to seek help, Ben's eyes went dark, leaving them shrouded in a film of dense, ashy blackness, unable to see anything actual or visionary. He began to pant short, diminishing breaths, none seeming to reach below his throat. A thick cud of lasagna spat from his mouth while his body lurched forward, attempting to use the table to pound the life back into his chest. For the first time in his life, he could see nothing, read nothing out of whoever's fate this was. His mind had somehow become lost in the darkness. His body was practically vegetative, head and arms sprawled out over the table, lifeless but aware.

Suddenly, he heard the high-pitched sound fuse into the clinking chimes of a bell. Not just any bell but a distinct warning bell, unmistakable to the one he remembered initiating his middle school's fire drill. Suddenly, his body jolted, manipulated and overpowered by the indomitable blast of another gunshot, followed by the sound of several children keening and more gunfire ... much, much more. The looming stench of gunpowder rose from his gut and bled into his nostrils. He could feel the soul slipping away from his body as he shuddered on the table. He could feel the warm, tacky blood drain amply from his gut. His mouth gargled the metallic flavor as he tried to breathe and stay conscious, slipping further and further away. His ears became muffled to the innocent yowls of children falling victim in the assassin's wake. Then he saw them, not people but two different lights, a red one and a blue one, pulsating with rage, scouring in the darkness, looking for more victims. It was then that Ben realized that this was not just another one of his usual dark episodes. No. This was different. This was a warning.

THREE

It had rained unusually heavy in Greeley, with the weekly forecast set to gloom. The senior back-to-school picnic had been canceled, as had most of the town's outdoor activities. The view of the mountains had been overtaken by a low, rippling sea of swarthy grays. Dismal clouds billowed and were surged over with even heavier ones, bringing with them a wet, humid scent that seemed to rise off the trees and asphalt until it became almost suffocating. The atmosphere began to tarry with depression until the despair was unbearable. All this had complemented Danica's mood for some time now.

She curled up in her favorite armchair. The side of her head rested on her hands, one over the other on the armrest, as her legs curled into her chest. She watched the rain drizzle down the living room's massive front window, beads of water racing like a flurry of shooting stars. Things had been vastly different only five months ago when the sun shone bright, and the birds serenaded her each morning. She now felt immune to all those deceitful feelings as she stared out at the horrific world beyond her home. Now it was common for a tear to creep from the corner of her eye, down her temple, and rest atop her hand. What she couldn't understand was how she got to this place. Was it that fate wouldn't allow her to react to one problem before another stepped directly in front of her? If so, as retaliation, all she could do was give up trying.

The previous night, she dreamt that things had never changed, the first decent dream she had had in a while. In her dream, she remembered thinking that she'd never take the joys of life for granted again.

She used to believe that if she remained kind to others, life would repay her with favor and success. She never claimed perfection but remained determined to strive for it. After all, she had the brains, beauty, and common sense to know what to do with both. Her long blonde hair reached down to the middle of her waist, and she had big, brown, doe-like eyes. She was the school's cheer captain and held a GPA at the top of her class. Still, none of that compared to how it felt to walk under a boy's arm who most girls could only drool over from across the quad, while etching their names within a heart on the jacket of their books.

She trusted him. So why did it have to be him who caused her dream to end so abruptly? So painfully. Every time she saw him walking toward her with that boyish grin, it made her weak in the knees, even after they started dating. That reaction quickly changed. Her subconscious knew something terrible would happen that night, and everything she observed indicated it.

Most nights, while she dreamt, she could hear faint laughter fuse around her. Always, she was at school. A plague of students walked past without acknowledging her existence, as if they knew she wasn't actually there somehow. Suddenly he was there, sundering the crowds around him, wearing his most insidious smile. His eyes gleamed with a blend of excitement and fury as they looked directly into hers. He began joining in the laughter, but the volume of his overpowered the others. A flash, and he was inches from her face. She stepped back. With brutal force, he pushed her, shoving the front of her chest without restraint, taking her balance and air from her lungs as she dreadfully fell back.

Every time, it was in the middle of that hard fall that Danica instantly jerked awake. The dream hadn't been a bad omen but a brief reflection of what had happened. It played with her emotions the same way her physical existence had. Nothing about it brought relief, but nothing about it could drive her further into such boundless hopelessness either.

She watched her dad's Lexus pull up into the driveway, remembering when she enjoyed weekday evenings when her parents were home. She studied, laying out her cheer outfit for the next day while her mom played music in the background. While her mom danced around the kitchen preparing dinner, her dad would sit at the table and earnestly share ideas, constantly pressuring Danica to share her own. His favorite topics had always been theology and economics. Probably because he worked as a deacon at the First Baptist Church and ran the small yet successful Briggs Hardware Store.

Her mother worked as a part-time event coordinator for an assisted-living facility. To most, she was quite stunning, with beach-wavy blonde hair that hung to the center of her back, soft brown eyes, and a figure that showed no evidence of ever bearing a child. Both parents became a staple in the community, highly regarded by those who knew them inside and out of church circles.

Her dad got out of the car and began swiftly moving plants to shelter as she dwelt on how thankful she was that her parents hadn't lost their admired status even when she lost hers. This made them somewhat oblivious to everything that had gone on in her life recently, which went into a domino effect by her first mistake, Justin Thompson.

She had known him since middle school, though she hadn't caught his eye until their sophomore year in high school. Right out of the gate, Justin came with a playboy reputation that took its mark in middle school and road it all throughout his academic career. It was becoming of such a fellow. He was an outgoing, charming, and charismatic young man who had dated the cutest, most prevalent girls. Popularity and a strong throwing arm expanded his horizons in that department.

In the beginning, Algebra II was the only natural setting where they had acquaintance with each other. She remembered vividly how Mrs. Atmore pointed her in the direction of her assigned seat. He was already positioned at the same table, observing everyone and everything but her. He was a prominent babe with sandy blond hair that he wore shaggily, and his baby blue eyes glistened even in a dimly lit room. When he grinned, his dimples never failed to gain notice by those who were looking back at him, like a whirlpool sucking in the room's attention. He sat hunched over, with his elbows on the table, exposing his biceps. She sat down and pulled out her algebra book, notebook, and pencil, acting as if she hadn't noticed. Only when taking dribbled notes could she bask in the exhilaration being seated next to him produced. Mrs. Atmore gave a quick introduction and then began writing out problems on the whiteboard, and this was when Justin spoke for the first time in her presence.

At one point, and without initiation, Justin leaned a hair in her direction. He muttered, "Doesn't Mrs. Atmore remind you of Mrs. Crawley from *Downton Abbey*?" while surveying the teacher from where he sat.

The sound of his voice startled Danica. She replied, doing her best to keep her focus straight ahead. "I would find that somewhat funny, except that it's not, especially now that I know you watch *Downton Abbey*." Danica felt the corners of her mouth fight to rise as she did her best to suppress a smile. From the corner of her eye, she could see his perfectly formed head slowly turn to look at her.

"It's a sophisticated show," he said as defensively as he could without attracting attention. "You seem like you might be the kind of girl who would appreciate a show like that."

Danica turned to face him; his expression was stern, but he had a glisten of humor in his eyes. Was that a compliment or an insult? She couldn't tell. But she couldn't help but smile back at him, fighting the urge to laugh aloud.

The next few weeks went just like this, hitting it off with jokes and slight hints of sarcasm. They both had a similar sense of humor, and their peers began commenting on how they would make a perfect couple. When the reality set in that they could eventually become a thing, Danica started dreaming about how they would climb the social ladder together and positively impact the school. After all, she was the cheer captain and head of the student council. And she already had influence over her social circles. It was only reasonable that the rest of their high school career would play out in supreme bliss with them together.

Early in their blooming relationship, Danica caught wind that he regularly attended youth group at Stonebrook Baptist Church. This was another checkmark on a long list of must-haves for dating potential. His family had made a small fortune off cattle and oil, though he never seemed to flaunt it. He presented the image of being humble and well mannered. He held the door for women and helped coach baseball for underprivileged youth at the YMCA, something that, Danica thought, won him major bonus points.

She recalled their first official date with mixed feelings. When her dad answered the door, Justin immediately held out his hand and introduced himself. Not being impressed, her dad asked him the usual father-type questions, such as, where are you going, what will you be doing, and when can we expect our daughter home. Justin not only answered all his questions with extravagant politeness but also showed enough backbone to ask her dad questions in return. He asked him if he'd feel more comfortable if they had a chaperone, or if he preferred, they stay at the house until they could acquire one. He asked him about his daughter and what kind of things she enjoyed doing. This impressed her dad more than the superficial "Yes, sir," "No, sir" responses that most boyfriends offered.

By the time Danica emerged from upstairs ready to go, Justin and her dad were laughing hysterically over a scene that had just taken place on her dad's favorite show. She folded her arms and leaned against the wall, entertained by their amusement. She watched them repeatedly replay the clip, laughing more intensely with each repeat. When Justin finally noticed her, his smile didn't fade but only changed in a way that hinted to her how much he enjoyed being there.

They decided to forgo a drive to walk half a block to a well-lit park. Justin looked up at the stars as they strolled down the sidewalk, not uttering a word for the first awkward minutes. As they walked, a whispering gust blew through Danica's hair and sent it afloat, just in time to spot an elderly couple taking their diurnal stroll in the night chill. Each step was taken with caution as they crossed paths, washed in gold streetlights. Bones quivered. Aged fingers laced permanently in each other's hands, as if they had been together for centuries and had never desired to let go. A blushing idea welled inside Danica—a thought that this night could very well be the first night of forever with the hand that held hers. She couldn't help but smile as her gaze drifted to her clasped hand and made a permanent memory of what she felt and what she saw. She was in love.

After a strand of laconic moments together, they got to a place where they felt comfortable talking and joking about school, family, and dreams of their futures. The quiet evening brought a calmness to the butterflies in her stomach. It was only after she felt comfortable that Justin told her, "I saw you." A shy smile crossed his face. "When you didn't think I did, I did."

A little embarrassed that he had somehow been in her head, Danica responded, "What do you mean? I didn't—"

He nudged her playfully on the side. "It was your confidence," he said. "The way you are with your friends. Most girls don't smile as much as you do—or lecture. You have opinions, deep ones. I can only guess you get that from your dad." He grinned, dimples set, and looked directly at her. "Not that that's a bad thing. Quite the opposite. You don't look at anyone as if you're comparing yourself to them." Danica's face settled on confusion, stopping for a time to process where he was going in all of this. Justin sighed, looking up at the diamond-encrusted sky. "Sorry. I don't know how to say it without sounding cliché." Now he looked down at his feet. "You're just you. I like that."

"You're such an idiot." Danica gently pushed his shoulder while laughing and went on walking. "I'm hungry. Are you hungry?"

Justin quickly caught up, taking the lead before turning to face her. "Okay, are you hot? Yes. So maybe that caught my attention first," he said with suppressed laughter. "But that's not a bad thing either."

"Well, you want to know what I first thought about you?" she asked.

"No, actually. I really don't," Justin said sarcastically.

"Well, you are going to hear it anyway," Danica replied. "I thought you were probably the most beautiful boy I'd ever seen."

Now it was Justin's turn to stop. "Wow! So you see me as just a boy?"

"Absolutely," she said. "You also probably lack something significant, being that you're too perfect in outward appearance and all."

"And … do I?"

Danica squished one side of her face as if she had to think about it for a moment. "Too early to tell, but there are definitely red flags." She chuckled.

Justin didn't respond as he escorted her over to the swing set. Danica scooted onto one of the swings as Justin held the chain links to hold it steady for her. He began pushing her gently. The rest of their evening, they continued the half-sincere, half-sarcastic conversation.

Later, they grabbed dinner at a small but sophisticated bistro, cluttered with locals and the soft glow of low-hanging lights. Small, circular tables dressed in tea candles offered a cozy sense of intimacy throughout the meal. Danica had spent most of the night gazing at Justin, bemused by his words, actions, and eye contact. At one point, Justin brought his face close to hers as he lifted his hand to graze his fingers gently down the side of her face. Anything he said or did from that moment was perfect, from "How's your meal" to "Good night" and his soft, subtle kiss on her cheek that he left her with as the gift for a sweet dream.

Three months into their relationship, most of her walls came down. He gained most of her trust by asking all the right questions and exhibiting the right behaviors. Yet he still held a bit of mystery that kept her on her toes. She enjoyed that about him. It kept her intrigued. When he'd give her a gentle touch on the cheek as he spoke to her or brushed her hair back, every touch and word made her fall for him harder.

One bright and clear day, Justin took it upon himself to drive her home from school, joking that he needed to accompany her to protect her from Mr. Grady's dog, a tyrant Yorkie who liked to try to nip at people's feet as they walked by. He drove slowly, keeping one hand on the wheel while the other was fused to her hand. They plunged into a light conversation, ignoring the matters of deep subjects like politics and family. After stopping, he idly walked her to her front porch and took a seat on the top step. She automatically sat down at his side.

"And I take it you believe in marriage," he said, a far cry from their previous banter. The statement almost sounded like a question.

Again, Danica was lost as to where he was going but felt compelled to find out. "Of course, I do. Don't you?" she inquired.

Justin unraveled a smirk. He took her hand and laced his fingers between hers. "Yeah. I just wonder why most fail." He paused for a moment and rolled their hands so that his lay over hers. "Do you ever think about that? Surely people go into it with the right intentions, and if you believe in true love, I don't know, it just doesn't make sense." He leaned over and grabbed a twig and gave it a good toss into some bushes.

Danica was concerned about his doubt but pleasantly surprised that he had opened up this much without quickly turning the topic into a witty remark. "It probably comes down to selfishness—maybe? People stop giving and start expecting too much." She wasn't sure if she agreed with her own comment, so she made no effort to elaborate while remaining in thought.

"Do you think people give too much before they're married?" he said, still hunched over but now looking at her with squinty eyes. Danica wasn't sure she understood what he meant, and her expression must have revealed it. He looked back down and continued, "I mean, with intercourse and all. Do you think people should wait?"

"I plan to" was her instant reply. She assumed he did, too, but now she wasn't sure. "I really want to," she solidified. "It's a sacred thing. Don't you think?" she pressed. Danica leaned over, keeping her eyes fixed on him as her hair cascaded over her knees and grazed the ground. "I mean, you plan to wait too, don't you?"

He took his time responding. "I like the idea of it, but I also like the idea of being with someone that I have felt … love. I could wait if I had to." Justin slipped his hand out of hers and stood up. He brushed off his thighs, throwing Danica into an emotional spiral. "Thanks for letting me be your bodyguard. Now you owe me one." He grinned.

"Or my heels do at least." She stretched her legs out and wiggled her toes.

"I better get going," he said.

She looked at him, baffled. "Are you coming by later?"

"Can't. My dad has me pulling crap out of the attic all evening."

"Ah, good. Building up those lumberjack muscles to survive this tough terrain we find ourselves in!"

"Sure. Something like that," Justin replied before lunging a finger down his mouth and making a choking sound. He then rested a hand on her cheek and gave her a steady kiss. With that, he was gone, leaving Danica to want him more.

Shortly after, a profound incident caused what Danica saw as a defining advancement in their relationship. The first of two occurrences would scar her life beyond mending. It was a few short days. The school day ended, and Danica was in the locker room getting dressed after practice. She noticed her duffel bag had been stuffed in the wrong locker, a mistake she could not recall making. Scouring the lockers, line by line, row by row, Danica tried to remember where a thoughtless mind might have misplaced her things. Never had she bothered using a lock since the only thing of value was her phone, and she'd kept that on her during rehearsals. Now that her time had been compromised, rummaging through walls of vacant lockers, a lock didn't seem like a bad idea. After all, Justin was waiting.

By the time she found her bag, the other girls had finished dressing. They shuffled out, saying their goodbyes, leaving Danica by herself. Her tank top cowled over her face when she heard the footsteps rushing behind her. Before she could turn, she felt one arm contract around her waist and another around her neck—both from behind. Someone's head nuzzled into her neck with a scent unfamiliar. Someone was clearly bigger and stronger than her, leaving her to push and scream. A semi-calloused hand sloppily covered her mouth. It tasted of leather and sod. She tried to bite down on any bit of flesh she could trap in her teeth, but not a morsel took. The assaulter's other hand began to slither around her midsection, playfully sinister. All the while, Danica's tank top still hung awkwardly around her face and shoulders. At one point, he spun her and slammed her back into the cool metal wall of lockers. He pressed against her, crushed her, skin to skin, violating his way from her face down to her shoulders and chest, clawing at her abdomen and leading straight to her—

"Danica!" She heard Justin call her name and then yank the culprit off her with extreme force. A heavy thud rattled down the lockers as he slammed the senior, Braydon, against them. "What's your problem, man!" Justin yelled in his face. "What the hell are you thinking!"

Danica stumbled back and fell to the floor. The sudden violation had struck her down to the marrow of her rigid bones. Justin grabbed a fist full of his shirt and began slapping him, palm cracking against cheek once, twice, three times over. Braydon looked from Justin to her, seemingly unremorseful at the sight of her dread.

Justin threatened, "If I ever see you in the same vicinity as Danica or any woman, I'll fuck you up so bad your mother won't even recognize you!"

Braydon headed straight for the door without looking back. Not looking in her direction out of modesty, Justin knelt beside her, took off his jersey, and draped it over her chest. He then asked if she was okay.

Never had she heard Justin speak in such a way. It was harsh, frightful, and violently intimidating—using words that made her cringe at the very sound. However, circumstances being as they were, she had very little reason to object to his methods of intimidation. If anything, it was a small dose of reassurance that he would do anything to keep her safe.

"I-I'm fine ... I think," she replied while pulling her tank top down under his jersey and buttoning her jeans, hands uncontrollably shaken.

"Thank God I was waiting for you outside the locker room. Who knows how long that shit stain has been hiding in here," he said in an aggravated whisper, keeping his eyes on the locker in front of him. "Probably getting off on watching you all change, that perve."

Danica didn't respond. Her voice lodged firmly in her throat as the events sank in. As Danica's trembling began to subside, Justin put his arm around her, drew her in, and held her tight. It felt good. He felt safe.

"Should we report it?" he asked faintly into her ear.

"No," she whispered, then hesitated. She confidently repeated, "No, I don't want to report it. I-I just want to go home."

In her plea, she convinced herself that it all would evaporate into nothing if she didn't play the victim. Justin nodded as if respecting her decision. He helped her to her feet and took her bag while holding firm to her jersey like her security blanket. "It's okay," he said. "Everything will be okay," he said to ease any doubt.

They only made it to the door before such trauma overtook her. The jersey slipped from her hands and fell to the floor, giving up a piece of the man to wrap her arms around the whole thing. Embraced, she wept.

The walls were down, and now she trusted him fully, evidence of this being revealed as she poured out her vulnerability in his arms.

The sound of her dad opening the front door pulled her out of the memory of that day. She quickly wiped the tears off her face and spread them over her lap. Looking back, it was only reasonable that such an event would cause the fear needed to let her guard down with Justin so that her heart would trust him completely. Now he had her. Now she felt she owed him everything. Only now had she realized it had been a well-manipulated test. And she failed.

* * *

It had been over a year since Mr. Nelson had found Ben lapsed atop the table—his pupils dilated, driblets of blood trickling listlessly out of his mouth, his breathing thin, and skin ghostly pale. The feeling of it all had set Ben on edge, bringing a paranoia not easily tamed, especially when adding four seasons' worth of dark episodes and exchanges. Every new day became harder to welcome than the last, as he dealt with the fear of not knowing what he had experienced or if more were to come. He wondered if they'd be more palatable or would only get worse.

Early sunlight lanced through his window blinds, exposing a lazy stream of dust particles that floated diagonally in the air. Within the beam came warmth and a solicitous comfort to the room. The pellucid odor of fresh cut grass seeped under the door and through the fissures of the windowsill, alluring Ben's nose with its mild fall fragrance. He opened his eyes to the sun's generous rays and let them wash over his face. Reluctantly, he mustered up the will to drag himself out of bed. His dysania anchored him down, and he made it as far as the dust-stained couch before collapsing lethargically over it. It was an adequate sofa for the room, picked up outside a college laboratory. Much like any other piece of college furniture, it had all the comfort and appeal of a stack of bricks, dressed in what felt like heavily starched burlap and decorated with a ghastly pattern of light pastels.

He couldn't help but feel that one vision was only the first strike in a brigade of hopelessness that would soon follow. It had been haunting him—the thought of so many dark episodes magnifying and growing stronger, coming on more frequently.

In part, he blamed the disease of social networking, a plague becoming rapidly ubiquitous. He recognized that a more sanctimonious mindset had been seeping into these poor souls, sinister words distributed in bulk, like a poisonous antidote for the masses. While everyone worked tirelessly to live by a fanatical standard to achieve this facade of ultimate pleasure, Ben could only see what lived beneath the flesh of these networking beasts. They had become a virus posing as a cure, feeding off the human spirit faster and more viciously than he had previously experienced.

With that, the need for exchanges had also come more regularly, fraying his body in a way that required more time to recover. Every exchange had become abnormally taxing on his health—if he could deem any of it normal. The scars and blemishes that healed within hours were now lasting days, multiplying and leaving scars on his body. Dislocated limbs were now having to be put back into place by hand. Gashes had to be bandaged and dressed. Tylenol and ibuprofen quickly became his new best friends, purchased in bulk. They held a permanent residence on his bathroom counter.

Ben decided to remain confined in his suite, with every intent to let the melancholy send him in and out of consciousness. Anything to settle the voices that had elusively lambasted his head. At first, he tried to fight them, using the sound of infomercials to suppress them from going any deeper. He glared at the screen, eyes remaining hollow and listless as the battle of voices swayed between the favor of the screen and his own mind. His mouth was gauzed in dry mouth, sucking in air to counter the chalky taste of acetaminophen and day-old water. His clothes stuck dingy to his flesh … three days overworn, ridden with oily sweat.

To add to his suffering, stations of impeccably dressed people spouting out their concerns for hours a day while presenting no sensible resolutions seemed to flood the channels. He had to watch as society was being torn apart by abandoning the idea of a middle ground for the power of absolutes. Violence seemed to be breaking out more than ever. Destructive behavior had increased the amount of incivility. At the same time, those highly praised held the most anarchist behavior, as if respect were the true enemy in all of this. Ben's heart broke to witness such despair flourishing. The war had been clearly leaning against his favor. And yet he endured it, all so that he had assurance that no one had spoken of the thing he feared most— "A mass shooting has occurred at such-and-such school today …"

It was the third quarter of the USC game. The Trojans were down by fourteen and showed no signs of turning it around when Ben heard the gentle knock at the door, followed by the sustained creak while it opened a third of the way. A gust filtered out a load of the stagnant ozone that had settled over the room for some time and breathed in a crispness that made Ben aware. He took in a long gulping breath of the outdoor air that whipped around him, hoping to wash the bitter taste from his mouth.

Gradually, the head of Mrs. Nelson appeared from the doorway, her eyes riffling over the room with concern as she called into him. "Ben … you in here?"

"Yee-uh," he grunted with a rasp in his voice, unmoved as he lay over the couch, letting his fingers toy with the half-empty water bottle rolling over the floor beneath him. It was all the action he could muster in his state—or at least cared to.

Mrs. Nelson crept in a tad quietly, as if she were checking on a sleeping babe. A weary yet affable smile formed over her face. "Jeremy called for you … again. He said you haven't been answering your phone the last couple of days."

"Yeah. I'll, uh, I'll call him back later," Ben said, languished, writhing his arms and feet as they attempted to stretch over the couch's armrests and touch the path of the breeze.

Ben flipped over onto his stomach like a lethargic slab of rotisserie meat. At the same time, Mrs. Nelson took another broader step. She heard malaise in his voice, a sickly timbre that seemed more common than not these days. "Are you okay?" she asked. Her voice was troubled, knowing the toll the exchanges had taken on him that past year.

He let out a whorled groan. "Yeah, I'm fine. Just exhausted, that's all."

She took a bite at the corner of her lip and gained another step closer, seeing the open bottle of painkillers splashed across the carpet. She loomed over the back of the couch, getting the best clear view of Ben in days. Her eyes widened worriedly, taking notice of the ill tinge that paled his skin. A broad line of perspiration divided his back's right and left sides. Seeing him in such a way made her think about the mononucleosis behavior she'd seen devouring him since that one dreadful day. "Ben? Hon? Are you sure you're all right? You look—"

"I'm fine. Trust me." His voice came out with a husk of nettle. It was grainy, faint, and short, and it rattled her. Ben reached for the water bottle, scooping a few more pills off the carpet along the way. A ghastly expression brushed over his face as he choked down his second helping that morning. "Don't worry." He coughed. "This will all pass. It always does."

"Well, okay. If you say so," Mrs. Nelson replied, composing herself while remaining unconvinced. She held a reluctancy yet stepped back anyway and turned to walk away. Wrapping her hand around the doorknob, she hesitated. "You know, Mr. Nelson and I talked, and we think that maybe it's time you told Jeremy the truth. I think he's earned the right to know. He deserves it. Frankly, I think you both do."

The room sat quietly for a moment as the TV seemed to flip over to another channel. Another game.

She continued, "It's a gift, I know. However, it's also a burden, and no one can do what you do on their own. I don't care how young and strong you are … or think you are. If you aren't going to lean on me out of concern for my family and me, can you please use someone like him to lean on? He's a good guy. He can handle it. Just something to consider, that's all." With that being said, she vanished into the outside world's brilliant light and shut the door discreetly behind her.

Ben continued to lie there with his eyes actively aflutter under his eyelids. He listened to her words play back in his head, discerning the contrast they held to his mother's words on her deathbed. Both spoke with validation and sincere interest in his well-being. The last thing he needed was more complexity, more urges to make changes and risk the innocence of those for whom he cared. Besides, he'd seen what damage his anomalous secret could cause. He'd been down that path and watched it culminate in destruction for someone he cared for deeply.

Ben could sense anger beginning to rise as his mind went where he could no longer control it. It was then that he recalled something he had forgotten. And yet it was so familiar he could practically see it hanging on his wall, just as it had in his mother's room. It was a plaque, pink with water-colored flowers dressing the borders. Inscribed were the words "Carry each other's burdens, and in this way, you will fulfill the law of Christ."

Wasn't this how it was intended to work, with so much isolation? Wasn't I the one looking after and not the one looked after? His thoughts battled those words in which his mother found value. The lost and hurt trusted him to abolish their pain, not to put such a burden on someone else. What kind of person would he be to even think of such a thing when it was ordained for him to be the one to take it all away?

"Swallow your fears and let someone else in," she said somewhere deep in his soul. Ben could feel her presence as if she were next to him, holding him just as her vibrant and lovely self had in his younger years.

Ben's voice trembled. "I can't do it, Mom. Not again. It's too much pain."

"On, my sweet Benny. You are so strong. This will not break you."

"Mom?" Ben said.

She was gone.

Ben gathered enough energy to pry his body off the couch and began a slow, swaying journey to the bathroom. He stopped when he reached the counter, resting his hands on its granite surface and allowing his head to hang for a moment. Lifting his head, Ben stared deeply in the mirror. It looked as if the years had passed by him. Part of him he could no longer recognize. Lines sprouted from the corner of his eyes, masked only by the parts swelled in blackness. His skin was blemished in sores and settled filth. Hair was set in shambles over an oily head. His face was covered in a hairy shadow that ran along his jaw, chin, and upper lip.

He grimaced with tremendous effort as he pulled his shirt up over his head, turning the shower on. Then, after stripping off the rest of his clothing, he gently and painfully washed his body. He had hoped that the cleansing water would also rinse his head sterile. In that, it failed to comply.

* * *

Danica gazed up at the ceiling fan, watching it revolve smoothly and swiftly above her bed. She tried to count each time it completed a full rotation but always lost count around the fourth rotation. It was the weather. The rain pelted her upstairs window. Lightning flashed, calling for rolls of thunder to shiver her breathing. Why it tied her emotions to her early days with Justin and instigated her to finish mentally reliving the relationship, she couldn't say. But if it must, it might as well happen in solitude over a posh bed and a stack of pillows.

There was no use in fighting it. The memory was a demon, casting its spell many times, sickening her to the brink of despairing possession. It had taken control of her—mentally, emotionally, and physically—searing pain in everything its vile fingers touched. And yet every ounce of her thirsted after it. As if it made her feel she still held onto a fraction of her humanity. Without the torment, she functioned in the land of the dead. She had become a lemures droning about mindless and hopeless throughout the house, looking for a plot to lay her corpse remains and just be done with it all.

It was supposed to be the party that memorialized her teenage years. One of Justin's more troublesome friends, Anthony Harper, had the whole thing set up. The boy's parents were out of town, celebrating another year of good fortune on some tropical island somewhere, which left their teenage son to run amuck with a hundred or so of his closest friends. Danica knew about the party. Everyone knew about the party. Rumors about it circulated quicker than a celebrity scandal and held a higher reputation than senior prom. She just hadn't expected to attend until she found out how close Justin and Anthony were.

Justin showed up at her door dressed in slacks and a nice buttoned-down shirt but with a Volcom cap set backward on his head. He shouted a polite but brief "good evening" while craning his head past the doorway. It was a far cry from the cordial greeting her parents had grown accustomed to. Before she could say a word, she found her hand clutched in his firm grip and tugging her out the door. It wasn't the first time he had acted this way. Haste in his demeanor had been brewing ever since the locker room incident but only with her.

The Harper estate was about an hour away in the foothills of the Rockies. During the drive, she let him talk without interrupting or giving him her full attention. Being her first real party, Justin took it upon himself to catch her up on the adolescent rituals that would most likely be taking place. An uncomfortable feeling stirred in her; he had never indicated behaving in such a way before. But conversations suggested that was not the case. Everything he said was laced with obscure, subtle hints about what she might expect, assuring her that it was all "natural" and "safe." Never had she felt the need to be someone she was not. Nor had he ever asked her to be before.

After many twists and turns, they finally curved onto a side road that led them over a wooden bridge before winding its way to a grand, mansion-sized cabin. Despite its impeccable size and magnificent lighting arrangement, the massive amount of trees and hills concealed the property well enough to be invisible if you weren't looking for it. The front yard was already crawling with lazily parked cars and a ruckus of teenagers. Danica's eyes were drawn to all the high-class vehicles. Audis, Mercedes, and Lexus sports cars, souped-up trucks, and SUVs adorned with customized plates littered the grounds and trailed down the long gravel driveway. Danica appraised the scene with round eyes and a mouth opened wide enough to consume it all. Never had she witnessed such a thing.

Justin opened his door, then came around to open hers. Pulsating thuds of music could be heard spurt out of the house. "You good?" Justin asked as he helped her out of the vehicle. Her face was always readable and honest. A bit of nerve was setting in, but it was mixed with mostly excitement. Danica gave him her best smile, briefly nodded her head, and then latched on to his outstretched hand.

Justin pushed through the crowd at the door, guiding Danica through the rambunctious crowd. Inside, a palate of fashion was on display, flaunting more money than any of Danica's friends had ever seen. She felt Justin grasp her hand tighter as they maneuvered through the crowds. When they got closer to the back, an odorous scent of weed contaminated the atmosphere, billowing out of rooms where she assumed joints were being passed around. Already there was regret in her choice of attire. She evaluated her dress—crème colored with lacing that went from the armless shoulders, hugging her frame as it cascaded down to the base of the skirt. At first blush, she found it too revealing. But now, seeing what the crowed had deemed presentable, she was practically a nun, even with her hair pulled back into a bogo-style ponytail.

Justin turned to face Danica and pulled her in close. "I want to find Tony!" Justin yelled in her ear, to which she replied with a closed-mouth smile.

They eventually reached the sliding glass door and stepped into the backyard. Even more music and a swimming pool full of teenagers greeted them. Some were swimming in bathing suits, others swimming in their underwear. Several kegs lined the back wooden fence next to a few tables and a stockpile of red Solo cups. A huddle of people had been drinking and conversating out in the garden. Outbursts of laughter spread across the field as some cute redhead blundered over herself and went tumbling into a bush, ass first. By the time Danica noticed, the girl's blouse had been well soaked in beer, and two of her closest friends had already started to pull her out.

"Hey … Justin!" Anthony hollered from the middle of the pool. He was relaxing on a neon pink floaty with a cup of beer that he held up in the air to get Justin's attention.

Justin let go of Danica's hand. He strutted around the side of the pool in a manner foreign to Danica, giving her the feeling of abandonment so that he might catch up with his friend. Danica scanned the area and noticed several girls who looked like they had stepped off the pages of *Sports Illustrated*. They stared hungrily at her boyfriend as he strolled by and embraced his friend. More nerve set in. They were the kind who made you know you were not just out of place but way out of your league.

"Care for a beer?" some guy said. He held a scrawny physique that only boasted when he held out his arms to display the incredible gap between his arms and sleeves. He was merely a hair above five feet tall, easily concealable in diverse crowds. And yet he had impressively managed to break through a gathering of people to acquire two brimming cups of beer. One cup he held out farther than the other. "I'm Logan, though pretty much everyone here calls me Lo. You know, because I'm not the tallest guy around, so … yeah. Anyway, I saw you over here, and I thought, *That's a lady who could use some liquid distraction.*"

Danica looked out to Justin, who seemed to be in a lighthearted conversation with one of the girls who flirtatiously braced herself over the edge of the pool, then back to the scrawny guy who had added an unsavory grin to his uncomfortable presence. Until that moment, she had never drunk before, nor had she cared to. Her life was intoxicated with goals and a certain standing, and she had always taken pride in that. To her, alcohol was a broken compass, a liquid designed to direct people off course. If she wanted a distraction from life, she had other means to do so. However, under such circumstances …

Danica snatched the cup from Logan's hand, eyes magnetized on Justin as he welcomed his new lady friend to have a taste of his ear. Logan stood by her in awkward silence, watching her heart begin to crack, face flushed with embarrassment and rage, blending into a compound that made guys like him lucky.

"So, um, where are you from?" Logan asked, trying to capture Danica's attention.

For a mere heartbeat, Justin cast his sight on Danica. He saw her anger and shame brewing and watched as the red cup in her hand gravitated closer to her tightly clenched lips. A smirk arose just before he turned his attention back to the girl for another round of flirtation.

The cup couldn't reach Danica's mouth fast enough as she chugged through half the cup. Her nerves welcomed the drink at every chug. She gasped, wiping the lines of beer that trickled down her face, and told Logan, "Thanks for the drink," before walking away and leaving him rejected.

On her way back inside, Danica witnessed Anthony hollering at another guy, saying something she couldn't quite make out but pointing in the direction of the kegs, then Justin. She waited and watched as the guy put the cup in Justin's hand. He destroyed the entire cup in no time flat. She became just a little more uneasy. She wanted to think she would never be a jealous girlfriend. She wanted to believe that she knew him. But as she put her cup to her lips and endured the sweet and bitter drink, she slowly realized she was wrong.

It didn't take long for everyone to have the time of their lives. Bottles and red plastic cups adorned every other hand in the crowded. They rested on tables, lined furniture, and mounded over the brim of trash cans. Furniture lined the living room walls, pushed aside to make room for dancing whenever a brave or intoxicated soul thought it fun to give their all on the dance floor.

As the night progressed, Justin's demeanor became more lighthearted as well. He laughed at Danica for sticking to only one cup of beer—a lightweight most his friends called her. But as the night went on and things became hazy, it no longer seemed to matter. Justin was more concerned with holding her, dancing with her, and introducing her to his friends and acquaintances, as if the pool scenario had never existed. But it had, and Danica never considered herself a fool regarding red flags. And this night showed he had plenty of red flags.

Around midnight was when the alcohol began to show its other side. It was a red-faced, sweat-glossed creature with a tipsy stride and a loose mouth. Danica found herself in the living room, sitting on one of the couches lined by a back wall. Justin sat immediately on one side of her, using her bare shoulder as a pillow, while Victor, a loud-mouth adrenaline junky with a buzz cut and tattoo sleeves splayed out on the other. Every now and again, she looked at Justin, this flushed, glassy-eyed version of a boyfriend, and saw all she had thought and expected of him unravel inch by inch, yard by yard. It pained her. It pained her to think he was something he wasn't, and it pained her to realize she fell for it like a well-orchestrated scam.

"Hey, girly," Anthony called, luring Danica's attention and arousing a disturbed grunt from Justin. His body teetered from the kitchen, no different than if he were walking on a ship. In his hands, two fresh cups of beer splashed over his fingers and on the wooden floor. "I say we toast," he proclaimed, thrusting one of the drinks into her hand and then raising his own. "To my new girly and her first real party." With that, he gave a salute and chugged every drop in his cup.

Danica offered back a grin, also saluting, but then paused and eyed the cup. Her stomach turned. Her mind and ego were at odds with each other. She didn't want to be rude, not to Anthony. He had been quite pleasant to her all night. And she felt that she could handle one more drink. But there was something about it. Something that—

Suddenly, and for no apparent reason, she stood up. Justin snorted to wake and asked, "Where are you going?" with a degree of alert paranoia in his voice.

"Only to the restroom. I'll be right back," Danica replied.

"Here. I'll hold your drink for you." He struggled to straighten up but managed with one hand on the couch for support and the other reaching out for her drink.

Danica handed him the beer and witnessed him taking a swig before setting off toward the restroom. Passed out bodies laid out as obstacles along the way. Amateur drunks puked in corners and vases, declaring they were all right in a repetitious slur. It was just around the corner when a slightly familiar voice rang out, "Hey, you!"

Leaning against the wall was a scrawny, flushed guy with eyes diluted by one too many drinks. Over the span of the night, a few of his shirt buttons had come undone, revealing just a taste of his boney chest. "Remember me?" he asked, stumbling the get her attention. "Logan? Or Lo?"

Danica tried to curtail him in a way that made it seem she never saw him at all, head down, cocked to the other side of the long hallway, her stride displaying her desire to not be bothered. However, as she began to cross paths with him, she felt the firm, boney grip of his fingers loop around her upper arm.

"Hey, wait a minute," Logan said. Danica stopped and gave him a cold, uninterested stare. Logan's face crooked to one side. "Ya-you …" He swallowed something that Danica could only fathom came up from his stomach. "Okay? You seem upset?"

"I'm fine," Danica replied, exhibiting disgust and annoyance while taking back her arm with a flustered tug. "I just need the restroom." She strode away.

Soon enough, she made it to the restroom, surprised to not see a body in the tube, and closed the door. At first inspection, she was rather impressed with how fresh her makeup appeared. On the counter, she noticed a vile of sea salt facial spray, and she helped herself to a few spritzes on her skin. Then she took a moment to relieve herself and clean up before strolling back out toward the living room.

Logan was gone, leaving the hallway void of any mindful life. However, upon entering, she saw Justin back on his feet, moving in a way that would only pass as dancing in the most inappropriate sense with a twiggy brunette girl wearing things that left little to the imagination. Danica felt her stomach drop. Rage settled in. She looked over to where they had been sitting and saw her cup next to his empty seat on the end table. Feeling as if she were losing some control over her emotions, she walked over without hesitating, took the cup, and guzzled down what remained inside. She slammed the cup down, startling Victor and putting an abrupt stop to her boyfriend's careless behavior.

Justin looked hazily at her. She glared back. "What?" he slurred, head swishing from one shoulder to the next.

"You're a creep, you know that?" Danica replied as she stumbled from the living room to the kitchen and out the sliding glass door to the patio.

Even in the crisp mountain air, Danica felt as if she had been suffocating. She paced the grounds with one hand on her stomach and one over her mouth. She wanted to cry. She welcomed it. Anything to subside this pain in her gut. Emotions sent the world around her spinning in a way that forced her to begin breathing deeply.

Danica's head began to pulse faster and harder than her heart. Her legs began to wobble, growing numb. She searched for a seat just as a slight wave of nausea entered her body. Her brain felt as if it were rupturing in half, pulling her skull apart and rendering her thoughts useless. Tunnel vision captured her sight and made the search for an empty chair nearly impossible. However, she managed to stumble over one just in time to fall into it. She brought her hand to her head and continued deep breathing. "What … is … going … on?"

Her head rolled back, looking out at the scene behind her. What wasn't black had become a blur. "This can't be happening. I need to go home," she insisted but couldn't tell if they were words or thoughts. Her limbs felt heavy and ceased to move. She looked up at the murky stars, watching them go dark as well. Suddenly, a shadow loomed over her. "Justin," she slurred. "Justin, is that you?" Her hand raised only to plummet. She swore she could feel him touching her face, her shoulders, and her waist. "Justin, please." Her words came feebly and slowly, drifting like her consciousness out of her mouth into the dark night sky.

Her eyes flickered open before the sun began to rise. There was groaning, but she couldn't tell if it came from her or someone else. For a brief second, she couldn't even remember where she was. With an ache, she turned on her side and stretched her arm out over her head. A jab of pain penetrated the triceps down to her ribs. Slowly, she rolled herself up, sitting with a pain that felt like she was sliding over rocks.

Damp fingers began to rub her eyes awake, putting clarity to the view that was last seen blurry. A few sighs, and she stored enough energy to push off the chair to stand. As muscles became aware, so did a plague of brutal soreness that attacked up her legs and thighs. Again, she heard the groans, only this time more confident they were hers. The pain alone made her feel she would lose her balance, and drowsiness had not been her ally. Fortunately, the muscles in her legs worked just enough for her to stumble toward the sliding glass door and brace herself up by the frame.

Danica looked through the kitchen toward the living room. The house had been ridden in cups, and bottles lay parched all about the floor. Some towered in bulks in various areas, particularly where kegs or trash cans had been placed. Stagnant haze loomed thickly like a fog all about the still residence, once lively with music and banter, now drowning in early silence. For Danica, the repetitious thuds still fevered her head with swishing vibrations, making the likelihood of a hangover overly plausible.

It took a moment for her to spot Justin, but he was still there, lying sluggishly up against the couch. Something about seeing him made her cringe from the inside out and elicited a pain that pulsated deep inside her abdomen. His peaceful slumber took to her like an assailant wallowing in his own victory, a con artist relishing in his most elaborate scheme.

She treaded into the house, holding herself up by the wall, then the table, and then any other pieces of furniture she could grasp while attempting to make her way to and through the living room. The room spun both clockwise and counterclockwise, a deranged carousel that refused to let her off. She slowly made progress toward Justin, realizing how much she hated the way she felt, the way her breath tasted, the way her thoughts came about jumbled. She could hardly stand the putrid stench of booze, let alone inhale its musty remains penetrating the flesh of all the lying bodies.

When she got to the couch, she slumped down beside him, eventually collapsing to the floor. More parts of her body writhed in pain but held back the agony for the sake of keeping Justin unconscious. She wasn't courageous enough to deal with whatever type of person he would be, and soon enough, she would have to somehow dig through his pockets in search of her phone. For now, she sat and waited for another round of energy, staring out the window, watching a moon abandon her behind the diaphanous caps of tall standing trees so that the sun could have its day.

Somewhere upstairs came a rumble. Like an alarm, it made Danica aware that it was time to get out of that house. She reached down into Justin's pocket, creeping stealthily with just a finger and thumb, and clawed her phone in their grasp. With precision, she extracted it from his pocket, stopping only once and holding her breath when his head shifted to the other side. Carefully, she pushed herself back up into a standing position, holding back a painful moan with every advance.

She crept toward the front door, stepping over crushed cups and warm bodies along the way. The house was slumbering, and she wanted to keep it that way. To her surprise, she found the door locked, fastened with three bolts that seemed to unlock louder with every turn. Danica twisted the knob. The door broke open.

"Ha, ha! My girly lives!" Right then, Danica's heart went into overdrive. She turned, slack-jawed, glimpsing a flushed-drunk Anthony, shirtless, staggering out of the kitchen with a trash bag full of Solo cups and other debris. His head bobbed and swished from side to side, blurting his words as if no one else was in the house.

Danica looked back toward the door.

"Whoa—hold up a minute," he slurred. She froze but didn't acknowledge him. "Come on. Chill with me a bit." Danica turned to face him. "You know I'm Justin's boy, right? So that makes me your boy as well." He smirked at her in a way that confused her already battered mind. "So I ain't gonna say a thing about … you know. But I gotta ask, how was it?"

Danica's eyes furrowed at him. She took one step in but left one foot at the door. "How was what?" she asked.

"You know, the ugh-ugh," he mouthed, suggestively moving his arms and hips.

Her eyes exploded. "No … no …"

"Oh yeah." Anthony laughed. As Danica turned and raced out the door, he raised his arms and called to her, "Augh, don't be like that, girl! I just want a bit of what you were giving out last night!"

Danica's face was crimson with shame and anger as she crumbled outside, leaving the front door wide open to collapse in the front yard. She began sobbing at the nightmare to which she had awoken. Her head pressed heavy at the ground, knees curled into her chest, balled up as a means of shelter from the hell storm. The yard was now mostly deserted. Her sight was wildly distorted under the acidic tears that collected over her eyes and ran down the side of her face. It finally made sense—her body, the feelings, the bruises. This was beyond alcohol. This was beyond a hangover. Every cell that constructed her limbs trembled as she inspected her body from her arms down to her feet. Daylight exposed the extent of her bruises. Dry blood crusted along her inner thigh. It was clear her body had been violated. And to add insult, Danica realized whoever had done this thing had kept a trophy of their conquest. Under her dress, there was nothing.

It was a little after five o'clock in the morning. Hands aflutter, she unlocked her phone and saw the list of texts and missed calls that peppered her screen. Most were her dad and showed a worry she had never caused him before, which caused her to break down even harder.

The weight of the night pushed her down into a sustained fetal position. It wanted to crush the life out of her. At that moment, she wanted it too as well. She used the bottom of her dress to wipe her face, knowing she needed a ride but not from someone to whom she was too close. It had to be someone who would care enough to answer the phone but wouldn't ask the questions she didn't want to answer. She had no choice.

Danica closed her eyes and prayed, "Oh, God, let her answer," and then speed-dialed the first trustworthy name she could think of. She hoped for the best but expected the worst, given the circumstances. It rang once … twice …

"Hello?" The hesitantly weak and raspy voice could be heard on the other line.

"Hello, Melanie?" Danica said, quivering, tears welling up over the dark smear of her mascara-stained cheeks. Heaving tears and an overwhelming supply of phlegm, she barely made out her words. "Hey … it's Danica. I'm … sorry to wake … you, but … is there any … chance you could … pick me up?"

Even now, she sobbed the memory of that day into her pillow.

FOUR

Distant thunder rumbled outside the window. A soft grayish hue breached the blinds of Danica's window, a sign that the storm was moving on but leaving behind mayhem in both physical and emotional proportions. Danica didn't know where to begin cleaning it up as she raised her head from her tear-drenched pillow and scooted out of bed. She crept down the stairs of the dim house, made her way into the kitchen, and flipped on the lights.

Caffeine was the first thing she wanted—the only thing she had wanted in days, hot and black and bitter. The pot had been waiting for her. Danica poured in the water, splashed a few scoops of grounds into the filter, and hit *brew*. Then she waited as the machine gurgled and popped to life. Its slow, smooth croon quickly let out an aroma that made her senses impatient, promising at least a small amount of vigor at the bottom of a cup. Insipidly, she reached into the cupboard and plucked her favorite inspirational mug.

While glazing over the print on the mug, she realized the words meant nothing to her now. Not much did anymore. She grabbed the pot and poured a cup full of caffeine into her mug. Danica held the warm beverage between her hands, drawing the flavored steam into her nostrils as she took her first long, burning sip. Much like everything else she held dear, its simple pleasure brought little comfort, but it was something.

After escaping the party from hell, Danica somehow mustered up the strength to stumble down to the main road. She waited until Melanie's Honda pulled up along the curb. Danica tried to open the passenger door, yanking on the handle with the bit of strength she had left. It was a needless struggle that gave her just another reason to break down sobbing.

Melanie reached over and popped the latch from inside and let the door swing open for Danica, just enough to let her slip into the car. Danica caught her old friend steadily gazing at her with no attempt to conceal her concern out of the corner of her tear-blurred eye. And yet she said nothing, as expected. It became instantly apparent to Danica that Melanie still had walls up, and rightfully so.

Melanie wasn't so popular with Danica's crowd. She was most definitely cute. Her natural beauty was mesmerizing, so that makeup would only weaken what God had given her. Chestnut hair framed the caramel tone of her skin and curled down to her shoulders, where a thin streak of turquoise peeked out the bottom of one side. She had long, natural eyelashes and freckles that sprinkled her nose and under her alluring eyes.

No sooner than Danica showed a glint of relief in the passenger seat did Melanie utter that imminent question, "Why me?" It had been some time since Danica had felt the sharp end of her cut-to-the-chase tone. She missed it. With Melanie, there was no guessing or reading between the lines. What she said, what she did, she set her life to be as transparent as crystal, and Danica envied that now more than ever. However, Danica refused to respond, undeserving behavior to her old friend. Melanie laid on the gas as she continued, "You see, I find it weird because I am fairly certain that the last thing you said to me was that you didn't want to be my friend anymore. You remember that?"

Melanie shot a quick glance at Danica and watched her fidget with the polish on her nails, breaking off bits and pieces of tiny flakes. The wee speck of a stud that adorned Melanie's nose twinkled a burst of morning light at Danica. Danica said nothing.

She went on. "If I were to guess, I'd say you did something that you don't want other people to know. And seeing that I have proven beyond a doubt that I can keep my mouth shut, I was the only sensible person to call. Does that sound 'bout right?"

Again, Melanie paused, allowing Danica a chance to state her case.

Instead, Danica shuffled a bit uneasily in her seat and moved her glare from her nails to her window, remaining silent.

Melanie sighed and shrugged as she kept her eyes on the road. "Well then, I think you should know that I won't be seeing you again after spring break." Danica's eyes broke from the window, and she quickly glanced in her direction. "I have decided to become a nun," Melanie said. "I report to the monastery on Sunday."

Danica couldn't help but let out a chuckle.

"See. I knew I'd say something to perk you up if I kept talking." Melanie laughed. A dash of remorse flavored her tone as she tried to keep upbeat. "But for real … my dad finally found a job … in Texas. Guess there's more work out there than here!"

Danica slumped lower in her seat and mumbled, "Wow."

"Yeah, I know," Melanie replied.

Danica turned so that most of her body faced her old friend. "Mel, I am so sorry. I shouldn't have let you take the rap. I was so scared, and, and I wanted to say something, but didn't know what, and—"

Melanie cut her off. "Oh girl, please. I get it. And I must admit, it was kind of cool to be known as a professional shoplifter at fifteen!"

Danica sensed a tinge of truth under the harbored bitterness in her statement. She expected much worse. "What I did. What I didn't do—all for the sake of reputation. It was wrong of me. And there is no excuse. I'm sorry, truly."

Melanie reached down and took Danica's fidgeting hand. "It's okay. I forgave you a long time ago. I only wished I got to hang on to my best friend all these years. Besides, I should have talked you out of it."

"No," Danica interjected. "It was my decision. Taking some childish initiation—for what?" She paused and took a moment to dwell on that day. Shaking her head, she went on, "There will always be stuff about that situation I won't understand."

The bitterness crept back in both their minds, leaving the car silent again. Danica placed her head against the passenger window. She began hacking away at her nail polish again, hiding another round of tears that moistened her face, not knowing how to make them stop. All she could do was keep brushing them away and hope the well would soon dry up.

After several more minutes of silence, Melanie finally asked, "You gonna be okay?"

"I don't know," Danica responded in a dry, lifeless whisper as another speck of polish flung off her finger.

Neither spoke again until they pulled up to the front of Danica's house. Melanie parked the car and turned to face Danica as she painfully and exhaustively began to exit. "Listen, I know it's not my place to say anything, and if you don't want to tell me what happened last light, that's your choice. But I really think you should tell someone."

Danica refused to look back in her dismay. She could already picture the concern in her eyes friend's eyes, the disappointment. There was enough of that welling inside her already. She refused to take on any more. Besides, Melanie was the only person she felt might have given a piss in a pail about her. And she didn't want to diminish the last memory of her friend any worse than she already had.

"Thanks," Danica simply muttered over her shoulder. She slipped out of the car and let the door shut naturally behind her. A second later, Melanie pulled away, leaving her alone in front of her beautiful house. She took a minute to gaze upon this thing that kept her family together, this structure that kept them safe all these extraordinary years. Limestone and cedar, a garden ridden in lush, elaborate colors, all reflecting the gold of an early sunrise and glowing in morning dew. But she couldn't see any of that. Not that morning. All she saw was a house and an atomic supply of remorse divulging inside her, cased in a shame and ticking away, ready to explode in the confines of her room.

As she walked up to the house, Danica eyed the garage, noticing that one of the cars was gone. Finally, a bone of relief. However, if only to be extra cautious, she went around to the kitchen door, where she knew how to make a discrete entrance. She crept up the stairs from the kitchen, agonizing over every aching muscle in her legs and thighs. A brutal yet straightforward journey, setting course for the bathroom at the end of the hall. Her feet sloshed over thick carpet, a plush hindrance that brought relief to the bottom of her feet. As soon as the door shut, she began to strip down and inspect her body clearly for the first time. She was a wreck, every inch of her, with her hair disheveled and matted and her face blotchy and flushed. She had mascara streaked down her cheeks to her chin, brushed forcefully along her face by aggressive hands. It chilled her to think they were not her own. Now her tainted mind couldn't help but wonder where else those hands had been. Who else had they touched in such a sordid manner? Why had this happened? Could she not wake up from this nightmare back into the sunset background of her sweet and perfect life?

Danica turned on the shower and stepped inside before it had time to warm; she scrubbed every part of her body only to do it again and again. She stepped out, draping a fresh towel around her body and using another to wrap around her head. It was no sooner than she went for the door that she heard the front door open, then slam shut. Fear washed over her as she stood there and waited.

"Danica!" her mom called up the stairway. "You up there?" The sound of panic and relief coated her voice.

Danica cleared her throat, attempting to make it sound chipper. "Yeah, Mom! I'll be out in just a minute!" she shouted back, trying to say it in her usual cheery tone, all the while forging an excuse that would keep her mom from asking too many questions.

Heavy thuds climbed the stairs. "I need to know where you have been—right now!" Frustration was clearly perceived in her mother's voice. "Do you know where we were? Reporting you missing to the authorities! That's where!"

Suddenly there was banging on the bathroom door. Danica's mind went into a spiral. Had they been out all morning looking for her? Was there a sliver of possibility that they had reported her missing? She couldn't fathom the idea that a single police officer would be out there at that moment with her father. She had only been missing one night. Who would they ask? Her friends? They didn't know anything. And if they were to ask someone, they might find that having a word with Justin would be worth the trouble. The very idea of seeing him being questioned by her dad and a peace officer was almost a thought worth pondering, wondering what he might say. Would he confess, spill his guts, break down like a little bitch and plead for mercy? Or would he say something else, play off his charm, and shift blame, using Anthony and all his buddies as alibies? And Anthony knew everyone. He had more friends there than she could count. If anything, it would be a hundred or so words against hers. Not very favorable odds.

Danica went on the defensive, offering an edited version of her night with a splash of a little fiction. Hopefully, it would reach her dad's ears before they found out from someone even less honest than her. "Mom, I'm really sorry." So she began, spinning a thin web of lies, small enough that it would hopefully not be seen from her small corner of the house. "I didn't know how late it was until it was too late. The party was a bust, so Justin and I went to catch a movie, and while we were there, we saw Katie … White … that girl I used to play soccer with." The lies spun so quickly and smoothly. She knew her mom wouldn't remember a thing like that anyway. She hardly remembered the girls on the cheer squad, and they were at her house at least twice a week after practice. "Well, one thing led to another, and we ended up at her house. Her parents were there, so you don't have to worry about that. But they thought it'd be best if we all just stayed there the night since it got so late. They didn't want us on the road with all those late-night drunks behind the wheel." She tried to be as detailed as she could without giving too much away. "I told Mrs. White that I'd call you, but we were so tied up in things, I sort of forgot. I'm really sorry."

"That's not good enough!" was her mom's instant reply. "We'll talk about your punishment when you get out!"

Lies had never become Danica. Nor had drinking. All she believed were her morals and standings she felt had been compromised by her unwary ignorance and a boy with a flattering tongue. And now he was gone, and so was her innocence. Gradually, her body collapsed over the bathroom floor. There she sat, knees wrapped firmly in her arms, pressed against her chest, letting the vanity lights judge her and expose the filth of all that had happened that night.

Danica took another sip of her coffee and walked over to the kitchen table to sit. Every movement felt automatic and expected, as if she wasn't in control of anything she did. She felt as if she were a doll in a playhouse, with a plastered smile painted on her plastic face, taking the abuse of some celestial child who had no care or concern for taking care of her things—so long as it entertained her. She brought her hand to her mouth and gingerly touched the soft curvature of her lips, confirming that the faux exterior wasn't genuine. At this point, she wouldn't be surprised if she found her skin to be some waxy chemical compound like one of those *Twilight Zone* episodes her dad used to fall asleep to. With a more generous sip, her head drifted back to the circumstance that soon followed that morning.

The week after the party, she was restricted to the house, a small but reasonable punishment she frankly hadn't minded. The other part was unintentional yet most severe. It was the voices, the ones that whispered to her when she looked in the mirror. To see herself became her enemy, a reflection that taunted her and beguiled her emotions. There was no more Danica looking back, the vibrant, beautiful young lady who would spend hours doing her hair, putting on makeup, or rehearsing for one of Mrs. Atmore's oral reports. Not at all. What she saw was a grotesque embarrassment of who she became that night. The same disgusting creature who whispered in her ear and chastised her own value before anyone else could appraise her worth. "You are not their daughter."

There was a disappointment in the way her parents now looked at her—one she'd never seen before. Guilt plagued her conception. They never suspected their daughter to be a liar. She never gave them a reason to. And yet something whispered in her ear, "They know. They know that you lied, and they know what you did. They know everything. And they hate you for that. You're not their daughter. Not anymore." The voice never ceased. All week it whispered to her, "They know. They all know," laying seeds of guilt and depression deep inside her, things her parents would not understand.

After a while, she thought Justin might call but didn't know why. She also couldn't make heads or tails of whether she wanted him to. Being that there was no recollection of what happened that night, Danica wasn't even sure how that conversation might go or if she wanted to know. But the fog still hung over her memory, and she hoped a little dose of clarity might help her move on, no matter how harsh it was served.

Days passed. No calls came. By the fourth day, she found the courage to dial his number. It rang twice. Justin's voice mail picked up. "You've reached the cell phone of Justin Thompson." His voice came over as lighthearted and confident. "If I didn't answer your call, I'm probably doing more important things. Sucks to be you. Leave a message or shoot me a text."

Danica used to remember when she thought his voice mail was rather funny and original. Now it just seemed sincere to her. "Hey, Justin," Danica began. Her message carried a tremble in her tone. "I really need to talk to you. I have questions. Call me back … please." She hung up hastily, ashamed of sounding desperate to such a person.

A few more days passed with no reply, leading to the final day of spring break, Sunday, the day Melanie would be gone forever. And yet all Danica was concerned about was if she would hear from Justin. It consumed every thought and feeling and every reason for everything she did. The opportunity to speak with him had become her own brand of heroin, and she needed her fix.

Danica sat out on the back porch with her guitar, strumming chords most sloppily. Not a word had been said to anyone about that night, friend or family. Anything at this point would be speculation, no matter how confident she felt about what happened. Still, she needed understanding. She needed Justin. Despite all the voice mails she left and all the texts, Danica received no response.

She sat, a drone with fingers that subconsciously did their thing as she stared blankly into the backyard. She knew, if nothing else, she would see Justin the next day at school. If only she had a chance to prepare for his reaction. She didn't even know if she should be angry with him or if he had a right to be disappointed in her. She didn't know what he knew, and she didn't know what to think. Her brain only worked well enough to keep her half-alive. She moped about and occasionally strummed random chords on her guitar. Then her phone rang.

"Hello, Jus … agh-huh … I can do that … Can you please just … yeah … okay … okay. I'll see you there."

Danica rushed to get ready.

The bistro was packed, as it had been most Sundays. Creme hue bled through the window and cast a soft, shapely glow on the sidewalk. Plates and silverware chimed under the fluttering conversations. Candlelight danced over tables. The cozy scent of coffee and fresh bread loomed and enticed a surge of salivating mouths in the room.

Danica waited at the small circular table on the deeper side of the bistro, hunched over, elbow to table and hand to face, her seat pressed against a rusted stone wall. Two napkin-wrapped sets of silverware and glasses of ice water sat on the table, sweating clear, circular rings around their base. Danica ran her fingers around one of the rims like the second hand of a clock, watching and waiting for Justin to appear around the corner. Suddenly, she straightened herself properly as he approached, cutting through the door with his hands in his pockets, appearing as if this was the last place he wanted to be. His face was hard, and his jawline set. What appeared to be anger reflected in his eyes. Again, she was being introduced to a new side of him.

As Danica waved to him, his face remained unaltered. He took a seat, interlaced his arms across his chest, and leaned back far enough so that only two legs of his chair were still on the ground. "You wanted to talk," he said, looking sternly at one of the glasses of ice water, as if he hadn't had a drink for days.

"You thirsty?" Danica inquired.

Justin replied, "I'm good," while taking one of the glasses from around the brim and sliding it over to his side of the table, leaving two trails of perspiration in its wake.

"Okay," Danica said slowly as she watched Justin lance a straw in the water and go on to empty the glass. She cleared her throat. "So I guess I'll go first."

"You called me," Justin replied, short.

"Yes," Danica said, "I did. 'Cause I wanna know what kind of games you and your friends are playing."

Justin looked up and met her gaze in the dead center of the table. "Playing?"

Danica leaned back. "Don't think me stupid just because you played me. I liked you, Justin, really liked you—at least I thought I did. But then I saw the real you with all your buddies, drunk, hanging over all these girls, embarrassing me like I'm this disposable accessory for you to have and then toss away when you've had your fun."

"Is that what you think?" Justin coldly replied.

"Yeah," Danica said, "I do. And if that's the kind of girl you're looking for, well, sorry, bud, but I'm not her."

"Fantastic," Justin replied. "So, are we done here?"

A stubborn look leapt onto Danica's face. "No, we are not done here. You should thank your lucky stars that I haven't already pressed charges on you and all your micro-penis buddies."

Justin chuckled, furrowing his eyes. "And for what exactly? The beer? 'Cause you were drinking, too, so don't think you're all innocent in all of this."

"I don't give a crap about the beer," Danica scolded. "God, are you so weak of a man that you cannot even fess up to me about what you did?"

"Fess up?" Justin blurted out, grabbing the attention of the tables surrounding them. "Okay, fine." His words began to spit out of his mouth. "I'll fess up just as soon as you fess up for being one jealous chick who can't handle other girls being around me at parties. Or better yet"—Justin put a finger to his mouth and charismatically looked to the ceiling— "how about you fess up for sneaking out on me to go screw Lo in the backyard of my friend's goddamn house!" he shouted, slamming both hands on the table so hard that everything on theirs and the surrounding tables rattled.

Danica went slack with shock. Her eyes blinked intensely as a rush of electricity fried every thought and nerve in her body. "But … I-I-I-"

"I-I-I," Justin mocked her display of confusion. "You're a whore! That's what you are!"

She cringed. Scanning the room, Danica could only see faces looking back at her. "No! I didn't." Her head craned forward and crossed her side of the table. "I don't know what happened that night, but I swear it was you that—"

"I came outside to apologize," Justin stated articulately. "Yes, me. I was the one who was going to apologize for my drunken behavior. But then I did not go have sex with someone I just met, did I? No. You did that!" Danica shook her head at the accusation. "Please! Don't even try to deny it. I saw you with my own two eyes, spread out on that lawn chair while Logan had his pants around his ankles, plowing you."

Danica wanted to either speak or throw up, or both, but only aches and sounds squeaked from her trembling lips. Her face began melting off her skull, dripping, hot, waxy flesh from her forehead and cheeks. The air in the room had the density of lead as she tried to catch her breath. She was glued to Justin's with nothing to say, reading the sincerity that stemmed deep in his eyes. This was not a trick or a bad dream or a lie. This was her new reality.

Justin cleared his throat and calmed himself. "Look, I don't even care anymore, 'cause this"—his finger bounced back and forth between them— "this is clearly over." Justin went on to push his chair back and stood over the table. Peering down at Danica, he gave his final peace. "And not that it matters, but Logan is a good friend of mine, and he told me what actually happened."

From there, Justin strode out of the bistro. Danica shot up from her chair. "Wait," she called out to his back, not knowing what she would follow it up with, but she would've said anything to stop him.

Justin didn't turn back. He didn't give her a second thought or consideration. He left Danica alone there to feel the full extent of that night cut her open from the chest to her navel and have her soak in the ugliness that spilled out onto the table.

Danica could still feel it, like the scar of an old war wound, as she set her mug in the sink and let her head hang for a moment. She didn't think she'd ever be able to feel a worse hurt. But then she couldn't predict the blindsided events that were destined to follow.

* * *

School had been winding down to its last remaining weeks before the holiday break. The homework had already begun to dwindle, and the assignments were starting to feel a little jejune even for seventh graders. Soon there would be ample time for video games, lots of video games. When there was a holiday, the only thing that would distinguish the hours of the day would be a hungry stomach or television programming, and even those could be overlooked.

Most kids itched with anticipation for any type of break, but none as much as Calvin and Travis. To them, it was much more than being able to sleep in or stay up late, days consumed with Call of Duty and Hulu binge watching. It was their release from a hostile prison and freedom from the endless harassment, the belittling, and the torture of not being a socialite in a school swarming with fractious affronts.

If elementary school was torture, then middle school was to be hell on earth, on or off school grounds. It was the last period of the day. The class cut out early, allowing Calvin a head start on his usual walk home. Leisurely, he paced down a couple blocks of suburban homes before cutting through a large park with a pleasant walkway that seemed hardly used before schools were officially out.

The overcast clouds brought cooler weather that caused him not to worry as much about his surroundings. Most times of the year, patches of flowers attracted swarms of bees that typically caused him to be on alert, keeping his eyes actively searching his surroundings. It only took one time for those little buggers to drive its stinger into his skin, a searing pain that would be difficult to forget. It swelled so quickly, forming over his shoulder like a water balloon. His skin stretched all shiny and thin, ready to burst at any given moment. His mom picked and tweezed at it for what felt like hours, determined to pull out the stinger, saying that that particular bee must have had some sort of vendetta against him. He remembered his dad being uncommonly proud of him as he witnessed his son refusing to cry out his pain.

I have at least one good hour to play Xbox in an empty house, he thought as he carelessly sauntered along. Keeping his eyes tenaciously suspicious had always been an essential part of his walk home, crucial, especially in places like a park. But being let out early made him slack. And out in that park, he might as well have been a lone buck standing in a vast meadow during hunting season.

Calvin's face was angled over the ground, watching the leaves crush under his feet. He failed to notice the boys he was about to cross. Suddenly he heard the snap of Travis's voice shouting in the distance behind him.

"Calvin, stop!" he cried shudderingly.

Calvin turned back to see Travis running toward him. His face was flushed, his expression terrified. His backpack thrust left and right in the air over his shoulders as he dashed toward Calvin as fast as possible.

"Run toward me! Now!" Travis exclaimed.

Calvin stood there, maintaining a long, perplexing look. "What?" he questioned, not waiting for an answer. "I was just going—"

Just as he turned to point to the opening of the walkway into the playground, he caught a painful glimpse of stained teeth inside a devilish grin. The next thing he knew, he felt the crush of boney knuckles connecting with his body, first to his face, then to the ribs just above his stomach. His nose, cracked under the pressure of the first blow, brought a hot rush of blood to his face. Suddenly, whiplash overtook his neck as his head was thrust forward by the velocity of how fast his body was sent to the ground. He crashed to the surface, back first, then his head and arms. The air instantly abandoned his lungs, too scared to return. He felt a heel press into the softer part of his gut and dig in. It was Brett, one of Gabe's pimple-faced thugs. As sound returned to his ears, he could hear Gabe rhapsodizing a scathing chuckle above him.

"Wha-happened Gardner? Had a widdle whoopsy?" Gabe tsked, strutting up to tower over him with his taunts. "Here, wet me help da baby up," he scoffed, reaching down only to drop a knee into the front of Calvin's leg and bruise it numb. Calvin rolled to his side, holding his breath to conceal his pain as they jeered. Blood spilled from his nose. Calvin felt it burn like lava as it gargled deep in his throat. "Oh, don't be such a wuss," Gabe mocked. "Get up," he demanded, cocking his chest. "I said get up, bitch!"

"Leave him alone, Gabriel," Travis called out, purposely pronouncing his name femininely. He slowed to a jog before stopping, standing alongside Calvin's back. "You ass."

"How 'bout you shut your mouth, Mason," Gabe spat, stepping over Calvin before giving a painful donkey kick to his back. He stood face-to-face with Travis. Though Gabe was taller, it wasn't by much, leaving only a thread of hot-tempered space between them as they stood nose to nose. "God, why don't you do your mom a favor and put a gun in your mouth like your old man did," he said.

Travis's temples began to throb. His face flushed, eyebrows jittering, as he stared angrily and nervously at his foe. He could smell the stench of early pubescence filtering off Gabe. It mixed dreadfully well with the moldering odor of his lunch breath. Travis pulled back his head a tad to grasp some clean air. "Why don't you do your dad a favor and tell your whore of a mom to stop handing out her phone number in the boys' bathroom," he replied, sparking a slightly red tinge to Gabe's face.

Gabe crooked his face down and returned full force with an uppercut to Travis's gut. His heinous friend looked on with amusement as the comparatively twiggy form of Travis plunged forward over his fist like a rag doll and then fell straight down to the ground.

Gabe took a cheap kick to the side of Travis's thigh, causing Travis to writhe and coddle his leg. "Hey, I gott'n idea for the both of you. Why don't your scrawny asses write your parents a nice letter apologizing for being such bitches. And then stick a gun in each other's mouths and pull the triggers. You can do it together like the faggots you are. I'm sure that would make everyone happy," Gabe said with ribald before spitting at the two of them and then casually strutting away.

Travis watched as they half skipped, half jogged out of sight, laughing about their handiwork. "I swear, if my mom didn't take my knives away, they would have felt the business end of a cold blade by now," he said, face flushed with a concretion of rage, suffering, and humiliation.

"Yeah, well, that's probably why she took 'em." Calvin gasped nasally as air returned steadily to his lungs by way of his mouth alone. Still spilling with blood, his nose had swelled to an unbreathable level.

"Shut up," Travis snapped as he rolled over, pressing his palms against the ground. He trembled as he hoisted himself up to sit and locked his elbows, arms angled behind him. He sat there for a minute that way, collecting himself. "What the hell, dude. Why didn't you run?"

"I didn't know what you meant," Calvin explained, snorting blood and coughing a wad of strawberry-colored phlegm. He cupped his nose and choked down another nauseating serving of blood before turning over and pushing himself up onto his knees. Already he began assessing the damage, finding no good reason to wait. He started with the hot, crimson liquid that breached the slits between his fingers. It had smudged all over the pathway around him in thick blotches, reminding him of the crime scenes they showed at the start of all those police dramas his dad watched.

"You didn't know what run means?" Travis snickered, authentically unamused, climbing up to his feet. "Dude, are you that stupid?"

Calvin hacked up another wad of the fiery phlegm. "Whatever," he said as he pried himself off his knees and took a wobbly stance. A specific spot in his leg writhed in pain and made it harder to stay up and walk. He used the back of his arm to wipe the blood from his nose, realizing the gentlest touch still felt as if he had been sucker punched all over again. He sniffed and crippled over to Travis. "Can we get outta here please? I'm about to puke blood."

"Funny. I thought you'd be used to it by now," Travis said, allowing Calvin to place his arm over his shoulder before limping together in the direction of home.

* * *

Groggily, Ben opened his eyes to loud banging on the front door. It caused reverberation to tremor down the walls and went on relentlessly. He sat up, rubbed his eyes, and then maneuvered hurriedly into his bedroom to throw on a few of the clothes he had piled on the bed. "I'm coming!" he shouted a couple of times in between the "Hang on" and "Just give me a minute!" The knocking persisted. He rushed to the door, pulling a shirt down over his head while trailing the short walk blindly.

"What the hell, Jeremy." Ben wheezed as he opened the door, annoyed at his friend's persistence. Jeremy looked at Ben with his mouth thin and uplifted on the sides. His pythonic arms crossed … swelling with some definition over his well-formed chest. His black brows dug eccentrically into the center of his face, enhancing his honey-colored eyes. No matter how hard he tried, he couldn't change their ever-gentle state.

"Seriously? Don't give me that. I've been trying to reach you for days. I should jab you in the throat, make you struggle for air." He dropped his arms to a neutral posture. "Where have you been, dude?" Jeremy asked, ignoring the social necessities, pushing past Ben with little effort and helping himself into the living room.

He had every right to be angry, and Ben knew that. "Sorry," he murmured as he shut the door. He used this reply more than he cared to think about. It now carried about as much clout as a dirty politician's apology. "I've been feeling like I caught something."

"Yeah, yeah," Jeremy rolled out, sounding weary of his hackneyed excuses. He plodded down over both seats of the sofa. "Well, you look fine now," he said, taking a few sharp sniffs over the couch. His face twisted a disgusted look. "Ugh, this thing smells!" He jumped up and then looked back at the sofa as if it verbally offended him. "I'm going to be real with you because you're my friend. Disregarding the fact that I'm a couple of years younger than you, you need to pull your shit together. Clean yourself up, man. Clean up this mess." Jeremy peered around the room. "And step out into the world. Right now, though, you should clean yourself up. Then we'll go grab something to eat before you get to work on this dumpster." Again, he surveyed the room on the last word.

"Sure. What were you thinking?" For once, Ben had no excuse, nor did he care to give one. He hadn't had a dark episode in a couple of days and felt vitality increasing in his body again. He was also starving and could use something to eat and some fresh air.

Jeremy looked taken aback. "Um … okay … awesome." Jeremy hesitated as if bemused by Ben's reply. It left him thoroughly dumbfounded. "Well, I guess I thought that taco place down the road sounded good, if that's cool with you?"

"Sounds great," Ben replied. "Just let me wash up really quick, and then we'll go."

"Please do." Jeremy assumed a spot leaning against the wall by the front door. He still looked bemusedly suspicious. "Hey," he hollered, "are you sure you're okay to go out? I mean, I don't want to get … whatever it is that's going on with you."

"Nah, I'm good." The shower turned on. "Just give me a few. I'll be out in a sec."

It was a short drive to the restaurant. Regardless of being busy, they managed to find a booth clean enough to relax while they patiently waited for their food. Whenever Ben was with Jeremy, they attracted notice. Jeremy was half-Asian, half-Caucasian, a blend that gave him unique but attractive features. He blended in well with college kids and could have had a free ride as a linebacker, but he chose to go a different route and headed straight into the workforce after high school. If anyone could do that and still be successful, Jeremy could. For him, college would have been a waste of time. It would have only slowed him down with general nonsense and distractions. He could quickly grasp anything he needed to know so long as it would advance his life somehow. And he wasn't ashamed to start at the bottom and prove himself along the way. So far, it was paying off.

"So, for real, how've you been?" Jeremy broke through the façade. "You know, 'cause I haven't seen much of you lately … or at all." He glanced around as he took a sip from his drink.

"Yeah, sorry about that," Ben replied. "As you can see, I am certainly alive."

Jeremy threaded his fingers and laid his arms on the table, occupying a good quarter of the broad surface. His eyes sharpened and his head crooked as he began to study Ben's face. Ben shifted a little uneasy. "Does any of this have to do with a girl?" He appeared satisfied with his question, as if he hit the nail on the head.

"No. Of course not."

Jeremy looked suspicious. "Then there's only one other thing it could be. You're like …" He considered his words. "Like a superhero."

Ben's eyes broadened slightly. He said nothing, feeling the ligaments in his fingers tighten to what might come out of Jeremy's mouth next.

"You see, you're like Clark Kent, right? And me, I'm like your Lois Lane," Jeremy continued.

Ben let out a soundless breath of air. "We're gonna do this type of analogy again?" he asked with a smirk.

"Dude, there are some good lessons to be learned in *Action Comics*," Jeremy said. "So shut up and listen. You might accidentally learn something."

Ben leaned back as he swiped his drink off the table. "Proceed," he said before taking a sip of his drink.

Jeremy settled himself in the booth and raised his hands to demonstrate his point. "Okay, so whenever Lois seems to need Clark, he's never around, right? Finally, he always has the same lame excuses when he does show back up. It's like he purposefully deprives them of any colorful situations, thus keeping his fake identity as the boring nerd reporter he wants to lead people to believe. However, the only problem with that was that it only became harder for the fans to buy into Lois's obliviousness as time went on. I mean, she is supposed to be Metropolis's crackerjack reporter, right?"

"So?"

"So, DC had a choice—to continue with the lame excuses and Lois's ignorance toward the obvious or spill the beans and let her in on the secret. Which way do you think they went?"

"You know Clark wasn't around because he was saving people, don't you?" Ben replied monotonously. "I mean, he's Superman. And he didn't tell her because it would have made her a target for his enemies."

"You're missing the point!" Jeremy said in a high, grinding whisper, which turned a few heads of the girls sitting nearby. He glanced at them and then continued. "I'm saying that even Superman's excuses wore thin to those who valued him most, his readers. Moreover, they knew if they wanted to keep the fan base up, they would have to let Lois in on the truth. You are in the same position, I feel. It's time to take off the glasses, pull back the shirt, and let another character in on the mystery of Benjamin Weaver."

Ben said nothing. Despite the horrible analogy, he did want to spill his guts in some obnoxious way. *Maybe I should take off the proverbial glasses of* *modern-day lore and share my secre*t, he thought but then instantly began to second-guess himself. *Would Jeremy even believe me? The only way to make sure he would is to let him experience it. Mrs. Nelson was right . . . he is strong enough. Just one transfer of a vision would be all that was needed to make him understand. But what if he couldn't handle it? What if it only made matters worse and darkened Jeremy's heart? I can't go through that again.*

At just the right instant, Jeremy broke through his train of thought. "You know, buddy, you can tell me anything."

Ben decided. "I'm not hiding any secret, Jeremy," he lied. "I get a little under the weather from time to time. It's exhausting, you know. It's not all bad. I have good days too."

As Jeremy nodded, Ben sat quietly for a moment, wondering if he had made the right decision.

"Numbers two forty-eight and two forty-nine!"

* * *

Danica imagined her past self being devoured in flames, burning slowly and horrifically and leaving a heap of ash before it resurrected into a clone of who she had previously been. She sat slumped at her desk, doodling a still image of it in her notebook while vaguely listening to the classroom lecture. For the couple of months following spring break, Danica's mission was to become a seasoned criminal at forging herself. The masterpiece would be hoaxing everyone into thinking that she had a decent spring break. She strolled down the reacquainted halls, suppressing every emotion that wanted to cause her to hang her head and cry. She sat at lunch with friends feathered around her as they peppered her with questions. They drank in her lies about how everything was going great. Miraculously, when asked about Justin, they accepted her shallow response that they had decided to take a break. She spoke confidently and pleasingly on the outside. But under that matte-pink smile, she harbored a lavish amount of depression.

A long weekend and time to herself produced evidence revealing that something wasn't right. As a tapeworm ate away at everything she used to be, her dank insides festered and began to seep through her exterior. She told herself repeatedly that she had everything under control. Still, involuntarily, her appearance slowly and mildly withered down. When school was in session, she received curious glances from fellow students and random inquiries about her well-being from teachers.

As more days passed, friends slowly began to distance themselves due to this unexplained deterioration. They started giving her space with a bit of genuine concern. Still, it quickly turned into snickering gossip as they relied on themselves to fix her problems without confronting her or even knowing the cause of her demise. Most mornings, as she strolled slowly to school with fingers gripping the straps to her school bag, strangulating the padded fabric while her focus blurred over the stone ribbon of pavement, nausea would settle in. It developed in the lower part of her stomach, just above that tender fold of skin where regret and shame had consummated their relationship. They had built a nest in her belly and graciously filled it with their eggs. Now those eggs were hatching—each one a gross, agonizing thought, spreading their gross, agonizing sensations all throughout her body in relentless, shrill chirps.

In dealing with all this, she also mourned Melanie's move. When Danica first confronted Justin and received the truth, a part of her was relieved that Melanie wouldn't be returning after spring break. For Melanie to hear about what happened, especially with their past falling out, Danica wouldn't be able to stand her friend looking down on yet another mistake. But now Danica yearned for that friendship. She felt she needed someone who knew that she was less than perfect, who had seen her at her worst and had still been direct and honest with her.

Gossip morphed into quiet rumors that diverted her ears for a short time and then progressively made themselves known. Snippets of them were tossed into conversations that took place in her presence. Even while at church, she realized that the dark shadow was walking one step behind her. People began to sit slightly away, recusing themselves from her. A few only offered sanguine smiles, hoping that she'd open up first and they wouldn't have to ask if she was okay.

Danica's pencil was applying shading to the flames when she began to feel Josh repeatedly kick the leg of her chair from behind. She was sure he was either attempting to annoy her or wanted to get her in trouble.

After a few failed attempts at getting her attention, he finally took it upon himself to whisper, "Danica."

"What," she whispered back, focused only on the artwork forming over her desk.

"I hate to be the bearer of bad news, but you might want to glance at the announcement board on your way to your locker."

"Josh!" Mr. Henderson snapped.

"Sorry, sir." Josh slumped back in his chair while whispering, "For real though, take a look."

The bell rang, and Danica swiftly flipped the hood of her hoodie over her head and wedged in her earbuds. She grabbed her belongings and dodged her way out of the classroom, not acknowledging Mr. Henderson's concerned glance. Scurrying down the hall, head cloaked and sunk low, she could still detect other students sporadically looking in her direction. Mouths were moving. Danica didn't know if they were talking to her or about her. She didn't care. She kept walking, never ceasing until the announcement board stood before her. The only way she'd look was if she dared herself.

Fliers of afterschool activities and drives cluttered the board in photocopy ink and fluorescent paper. Black-and-white pictures of students cut from newspapers, primarily athletes, had been pinned under decade-old headings, faded by years of the elements. Somewhere among the bottom of all the school spirit hubbub was a postcard. The ink was fresh and seasonally colorful, dressed in a snowman and mistletoe and yellow cartoon bells. It read:

Party at the Thompson's!
Saturday @ 7:00 p.m.
5517 Preston Avenue
This is a teen party, no sex workers allowed. Sorry, Danica.

Danica rapidly turned her head away only to lock eyes with Justin, who was with his clan, including Josh. They lounged against the lockers every day right across the hall after the fourth period. That day, they were smiling directly at Danica, waiting for her attention.

"Truth hurts, doesn't it!" Justin hollered nonchalantly over the traffic at her. Some students turned their heads in her direction. A few laughed with the group.

"They know," the voice whispered in her ear. "They all know. You are not Danica. You don't deserve such a name. Whore! That's what you should call yourself. A filthy whore!"

Discreetly, she put her head down, turned up the volume on her playlist, and made her way to her locker. She wasn't ready to face him yet. She uncoded her lock, lifted the handle, and lowered her backpack to begin pulling stuff out to shove it in her locker. That's when Zoey approached from behind. Danica felt the tap on her shoulder and turned. Right away, she noticed a few others from the cheer squad ganging up behind Zoey, waiting for Danica to remove her earbuds.

"Hey, Danica," she began with alacrity. "So … yeah, I don't know how to not be confrontational with the information I have, so I'm just going to lay it out there." She paused for a quick second to glance back at the rest of the squad. "It's been brought to our attention that you've exhibited some improper behavior over spring break." Danica turned and continued to put her stuff in her locker. "Also, you missed the last practice without prior notice." Danica finished putting her last book up, shut the dented metal door, and then turned to face Zoey.

"What do you want, Zoey?" Danica said, cutting the longwinded civility out of Zoey's formal speech.

"We've voted, and you've been ex communicated," Zoey finally said bluntly.

"Fine." Danica pulled her backpack up on her shoulder and walked past Zoey, brushing her arm along the way. With a gasp and a sneer, Zoey shouted after her sarcastically.

Danica strolled theatrically up the walkway to her house at the end of the day, practically sprinting through the front door, and then threw it shut behind her. She slammed her backpack on the ground and then kicked it with all her force before walking into the living room and breaking down. Tears flooded over her hands as she wailed without shame, screaming between gasping breaths. She didn't care who heard. She wanted the pain gone.

Her dad ran in from the back room and grabbed her, holding her tight as she let emotions flow out. Even her parents began to look questionably at her. Even so, she refused to let them in. But now she couldn't resist it. She was breaking apart. The tapeworm had thoroughly hollowed out her insides.

* * *

Ben was stone. He sat that way for hours in the silence of his room at the edge of his clumpy bed. His eyes cut into the darkness with nocturnal ease. His feet were planted, his body bent, mouth twisted, and arms resting on his lap. He cupped his hands. A jittering, fleshy clam glistened in torment and perspiration as he listened to the overwhelming sound of his heart thumping in his ears—*thump-thump … thump-thump*—hot as a furnace against his face. His chest hitched as if he had just attempted to run a marathon without any prior training and gave no evidence of slowing down. He rubbed his face intensely, washing it with the sweat of his hands, offering nothing more than a dingy condemnation that smelled of salt water and some brand of coconut shampoo.

Ben sat there for a half second longer and tried to calm his nerves. "I can't," he panted, trying to hold it together by aggressively rubbing his hands back and forth, legs shaking profusely, burning a hot stare into the ground between his feet as he stood and staggered drunkenly out the door.

It didn't take but a desperate minute or so before Mrs. Nelson was sitting across from Ben, with two cups of chai tea steaming on the table between them.

"Ben?" Mrs. Nelson said. "Look at me." He hesitated and then met her eyes. "You have to talk about this." She studied Ben's face, thinking that she'd never get used to seeing him in pain. Still, she wanted to do him this favor after everything he'd done for others and what he did for her. Their eyes met briefly, Ben's revealing both the tremendous strength and hurt he carried. "It's Allie, isn't it?" Mrs. Nelson spoke as if it were a question but not quite. Mrs. Nelson became witness to the name's mnemonic effects as some invisible knife plunged into his chest.

"I've heard you call out her name when you sleep." Her hands grasped her cup and rode the brim with her thumbs. "I remember her. A pretty girl. Petite. You two used to do everything together before she—" Mrs. Nelson stopped at the sudden realization.

Ben cleared his throat and fixed his eyes on the table's surface. "She was beautiful, wasn't she?" He smiled faintly at the thought. "I've hardly ever seen features like hers. I used to tell her that her hair was as dark as midnight and her face was the color of dawn. Her eyes had a unique shape too. Did you ever notice that? It was there"—Ben pointed to his own eyes— "the way the corners turned just so. What do you girls call that? Almond shaped? I don't know. I don't know, but they always reminded me of those old Egyptian paintings. Especially when she smiled." Ben's thoughts drifted from him. "That one fantastic smile. It was like a pause button on the rest of the word."

Mrs. Nelson witnessed him drifting away from her as he mentally traveled to another time and place. She made every effort not to move, biting her tongue as if not to accidentally bring him back. She felt like he needed to go there and revisit old ghosts.

* * *

Ben's memory fell further back. He remembered when he met Allie. It was impossible for him not to. It was back in their junior year of high school, shortly before they expelled him for too many missed classes. Though she was petite, she was equally powerful and athletic, with enough spunk to keep him entertained. That morning seemed particularly bad for Allie. He watched from the steps as she ran intermittently across the school's front lawn. To be late for him was nothing new, though he'd rather miss the first period entirely than go in five minutes past the bell. Late attendance always triggered such snarky responses from the teachers. But for Allie, this was an inexcusable offense, and it amused him to watch someone in a state of frenzy over such an insignificant infraction. Allie tugged on her backpack, shifting her stuff from one side to the next. Ben watched on, curious.

A few short yards in front of him, Ben watched Allie fish a pair of running shoes from her bag. She slipped off her sandals and brushed Pacific sand off her feet. Then, as she bent over to slip her shoes over her toes, the unthinkable happened. Everything poured from her bag, over her back, and spread across the ground. All her pens. All her books. All her makeup. Everything. Ben rushed over to help her. He wanted to chuckle, but something told him she wouldn't have found it as adorable as he had.

"Need a hand?" he asked, already kneeling and collecting an assortment of knickknacks from her bag.

When she smiled, he witnessed glittering microbes of constellations.

"Thank you for helping," Allie replied. "I'm sorry. I'm such a wreck this morning."

Ben handed off the clutter, looking her in the eyes for the first time. She smiled. His heart stopped. Never had he seen such a creature, at least not up close. From that distance, he could witness the glittering microbes of constellations twinkling in the iris of her eyes, appreciate how her shoulder-length hair widened out at the bottom before tucking in at the lowest point of her neck to frame an aura around her beautiful face, and indulge in the sweet scent of vanilla and nectarines around her.

He found it hard to look away as she shuffled papers back into her bag. Allie started rambling about how she was new to the area and how far the beach was from there without instigation. How she used to surf every morning, but now it took her too long to get there on time—and on, and on, and on. And Ben loved every second of it. He didn't respond; he didn't have to. At no point did she show a sign of coming up for air. Besides, he was still hung up on the first thing she said … about her looking like a mess. That was the furthest thing from what he thought. He was infatuated with her.

Ben made it his mission to find out everything he could about her in the days that followed. He learned her schedule and orchestrated a few convenient crossings of paths about every day he was there. Ben had even taken the time to jot down a few clever icebreakers to boost his confidence. Some even made her laugh, though he was never sure if it was because they were funny, or he screwed them up.

There were no dark episodes when Allie was around, which made Ben more open than he had with most people in his life. He didn't mind when she bombarded him with questions. On the contrary, Ben appreciated her curiosity and found love in her unwillingness to accept his vague responses or excuses. However, he hated when he had to lie. She challenged him in every way possible and dove deep into his life without fear or reluctance, traits he hadn't been around since his mother passed. It was like he had come back home with Allie, which caused their relationship to flourish quickly.

It was the week before Christmas when everything changed. A dark episode, the first in some time, fell over Ben. The girl he was to make the exchange with was young, too young to be thinking about doing something so terrible to herself. She had spent the season as she always had ... in the company of her passed-out, alcoholic mother and a withered old Christmas tree she had hoisted out of a dumpster. It was now shedding a brown thicket of needles over their stained carpet. The house was freezing, a run-down heap of old planks, torn industrial carpet, and rotted-out windowsills. Most of the windows were taped over with cardboard after being blown out from her mother's umpteenth fit that month.

Food was bare. A few boxes of generic crackers had been left staling on the table and counters, along with jars of peanut butter, of which only a child's finger was small enough to scoop any remains. The fridge had been emptied for some time and yet gave off a decomposing odor caused by dead rodents or rotten meat and curdled milk.

It's a Wonderful Life was left on repeat from one of the local stations, feeding what little hope it could into their living room to keep up the bleak holiday spirit. At the same time, her mother slept off the long day of booze drinking and anxiety med popping. There were no presents that year due to the rule of the house—if mommy came across any extra money, it was only to be spent on Uncle Jack Daniels. Even what her dad sent had already been pawned and contributed to mommy's drinking fund.

Ben had seen her in the vision, alone, locked up in that trash heap, shivering in ragged clothes with more holes in them than a guilty man's alibi. Her dark, curly hair had been muddled, damped with sweat and tears, exploding from her scalp as deranged as the outburst that caused it. One of her eyes shone purple and green under the dancing glow of the black-and-white movie, swollen to the point of being nearly useless. While mommy slept down the hall, what should have been her reason for breathing Ben saw climbing onto what was known as "the good chair." Her tiny feet were purple and bare. Her toes were numb to everything they touched. Ben could feel the electric chill of frostbite settling as she discretely tied a rope around the banister, trying not to make a fuss in the room. With her tiny bit of weight, the little girl tugged tight, practically swinging on the rope to ensure that night wouldn't fail.

"Quit your whining, you selfish brat." Mommy's words rang brutal in her head. *"Do you think that hurt? You ruined my life! I would have been a star if it weren't for you … a goddamn diva! Instead, I'm stuck in this dump having to take care of your useless ass!"*

Ben felt her soft mocha skin shudder as her bruised arms reached up and repeatedly threw the rope over that banister. Her dark, curly hair was still dank and dripping with the sweat and tears caked on from every kind of abuse.

"Daddy? You want your daddy? What, you think he loves you? He doesn't love you! How could he? No one loves you! You're a waste, just like him!" mommy scolded as she threw back a few more chugs from the bottle.

Ben scoured the internet for his way to get to that little girl, searching events and charities, burning through classifieds for some excuse to be where he was needed as a front to minimize his risk of being arrested. At last, he found an outreach program looking for volunteers to bring food and gifts and a little bit of holiday cheer to those less fortunate. It was the perfect means to reach the girl. With his tiny amount of charm, he finessed his way through a series of social channels to secure a place on the delivery team scheduled to drop off goods on the girl's doorstep that night. He only hoped it wouldn't be too late.

At the last minute, Allie decided she was coming too. Unfortunately for Ben, charities didn't usually turn down volunteers, and her decisions were always set in stone. The truck that carried the donated goods only happened to be a two-seater, which already made the drive snug. They assigned Ben to a festively plump man they called Buck. He had a gray, wiry beard and a red, well-used stocking cap that made him look hilariously like the jolly, old fat man. When Ben showed up with Allie, there was no opposition. "The more, the merrier!" Buck smiled and said, "But you might have to take your own car."

Ben sat shotgun in a recycled appliance truck with a man who had just retired from a long life of working in the construction industry, while Allie followed behind in her posh BMW. After a few debated alterations to the schedule, the girl's house came as the fourth stop on their list. The evening light had already taken its rest for the day, leaving the unkept path into the housing complex dark. They pulled up to the house, stopping parallel to a weed-ridden front yard.

Buck stretched the age out of his back with a grunt, then gave out an "I'm too old for this" yawn.

"Hey, Buck, why don't you relax in the truck and let me take this one," Ben suggested.

"Nah-nah. I can't let you do that," Buck replied, the last of his yawn still muzzling his words.

"It's not a problem, really," Ben insisted, keeping an outer calm while acting fast. "Save your energy for the next drop-off."

"If you're sure? That stuff's awfully heavy. And if you thinkin' that girl of yours can help, well ..." He leaned over the passenger seat as if Allie could hear from inside her car. "She ain't much heavier than two bags of feathers. Ain't no way she could carry most those things."

"She's stronger than she looks," Ben said, speaking from bruised experience. "She'll get the food, and I'll get the heavy stuff. No big deal."

Buck adjusted his cap. "Well now, I guess I could use a little break," the old man said before murmuring, "This old sack of bones ain't quite as nimble as it used to be, but I-I don't want to be a—"

"We got it, Buck. You stay put," Ben said while he opened the door and hopped out.

Ben jogged around to the truck's back end and rolled open the sliding door. By then, Allie was already out of her car, waiting, and asked if everything was all right. Dragging out one box after another, he assured her everything was fine. Ben loaded her up with the sacks of hot food before sliding the door shut and heaving the oversized box of donated goodies off the fractured pavement. Together they stalked up the walkway, arms working at full strength not to drop the food and presents.

With great difficulty, Ben knocked with his feet, kicking the base of the screen door. The aluminum door rattled feverishly. Nothing. Again, he knocked.

"Seems pretty dead around here," Allie said. "Maybe no one's home?"

Ben put the side of his head to the door. A heated argument between George Bailey and Mr. Potter could be heard blaring in stereo from the TV set. Under that, his ears picked up the faint but recognizable sound of a chair being dragged over cheap tile. The unsteady woes of a young girl arose, trying to keep her balance on the rickety old chair long enough to secure the rope and pull the noose around her neck. There was no time for a third knock.

Ben dropped the box, pulled open the screen, and gave one forceful kick to the door. The door cracked at the blow and burst open. An explosion of brittle wood sent shrapnel of door jetting all over the living room. Ben rushed inside a house as cold and as dreck as the misery that filled it.

Allie peaked in, letting her eyes widen into a state of absolute shock before coming in after him and becoming more jolted at the sight. She saw this beaten-up little girl who, only a blink ago, kicked the chair out from underneath her. The desperation that had long built inside her had now hung on display.

Ben was already at her legs, holding her up. The girl's body shook, lamenting and traumatized, direly frail and begging to amend the idea of her final decision. "Untie her, now!" Ben hollered back to Allie as she stood, horrifically pale, at the doorway.

The bags readily plunged from Allie's hands as she rushed to his aid and shudderingly began climbing up the chair. She attempted to loosen the noose from around the girl's neck. The sight of this frail child up close—with eyes bulging an unspoken cry for help—had Allie rattled. The chair legs shivered over the floor, tapping out the urgency of loosening the rope as Allie went to work pulling and unraveling the noose, loop by deathly loop.

Soon enough, the girl's head slipped through, and she fell into Ben's grasp, lifeless. He immediately began the exchange. Never had any of his exchanges been so close to death. And most definitely not in the presence of someone else. It was always too dangerous. If he passed out and someone else touched him, even for a second, the things they would see and feel, Ben would have no control over.

Allie looked down from the chair as Ben began to struggle for breath. His face turned pink, then crimson, then a plum to somewhat blue. The little girl slowly regained consciousness as Ben's began to fade. Suddenly, her eyes exploded open, looking up toward Allie, but they were bursting with an illuminating white. She wrapped her bruised arms around Ben just as his arms were beginning to slip, taking in all he had to offer. Small trickles of diamond-coated tears leaked from the girl's eyes.

Allie stood on the chair and watched, a white-knuckled hand gripping the rope, petrified, as the exchange played out beneath her. What she witnessed just then was nothing short of fantastic. She felt her eyes betraying her as the bruises on the girl's body faded from her skin under a blanket of steam, only to reappear in the same place on Ben. The green and purple around her eye softened to a restored, flawless mocha, her black hair volumizing with a spurt of life. Her cut lips had become soft and vibrant, reigniting with the plump color of ruby-kissed rose petals. At the same time, Ben's appearance had begun to fade as gashes and sores speckled his body, trading the color of life for a graver pastel shade.

Ben's body would plummet to the floor in the next few minutes, bruised and lifeless, as life revived the young girl. She began to weep frantically with a chuckle, terrified and excited. Conflicted emotions teetered her between a shower of tears and this unwavering smile that had befallen over her face. It was the first smile she had shown in years, exposing a set of milky white teeth.

Allie cautiously stepped off the chair and rushed down to prop Ben's head in her lap. She called to him, pleading with him to wake up. His breath wheezed thin in her ear. Around his neck, the raspberry markings of a tightening noose singed his skin. The little girl looked down and saw him for the first time in Allie's lap. She took no time rushing to find a warm blanket to drape over his body. With a flick, both the blanket and the girl dropped over Ben as she spread the covering over his body before gingerly setting her hands over his chest.

"Is he an angel?" the little girl asked. Her voice was perky and full of life, her eyes full of wonder.

She got no reply.

After several minutes, his eyelashes fluttered, and his fingers started to curl. Allie laid her head over his and prayed, "Come back to me, Ben. Oh God, please let him come back to me."

What happened at that point was nobody's fault, but Ben was still working to convince himself of it. Allie's expression shifted from relieved to sadness when his eyes opened to look at her. He realized she was clutching his hand tight. He could feel the pain leaving him, the anguish, and the utter hopelessness, as it was muddying the green in her eyes. He tried to pry his hand away, but it was too late. All he had taken in was transfusing into her as he watched it fall over her face.

Allie was never equipped to handle such pain, not even a fraction of it. She wasn't like Ben or the little girl. She had never felt a cold, abandoned night, the clenched fist of an abusive parent, or the sharp stab of real hunger. That kind of misery was something that didn't exist in her world. She had grown up with enough love and support to last ten lifetimes.

Allie began weeping in such a way that only the horrid things in his head could cause. Her nails burrowed in his pale, clammy flesh, ensnaring his hand like a bear trap. He tried to pull away, but she was so strong, and he was still too exhausted. Her image at that moment would haunt Ben for what felt like the rest of his life, no matter how short or long that would be. The way her tainted eyes loomed up to the rope still tied to the banister, the way she shuttered at every nook of abusive history in the room. She dragged her body across the trash-ridden floor until she discovered herself cornered between the table and a wall.

Brutally she pleaded for him to stay away, kicking and screaming uncontrollably as if he were a monster. Even the slightest attempt from Ben to calm her shook her nerves as she screamed at him and threw a firm hand into his chest, demanding to keep away. Buck heard the screaming from outside and promptly called 911. By the time he rushed in to see if everyone was okay, Ben had already regained the strength to fight Allie's terrified blows and hold her down long enough to take it all back. But it was too late. She had already felt life's venom rush through her veins. Though the visions were gone, its emotions were all too strong. They clung adamantly as if none of the abuse had happened to her. Yet the knowledge of its existence was deeply engrained.

The way Allie saw the world changed after that. How she acted toward her life, toward him, all changed. Allie now possessed emotions that left a permanent hole in her ignorance, leaving her with a fragile heart that not even Ben's gifts could help strengthen. Now she knew that the sun had set on some people out in the world. And for some, it never rose.

The grinding sound of the espresso machine brought Ben back to the coffee shop. He was still staring down at the table, only now Mrs. Nelson's hand rested on top of his. He looked up to be sure he hadn't caused a scene. The ceiling fans cooled his cheeks, leaving salty trails where the tears had been coursing.

"You're doing well," Mrs. Nelson reassured. "Let's walk." They arose from the table and sauntered out of the shop. Mrs. Nelson gave the staff a quick thank you as the door shut behind them.

Outside, darkness cloaked the sky, leaving the air significantly colder. Traffic dwindled down to the tiresome few as Mrs. Nelson and Ben strolled down the lit sidewalk side by side. Ben knew Mrs. Nelson well enough to know she wouldn't call it a night until he spilled it all. "When did you first notice the changes?" she asked. Ben was pretty sure she had asked it before.

Ben skimmed the ground. "Some of it I noticed immediately after the exchange. I wish I could say it all hit her that night, but I would be lying. The worst of it was cooking inside her. Those things had slowly been revealed through her demeanor and some of the things she would say."

Only minutes after the incident, sirens could be heard screaming into the complex. Buck, Allie, Ben, and the little girl were all outside, waiting. They were still sitting in the same spot when the police dragged a listless mother from the house. She screamed in a drunken fit for her baby, kicking the air with her hands cuffed behind her back and two officers at her side. She fought them all the way to the back seat of a squad car.

They took statements, a tradition Ben had been quite accustomed to by now. He had learned to give just enough facts of the situation. When blended fluently with the insert of small lies, it made enough sense for them to find no need to investigate further.

As he spoke to the officer, he kept his focus on Allie. She kept her chin against her chest and held a blanket around her little body. Whenever anyone addressed her, she looked up in surprise, as if she had forgotten where she was for a quick moment. Her responses were very brief, as were Buck's and the little girl's.

When all was handled, Ben rode with her back home. He tried to ask her what she was thinking but couldn't get her to open up. He hoped this was due to her being extremely overwhelmed. That wasn't the case.

It was subtle at first, though she had grown a little distant. Ben and her friends still had the capability of raising a positive reaction out of her from time to time. In between the silence, she still went about the day appreciating the beautiful things in her life. He frequently caught her laughing with friends, smiling at nothing, joking, skipping.

Where once stood Allie, there was now a shell gradually becoming void of all that made her beauty. She fell mum in the middle of conversations. She didn't ask questions. She didn't oppose his vague replies. He could tell something was disintegrating inside her. She wasn't as all right as she posed. No one could be, not after what she felt. Inside, Allie was this stamp of that little girl, isolated and depressed, littered with the emotional asperities brought on by the life of this abused child. The same patterns Ben had used to uphold his secret from others could now be witnessed in Allie.

Guilt overran Ben as he began to see bitterness extend toward him for what he had cost her. With that came avoidance. Soon, phone calls were unanswered. Engagements were unattended. When he did get to see her, it was brief, just long enough for her to assure him everything was fine, as she lied through her teeth while her eyes kept a standoff pose that told him the truth. Nothing about her was fine.

Allie's departure came quickly before the end of winter. He breathed, and she was gone, carried by the gust of a new season. He thought maybe she was stronger than the others were, and perhaps all she needed was time to let it filter through, just like he had to. Then she would return to him, and everything would be as it had been. Only she didn't heal the way he did. And she hadn't endured these burdens for as long as he had. In the end, no excuses were given. She left no note or goodbye message. Only through the tender sympathy of a mutual friend did he find out she was on her way up north somewhere where her grandma had a room for her and a new life.

As Ben digested the sudden news, two things became clear: that no one should ever again share what he felt, and he was sure to never hear from Allie again. He liked to believe she would end up finishing school, get married to a doctor or someone of that sort. He could imagine her years older, with three children running around her legs. They would grow up to look more like her every day. He liked to believe she'd be happy again, living out the rest of her days in stable, loving bliss, and every year that passed would only prove to be better than the one prior.

But not all things work out the way we'd like to believe they should. And Ben's heart shattered when he heard the truth. Allie never made it to her grandmother's house. They called it an accident ... poor judgment on a long, secluded road with dismal visibility and a diurnal landscape that stretched into infinity. Things were said, excuses he called them. She should have never made the drive alone. The roads were too narrow, the curves too treacherous. That drive was too exhausting for even two travelers, let alone one. Accidents happened on that route every day, most of the time around the same hour as hers. Ben didn't see it that way, and none of those comments persuaded him otherwise. The truth was he allowed things to enter her, things she couldn't handle on her own. He should have been more aggressive, looking past the skin-deep smiles and the hollow laughter, and confronted the truth that spoke plainly in her eyes. Somehow, he should have been able to see her fate and change it.

* * *

In the short time it took Ben to walk back to the guesthouse, he couldn't recall a single word Mrs. Nelson had said over the chai tea. Every time her hand reached out to blanket his, he felt nothing—a numbness, like some inner means of anesthetic designed to block out any means of empathy that might intrude his guilty thoughts and have him consider the alternative. *It was not your fault, Ben.* The anesthetic spread its numbing effects to every notch of his body, only stopping at the cusp of his emotions. Those he felt with absolute clarity.

The door felt like hinged iron as he pushed it in with his entire body and did the same to make it shut. He sluggishly wallowed his feet over the main room, down the hall, and over to his bed. His body twisted, attempting to stretch out the memory of Allie for the night, and pulled back the sheets. His feet slid deep under the blanket, feeling the cool comfort of the end of the bed. With the click of the light, his room vanished in darkness, leaving him to let his head fall back into his pillow. He closed his eyes. From there, all he could do was try to sleep.

* * *

A wall of light cut diagonally across the room. "Hey, Ben," Jeremy called as he inched open the door. "Mrs. Nelson told me you had a bit of a rough night. How are you holding up this morning?" He crept inside and shut the door behind him.

Ben sat on the sofa, taking in mindless television banter. "I'm okay. I knew I had to come face-to-face with it at some point." Reflecting, he said, "I saw her, Jer. In my dream. It's just …" A grumble rattled in his throat and flared his nostrils. "It was like I was living the whole thing over again."

Jeremy pulled up a chair he had grabbed from the far side of the room. Sitting down across from Ben, he responded, "You know that whole situation was not your fault," he said slowly, precisely, and matter of fact. "You must come to grips with that. If you don't, you'll never move on."

Ben heard what he said but knew Jeremy could never fully understand what bred her demise. As far as Ben could help it, Jeremy never would. Jeremy would never see and feel the depth of that terrible darkness and possess the weight of its knowledge. Allie changed over time. He didn't and couldn't understand what caused those changes. Ben also couldn't tell him that, despite how many he was able to save, he failed when it came to the one person he loved most in the world.

"There is another reason I came by," Jeremy said after a couple minutes of silence. "I wanted to tell you something, ask you something in person, and give you time to weigh it out a little," he said earnestly. His eyes pulled Ben's attention to him. "You see, it's kind of a big deal."

Ben gave off an almost stoic look before giving Jeremy a minimally gestured signal to continue.

"Okay, so you know how I've been working tons of overtime to try and move up at work," he said, looking into a slightly involved expression droning back at him. "Or maybe you don't," he uttered under his breath. "Anyway ... I have. And ... well, I finally got it."

Ben said nothing, but his face blurted out the confusion.

Jeremy, a trifle perturbed, clarified, "The promotion. At work. Me. I got a promotion."

Embellishing his grainy burst of excitement, Ben replied, "That's great. You've been working for them for like, what—three, four years? Right out of school, right?" His thoughts were shambled, hardly worth anything, but what they were worth in the moment still belonged solely to Allie.

"Four years, yeah," Jeremy said. "Can you believe it? I feel like every waking moment is dedicated to that place too."

"Well then, maybe it's about time. So you're going to be doing what now?" Ben asked.

"I'll be a district manager. I get a company car. They have good health care and everything," Jeremy exclaimed, watching Ben's head bob in synchronization while his eyes faded from Jeremy and back to the TV. "Plus, I'll be making a boatload more money. And I get holidays off—we're talking post office holidays. It's going to be awesome. There is only one thing that I could have done without."

"Oh yeah, and what's that?" Ben looked as if all his focus were now on the screen.

"They want me to relocate."

Silence hung in the air for a minute. Ben's brows crooked and waggled as he shifted his attention back to Jeremy. "Really? Where are we talking? LA? Burbank?" His lips curled as one more popped into his mind. "Lancaster?" he said melodramatically. "Oh, please don't say Lancaster."

"No, not Lancaster," Jeremy said, letting the sound of his voice gradually wither. "It's, um, Denver … actually." He looked down as his feet shuffled a bit over the carpet.

Ben froze. "I'm sorry. Did you say Denver? Like, Denver, Colorado, Denver?"

Jeremy looked back at him. "Denver, Colorado, Denver," he confirmed.

"Well … crap, dude," Ben replied with the first sincere expression he made that day. "So where does that leave me? You're like the only real friend I have."

"Don't I know it," Jeremy replied with slack on his face.

The pupils in Ben's eyes began to bounce side to side. His brain was working overtime, trying to figure out what this would mean. "So, when do you leave?" was the only thing he could think to say.

Jeremy's words were as direct as his glare. "Four weeks."

"Four weeks! And you're just telling me now?"

"Don't lose it on me. Four weeks isn't that bad. Besides, it's not like you're the easiest person to get in touch with or aren't always in some weird-out mood. I've been trying to tell you for a while; it just never seemed like the right time. Even when you're here, your mind is always on something else."

Ben was hurt, as the truth often did when confronted with it. "Yeah, but does it have to be four weeks? Can't you postpone it for another month or two?" As if that would make any difference.

Jeremy's head shook. "No possible way. I gotta go up for some training seminars, scout out my territory and all that, find an apartment, sign paperwork—"

"Okay, okay," he said, stopping Jeremy. "So now what? When do we say goodbye?" Ben felt that he was being dumped by this transition into a long-distant relationship.

"Shut up. We still have time, and it would be nice if we could hang out more while I'm still here—act like we really are friends," Jeremy said, to which Ben nodded slightly. "Or …"

"Or what?" Ben asked, breathing a long reluctance out with his words.

"Well, that's the thing I wanted to ask you about. You see, I was wondering, a-and I know it's a big decision, so I want you to think about this. Really think about it. I was wondering if you might … you know, want to come with me? I was thinking about it, and I could probably get you a job somewhere in the company. We could find a two-bedroom apartment. Do our homeless ministry out there. It really could be great if you think about it."

Ben's face dropped. He was silent, as was Jeremy, searching his face as he tried to read his mind.

"I … don't … know …" Ben's mind was lost, becoming a washed-out blur as every thought raced through his head and then vanished just like that.

"What do you have going for you here anyway?" Jeremy asked. "You have no job … clearly. You're living in some family's guesthouse rent-free, which we both know can only last for so long, and Lord knows you haven't put in the effort to make any friends. Right now, you're barely hanging on to me." His words cut deep with a blade of honesty. "If you think about it, what are you really losing moving to Denver?"

The truth rolled over in Ben's head before he spoke up with the only reason he could think of. "My mom." There was a degree of shame in his tone, as if simply thinking of leaving his mom out in that cemetery alone was an unforgivable disgrace. "I can't leave her." He froze, then said again, "I can't," as a commitment to his decision. "She raised me here. She made this place the most familiar, comfortable place in the world for me. It may not have been intentional, but what if it was? What if I'm meant to stay here?"

Jeremy's eyes clenched at the thought. He had lost no parents and couldn't imagine having one slip away the way Ben's mom had. He took a breath and held it. "I get that. This is home to you," he said. "Yeah, that I can understand." Jeremy's tone expressed substantial doubt. He scooted closer to Ben, quieting his voice to a somber whisper. "But I believe ... I truly believe that your mom would have wanted you to get on with your life. Both your parents would have wanted you to be your own man, to experience all the world has to offer. Not sit in a town that is doing nothing for you because something inside has you believing this is where she meant for you to stay. What if you're wrong?" He paused. "Wouldn't it be nice to have a change? To be somewhere new? To do something new?

"Look, I'm not asking you to choose right away." Jeremy's voice was tranquil. "Go see your mom. Talk to her. Ask her what she'd want you to do. I'm sure she'll see that I'm right about this." His eyes brightened a little.

Ben looked back at his friend, knowing he may be right. But what if he wasn't? What if moving away meant losing the sound of his mother's voice, her presence, her guidance? What if there was no Mrs. Nelson there to watch over him after a taxing exchange? What if he couldn't heal? Ben turned several considerations over in his head, realizing he didn't want to lose Jeremy, but he didn't want to risk everything certain about his life either. He didn't want to compromise all he knew for the unrecognized. He didn't want anything to change.

FIVE

The house was dim and still, lit only by the tawny glow of the late afternoon as it filtered in through the gossamer drapes that covered the windows. He locked the door behind him, slipping his shoes off, heel to toe, and abandoned them by the unused coatrack. His backpack slipped off his shoulders with desperate ease, creating an ephemeral thud as it clumped onto the hardwood floor.

The sound of the five o'clock news reverberated from an unwatched TV in the living room. It blended in his ears with the rushing blood pouring liberally from his nose, forming a palm-sized pool of snot and blood that foamed in his hand. His entire face felt on fire. His eyes swelled with an outburst of salt water. He hobbled, body crooked, to the side where Gabe's foot had booted. Breathing hurt. Walking hurt. Everything hurt. And yet miraculously, nothing was broken.

Calvin felt strongly that he could mend most of the damage before his dad noticed. It was keeping his blood off the carpet that really worried him. A trail of crimson footprints leading to the bathroom would stir more trouble than the state of his face, though Calvin's dad didn't take too kindly school brawls, especially when blood was drawn. His solutions seemed to do more harm than good in the matters of bullying, calling for another fun-filled meeting with the principal. Of course, the other kids' parents would be there, hashing out a façade of a peace treaty. Undoubtedly, it led to more bullying, which led to more bloodshed and even more creative ways to make his life a living hell. If only he could make his dad see that.

Calvin raced to the bathroom to address his wound, gliding over the emerald carpet in his white cotton ice skates. One hand was cupped under his nose to prevent blood from dripping to the floor. A small red lake filled up his palm in a short while. Soon it would breach the space between his fingers. He darted past the living room, where his dad let out a long day's worth of grunting snores. As sure as eggs were eggs, he was stretched fully over his dad-only recliner to sleep off a week of graveyard shifts under the erratic glow of the TV screen.

By the time he reached the bathroom door, the blood had already seeped between his fingers and created several trails down his wrist. Luckily for him, it never touched the carpet. He abdicated the light switch for the natural glow that still beamed in from the milky-glassed windowpane. In haste, he leaned over the sink. A tarn of blood poured out of his hand and dripped from his nose, painting the bowel of the sink in a Pollack display of deep cerise.

He turned the nob to let a cool stream of water begin clearing it away. He then took a cup of it in his hands and sopped his nose. The cool water stung just a bit. He watched as the water dribbled down with a pink tinge to it, flushing blood and snot down the intestines of the drain. He then refilled his hands and did it again and again. Finally, he stepped back and reached for a roll of toilet paper, cupping a hand under his nose to catch the diluted blood still teeming from his nose.

At first glance, it jarred Calvin to see the early buildup of a fat, arching bruise as it developed over his nose and horned beneath his eyes. It formed into a sickly sallow tone, hinting a bit of a moss green undertone, but was quickly swelling and would soon roost over his face in a more settled dark purple.

"I can't let my dad see this. I can't." He grimaced while surveying the bloody mess he left splattered over the counter. He ripped off a generous amount of toilet paper, then proceeded to roll it, wet it, twist it, and wrench it into his nostrils. He turned off the water and wiped the sink down with a second handful of toilet paper before flushing it down the toilet to erase any suspicious evidence.

The bathroom was clean, but it was inevitable that his parents would see the bruise. That, he could not wipe away. And when they did, they would ask questions. Calvin brilliantly formulated a reasonable answer too sensible for there to be any suspicion.

"I'm a klutz." He shrugged. "Plain and simple. They know my mind wanders all too easily. And sometimes I'm just not paying attention to where he is going. Next thing you know, there's a trip or a fall. A run-in with a tree branch or some low-placed sign. Yes, that's it. Dad always told me it was only a matter of time before I'd run smack-dab into some blasted thing perching over that sidewalk. Well, Dad, today is that day. And the brilliant thing about this excuse is that it's so simple. It just makes sense," so Calvin reasoned.

He made his way down the hall, snorting water and blood and forcing it down his throat. Each gulp was liquid knives lacerating his esophagus and chest. He crept, holding his breath for as long as he could. He didn't want to give a hair of reason for his dad to leave his cozy post to see what he was doing.

It wasn't until his fingers had wrapped the brass knob of his bedroom door that a stir came teetering out from the living room. He could hear the stretching grunt of his father, now mobile, followed by his deep, somnolent voice. "Cal? Is that you back there?" his old man hollered as if the soft click of the knob reverberated into a shattering commotion by the time it reached the living room. A deep, resonating belch and a gratifying breath of relief followed.

"Yeah, Dad," Calvin hollered back, digesting another gulp of watered-down blood. His voice cracked all high pitched and nasally. "It's me. Got a lot of homework and stuff so …"

The recliner squeaked, leaning back then forward as old metal flexed under a grown-up amount of pressure. Another grunt followed with the leftovers of a belch. "You just getting home now? It's awfully late, don't you think? I couldn't imagine it taking you more than half an hour or so."

Like you would know, Calvin thought with a sigh. He said, "Yeah, sorry. I met up with some guys after school." Abruptly, he choked on an execrable cocktail of tap water and blood he had not prepared for. "I lost track of time and all that." He didn't lie. At least not according to his standards. He did, in fact, meet up with some guys, only he preferred to call them goons. Moreover, as far as time went, well, it always seemed to baffle him how it felt like time stood still while he was being royally pummeled by Gabe and his cohorts of misfits.

"Ah-hah … listen, you feeling all right? Because you sound a little … not yourself."

Calvin tightened his gut, puffed out his chest, and snorted a shot of diluted blood to clear his throat. "Oh yeah. I'm feeling just dandy," he said as familiarly as possible while residue gargled in his mouth. Its sound wouldn't even convince him, which meant it stood no chance of convincing his hawkshaw-eared father. "A little tired is all," he tagged at the end, a plausible excuse for such a nasally tinctured voice. Unlikely but plausible. As plain as he could conjure, he doubled down. "It's been a long week, you know." He threw in a "Hey, is Mom here?" knowing darn well she wasn't but launching that Hail Mary to throw off his suspicion.

His dad chuckled. "Yeah, right. She's working a double again. Hey, you wanna hear about a long week? I got some good ones. Three domestic disturbances, two attempted robberies, and … I dunno … like a boatload of intoxicated drivers—every single one of them underaged. I thought it would never end." Calvin's head drooped. His shoulders slunk, dropping his hand off the knob as he listened to his father go on. "I don't get it. Why do you kids feel the need to drink? And then have the retarded idea to think you can drive yourself home after binging all night? I know, I know, I shouldn't be one to talk. But come on! Call a damn Uber or something. You guys do it all the time anyway."

"I hear ya, Dad," Calvin said, instantly regretting it as the bloody phlegm bubbled in his throat and traced over his tone.

Again, he heard the squeaking rock of his dad's recliner, then the creek of the floorboards, and finally the clod of bare feet tracking across the living room. Calvin suddenly began to fret. He was sure his dad was heading that way and even more confident he would flip when he saw the blood-ridden toilet paper shoved up his nose. After a brief silence, his dad called, "You sure you're all right? 'Cause you don't sound too good to me."

"Fine," Calvin said.

"What on God's green earth are you doing back there anyway?"

Calvin had to say something to hold him back. At times, his old man was an inquisitive SOB and downright nosy at others, especially since laying off the booze. It was his way of making up for a lost time, like when he took him on a fishing trip during spring break. Four days of peppering him with questions about school, girls, and what sport he wanted to try out for that summer, as if he didn't know his son. The truth of the matter was that he didn't.

Calvin knew he had to come up with something a hair duplicitous. He had planned what he would say if his dad saw him but not what he would say to keep him away. It had to be something extreme, something so out of his father's range of interest that it would absolutely repel the old man.

He blurted out the first thing that came to mind. "Just eager to play some Call of Duty. You can join in if you wanna," he said, knowing there was no way in hell his dad would take up that invitation. Asking that man to play video games was like asking him to voluntarily have a root canal on a perfectly good tooth without Novocain. He could hardly sit comfortably watching his son play, let alone join in. For that man, it ranked right up there alongside watching chick flicks, sitting through a dinner party, or tolerating any meal that didn't provide a monstrous portion of red meat.

"Right," his dad mumbled, then rattled his never-ending discourse about mindless entertainment and how it created a lack of character in today's youth. It was a speech more commonly heard on lazy weekends.

Calvin waited to hear his dad's body thud back into his chair and crack open a can of diet cola, the only thing he ever drank these days. He sighed out of relief and opened his door, just as his dad called out one last time. "Oh, yeah … I thought we could order a pizza for dinner tonight. Pepperoni and sausage good with you?"

"Sounds great, Dad," he lied. Calvin hated pepperoni and sausage nearly as much as he hated all the double shifts his mom had worked. He figured his dad would have at least known that by now. They'd only lived with each other every day of his natural-born life. "I'll be in my room if you need me," he said and then stepped in and shut the door, locking it behind him.

The flip of the lights unveiled a room that put a cavernous aura on the environment, marking it as the house's darkest, most isolated corner. His window had been shrouded over by a dingy old flag with a yellow smiley face, wearing a bloodied-up bullet hole on the corner of its tilted, smiling head. The tarp left the room to be seen only under the glow of three out of four bulbs still working from his ceiling fan. The walls were obscure, with a gallery of sci-fi and music posters. Comic book memorabilia lined shelf tops and dressers, most of them encased in glass. Old dishes and video game cases sprawled over the floor, cluttered with a blend of undistinguishable dirty and clean clothes. An assortment of fishing equipment still left out from the camping trip had been crammed in the far corner, grouped as a cenotaph to one of the few times he felt connected with his dad. Somewhere among the disaster was actual carpet, a bed, and a desk with his computer on top.

He trudged across the cluttered floor, kicking away papers and cans and who-knew-what to form a trail from the door to his desk. He pulled back his chair with surprisingly little effort and sat facing a blank computer screen before finding the switch and turning it on. The sudden brilliance of the screen seared his eyes for a brief spell as he adjusted to the light contrasting the dim and then instinctively began to tap in his password. From there, he opened the page on Facebook.

Then one for Twitter.

Then one for Instagram.

He scrolled over the endless pictures of people he knew. They were primarily family members—grandparents and aunts and uncles, a few cousins—with a mixture of fellow students posting activities inside and outside the school. There were short videos of spring break activities, photos at the beach, selfies at Disneyland, and family photos taken in front of the Grand Canyon or the Washington Monument. Extravagant vacations (according to his folks) flaunted over pages of followers for people to like and comment on. Everyone he knew was connected on that site, whether they liked him or not. That is, everyone except for Travis.

Of the many pictures, Calvin made the short scroll down to the one he had posted that morning, surprised to see that it was still up near the top. He clicked to see three-fourths of the screen become consumed with his picture. Under it, his own title, "Greatest day with my dad," had been typed out as his creed to that specific day. It was on the shores of Riverkern Beach, on the eastern bank. Calvin was touting a rainbow trout, a good-size one, about seventeen, possibly eighteen inches long, and weighed at least three pounds in the picture. Behind him, gnarled oak colored the landscape. And at his side was his father, standing proud, a sight worthy of remembering.

It was a beautiful shot. The river glistened like a blanket of diamonds being dragged under the high noon sun, languid and steady. Sandy rocks glazed in spring water, rising into a mountainous backdrop behind them. Pine trees amassed over shrubbery, adding a magnificent array of greens to the mix as they climbed into a single-toned sky.

Between them, Calvin's fish dangled from a stringer. Both of their faces were sun-kissed with a glint of copper. Their grins of a genuine smile stretched from ear to ear. On this rare occasion, when he felt the embrace of his dad's arm wrapped over his shoulder with pride, he didn't have to worry about what the next day would bring or what excuse his dad would give for not being able to be there for him. And he didn't have to pretend to be interested in some team or game or whatever his dad typically went on about. The planets aligned at the perfect time, and the universe came together to make this one spectacular moment. Even as he sat in the trash heap of his room, overwhelmed by the paraphernalia that filled his day, that photograph made him smile.

Below the picture, a handful of thumbs-up and comments were listed. Some from people he knew. Others were from people he didn't care to know. Still others were those kinds of people who would comment on anything, just because, regardless of if they knew him or not.

Calvin read through them. "Nice fish," some said, while others wrote, "Good catch" or some other positive words. He continued to scroll down the list:

"What? Am I supposed to be impressed?"

One wrote, "I don't know what's uglier, the fish or the girl that caught it. Oh, wait. That's a guy!"

Another said, "Nice to see an innocent animal being hung by a thread and hooked for your own amusement, sadistic creep."

And another said, "It looks like you should be the one on the line."

Yet another said, "If this was the greatest day of your life, your life must really suck."

The scathing comments went on, disintegrating his feeling of that day into a vicious joke.

To Calvin, it felt as if the harshest of comments came from the minds of those from his school. There had to be ten negative comments for every positive word, and at least every third posting was tied to a face he'd see Monday through Friday. The smile gradually started to dwindle from his face as he read the nimiety of comments left by people he hardly knew.

"Are you such a fool that you thought someone might actually care to see your pathetic attempt at life?"

He heard a voice billowing up from somewhere in his head. It had the timbre of his father's, back when he loved the drink more than his wife and son and wasn't afraid to give a thorough beating to prove it. Back when the only words he spoke were derived out of conflagrated rage. Back when Calvin had to wear long-sleeve shirts outside the house, and his mother, in duress, would rather furnish another excuse for her husband's behavior than acknowledge the truth ... he had a problem. It was that same execrable voice, only soberly keen. *If you're that stupid, you deserve their animosity.*

"It was just a picture. One picture," Calvin said to himself. "A good picture."

"That's right. It is just one picture. The only picture, too, isn't it?" it hissed stridently, snorting disgust, scouring every nook of his head. *"But good?"* it tsked. *"Let's not kid each other. The only thing more pathetic than*

this picture is that you don't have another one of you and your dad together. S, all you're really doing is showing the world how miserable you are at being liked even by your own father."

"What are you talking about?" Calvin protested. "He's been great ever since he sobered up."

"Great? Really?" the voice considered with askance.

"Well, I mean, sure, he's been a little busy ... and tired, but—"

"For you, Cal. He's busy and tired for you. Don't sugarcoat it, buddy. Don't do what your mom did and make excuses for the man. The only reason why he's so busy and tired is that, for him, it's better than the alternative, which is spending time with you. He sees what a loser you are, Cal, a wasted pile of flesh, a mutated sperm that somehow managed to dumb their way through life, just like he did when drunk ... What? Did you honestly think sobriety would change his opinion on that?" The voice tsked, *"Oh, no, no. For him, you're still a turd stain of disappointment."*

"Why are you saying this?" Calvin asked.

"Because, Cal, you are being unbearably naïve, and it's sickening. It's time you embrace your reality, not cower from behind a crapshoot photo in your room. I'm helping you find the balls you never had, Cal. That's right. It's time to face the truth, and the truth is, Cal, nobody likes you ... never had, never will. You, buddy, are a worthless specimen of a human being. Truly and utterly worthless to the rest of the world."

"I-I'm not worthless," Calvin said, uncertain. "I-I have friends. Travis. He likes me, and so do my parents. You don't even know what you are talking about. They work hard for me. I've got everything I need thanks to them."

"Except for their time or affection, you can't deny that. The only reason they work so hard and throw all this crap you have your way is so that neither of them must spend time with you. Do you think your mom works doubles to help pay the bills? Your dad's a friggin cop. Been so for over a decade. I'm sure he's making enough to afford all this by now. Come on, Cal. I'm trying to be your friend here. Face the truth. You'll feel much better. Don't make your old man put on one more sham of a smile when it takes everything he's got to hold back his own stomach from spewing his disgust all over the floor.

"Oh, and as for Travis, please. That kid is three eggs short of a rotten dozen. Still, the only reason he hangs around you is because you're even more of a loser than he is. You make that sorry bastard look pretty good. Consider yourself a buffer to the detestation that would naturally belong to him if you weren't around.

"Don't you dare shake your head at me, Cal! You look at him! Look at that smile on your father's face!" Calvin looked, though he didn't want to now. *"You see it, don't you? Don't you?"* The voice brought Calvin to shudder. *"Tell me that's not a fake!"*

Calvin mumbled, feeble under his breath, "It's not a fa—"

"Don't lie to me! They've all been fakes, and you know it! Every day, he's had to put up with your worthless existence. He wanted a strong son, an athletic son. They both did! One they could be proud of, and you've brought none of that to the table. All you've done was burden them with disappointment. You were the reason he took to the bottle so readily in the first place, the reason why it was so hard for him to quit. You keep your mom away from home and push her to take all those extra shifts. All of it was because of you. So don't you dare tell me that's not a fake, you bastard!"

Calvin reached toward his chest and clutched the wooden ornament on his necklace. His mouth bent at the sides, quivering, realizing his palms were nervously damp. He wasn't talking to his father or the thought of him. Not on one of his worst days had his father spoken to him this way. There was something else inside him. Something baneful. Something that despised him absolutely and knew what could hurt him far worse than anyone ever had. It was a part of himself. The amount he had been harboring in dark places, locked away and concealed from his family and friends.

"That's right, reach for your blanky. Suck your thumb and cry for your mommy, just like you've always done, but in the end, no one will be there for you, and there'll be only one way for you to rid yourself of this. One way to make it all … stop."

"No," Calvin said, clenching his eyes shut. "That's not true."

"Aww, what's the matter, Cal? Truth hurting a little too much? Cuts a little too close to the bone? You should be happy that at least I care enough to

offer you a way out. Who else has done that for you?" Calvin held his eyes closed, whispering prayers. *"Yeah, try that. See if God answers. He never does, not to kids like you. The good news is I know a direct way to talk to that God of yours, one where He must answer. You know where daddy keeps his gun, don't you, buddy? Pal? Kiddo?"*

"No." Calvin shook his head, teeth grinding, veins bulging from his neck as his head craned over the keyboard, dangling over the precipice of tormenting gloom. "No, I won't do it."

"Why don't you go grab it for me, Cal? You know you want to. Just trust me. Once you feel that gun in your hand, your boney little finger is pressing against that trigger. Ooh, you'll want to do it. Hell, they all want you to do it.

"Ah, come on," it taunted. *"It'll be really quick, super quick, and then I'll go away, and everyone will be happy. You want them to be happy, don't you? Yeah … of course, you do. You're a good boy, aren't you? Then do it."* The voice turned commandingly brazen, *"Do it, Cal, do it … do it!"*

"No." Calvin gave out a short, ululating wail. Tears surged out from the infinite darkness of fastened eyes, boiling with rage and sadness. Mixed emotions stirred a conflict that tussled inside him. "I don't want to. I don't." Calvin's voice rose to a belting howl as he swung a fist and batted something breakable across the room to shatter against the wall over his bed. His blood was a conflagration sweeping through his veins, boiling and scorching every inch of his being, steaming his breath into a piston of exhales. His fingernails dug into his palms like feral, unrestrained, and savage claws. Something had broken free inside him and had refused to be put back in its cage.

"Cal, buddy. You okay back there?" his dad hollered from the comfort of his chair, unmoved by the clamor of his son's struggle.

Just then, his cell phone rang. He opened his eyes with a cruel, stony gaze and looked down to see a picture of Travis's face looking back up. The voice had fled just as swiftly as it had come, leaving an echoing memento of its dark impression for him to reflect on.

"You see. I bet the old man didn't even lurch out of his chair. He has no concern for you. It really is pathetic, Cal. Admit it."

"I-I'm fine," Calvin hollered back, swiping the screen on his phone and raising it to his ear.

Calvin fought his nerves into calm submission. He wiped his eyes and choked down that giant ball of enmity he had toward himself, grunting his throat clear to speak. "What's up, man?"

"Hey, whatcha doing right now?" Travis said, whispering.

He took a gulp of air, held it, and then let it go to calm himself. "Nothing," he lied. "Just looking at crap on the internet."

"Anything good?"

Anything good? Calvin thought. *Are you kidding me? Why the hell don't you get on and post a picture and see if there's anything good on, you piece of…* He wanted to caterwaul and obliterate the phone by smashing it on his desk. However, Travis wouldn't know of such things. His house didn't have a computer or pretty much any other modern-day device. Even his cell phone was pushing the legal driving age, but that was probably for the best. A page like Travis's would likely be shut down before anyone had a chance to be victimized by its content.

"Is there ever?" is all he simply said. "Why, whatchu doin'?"

"Yeah." Travis wafted a fragmented chuckle within the word. "I need you to come over, like right now. I have something you've gotta see. It's killer, dude, totally killer."

"Ah, man, I-I can't," Calvin protested. "My dad's home. He's gonna order us dinner and—"

"Oh, come on, dude. It will only take about ten minutes—fifteen tops."

Calvin sighed. He looked at the time on his phone. "Ten minutes," he said hesitantly. "That's all."

Travis replied, "Cool. Ten minutes is all I need. Now get your worthless butt over here."

"All right. Later," Calvin said and hung up the phone. He turned off the screen to his computer and pushed his chair back, taking a few pieces of debris with it. Calvin then turned and went straight out of his room, down the hall, and into the entryway. He could hear his dad fixing a drink in the kitchen, hopefully nothing more than another diet cola.

Either way, it made it easier to tell him what he was doing when they weren't standing face-to-face.

"Dad, I'm going over to Travis's for a sec. Be back for dinner," he said nasally as he rushed out the door.

"What's that?" his dad called back just as the front door closed. "Cal?"

But Calvin was already gone.

* * *

Calvin approached Travis's doorstep just as the sky turned periwinkle and the first star blitzed its presence in the sky. The short walk soothed his nerves more than staying at home ever would. The tissues had dried out in his nostrils by the strident breeze wafting over his face. He pulled them out three houses down from Travis's.

Travis waited outside on his porch, wearing a smile no less grotesque than the tissues in Calvin's hand or the manner of the house. The property was isolated by a strand of wood fencing that had a good part of its brittle teeth knocked out. It was a seemingly sizeable unattended plot with a small, one-story house smack-dab in the center. Wood paneling ran from the roof to the base of the windows, flaking off paint like sunburnt skin. Initially, the wood had been painted in lime green, but time and dirt had disgraced it into a color resembling a one-year-old's soiled diaper. Below that, sandpaper brick stacked, zigzagging down to the scorched grass and garbed in ancient mud.

"Come on, hurry. It's in my room," Travis said as he held a screen door with his back that was as beaten as the fence, twisting outward at the top corner so that it would get jammed half a foot from closing. Even if that hadn't been the case, a plague of flies could swarm through all the holes, punched and kicked and cut into that rusted old piece of crap. He opened the front door and instantly slipped out of view and into a dark entryway.

Calvin followed, the screeching of rusted metal and old aluminum closing in behind him.

The inside of the house proved just as dark as it appeared to be from the outside. The stale musk of several extinguished cigarettes and half-drunk glasses of scotch caught his nose and throat, bringing his eyes swiftly to tears. The aroma hazed the entirety of the house as far as he could tell, in the spirit of a biker bar just before the last call. It was a hardly modish residence. Inside was the accumulation of things leftover from the eighties, filled with avocado- and harvest-toned appliances and oak. Walls dressed in faded taupe wallpaper, dingy, showcased their wear with several loose flaps and heavy curls peeling at the seams. Stains patterned the powder-blue carpet with foreign shades of brown. A nicotine tinge died the popcorn ceiling above to match the bottle-glass cabinets and bricks that divided the rooms.

Well into the haze, Calvin could just make out the living room corner, where a glass-tubed TV rested on the ground, decorated with hotel room flowers and a towering stack of faded magazines. Beyond that, a blue, floral-patterned couch gathered dust under a window dressed in the ghastliest mauve-taupe combination of floor-sweeping drapes.

"Travis?" Travis's mom hollered blusteringly, coughing out the phlegm of her umpteenth cigarette that day. "Who is that? Who you got with you?" Calvin and Travis could taste the decades of tar on her breath even at a distance.

"It's Cal, Mom," Travis hollered back. "I asked him to come over."

"Dammit, Travis!" she cursed asthmatically, wheezing louder with every word. "I got enough on my plate right now. The last thing I need is you filling my house with your delinquent friends!"

"He's not a delinquent. And he'll only be here for a few minutes."

She coughed, sounding like an entire black lung was being expelled from her mouth, saying, "I don't care how long he'll be here. Now you hear me good; I want his grungy ass out of my house! You got that?"

Travis's face turned crooked with irritation. His hands balled into fists, popping knuckles with his thumbs. "Why don't you get off your fat, lazy ass and make him!" he screamed and pulled Calvin into the hallway that led to his room.

"You little piece of tragh ... tragh ..." She hurled up the other lung, trying to scream, "Trash!" She hacked, wheezed, grunted, and wheezed some more. "I will end your existence right here, right now—you hear me! I will beat the disrespectful shit outta you! God help me, they won't be able to identify your body! You hear me, Travis!" She hacked again and again. "Travis!"

"Like God would ever help you!" Travis yelled from his bedroom doorway with a trace of entertainment in his insolent remarks.

"Whatchu say? I said whatchu say?" his mom hollered as the door slammed to a close.

Screaming rants continued to muffle through the closed door as Travis ignored every word to say to Calvin, "Dude, let me first say … you look like shit."

Calvin gave a reserved nod to Travis, dumping his cigar-shaped tissues in a wastepaper basket brimming with junk food wrappers and crushed soda cans. He then began surveying the room, trying to block out the convulsing slurs that rumbled through the walls from the other side of the door. Unlike Calvin, Travis found it fortunate that all his bruises could be hidden under a layer of clothes.

As Calvin rummaged his sight over the room, he fell onto some boxes crammed with old junk Travis had been hoarding against one side of his room. They peeked from under a mounted lineup of seasonal jackets, months away from being used. In the top box nearest him was a bundle of worn-out shoes he appeared to have collected from the goodwill store. Calvin fished one out by its shoelace and gave it an awkward eye.

"So, what was so urgent that I had to come over tonight? Keep in mind that I'll probably be grounded until I'm sixteen for this," he said, dropping the sneaker back into the box and then wiping his fingers on his pants.

That same outdoor smile resurrected over Travis's face as Calvin curiously watched him hold up a finger and step away from behind his bed. Kneeling, he reached under the mattress and retrieved something that left Calvin more uncomfortable than before. It arrested his gaze with its matted black presence, catalyzing a nervous sweat in his palms. He pursed his lips nervously, knowing that its one black eye had the power to foretell the end of someone's existence within the depths of a single firing glare.

Travis couldn't have smiled brighter. "It's called a Glock 43. Freakin' sweet, right?"

Calvin's eyes were frightfully glued to it. Black steal, 159 millimeters, and an unforgiving barrel. And it rested a little too comfortably in Travis's hand. The gun looked remarkably like his dad's. Significantly. Close enough for Calvin to have a hard time sitting in the same room with it.

"Where did you get that?" he asked, sidestepping around the room with funambulist precision, gripping his finger and twisting his nerves out of it.

"It's my brother's. Or, should I say, was my brother's." His head nudged slightly to the side. "And this ain't even the coolest one he's got neither."

"Your brother's?"

Calvin knew Travis's brother, Garrett, as an intolerant, temperamental, and all-out malicious criminal who slept in the room across the hall. And if Garrett ever caught Travis with anything of his, there was little doubt that he would punish Travis in a way that eclipsed anything of which Gabe was capable. He was always bad, but for Garrett, bad turned to worse when he dropped out of school his sophomore year and saw the benefit of dealing drugs over schoolwork. He'd raid his mom's stash of pain pills as routinely as taking out the trash. His mom was none the wiser. She made it her passion to maintain a blood alcohol level that never dove below .01. She would always rant and rave about her boys stealing from her in one of her drunken frenzies. However, Garrett had a talent for persuading her that she had been taking them and simply forgot to refill her prescription, wrapping his words in a shallow "I love you" and bestowing upon himself the task of correcting her forgetfulness by taking the time to roll down to the drugstore and refill the bottle. However, after Garrett found their dad napping in the car with a hose running from the window to the exhaust pipe, he decided to graduate to the more hardcore brand of drugs.

"Dude, you gotta put that back—now. If he finds out you snaked it from his room, he's gonna use it on the both of us." The scary thing was that Calvin wasn't exaggerating.

Travis shook his head. "Mmm, I don't think so," he said, biting down on his lips as if he were on the brink of exposing the biggest scandal of all time. "Garrett's gone. Like, gone-gone. The fool got picked up this afternoon for possession," he said, closing one eye and focusing the other straight down the gun's barrel. "And now they're all mine, each and every one of them."

"Possession?" Calvin replied. "I don't get it. Possession of what?"

Travis rolled his eyes, taking his sight off the barrel. "Cocaine, bro. Lots of it. And they added intent to sell to minors. What an idiot, right? Apparently, he was peddling the crap behind some old gas station along Sierra Highway. Had a stolen handgun on him too." He lowered the gun, ebbing away a sliver of uneasiness from Calvin as he brought his voice to a loud hush. "And this isn't his first offense either." Shaking his head, he returned the gun somewhere back under his mattress. "Who knows how long they're gonna put him away."

"So, what are you going to do with it?" Calvin asked, breathing in a bit of ease and the permanent odor of burnt tobacco.

Travis shrugged. "Shoot it," he replied quite simply. "I figured we both could. You know, set up a couple of bottles out by that old barn where we use to shoot our air rifles and fire off a couple of rounds. It would be fun. And," he said at length, "I thought you could give me some pointers, seeing how your dad taught you how to really shoot."

Calvin's dad had indeed taught him how to use a gun. He had also taught him to respect it, fear it, and handle it safely in a controlled environment—not out in some field with an abandoned barn. This was far from what his dad lectured. He looked askance. "Dude, I don't know about this. I never liked shooting all that much unless it was from a controller. And to be honest, it seems … wrong."

"Seriously," said Travis. His shoulders slumped, drooping his head to give Calvin a drowsy, boorish look. "It's not like we're going to go out and shoot stray cats or anything. We're just shooting bottles. If anything, it'd be like a cool way of refining our Call of Duty skills."

Calvin shook his head. "No. It's not. This is dangerous. What if a stray bullet fires off and hits someone? What if someone gets hurt?"

"Dude, no one is going to get hurt. It's practically in the middle of nowhere, and there's friggin' hills surrounding the whole place," he argued, pointing his thumb at a random wall. "Besides, it's not like we're going to shoot his bigger guns, just this one."

Calvin stood reserved, showing reluctance by the look on his face as he returned to twisting his finger.

Travis sighed, making his way back around the bed. "Look, come over this weekend. We'll go out, I'll have the whole thing set up, and you'll see. It'll all be totally safe, okay?"

Calvin was silent.

"Okay?" Travis said a notch louder.

"Yeah, okay," he conceded, still holding his reservation. "Listen, I gotta go. My dad's probably wondering where I'm at."

"Sure, whatever," Travis said. "Remember, this weekend, okay?" He placed one of his hands on Calvin's shoulders. "And don't go telling nobody, you hear? No-bah-dee."

"Got it. No-bah-dee," he mimicked. "I'll see you at school tomorrow."

* * *

There is one benefit to having a complete breakdown. It forces a person to choose between life and death from rock bottom without anything left to lose. To make the tough decisions to put the pieces back together or throw in the towel and cur into a useless pile of flesh and bones, practically becoming a blob of nonexistence.

Danica had finally decided to confront the culprit who took advantage of her. She felt a small amount of power and life leak back into her soul when she chose. Her parents even noticed a slight improvement in her demeanor when they caught her sitting on the couch, writing diligently in a notebook, as if she had a purpose. What they didn't know was that she was planning to get in contact with the villain and confront him in a way that would bring the fear of hell upon them.

Step one involved her getting their contact information. Justin admitted that they had been good friends, but did she have the courage to approach him again? She began to rack her brain for another option, tapping the pen gently against her cheek. Then it came to her. Anthony would also be able to get her what she wanted. The only difference was that she had a little bit of leverage over Anthony. Justin could refuse to comply and probably would after such a false accusation. After that, she'd have no tool to convince him otherwise. Anthony, on the other hand …

She began scrolling through old text messages. She had sent Melanie his address when she needed to be picked up. She plugged it into her Google search with his name. After some diligent scrolling, she finally found a phone number connected to the information that matched his.

"Danica," her mom called out. "We're heading up to the church for a council session. You good being here on your own?"

"Of course," Danica replied. "Drive safe."

As soon as she heard the door shut, she called the number, knowing that any delay may cause her to chicken out. The phone rang a few times before a woman answered, "Hello?"

"Hi!" Danica attempted to sound cheerful. "This is a friend of Tony's from school. Is he home by any chance? I was supposed to get in touch with him about an assignment."

"Uh … no, he's not in right now. Do you have his cell?"

"Unfortunately, I don't. I'm such a goober that I plumb forgot to make sure we exchanged numbers before we left. If you don't feel comfortable giving it to me, I bet I could grab it from Ryan." She just threw any name out there, hoping it would work.

"I'm sure he won't mind. Give me a sec," Anthony's mom said, retrieving her son's number before continuing. "Okay, are you ready?"

"Absolutely." Danica sighed with relief. She jotted down the number and then responded with a quick thank you before hanging up. She promptly dialed Anthony's number and heard it ring several times before his voice mail picked up. She hung up without leaving a message and began texting.

"This is Danica Briggs from the party. I need you to call me back right away. It's about what happened at your house. If I don't hear from you immediately, I'll get the law involved."

Less than a minute after hitting send, her phone rang, "Hey, it's my girly girl! Sorry, I didn't recognize the number. What's up?" He sounded unreasonably upbeat, which made Danica uncomfortable.

"There was a guy at your party. His name was Logan. I don't know if you knew him or not, but—"

"Hells yeah, I know him," Anthony replied celebratedly. "You, uh, looking to move on already? Gonna be honest. Going from Justin to Logan is a sturdy step down."

Danica replied, "No. Actually, I need his phone number to discuss the sexual assault charges I am considering pressing." The line went silent. "And if you don't give it to me, not only will your parents know all that went down at your house, but law enforcement might get a nice little phone call about it as well."

Why Danica thought she'd hear the edgy tremble of Anthony's voice ramble off ten specific digits was most likely due to several rounds of mental practice. That was not what she got. What she did hear sounded more like a building snicker on the other line.

"Look," Anthony replied passively, "frankly, I'm tired of Justin pulling this shit at my house." Danica's eyebrows furrowed. "If you talked to Logan even for a second that night, you would know that that kid is the biggest moron and sissy you will ever have the pleasure of knowing. I feel sorry for the guy, I really do, and he's my friend—but come on, the guy can hardly manage to look a chick in the face. Trust me when I say he's not at the top of anyone's list on masterminding sexual domination over someone. Having said that, and only because you are my girly girl, I will let you in on a little secret. That little turd ball didn't do anything to you that night."

"You mean, I wasn't—"

"Oh, come on." Danica could hear his eyes roll over the phone. "Just because you're a blonde doesn't mean you have to be a dumb blonde. Danica, think about it. Does Logan seem like that kind of guy? No, he doesn't. And I am pretty sure you could take him on even on your worst day." Again, silence. "Look, all I can say is that he didn't do it. So, before you go around pressing charges, you might want to reevaluate your situation."

"And why should I trust you?" Danica replied.

Anthony chuckled. "God, every single time—you guys make this too easy for him, I swear," he mumbled. "I dunno. Maybe you shouldn't, but I could just not give you Logan's numbers if I wanted. I could have not called you back. Hell, I could deny everything completely. But I didn't, did I? Seriously, why would I contradict what you've been told?"

"I would call the cops—"

"You wouldn't. You know you wouldn't, and I know you wouldn't. There were other witnesses. Plenty. And if you found out the truth that way? Woo-wee, now that would be embarrassing. Here's what I suggest. Do some actual digging." Anthony then sighed. "Look, I've gotta go. I am sorry. I really am. Just do me a favor and reconsider what you think you know." With that, Anthony was gone.

Danica set her phone down on the couch and stared at it. *"Doesn't mean you have to be a dumb blonde, Danica."* His words echoed in her head. She mentally replayed the conversation over, nitpicking at every word Anthony said.

Something about how Anthony spoke caught her off guard. Danica hit the pause button on her recollection. She played the conversation, breaking down what was said and how it was said. But what stumped her the most, what really caught her off guard, was when Anthony said, "I'm tired of Justin pulling this shit."

Did I hear him right? she thought. *He alluded to Justin being involved, but he didn't accuse him of anything.* She reviewed what events she could remember of the night and who may have been around. If it wasn't who she was told it was, could it have been …? She rubbed her head with her thumb and forefinger. *He wouldn't have. He cared about me, took care of me. He even saved me from …* She put her hand to her mouth and pondered for a minute longer. *There's no way Justin could have set that up. Why would he? I was with him all night, except when he hung all over that little hottie.* She thought again about the last few moments she could still remember from that night at Anthony's. *He was the one who offered to hold my drink when I went to the restroom, but he wasn't near it when I returned. Anyone could have slipped. … unless he wanted me to think someone else … but he wouldn't. Right? No … no. Please, God, no!*

Anger built. *He went straight to that skank as if he had plans to meet up with her. And every time I left where they were, he stopped hanging around her, as if he was using her only to goad me to drink more. He knew I would. He only had to wait for me to put my drink down and leave it where I couldn't see it—or him.* The pieces began to connect, and her train of thought started over as she pushed them into place. *What if he set up the attack in the locker room with Braydon? He would have learned that I'm not the type to quickly go and report these types of things. He also knew that in defending me, he would gain my trust. He took me to the party, lecturing me about how I needed to act more outgoing and be open to new experiences. He created tension and then shoved that drink in my hand to escape it.* Danica's thoughts were rolling out fluently. *He took my drink when I walked away, giving him time to put something in it, and then acted in a way that he knew would set me off when I returned. Of course, he'd place the beer where I would see it, far from him and close to anyone else. It just so happened Logan was that anyone to pin it on. That bastard!*

Danica couldn't believe what she was realizing. Her eyes were shifting about the room as her anxiety built. She felt like she was going to explode. Anthony gave her a more significant piece of what she needed to know than he realized. If it was all true.

* * *

The world turned faster for Danica than it had for everyone else. A grueling speed, aging her shrill, chirping fledglings into monstrous, carnivorous buzzards that picked and shredded and guzzled down whatever inside her they found appeasing. She knew she would never be the person she had once been. That giddier, more ignorant version of herself had been shredded into thin slices of meat under the buzzards' talons and had long been consumed. With that, isolation bred a melancholy silence that filtered her words and actions. At the same time, Justin's eloquent tongue proved more fluent and persuasive when speaking in lies, so much that even the most loyal of friends had broken ties with her.

Every day, she tested the waters by walking down the hall with her earbuds in but not on. She would listen to what others were saying when they thought she couldn't hear. She'd watch to see the crude gestures, the weighty glares, and scourging wrath persist. Most days, she didn't know what would have been worse, the sharp, face-to-face, brutal surmise of her once-loyal peers or the more popular behind-the-back snickering of gossip that never seemed to lose trend. Either way, she took it all in, absorbing it to use it until eventually she would break and address it head-on.

That breaking point came when she spotted Justin at an unusual spot right before fifth period. He rested lazily against the brick wall of the gymnasium, half a campus away from his next class, surrounded by a group of friends. It was as if they had expected a fight and were waiting for it to come. The group jabbered nonsense and pushed each other around like a pack of baboons. Justin looked supreme to the others as he watched them do their thing without making even the slightest effort to join in. Danica curtailed one corner, weaving through a small group of choir students to cut behind a tree and hide. She dropped her bag to the ground, fetched a giant, face-covering book, and went on pretending to read it while observing him and his crew from a distance.

Just then, Leah Jefferson's obnoxious giggle could be heard as she pushed her way out of the gymnasium, drawing the attention she always received. She wore gym shorts with her name scribbled on the side and a crop top white T-shirt that exposed the pattern of her sports bra. As she walked by the boys, she smiled confidently, saluting them as she passed with a flick of her hair. All the boys, except Justin, howled and grunted, acting like the primates they were. Still, Justin remained cool and gave her a slight nod while maintaining eye contact until it almost pained her to look back at him. When she turned to face where she was going, Justin's eyes scanned down her backside.

As soon as Leah was out of earshot, Danica could hear the lewd remarks they all made behind her back. She discreetly slid her book into her bag and flung it over her back. Quickly and discretely, Danica brushed her hair to cover the sides of her face, creating a threaded wall between her face and Justin. She gripped the straps and hiked the bag up, taking a heavy amount of confidence before making her first bold step toward him.

They hadn't noticed her coming at first. Then again, she hadn't sounded a horn the way Leah had. Their eyes were drawn to one another as they continued their foolish banter. One by one, they noticed her and sneered, shoving those not paying attention so that they, too, would cast a crude look her way.

Her feet weighed heavier the closer she came, but she worked hard to keep an overly confident expression on her face. Random smirks blossomed over their faces, flashing the wantonness in their eyes as if she were there for a more erotic purpose. She pushed through the flexed arms that were out to hinder her way toward Justin, enduring the occasional cough that hardly did a sufficient job masking their snide remarks. "Skank," "Whore," they'd phlegm out of their mouths, getting a cheap laugh from some with few enough brain cells to find it entertaining.

"Hey, Danica," one guy said, gaining her attention. "I know of a party I'm sure you'd like to attend." He reached down and grabbed his crotch, intending to be ribald. "It's right here in my pants," he jeered, whirling another outburst of laughter from his peers.

Disgusted, she turned to look at Justin, just in time to see the smirk wash off his face, and then he gave the tickled, cursory, "What's up?"

"We need to talk," Danica said, flustered, outright steaming.

"I'm listening, so talk," Justin said, boldly snide. His attention wandered over every person he could see. Everyone except her.

Danica bit her lip. It was all she could do not to punch him square in the face. "I want the truth."

"Sure. You're a whore," he replied.

"Get off it. I know what you did, Justin. Did you really think you'd get away with it?"

Justin gave a manufactured shocked and innocent look. "You were pissed drunk, and you flirted with my friend, somehow getting them to sleep with you, so I guess it's past time I ask you, why'd you do it, Danica? Please, please tell me why." His words sounded as insincere as they were, but what did it matter? His friends didn't care about the truth. No one did except her, and she needed it.

"That's a lie, and you know it," she said, not expecting to be on the defense, but she was there, nonetheless. It didn't take much for her to lose control. Justin's grin widened as he read her expression. Inside, she was out of control and couldn't grasp her thoughts.

"You want to get real, Danica?" Justin pretended to drop the game. "Let's get real. After you started drinking, your legs were practically open the rest of the night. You were begging for it. Hell, I bet you would have taken it from anyone. I was just the fool who was suckered into giving it to you. It takes a real con artist to pin it on me and take zero responsibility."

Her nose flared while Justin held his grin. "I'll tell them," she said with the edge of her voice, gritty from the influx of tears she was holding back. "I'll tell the school, your church, even your parents. I swear I'll rent a freakin' billboard with your face plastered on it if that's what it takes."

Justin's lips twitched with duplicity. He clasped his cold hands in front of his mouth as if to pray. "Uh-huh, and exactly who will believe you? You drove everyone away, Danica. Look at yourself, like one of those trashy emo girls. You're not the head cheerleader anymore. You're the poster child of *Skank Digest*."

Danica looked down at her black hoodie and ripped jeans.

He continued. "I haven't changed," he said before leaning forward to whisper, tasting the nervous salt over her ear. "I'm still practically a god to these people." He leaned back again to taunt her in front of his friends with his calm assurance, "You're nothing. Hell, even your parents respect me more than you. In fact, I bet you didn't even tell them. Did you?"

Each word came as a blow to the face. Danica stood back, frozen in her own dubiousness and blizzarded over by his overwhelming sense of confidence. She hadn't told them. She was afraid of what they might think, of what they might do. Mentioning them only threw her off more. Justin grabbed her arm and pulled her along with him, away from the rest of the group. Still, he allowed them to remain in earshot.

"You know goddamn well that if anyone should be mad, it should be me," he continued. "That was the worst lay I've had in my life. And trust me, I've screwed plenty enough bitches to know when I've had a bad lay." Every word came out trivially entertaining to him.

Danica was dazed. She was hanging by a thread on the ropes, not seeing clearly enough to hit back. Even the vulgarness lacing his confession was omitted from judgment.

Justin continued. His final blow came louder than anything else he had said. "I mean, who lays there and does nothing but cry when having sex … honestly?"

The words smashed across her face like a freight train. It was over, and she could no longer hold back the tears. She could hardly breathe. Part of her would have liked to think she had something more to say, but her chest was hitching so badly she couldn't speak even if she wanted to. How could she stand there and pretend it didn't hurt when it hurt so much? Her eyes glazed and burned under the cumulative tears. They glistered and blurred as the person who was supposed to be the love of her life was now wearing the smile of a handsome monster. He beat her down into nothing more than a bruised sack of flesh and bones. She was beyond heartbroken, and he knew that. He turned and walked away before she could and before the final blow.

"Oh, and hey, Danica," Justin hollered without looking back, confident she was still standing there, "I think we should see other people. Don't worry though. I'm sure plenty of guys would get a rise off a damp piece of wood like yourself."

Danica put one step in a direction, then another, and then another. She began to walk, tumbling into a jog that eventually fell into a shambled sprint. Her world had altered into a blur of colors and unidentifiable structures and faces. Her shoulders pelted off stone and metal as she urgently plunged into the women's restroom and crashed into one of the stalls. Collapsing onto the toilet seat, she went to sobbing perpetually with no end in sight. Her face was rashed in tears and sweat, her nose runny, her hands a jitter, covering her face as if not wanting God to see her cry while the tears sopped her jeans a shade darker.

When her wailing turned into silent sobs, she heard the door swing open, and two chatty girls came lolloping in. Their conversation was shrouded in vile pleasantries and screeching cheeriness that settled on Danica's ears like nails on a chalkboard. Their nasally arrogant, high-pitched carp resonated through the bathroom, unconcerned by whoever else might be around to hear them. Danica gripped her sobs and choked down the tears. She forced herself to become reticent in her sorrow as she spied them approaching the mirror through the space around the door. One was short, trim, and curly haired, while the other, a few inches taller, wore her hair straight with a slight outward curve just below the shoulders. Danica knew them, had seen them around, but never dared to speak to them. They, too, were seniors but the kind that might've put a question mark on her social status had Danica been seen associating with them. She never thought about how stuck up that seemed until now, seeing that she was the one with whom no one wanted to associate.

Their heels clicked sharply over the dirty concrete floor, cutting the air in echoes, stopping only when their backs faced parallel to Danica's stall. Within seconds, they began reworking their makeup.

"I mean, did you see her? She was all, like, crying and whiney. In front of everyone," she heard the curly-haired one carp.

"Oh, I know," the other said, exaggerating shock. "I heard she tried to stick it to Justin, and he called her out on her two-faced crap. Little miss popular, always thinking the world belongs in her back pocket. It's about time someone called her out on her BS. Bitch needed to be taken down a few notches. I say if she wants to go and run and cry and throw a tantrum down the halls, let her. It's not like anyone's going to feel sorry for her anyway. She put this on herself, right?" The other girl nodded, fanatically engaged. "I mean, if anything, it's kind of funny."

"Yeah. But you gotta admit, she had you fooled," replied the curly-haired one.

"She had us all fooled, playing miss Goody Two-shoes all these years. I just feel sorry that Justin had to go through that to find out she was a slut this whole time."

"You know who I feel sorry for … her parents. Could you imagine? And they go to that church down off Maplewood too. I bet they don't even want to be seen with her right now."

The comment instigated a reply that sent the girls into a light chuckle. "Right? I mean, who would?" she stated. "You know Claudia from Mr. Bingham's class? Well, even she told me that the only reason why any of her friends hung around here as long as they did was so she didn't go all desperate and mental on everyone. They were afraid she was going to go all Carrie on everyone. Could you imagine having to put up with her, pretending you still wanted to be her friend just so she doesn't snap?" The girl's body shivered, curling her shoulders up over her ears. "Glugh," she said while mimicking a hurl, driving a finger into her mouth. "I think I'd end up wanting to kill myself."

"No kidding. I want to puke just sitting behind her in English." She gasped. "Do you think her skankiness is contagious?"

More laughter ensued from the other side of the stall door, crushing the lungs of what fragile esteem Danica had left living inside her. In the beginning, she held her breath. In the end, she couldn't catch it no matter how hard she tried. Danica's feet quaked over the stained tiles. Her hands clasped, fingers contorted in all sorts of ways, threading anger and misery, shame and pity and despair in and around each other. Sweat began to replace the tears pouring from her face, turning red, then violet, as she held so much back, pleading to God that they would just leave.

Makeup containers clicked just as one of the girls said, "Oh shit! I am going to be *so* late. I better get going."

"Say hello to little miss slut-slut for me," the girl with the straight hair chimed jeeringly.

"Ew." The other gave out a nasty moan. "Not even funny."

The other girls laughed as they all repacked their cosmetics, cackling until the sound of their voices had been blocked by the door's juddering close. Once again, it had become silent. Danica gasped and sniffled, nursing the wounds left by their words while she still had Justin's fresh on her mind. They had bludgeoned her soundly with shame as their residue continued to tarry over her, overbearing her emotions into a state of emotional disarray. It was as if the girl was right; she was contaminated, the carrier of some awful disease. She could feel the mycobacterium feasting on her from inside. She could practically see the pale lesions developing over her skin, marking her for all to see. She watched her extremities become deformed as they rotted with disease too contagious for anyone to be nearby.

They're right, Danica thought. *Justin is right. I have become nothing.* Her mind swelled with beguiled reasoning, layering one dramatic conclusion after another. *No wonder my friends can't stand to be around me. Look at me. Look at what I've become. What has happened to me?*

The bell startled her. There were five minutes to get to English, and Mr. O'Neil was strict on tardiness. She didn't care. She wasn't going back out there, not to sit in front of that girl. What was her name again? Braxton—the curly-haired one—just to be taunted and ridiculed under the loom of icy glares behind her back. No. Not now.

Not possibly ever, she thought ... for the first time in her life.

SIX

The evening had fully developed. Ben and Jeremy stationed themselves on a familiar street corner in Westwood Village, accompanied by a couple of Jeremy's friends and four large boxes crammed with food. The ever-growing lines of homeless people swayed on and off the sidewalk but moved along steadily. A couple of years ago, no more than a handful or two would come out for a free meal. But word spread quickly, and the line kept growing and growing until two lines of homeless Californians covered a city block. Tonight, bags of cheeseburgers and fries and store-brand water bottles were being handed out. Ben stood directly beside Jeremy, barely uttering a word as the two lines progressed smoothly.

An awkward and silent tension formed throughout the evening, masked in short phrases and customary glances toward each other. Ben did what he could to hold his tongue. He wanted to fulfill his promise to give it time. He said he would give it real consideration. But when you don't feel it, you don't feel it. And it was that cut and dry.

It wasn't until later in the evening when Ben finally broke the news, handing another bag of hot food to mucky hands. "I don't think I can do it," he said, eyes focused on the withered old fellow smiling back at him, toothless, in an out-of-season overcoat. "I know you're skeptical when I say this, but I really get this feeling that I'm meant to stay here." He avoided eye contact as he spoke.

Jeremy gave a cheap laugh, handing the same man a bottle of water. "Wow, you thought deeply about it, I can tell. That took like what, four, possibly five hours to decide?" he said with frivolousness in his tone and demeanor. "Appreciate you giving it the time and serious consideration you promised."

Ben discerned the tinge of hurt in Jeremy's response and felt helpless to console it. "The thing is I just don't know if Denver is the right place for me at this time. We have all this going on, and then there's the … um …" Ben tried to dig up another excuse, finding it hard without first unearthing any part of his secret. "Well, there's the Nelsons, and they count on me."

"For what?"

Ben screwed up his mouth, reaching in the box for another paper bag of food. His mind went blank. "I don't know. Things," he replied.

Jeremy gave a long, silent look and held it while a disheveled man stood patiently waiting for his water. "I see," he said. He handed over the water. "Them needing you to do things does sound awfully important. You just be careful, or they might start having you do stuff as well."

Ben looked at Jeremy's flamboyant expression. "Please don't be mad, Jeremy. I just need you to trust that I'm trying to do the right thing here."

Jeremy's expression softened. "I love you, man, but that doesn't mean I'm going to quit saying that you gotta get your crap together and stop making up all these excuses. You're a good guy. You're smart. You're as lazy as sin, but …"

Ben grinned.

"This is a real opportunity to finally start your life. Your own life," Jeremy urged. He spoke slowly and quietly while eyes held their own voice in one of those "listen to me, bro" sort of ways. It was his signature close. "It's a chance to let go of the past and all that drama and move toward something greater. I know I'm being unusually serious, but you deserve this chance. You do."

"I'm sorry, Jeremy. Not right now."

Jeremy sighed. "That's fine. It's a big decision. Hell, I'd be lying if I said I wasn't nervous about going myself. Leaving my family, all my friends, not to mention what would happen if I blew it at my job. There's a lot at risk here."

Ben lightly chuckled.

Jeremy continued, "But at least I am taking the step of faith. You really should give yourself more time to think about it." He handed off another bottle. "Give it at least a few weeks. Heck, I'll even fly you up when I get settled in, and after that, you can make your final decision."

"And if I decide not to go?" Ben muttered.

"Then at least you gave it time, and that's all I can ask of you," Jeremy replied.

A ruckus was heard from far back in the crowd as a small, unseen burrower worked his way through the line, barging and upsetting the passive flow. A boy appeared from the now unorganized formations and approached Ben and Jeremy from the sundering crowd. He had rips in his clothes, and a disheveled mop of hair rested on his head. He was a kid who looked like he should have been chubby yet wasn't. His feet bit the ground, pushing back those older than him with only his leg muscles and back. Boldly, he displayed his garnered strength acquired from his time fending for his survival. He held out a pair of grimy brown hands, impatient for his chance to dine on a barely warm cheeseburger and a small bag of now cold fries. His fingers flickered at Ben.

"Please," the kid whimpered insincerely, giving a hardened trace of distrust in his look. Ben reached for one of the paper bags. The kid watched with a starving gaze as Ben placed food in his hands, only glimmering a slightly solicitous smile once he held on to the only thing he came for. The boy stared down Ben as he stuffed the fries in his pocket and hid the burger behind his back. Once again, he reached out his other hand. "I got's a friend too, ya know. He be hungry s'well."

Ben couldn't help but smile. "Really?" he said, peeking around the kid's back. The kid turned with accord to Ben's eyes, making sure the unwrapped burger couldn't be seen. "And where is this friend of yours now?"

The boy stretched out his grimy finger and drew an invisible line, stopping across the street on a small shack of a home rotting on the other side. Ben had noticed the house before. Something about the place haunted him with a dark spirit. It was the kind of spirit that became uncomfortable whenever he saw it for too long, like staring down a terrible memory dug up under years of suppression. Even now, an uneasiness turned in his stomach and froze his spine. In every way, it should have been condemned. Probably was.

The brutal glow of a flickering streetlamp haunted the lot. The blue paint of the house had long dried and peeled away from most of the outside. Timbering weeds littered the front yard along with other people's garbage. The walkway had been overtaken by substantial cracks and colonizing vegetation. Shingles were evidently missing from the roof, with rails and beams rotting out. The windows, all but one, were covered in old bedsheets or cardboard boxes with the stains of things one would probably find festering away in a dumpster. An imping three-foot-high fence surrounded its property with a slight lean and was one swift gust away from toppling over entirely. It looked like a house that hell possessed. It churned in Ben to think how anyone could reside in such a rancid-looking place.

"He's in der. Dad too, but he's asleep from all dat needle stuff he be doin'," the kid said, never losing the face of a sympathetic pauper. He glanced once more at the box of food in front of Ben.

Ben couldn't help but think this was a setup for dastardly people to do wicked deeds. An elaborate mugging or another stratagem of that nature played out as a likely possibility in his mind. The more he processed the house, the more he felt the wrenching potential that this could very well be a trap, yet this reasoning shed a potent amount of guilt.

"Why don't you get your friend out here, and then we can get him a burger too," Ben suggested.

The kid shook his head dramatically. "Nope. Nah-uh. Can't. He's sleepen' too. His dad feed 'em dose pills that make him sleep aw day. Dey makes him feel better doe."

"What pills?" Ben asked before he could stop himself.

"Da cankar pills, dugh," the kid huffed, snatching some fries and another burger from a bag inside the box at Ben's feet. He quickly bit into the paper wrapping before Ben could take it back. He chewed and smacked on the burger and waxy paper while smooshing a wad of fries into the corner of his mouth. "He got cankar bad. Makes his head hurt but good too. Gut all spittin' and stuff. Innit be gross too."

Ben looked out at the house, then back at the kid who was now studying the burger's contents. A few fries' ends wiggled from the corner of his mouth like the tail end of some unknown rodents. Suddenly it came to him. "Cancer," he uttered. "That's what your friend has, isn't it? Cancer?"

The kid nodded. His eyes burst wide to reflect the speckles of light drawn from the lamp overhead. "Ugh, duh? Dat's what I said … cankar." The kid swallowed, then pried open what remained of the burger and gave it a good hard look before turning it and raising it up to Ben's face, exposing its contents to him. "Is dat a piggle? 'Cause I don't like piggles."

Ben looked back to the house. "And he's there? Right now? Your friend …" He paused to think. "And his dad?"

"Yeps." Meat and bread sprayed out the kid's lips with no regard as to on whom the speckles would end up. "Dey both der. Dat's where I juss comes from. Hey, you wanna meet 'em?" The kid's eyes flashed with excitement.

Ben evaluated the kid. If this was a trap, he was ignorantly unaware of being a part of it. Another bite had already cluttered his mouth before the last one made it down his throat. His cheeks bulged to the point of exploding and sending shrapnel of bread, meat, and ketchup all over the crowd. "Can I? Would they mind?"

"Naw," the kid said, "long as you bring 'em der food an-an wadder. Come on. Yous can follow me."

Ben picked up food and then reached into Jeremy's box to fetch a couple bottles of water. He caught a concerned eye. "Are you sure you know what you're doing?" Jeremy asked as Ben put a water bottle in each of his pockets to take with him.

"Yeah … sure," he said, shrugging as if it were no big deal.

"Bro, you must be out of your mind."

Ben's eyes wildered to the kid, realizing he had already dashed haphazardly across the street, past the gate, and was now hopping gaily up the languished steps of the porch. He watched as the kid ducked his head through the gap in the doorway. He disappeared for a second or two, only to reappear and wave, touting that everything was good and signaling Ben to come over.

"Most likely," Ben said to Jeremy while gazing at the boy. Ben took a few long strides, building momentum, then ran across the four-lane road. He walked across the overgrowth of the crumbled walkway and made his way up the porch, one creaking, rotting step at a time. The kid was still waiting by the door, picking the last few slivers of fries out of the bottom of his sack and gnawing on them like a chipper squirrel. The kid looked up and smiled as Ben ascended onto the front porch, dropping the small, empty bag by the door before dashing swiftly inside.

Ben held a certain amount of caution as he peeked through the doorway, head barely nipping the inside of the house while knocking a heavy fist against the wall. The wall shook along the front side of the house loud enough to gain anyone's attention, asleep or awake. "Hey, kid," he called out. "Anyone?" His entire head made its way inside while scanning the dusk underbelly of the house.

"Blake! Hey, Blake! I gots you food!" The kid's voice bellowed like the wails of a phantom, drifting down a long, dark hallway.

Ben continued to be cautious as he stepped inside, as if walking the charred planks of a second floor inside a freshly burned house. The only light to guide him streamed vaguely through the open front door, but that only went so far. He flipped one dusty switch after the other as he made his way through the front room, giving one, two, or three courteous tries, only to receive a dead response. Ben found no surprise. The touch of abandonment had left a skirt of dust over everything inside.

It was a bit haunting to see that the house, despite all outward appearance, had been meticulously decorated to fit someone's taste. A matching couch and love seat were placed just so to face a relic television set, and an antique coffee table was placed evenly between them. Small, knitted throws were draped over the tops and perfectly centered. Framed pictures lined characteristically angled, stair-stepping up the walls, yet they were too dark and dust-ridden to make out.

Dead plants in well-designed pottery were stationed at every corner. Branches and leaves stretched over the brims. It was as if the plants had made some desperate attempt to crawl out of the pots, hoping to drag their way to nourishment but failed. Three stood in corners, while another two sat on either end of the mantel above the fireplace, accompanied by bibelots and heirlooms. The kind of items no one would fathom wanting to leave behind.

Ben's stomach began to twist more as he was now beyond the outside light and passing an area that would only make sense as a dining room. Dishes molded with ancient meals that held the remaining eloquence of a toddler's hand and not so much of an adult. Peanut butter sandwiches with crusts left unscathed. Bags of chips exploded across the table and floors. Molded slices of cheese. Coagulated juices and milk left a putrid scent that had attached to everything without discrimination. All were the messy leavings of a hungry and unattended child.

He turned down the dank hall where he couldn't see much other than three shut doors and a room masked off by a pinned-up sheet, stained and old and still rippling from the disturbance of a spunky intruder. Ben pulled back the sheet to find the kid from outside kneeling by an old, race car sheeted bed, alight by the streetlamp that stood flickering no more than a few yards outside the window. What looked like a rolled-up quilt sat, bulging and oblong, in the middle of the mattress. Moaning proceeded out of it in response to the words being fed into his ear with a nursing whisper. Ben crept in quietly and discretely. Along the way, he familiarized himself with the scant surroundings of the bedroom. Broken toys, scattered clothes, crayon pictures of a family and animals, and fantastic imaginary things sketched on paper and wallpapering the bottom half of the room.

A face steadily came into view at the end of the rolled-up quilt. It was young and gauntly pale. The child's hair looked like random bits of chaff on his head as laved phantom blond strands haunted parts of his scalp. His eyes were skeletonized by their dark indentations of an impatient disease. The atmosphere had been cold and unforgiving, swooning with apathy, dressed hoary in grave silence. Ben knew this presence well. Death was in the room with them, watching and waiting for the boy to give up his last, exhausted breath.

"Come on. It's okay," the kid said to Ben as he proceeded mutedly into the room and knelt by the bed, placing the food and water along the base of the bed for safekeeping. The very sight of the child's ailment scoured Ben inside and out as he looked down at the fleshy anima of the child's fatality. "He's bin like dis for long time. But I's bin taken berry good care of him, I have." The kid slid his hand over the boy's head like a parent would with their own fevered child. The kid wiped the perspiration off his ailing friend's forehead onto a small, sweat-stained pillow, then flung what remained with a whip of his hand.

Ben nodded, silent. The sick boy's eyes were deficiently open, and short, wheezing breaths proceeded out of him as he looked up at Ben. Ben shuddered.

"Help him," a voice whispered from all around, coming in and out of the room as a wafting plea. It was a wraith, childlike tone, practically a toddler, innocent and yet in horrible pain.

Ben's ears perked to the sky, listening as it called again in a drift. *"Please help my daddy."*

Ben looked down to see two condensed beads of light reflecting off the blackness of the kid's eyes once more. They were looking straight at him.

"I want my daddy. Please help him. Please."

Ben looked to see the other kid still whispering in his friend's ear, already forgetting the food Ben had brought in. Gently, he knelt and practically crawled up beside him. "What is your name?" Ben asked the child.

"Blake." His voice came and went.

"What you need from me, Blake," Ben tried to explain, "I don't think I can give you."

Blake continued to eye him as his lashes closed ever so slowly and then opened. *"Please, please. I need you to help my daddy. He's sick, and he's all I gots."*

Ben peered around the room for nothing in particular, as if there were anything there to help. "Where is he?" His thought came out loud.

"In his room. He only does it in his room."

Ben rose. "Where's his dad's room?" he demanded of the grungy kid, still whispering in his friend's ear.

The kid looked up, wiping snot from his nose with the sleeve of his shirt. "It be down dat way," he said, pointing at a wall. "But he be sleepy too wiff that needle stuff he bees takin'."

"Watch him," Ben said and rushed out of the room, throwing the sheeted door in the air and turning the corner.

Ben made his way to each room, pushing open doors without an ounce of restraint until he placed pressure on the one at the very end of the hall. Each time he tried, the clamor of several things built a tighter resistance to his efforts, cluttering tightly on the other side of the door. It opened a little more, bit by bit, in hairline increments. With the first sliver of access, a festering aroma of all sorts of vile stank poured from the room. A potent synthesis of vomit, urine, and decay. Finally, after several more strenuous nudges, he skulked his head past the door enough to see a large bedroom.

Spying the room, he could see the work of a timeless, ash furniture set dressing the inside. Farther in, he noticed an array of pictures on the opposing wall, heavily centered over the smaller of the two dressers, clean enough to be made out, unlike the ones in the living room. It seemed they were of happier times, belonging to what was once a family. There was one of them in the stands of a ball game, all wearing the same team hats, holding up their gloves and inflated bats in the air. Another was all three at an amusement park with a looping roller coaster and a carousel behind them. Hand in hand, they stood, father and mother and son all together, a picture of a perfect day. There were also a few birthday party pictures, one or two from a Christmas morning, and all sorts of portraits taken at a department store studio. Each one had them dressed in their Sunday best and with matching attire.

The only oddity to the room was how the queen-size bed, dressed ever so elegantly, was left disheveled. An array of pillows were bunched over to the side closest to the door to keep the secret of what lay at the other end. Ben peeked in farther to get a better look. He noticed an empty can of beer with a lighter and several used syringes, all glistening under the last dying flickers of candlelight. Below on the floor, directly under the nightstand, lie an old leather belt, a strip of elastic rubber, and a spoon.

There was a body in that room; Ben knew it. He could smell it and shuddered at the thought of its condition. He withdrew his head, took a few steps back, then returned with a single shoulder striking a hole in the door as he plowed into the room. Sure enough, it lay just where he expected it to be, on the far side of the bed, where the pillows and blockaded door would keep it concealed from young eyes. He was thin and boney and pale, with no shirt on, only jeans that looked to have fit him at one point, possibly back when he was healthier. Now they showed to be a few sizes too big. The man's feet were grungy, his mouth dry with slight traces of tawny froth at the lower side of his white, cracking lips. He wore a tattoo sleeve on his arm with two faces contiguous to each other, with their names reading out *Blake & Emily Forever*, scripted below in cursive. His eyes were open with deep pits darkening around them, though they were harder to spot under the dank strands of hair. What's worse, they were looking away from the door, away from Ben, listless, as if bound by something more robust than the influence of the needles.

Ben roweled up the nerves to lean beside the body and tried to listen to see if there was a breath calling to him the way Blake had somehow managed. There was nothing, nothing at all. "Hello," Ben uttered. He scooted his feet a hair closer, kicking over more bottles and other strange paraphernalia just before noticing the pile of clothes blocking the door. He perched his mouth over the man's ear. "Sir, can you hear me? I-I'm here to help."

The man stared on. His eyes, dilated to almost complete blackness, failed to shift or blink. They were empty, glazed in black death.

Ben looked him over, turned off by the descry of his lifeless arm flapped over the bed. It was still punctured by a syringe, lying encrusted by the dehydration of age and abuse and dressed in a thin ribbon of dry blood. He choked down nausea and managed to move the arm off to the side. Ben's deft eyes shortly took notice of a small, triangular corner of what looked to be an old, rumpled photograph peeking from under his shoulder. It was nothing more than a glossy corner. Still, it screamed noticeably between the salmon-colored quilt and the man's sallow body.

"Sir?" He tried again to listen in his mind, searching through a sea of grim silence for the slightest beacon of utterance in response. He got nothing.

Ben placed his hands on the man, one over the upper shoulder and one on his thigh, and gently rolled the man over to face the ceiling, unburdening the photograph from his dead weight. Gingerly, he picked up the photo and angled it to meet the light. There was the same man looking dapper and dancing softly in the glow of candlelight while kissing his bride on the cheek. It was a healthier, heavier version of who he had been. Well dressed in a fitted tuxedo and standing under a New England arbor studded with lights and a profusion of white magnolias and sunset poppies, skillfully arranged just for a wedding photo. A beautiful young woman with a face that glowed radiance in the light had been embraced in his arms. Her sanguine lips gave the camera a most awing smile.

Behind the two, just past the point of a blur, was a lineup of wedding party members looking on. Most were women, a few were men, and one held a strong resemblance to his father. In fact, as he studied the picture in depth, it was uncannily similar to the same image his mother had of him back when Ben was merely a child. Through the blur, the man had fashioned the same beard, sculpted the same chiseled shoulders and arms, and posed the same authoritative stance his father had in so many of his mother's photos.

Ben took another look at the man on the bed, seeing him differently, affectionately. He placed the picture respectfully on the nightstand and looked at what had become of Chad. He wondered if this had been the same fate for Emily. He wanted to know if that man in the photo was indeed his father, and if so, why was he there? How did they know him? But more so, he wanted to know what his relationship with Blake was.

"Sir," he uttered again, voice trembling, chastened by the thought of why that was the last photograph Chad had chosen to lay eyes on. Was he giving his final farewells surrounded by the dark, somber, and candlelight? Could he have possibly been asking for forgiveness from his love for not being strong enough to go on, for leaving their child behind, sick and alone?

His heartbeat was sorely within his chest. To no avail, he gave a few meager pokes at Chad's shoulder, letting his finger rest unsteadily on the cold flesh longer than he would have liked to. Of course, there was no movement and no voice. Not even a heartbeat. Other than Ben, the room was gravely still. He glanced down one last time into the man's empty eyes, looking to find his way into where the man's soul would be, praying to find something there. All he saw was the irreversible certainty that there was no longer a father to be saved.

* * *

The door chimed as Calvin pushed his way inside the noisy restaurant, revealing a pleasant crème hue lighting, which was a stark contrast to the purplish darkness outside. He knew he was walking in during the evening rush. Every table seemed crammed with people and roadhouse cuisine. Silverware clinked and scraped eagerly over generic-colored plates. Cups tapped on wooden tables as a slew of banter swirled together in the air to create a spool of noisy ruckus. Clearly, it was the wrong time to come and see her, but he took his chances anyway.

"Hey, Cal," the young, familiar beauty from behind the hostess counter called to him. She had dark hair, dark eyes, dark lipstick, and ivory skin, bordering on Goth to the older generation. A slew of metal rings traced the outer realms of her ears, with one more perching the pencil-thin corner of her right eyebrow. Over her right breast, the tattoo strand of rosebuds and thorns peeked out from the open part of her blouse. Calvin tried hard not to stare. He failed. "What brings a cutie like you here at this time of night?" she asked, seducing him with her words like a vampire luring in her prey. How he wished she were.

"I'm looking for my mom," he said, struggling to keep his eyes tethered to hers and not the tattoo. "Have you seen her around?"

"Oh, well, she's pretty busy, hon. Maybe it would be best if you waited for her to come home. I'm sure she'd love to chat with …"

Out of the corner of his eye, Calvin saw his mom pushing herself out of the kitchen. The backside of her black skirt first, followed by a white, dress code–style blouse, and finally, two hands weighing the oversized serving trays they used to carry out food. Once clearing the path of the swinging door, she turned and began walking toward him. The room was too busy for her to notice her son. It always was. She dressed her face in her best "it's a pleasure serving you" smile and stopped four tables away from the hostess counter. He watched as she chatted lightly with the party of young adults, chuckling as if one of them cracked a joke bearing a trace of humor. She laid the food before the group, neater than anything he had seen her do at home. She then stood at attention just long enough to ensure they were all satisfied.

There was a lethargy she wore and hid somewhat well under her uniform manners. A spell of exhaustion caused by too many doubles and not enough rest. It was in the slant of her eyes—they dipped just along the tip—and how she held out each blink longer than usual. It was in the dryness of her makeup. How her face revealed a few extra wrinkles branching over her brows and from the corners of her lips when she cracked a grin. It was in the slight hunch that creviced her back and tilted her head slightly downward. Most people wouldn't notice such things on her. Calvin did.

With one final smile, she turned from the table and Calvin as well. She headed back toward a little walled-in station at the end of the restaurant, nestling her trays under her arms like black circular wings. Calvin gave the hostess a dashing thanks—for what, he wasn't quite sure—before stridently following her. He lost his mother for a glimpse as she curtailed the wall and ducked into the station. Still, all it took was that glimpse for him to notice another person was equally eager to catch her before her next table.

He was a big man, in height and girth, but in a way that one couldn't quite tell if it was fat or muscle. Either way, it gave him an intimidating disposition. He wore a business suit that could have come off a clearance rack from the starved bowels of the last surviving Sears. His tie hung loosely around his neck, and he wore his hair short, letting the grays blossom where they may. When he turned to sip on his coffee, Calvin caught a smile at half mast, creeping up one side of his face, while the other side remained composed. Something about it pissed off Calvin.

He watched as the man set down his mug and trail into the station. It didn't hinder Calvin's stride in the least. He negotiated the aisles, skirting around customers, other waiters, and waitresses, dodging trays until he finally rounded the wall. She was there, and so was the man, with his hand gently stroking his mother's arm. She quickly pulled away the moment she saw her son standing there, but the pleasure of his touch still tingled the muscles in her face.

"Calvin," she said, shocked. Pink swollen leaves of skin framed the exhaustion of her laboring eyes. An exchange of looks had been divided between the three. Calvin's mom took one good step around the man as he lowered his hand. "What in the good Lord's name are you doing here? Do you have any idea what time it is?"

Calvin stared into her eyes, expecting her to be taken aback by the stained bruise over his face. She wasn't. She hadn't even seemed to care in the least.

"Do I get an introduction?" The man stood upright with his hands on his hips, exhibiting the full extent of naivety within his confidence.

"Tom, this is my son, Calvin. Calvin … Tom. Tom … ugh … is visiting from corporate," she said. His mother's attempt at confidence was faulty compared to Tom's, hiding nothing.

"Hey there, sport," Tom said, throwing a hand over Calvin's shoulder and then giving his back a couple heavy pats. Calvin couldn't help thinking he probably called him "sport" because he already couldn't remember his name, even after his mother used it. "What a solid lad you are."

Calvin winced out a smile. He didn't like Tom.

"Where is your father?" his mother asked … demanded.

"He's at home," Calvin replied shortly.

His mother took a step forward to speak to him more directly while remaining oblivious to the bruise that colored his face. "Well, then how did you get here?"

Calvin shrugged, fighting against his mother's stern grip on his shoulders. "I walked from Travis's house."

"You walked all the way here from Travis's house at this time of night? What the hell were you thinking?"

Tom gave his mother a light pat on the back before trying to sneak discretely away, sidestepping his way out of the station while letting the hand on her back linger. Calvin eyed him with disdain as he walked past.

"I wanted to see when you were coming home." Calvin's focus shifted back to his mother. "Dad keeps ordering pizza with meat on it, and I don't like—"

He watched his mother's expression twist in disbelief. "Oh, for goodness sakes, Cal, who cares! Do you know what could have happened to you coming here at this hour of the night? You could have been kidnapped or … or hit by a car or heaven knows what else. Bad things begin to happen about this time. Do you realize how stupid that was? You've got to use your head, son." She sighed, releasing a flutter of aggravation. "I will be home when I get home," she said slowly and at length, pushing him off, out of the station, and back into the busy restaurant. "You get your butt home before it gets any later. We'll talk about this later with your father."

Calvin turned, flustered, and tromped away, not caring whose meal he might ruin on the way out.

"And I better not hear of you wandering the streets before heading home. I know how long it should take you to walk," she called out, causing embarrassment to flush Calvin's face.

* * *

Ben rushed out the door, his feet shambling down the steps of the patio, catching Jeremy's attention from across the street. One hand cupped along the rim of his mouth while the other swung high in the air. "Call nine-one-one, now!" he shouted and then turned and dashed back inside.

He turned and dashed back into a house with a new level of somberness to it now that he'd seen how it tasted the bereft flavor of death. It settled within his stomach quite uneasily. He held his breath and charged down the hall until he was past the sheet door and back in the presence of the grungy kid who had been left keeping vigil at his friend's side. Even now, the kid remained fastened to the corner of the bed. Only the food Ben had brought in had been tampered with and was one cheeseburger short.

The kid peered up at Ben, revealing a blotch of mustard and ketchup that spread around the corners of his mouth, "He be said dat his dad don't mind if I eats his burger. He be said dat he didn't tink his dad don't needs it no more."

Ben rushed over and collapsed to his knees before crawling to the side of the bed. "What can I do for you?" he said softly to Blake.

"Help my daddy, please," the childlike voice pleaded in Ben's head.

"I have an ambulance coming for him now," Ben whispered while avoiding eye contact.

Blake's voice continued. *"I have the dark stuff that took my mommy. It all hurts so badly. I wannit to goes away. Can you make it goes away? Please?"*

Ben reached over and embraced Blake's hand, coddling it with his own. The boy's hand was so feeble and delicate that it felt as breakable as a dry leaf. Ben gave a noticeable amount of remorse, looking down on the child. It made the boy's eyes begin to swell.

"He's gone, isn't he? Daddy?" Blake's voice quivered in Ben's head. Ben gave a gentle nod. Blake crunched his eyes tight, cutting off a tear that had been forming at the corner of his veiny lids for some time. Ben watched as it trickled down his gauzy cheek.

Fluttering pricks scoured Ben's lungs as he held his breath and then exhaled. He laid his head and all his focus on Blake to see what, if anything, he might be able to do. Something about this child was different from the others Ben had helped before. He wasn't called to the boy, at least not in the bizarre orthodox fashion he had grown accustomed to. And Blake wasn't trying to take his own life.

Ben tightly shut his eyes and prepared to search deep for the perpetrator, not knowing exactly how he would do it or what he hoped to find. He had never attempted to exchange cancer for health before, and even if he did find it, he wondered if he could even make the exchange or survive. There was no telling what kind of toll an attempt like this might have on him.

He concentrated, feeling the weightlessness of his conscious float readily away from his body and into the child. At first, he saw nothing, but this was not uncommon. He recalled a few he helped with a similar amount of darkness, blacker and heavier than the deepest cave of the ocean floor, consuming the individual as they neared their end. Ben had experience in navigating this midnight terrain.

Suddenly he heard the abrupt giggle of Blake's voice calling from far away. There were no words, just laughter, faint as if caught in a gust of wind, but pure. Through absolute darkness, Ben began to feel his body moving up, and then down, and then side to side, a kind of g-force moving him in multiple directions. Children and adults were building an entertained ruckus in front and behind him. Music started to orchestrate from somewhere below: an organ and chimes playing only the happy notes in lullaby fashion. *A carousel*, Ben thought. Suddenly he heard a long, repetitious clanking sound. His gut began to drop with nervous anticipation as his body leaned back, facing up to where a sky should be. Effervescent voices were starting to scream, rhapsodizing in excitement as the clanking slowed at the apex of the incline. Ben felt his body rotating downward before plummeting swiftly down, his hands clenched to a bar. At the lowest point of the drop, he picked up the scent of buttery popcorn. As he jerked to the right, he picked up a fonder scent, something he found cozy and quite distinguishable, like patchouli and peach with a hint of almond. A soft, gentle hand rested on top of his, its fingers interlaced. His stomach wrenched as he rose unexpectedly into the air and came down into an abrupt and jerky stop.

Ben was not surprised that he arrived at a joyous memory, especially if this was Blake's favorite one. It was safe to assume this was where the picture hanging in his father's bedroom was taken. Still, Ben realized a surfeit of blackness hazed the entire memory, something Ben hadn't experienced before. His concern grew as he could hear the laughter fade and the shrouded surroundings change. The perfume, too, diminished, leaving nothing more than a lonely cavern of thick darkness and stale air.

He felt it necessary to concentrate more if he was going to reach the stem of Blake's ailment and make it his own. He worked physically and consciously to dive into the core without crushing the poor boy's hand by mistake. He pushed through the overshadowed memories, reliving a few blindly. In contrast, others appeared to be locked away in places Ben couldn't access. It was as if the boy knew he was there and willfully kept them away from his prying. It became apparent to him that he saw no future in all these memories, the one thing he needed to grasp before beginning his final task.

The deeper he went in, the less he found. Memories became scarcer, on the brink of nonexistence. It was as if the cancer had been living off who he was, and now, being within its final stages, Ben realized it had almost completely wiped out who he might have been. As Ben reached the core, he found there was nothing, not noise or a glimmer of Blake's past, present, or future. All parts of Blake's life were simply nonexistent. Ben struggled to try to understand what this meant.

"Ben," Jeremy called from the hallway.

Ben opened his eyes and slipped his hand out of Blake's. "We're in here," he cried.

The sheet ripped from the doorway, revealing an out-of-breath Jeremy holding a phone next to his ear. His face was distorted, slack with shock as he took in the sight of the room and the boys. "What the hell?" he gasped. "Is he all right?"

"For now," Ben replied, standing up. He walked over to Jeremy and pushed him back out of the room. "It's his dad ..."

"His dad?" Jeremy questioned, taking an urgent glance around Ben into the room.

"He's in the room down the hall. The one with the door open. He's—"

Jeremy read Ben's expression and plugged his other ear on impulse to respond to the dispatcher. "Um, yes, I'd like to report an emergency." He breathed. "There is a young boy and a man. Um, his f-f-father ... we believe ... Yes, we found them in a house, a-a-and they don't look good. We need someone over here, STAT."

Ben immediately refocused on Blake as Jeremy went outside to communicate with the dispatcher. He hoisted his determination and took hold of his hand once more. "We'll get you all better," Ben assured him. Blake's eyes opened and sat dormant long enough for Ben to take notice of a glassiness he hadn't seen in them before. His eyes were nothing but sclera, white and uncomfortably close to looking at death.

"I don't think my friend gonna be here no mores," the grungy-looking kid said, reminding Ben that he was still present.

"Come on, little man," he said to Blake, chewing on the corner of his bottom lip. His eyes riffled over the sickly body, hunting for something that he felt should be obvious to see. "I need to know where the cancer is."

"In my head," the boy thought feebly. It came and went with a knackered-out blink.

"I can't see it," Ben replied, rubbing his hands through his hair in frustration. "All I see in there is blackness."

"That's it," Blake thought. *"It all hurts so bad—so very bad. Please take it away. I don't wanna hurt like this no more. Please take it away."*

"The blackness. You're saying that's all cancer?" Ben looked at him intensely.

Blake blinked and notched his chin downward at the same time.

Ben readjusted his grip over Blake's hand while the other rested gently on the boy's forehead. "I need you to open up all the way. Let me in, okay? I need to see everything. Can you do that for me?"

Blake wispily shut his eyes.

Ben felt his presence whisked somewhere deep into Blake's consciousness with a rush of ethereal air, thwarting off several irrelevant memories to cut deep within the palimpsest of experiences to a destination already set in place. It was as if Blake knew where Ben needed to go and was dragging him there with what little energy he had left. The draw of iodoform and urine started to burn Ben's nostrils. He came to a standstill, gagging on the obtrusive odor under the slow, mechanical sound of a respirator beeping. Faintly underneath the foul smell, Ben could pick up the familiar scent of patchouli, peach, and almond. Oxygen pushed through a machine, forcing sterile air through plastic tubes as it counted down the seconds with its insensate tone. *Beep … beep … beep.* His feet were burdened with the pressure of standing over a cold tile floor for what felt like hours. His body was blanketed in the awareness of the still, stale air found only in a sickening room. It was one of the memories Blake had previously locked him out of, and for a good reason. It was a bad one, one that a kid like Blake would fight against having to relive, making it a perfect spot for his cancer to nest.

The muffled sound of two voices could be heard conversing behind closed doors. They were less than an earshot away, seemingly unaware that there was another set of ears listening in. One voice penetrated in a trembling tone, overwhelmed by heartbreak. He was a young parent.

"She's in the final stages of her cancer now," a man said, voicing a morose demeanor, yet far from anything resembling sympathy. "I'm sorry, Mr. Johnson, but we've exhausted every option. There's nothing more we can do for her other than make her as comfortable as possible while she's still with us."

As Ben took in the struggle of Blake's grief, an emaciated voice fluttered into his ears. "It's okay, baby." Her words fell between life-draining pants of wheezy air. Ben tensed as a wisp of his mother's presence could be discerned. He felt the texture of a cold, fragile hand reach out to rest against his arm. It could only forge a meager movement as it lay arthritically feeble against him.

He finally glanced up to take in her appearance and saw the pale face of his own mother. She looked identical to the way she had when he'd last seen her. Tears began welling up in his eyes. Was it her hand he felt against his arm? Was that her voice that tried to ease him just as she always had? Whose mother was this, Blake's or his own?

Ben backed away. He needed a moment to regroup and realize that the memory may serve as a puppet to the disease, playing the stage of his own past to distract him or hold him back. Ben could feel it trying to take over his mind within the room, having a solid grip on his memory. He felt that it actually had a chance to link the two and spread its residence. Ben decided that if he were going to win this and take Blake's cancer from him, he would most likely have to relive his own dark memories as well.

For too long, the disease stayed concealed, like a monster under the bed, waiting for night to fall. But Ben could hear its snarl. He could hear its grunt as it nipped at the air to catch a flavor of who this stranger was. It watched with phantom eyes to see if Ben would have the courage to put himself in place of the boy to draw it out like a pack of wolves tired of gnawing on dried bones. To be the bait and lure such vicious teeth.

Ben clenched every muscle in his body and took all the dark memories of Blake and his own, pulling them up by the roots. The usual tingles of electricity had overwhelmed themselves by a surfeit of gashing pain, jagged and surging from his head down to his toes, reaching into the marrow with inexplicable agony. He accumulated the smells, setting his head on fire, trying to take it all in. Several volumes of previous exchanges had been pushed out into the beyond to make room for such a monster disease. It clawed at him, fed off him, and sacrificed all its holds on Blake's memories for a taste of Ben's own horrible past. He pulled and caged it all within himself, leaving him lost within an expanse of transparent nothingness, struggling to tarry in the savagery of this disease for an unforeseen amount of time.

His mouth became gaping, and his lungs scoured and filled with blood as they took in the air like molecular shards of glass. The exchange and disease consumed him from the inside. His bones felt crushed under sharp jaws. His gut felt brutally torn and feasted on. There were no tight hugs. No transference of emotions or replacing evil thoughts for good ones to come into play. He felt no noose around his neck, no choking down water, or anything of the sort. It was just havoc—pure, unrelenting, inner bestial havoc.

Blake's eyes burst open. His pupils shrunk as his iris's spooled under a vapor of steam, like the stirring of hot chocolate. A fresh coat of brown painted his eyes. Frail skin swelled, becoming plump, moist, and pink. His bones strengthened, muscles tightened, hair flourished and revitalized, and lips became red and soft and damp. He blinked once, twice, feeling his lashes tap each other with the thickness of life. A youth came back to restore that which the disease had taken away.

Blake gasped with excitement and tossed himself on Ben's unconscious body.

Ben lay in darkness, barely able to move. He heard something like a ripple across an abyss. *"Follow me! This way!"* a voice echoed. Ben turned his head to see Blake signaling to him from afar. Ben reached out his arms and pushed through the nothingness, kicking his legs to swim toward the vision. *"Hurry! You gotta get out!"* Blake hollered.

Suddenly, a dark monster screeched and howled at Ben's feet, reverberating in the bloodcurdling wails of a banshee. It had now realized that Ben had succeeded and was unwilling to let go of another meal. Ben struggled to keep as much speed as possible as the atmosphere continued to gnaw on its prey. He felt his legs tangle within something that resembled barbed wire. He felt claws gashing into his arms and torso as the monster tried to keep Ben in its grasp.

"You gotta hurry! Gotta get outta here!" Blake cried with frantic desperation in his tone.

"I-I can't," Ben struggled to say. "Let me hold it while you escape. It wants to come after you."

Blake closed his eyes and placed his head on top of Ben's. He clenched his fists and screamed, *"Let him alone!"*

Blake's voice blew triumphantly through the abyss, shaking the very atmosphere around Ben into a quaking shell of frail earthenware. Large fractures of blackness fissured and crumbled, sending in lances of brilliant light from the beyond. Every piece that fell sent beamed light over Ben's body, forcing the black monster to borrow deep within Ben as it howled and writhed in pain. Its claws blistered and seared at the light as it penetrated deeper and deeper.

Ben's body shuddered to life. His eyes popped wide open as he gasped for air. His heart raced—*thump-thump... thump-thump*—letting him know he was still alive. His face took a sallow tone, glistening with sweat as if he were about to lose his stomach all over the floor. Ben coughed and hacked and spit a bitterness from his mouth as he reacquainted his lungs with the dusty taste of air. Finally, he attempted to push himself up by the bed. His body gave out under him, sending him to the ground and disturbing a layer of dust on the carpet. Again, it all went dark.

SEVEN

The ride home was laden with silence for the most part. Jeremy drove well above the speed limit while one of his friends struggled to keep up behind them in Ben's puttering green truck. It took some time for statements to be collected. Protective services had arrived with their own batch of questions, leaping from person to person while everyone was adequately tended to or getting ready to be shipped off to hospitals. The roads had become a late-night stream of abandoned asphalt, leaving few vehicles drifting along on the lengthy drive home.

"I wouldn't sweat it, really," Jeremy said steadily. Streetlights swept above them, flashing over the dirty windshield in an extraterrestrial blur that brightened his face with every grainy, strobed motion.

Ben could feel the weight of his eyelids dragging them closed, dropping from a load of sleeplessness he customarily felt. His head still burned with the fever of Blake's disease, swelling from the inside, pushing against his skull as if fighting to escape. He wasn't interested in talking, even less in conversing about what happened that night. He had questions, but unfortunately, Jeremy was not the one to answer them.

At that moment, all Ben cared about was fulfilling his appetency to have his head deep within his pillow. His body craved to be buried under familiar sheets and let exhaustion have its way. Unfortunately, they still had a long way to go to get there.

"The guy who checked you out said lots of people faint in situations like that. For heaven's sake, dude, you stumbled on a dead body," Jeremy exclaimed as if that was something to brag about. "How you didn't puke at the sight of that thing is beyond me!" A few more lights flashed overhead. "You ever seen one before?" he asked. "You know, like in a morgue or wake or something?"

Ben gave neither a look nor an answer. Jeremy turned and faced forward.

"Yeah, me neither," Jeremy muttered under his breath. "Hell, I'd have probably fainted too had I been the one to come across it." Jeremy crooked his head slightly to give a sideways glance at Ben. "Not only that, but you probably saved that poor kid's life. You know that, right?"

"Blake," Ben grunted.

Jeremy turned his attention to Ben. "What's that?"

Ben said, "His name is Blake. His dad's name was Chad Johnson, and his mom's name was Emily." Ben turned to face the passenger window, rolling his head to stretch the jagged pain out of his neck. "He looks a lot like his mom … a lot like my dad as well. I had an aunt named Emily."

Jeremy gave an unsure look. "Huh," was all he offered.

Ben continued to wrench the pain out of his joints. Every muscle in his body felt like it was being ripped into strands of fiery brisket. Everything that could bend popped as he turned from one side to the other and went on saying, "I never knew her, but she lived around these parts. And I saw my dad. He was with them at their wedding. He was in an old wedding photo of theirs."

Jeremy gave his attention to the road, glancing back briefly to make sure the green truck was still behind them. "You were seeing things, bro. That's all. You came across a dead man and a kid all by himself. Stress plays games with people in those situations. And you lost your dad when you were a kid yourself, so it only makes sense that you would imagine seeing your dad in some old photo. Besides, suppose you really think about it. Your mind is probably trying to find another justification for you to stay here."

Ben went silent.

Jeremy's eyes sharped on the road ahead. "Man, that kid would have probably died had you not rushed in there like that. Do you understand how crazy that is?"

Ben didn't reply. He only offered a morosely stoic look before reacquainting the corner of his head with the door's window. The cool glass began nursing the fever that ravaged his brain. *Probably*, he thought. *There was no probably about it. That kid was one fatal sigh away from never seeing daylight again.*

A construction sign developed with a dawning glow, posting a slight change to their merge onto the I-5. Jeremy grumbled a quick subject change. "You gotta be kidding me." A swift merge into the detour lane sent the vehicle rocking. Jeremy watched through the rearview mirror to ensure the puttering green truck had done the same. After the vehicle settled, Jeremy asked, "What do you think he meant when he said, 'I can see what you see'? That's weird, right?"

Ben rolled his head off the window. "What are you talking about?" he murmured.

"That kid … in the bed … Blake. Before they loaded him up in the ambulance, he said, 'I can see what you see.' What did he mean by that?"

Ben rolled back to continue watching the streetlights. "I'm not sure, really," he lied. "Kid's been through a lot. Probably just senseless rambling, that's all."

"Hmm, I suppose," Jeremy responded, not entirely convinced but not finding ample amount of evidence for a reason to push the subject further. He flipped on the radio. From that point on, neither said a word.

* * *

Now that school had developed into a prison of resentment, truancies became more routine by the day. Danica realized she had lost the ability to care about anything. Her grades plummeted about as fast as her popularity, and her morals and values were on life support. The offensive words and merciless cold shoulders abused her like detestable children with sticks, poking and prodding her into the corner of some emotional alley, unleashing a creature of vileness in herself.

The last period had just begun a few blocks away from her house, but Danica wasn't there. Instead, she held her head over the faucet and rinsed the dye out of her hair. There was a satisfaction in watching the ink-like mixture spiral down the drain. She saw it as all those rancid words filling her head, exfoliating from her scalp, leaving a residue on the white porcelain as dark as the minds that put them there. Her gaze lifted while her head hung, eyes hiding under the cut of her newly chopped locks. Whoever it was in the mirror no longer looked like her. This girl was different, first inside and now out.

She grabbed a towel while recalling how distraught the stylist's expression was earlier in the day when she explained that she wanted a shoulder-length bob.

"Please tell me you're joking!" the stylist said, wide-eyed, holding up a piece of her long hair. Danica's desire to justify another part of herself was depleted to the point of irritation. It only took one weighted glare for him to pick up on that.

She lifted her now wrapped head from the sink and took a long look in the mirror, in her own retina. All she saw were the features of a stranger. The change she starved for had begun taking shape, leaving her to wonder if it was possible to feel empowered and hopeless at the same time. She felt both.

"Danica? For heaven's sake! Please don't tell me that's you?" her mom abruptly called up the stairs.

The corners of her mouth crept up, maddening and satisfied. Inside, a tormenting pleasure, her own method of flagellation, reached over to take the deepest red lipstick from the vanity drawer. She began scribbling over the mirror words her lips had never conceived of speaking a year ago.

"Danica?"

Danica paused. Her fingers lingered at the end of one word she had become sagaciously familiar with—the sum of everyone's belief about who she was: whore.

"It's me," Danica replied, apathetic.

Her mom's footsteps had already been heard climbing the stairs. They were minutes away from standing in the bathroom doorway, a state of shock on her face at what her daughter had become. No longer blonde and no longer the sweet Colorado cheerleading Christian she had raised. Danica unwound the towel, revealing jet-black strands as sleek as the body of a black widow. She reached over for a comb and began working out some of the tangles.

"What have you done?" her mom shrieked as she poked her head into the bathroom.

Danica ran a few last strokes through her hair, then gently set the comb down. "What? You don't like it?" she toyed as she brushed passed her mom, grazing shoulders confrontationally on her way to her bedroom.

"This can't continue! We can't live like this," her mom hollered louder than necessary. Her arms danced frantically in the air, marching after her daughter.

Danica moved like a specter, without care for the living in the house. *Poor Mom*, she snidely thought. *She can't live like this. The woman has no idea what I'm living with.*

Danica pressed her torso against the stained wood and leaned over her antique dresser. She went on to look intensely in the mirror. She swiped on a wild layer of eyeliner before crossing the room to grab a jacket from her closet.

Danica's mom had absolutely no experience with rebellion, which gave Danica a smug amount of confidence. As she drew a fresh layer of bloody lipstick over her mouth, her mom stood in the doorway, arms crossed, trying to express some amount of authority.

"Danica! Are you listening to me? Something must change." Danica couldn't recognize her mom in that tone. She was forcing herself to go into her calm, reasoning phase. "Do you have any idea the stress you are putting on our family right now? These mood swings, getting a phone call every other day to let us know you didn't show up for another class, missing meals, locking yourself up in this room. It's exhausting."

"Sorry to be a disappointment, Mom. Maybe I should just disappear." Danica strolled past her mom, determined not to look at her.

"That's not what I am saying … Danica … Danica, please," her mom pleaded.

Danica would hear nothing of it. Every step down the stairs came with a bitterly sharp stomp as if she were trying to plow her foot through the finished wood. Determination drove her to the door. Rage took her past it and gave her reason to slam the door behind her.

She stuffed her hands deep inside her jacket pockets and briskly walked down the sidewalk, cleared fresh of a recent tempest snowfall. She felt lighter, her hair fluttering in her face with the cold breeze. Seeing the dark strands made her feel like a completely different person. She wanted to own it, being that up until this point, her life had morphed into her own personal nightmare, flowing with a distortion of what she saw, heard, and felt.

Her parents were only starting to realize that their precious daughter had died and resurrected into this monster. They were helpless, not understanding the root cause. But she didn't feel bad for them. Why would she? No one felt bad for her. It was clear they were only concerned about how it would disrupt their comfortable lives.

She turned a corner and walked a couple more blocks before jogging haphazardly across the main street to a familiar shopping strip. Seasonal styles hung prematurely on display in most windows, enticing those early holiday shoppers to step inside. Cozy attire posed in lively or flirty postures, giving application to its wear during the seasonal chill that the week had held.

Danica strode past the first few doors, arms now crossed over her chest, shielding herself from the nip that gusted in the air and trickled down her blouse. Her toes began to feel numb as each step sank into the damp residue of the surprise storm. Her jeans, too, provided slight deflection to the biting air as her legs pimpled with goose bumps under the spandex denim. One sudden shift in the air, and Danica surrendered. She took shelter in a small boutique she would have passed right by without consideration had it been any other day.

The clinking of the door was pleasant to her ears. Her face went flush with electric sparks as it immediately began to defrost. The room was coated in the scent of wintry precipitation and radiator heat. She stepped in closer, transferring the warmth of the fabric merchandise into her hands with a wary touch.

"Miss … can I help you?" a well-dressed lady politely spoke from behind the counter as Danica pushed her way deeper inside the boutique.

She was on the younger side of middle age, with intentional silver hair with blueberry tips that blossomed from a high-sprouted ponytail. The outfit she wore came straight from one of the racks Danica had passed on the way in, a rebirth of sixties fashion with a modern twist.

Danica grinned but otherwise chose to ignore the lady and walked on, generating a suspicious look. She could see her out of the corner of her eye, leaving the counter and walking toward another lady folding blouses on the other side of the store. Danica glanced back briefly to see them whispering to each other. Each took turns to reflect in her direction before looking down at their own feet and continuing to whisper.

Danica turned around, chuckling. "Of course, they would judge me," she whispered, sifting through high-rise jeans on a rack, relaxed by the soft music and breathing in the scent of fresh material. Her hand flowed down the fabric of the last pair before slowly making her way to the lingerie, while glancing at items hung high on the wall. She picked up a couple of hipster-style panties, inspecting each of them at eye level before glancing over her shoulder to see the first lady was back behind the counter. The woman was still looking up at her through the tops of her designer glasses, even when Danica offered a complacent smile. She set the panties back down and brushed her hands across the lace, turning toward the tops on the other side of the store. Everything felt good to touch. It was far from anything she'd ever wear, making it more desirous.

The glass door clinked twice as another set of customers walked in. Decades separated the two, linked by remarkably similar features. Danica surveyed them together. It was clear that the pair were mother and daughter who held an equally deep connection in conversation as they did in physical traits. It was that type of connection Danica used to have with her mom on the days when nothing could go wrong. Danica weaved between racks, watching them for some time as they smiled and giggled, holding a medley of blouses against each other to see how well they complemented their natural features while continuing to chitchat. The scene took to Danica like an old family video, recalling nostalgic moments that were never to return. It nauseated Danica and turned her stomach beyond her tolerance. She missed that feeling so much that she diverted her eyes any way she could in the small boutique to keep them from tripping over the painful sight of these joyous strangers.

She began to graze against fabrics of different textures, running her shoulder down to her hands and thighs against the hanging clothes. Fingers scrolled over occupied hangers like a drawer crammed with folders, peeking at one after another. Suddenly a maroon top caught her attention, and she snagged it off the rack.

Danica moved briskly to the lady folding blouses. She drove straight to one of the dressing rooms and pulled the flimsy door open without hesitation or consent. The door sprung open and bounced back as Danica stepped into a long, narrow box that looked more like a bathroom stall than a changing room. She secured the latch, staring down an antique cheval mirror that seemed eerily similar to the one her grandmother had in her upstairs guest room. It was angled in one corner to reflect the whole stall, as if there was something other than a few metal hooks to promote.

Danica slipped off her jacket and slingshot it over the mirror before doing the same with her shirt. She then went to work, dropping the new one over her head and tugging it down. Something about its V-shaped neckline and how it hugged firmly around her midsection stirred within her a cynical pleasure. She turned on her toes slowly, rotating and inspecting her waist and backside. She let her heels drop and then abruptly reached up under her arm and ripped the tag off. Crumpling the little slip of paper, she took her own top, hung it on the hanger, put her jacket back on, and shoved the crumpled tag in her pocket. Lastly, she zipped the coat from the bottom up, high enough to conceal what was underneath.

Danica reached for the door and discretely pushed it open, surveying the room to make sure no one had been suspicious enough to keep an eye on her. She leisurely walked out of the dressing room, observing the woman who was once folding blouses now engaged with the other customers. Arms whirled and swished in front of her, painting a dramatic picture of something that had to do with her own daughter. Danica couldn't help but listen in as she swiftly hung the shirt on the return rack behind another top. She casually made her way past that first section of racks, oblivious to the other employee who stood behind the counter and glanced in Danica's direction.

"Did you not like it?" the lady behind the counter rang, jolting the deepest nerves in Danica so that she shivered and turned at the same time. The lady continued, "That blouse looked like it was just your style. I thought for sure you would've liked it."

Danica ran her fingers up her jacket in search of her zipper and confirmed that it held snug up at the base of her neck. "Yeah, but it was too small," Danica replied.

"Well, we might have that one in a different size. In fact—" The woman shifted and set her sights on the return rack where Danica had left her own blouse.

Flutters began to explode in Danica's chest. She caught a quick glimpse of the other employee looking at her with accusing brows. "You know, it's fine. My mom called, and I have to go anyway." Danica's words tripped over each other as she backstepped to the door, bumping into every single line of clothes along the way. "But I will come back later and, and then maybe you can help me find one in my size. Okay? Thank you." With that, Danica kicked the door open and slipped outside.

No less than a hair after she passed the window did Danica sprint across the parking lot. Part of her felt like she was flying, hopping over a couple of parking dividers before taking a mild skip over a curb and darting down a suburban neighborhood. She began to laugh from within her gut. Her slightly damp scalp felt ice cold as the wind rushed past. She watched her Converse hit the pavement with rhythmic thumps and didn't stop until she felt completely out of breath.

Danica's breath transformed into a wheezy chuckle as she collapsed and sat on the sidewalk in a quiet neighborhood. A few minutes passed in silence, her back resting against a cinder block wall, listening to a breeze uncontaminated by the hum of traffic or the nuisance of people. She closed her eyes and pressed her head against the wall, taking deep breaths, soaking in all the exhilaration she had now experienced. The afternoon sun gleamed through her lids. She didn't know how long she could sit there, but forever would be nice, frozen in that moment and undisturbed by the rest of the pesky world.

"Miss?" An authoritative voice rained down on her.

Danica opened her eyes to see a cop standing above her with his hands on his hips. The static of several other voices rambled out of a little black radio over his shoulder. The butterflies returned, only now they felt a little more like maggots invading her intestines and crawling up her throat. She struggled down one last helping of air as the officer silenced the voices to confirm he had found the shoplifter in that little black box over his shoulder.

The officer knelt and put on hand on Danica. "I think you had better come with me."

* * *

A faint light began to break through the concrete blackness, with Ben finding himself still sitting in the passenger seat and Jeremy at the wheel. It was night. The roads were still lit with the extraterrestrial glow of hovering streetlamps. A one-sided conversation was going on and on about something Ben couldn't quite make out, a jumbled series of nonsensical words spilling out of Jeremy's mouth. Suddenly, yellow and black signs began to form in the distance, with flashing orange bulbs warning of another detour coming up ahead. "Aw, crap. Seriously!" were the only words that came out of Jeremy's mouth that made sense as he flicked on his turn signal and merged to the left for the second time. Concrete walls would now guide them from both sides.

Claustrophobia set in as they merged into one tight lane, bordered and unnecessarily curved. Ben could feel his gut rising and ball up in his throat as the accelerator revved 3,000 … 4,000 … 5,000 RPMs, redlining it even at the turns. The lane narrowed and grew curvier as the speed increased, turning everything into a shooting blur.

Jeremy maintained his calm demeanor as wheels screeched and tread burned against the asphalt. Sparks splashed over the side of the car as they tapped against the lower slope face of the barriers. He remained unfazed as he lost control of the vehicle. Ben knew things weren't making sense but felt numb to respond, his mouth refusing to function. Jeremy's hand yanked the wheel left and right while the other hung loose out the window. Ben sat, succumbed to the pressure of the vehicle's speed.

"What the—"

Before Jeremy could finish his thought, he slammed the brakes and yanked the wheel. The car slammed into one of the concrete barriers, blasting away the hood, shattering glass, and sending them spiraling toward the other concrete barrier. In the glimpse between one wall and the next, Ben made out the image of a boy standing idle in the center of the street, unperturbed by the vehicle that now bashed and flipped around him. Ben could feel his bones snapping just before gravity left the car in a midair roll, with debris flying around them like fireworks. More glass, plastic, and metal shattered in their faces as the vehicle plunged to the ground and finally came to a grinding halt. Oddly, Ben couldn't feel anything except his toes growing frigid. Blood swelled his head faster than he could realize that he was hanging upside down and dangling from the seat belt.

Outside the car, among the silent backdrop of what seemed like early morning, he could hear a pair of bare feet walking steadily over the broken glass and fluid-drenched asphalt. The sound was horrendous, but he could eventually see the tiny feet walking over the shards as carelessly as if it were a patch of lush grass. Whoever it was stopped beside the passenger door. The next thing Ben discerned was a dank, melon-shaped head ducking partially through the shattered passenger window.

Blake. He was dirty and sallow, flesh corroding along his forehead and jaw, exposing carmine bone and rotted gumlines where soft pink flesh should be. His eyes were smoky and gray. His mouth and teeth were all black and coated with an oily substance that dripped from his mouth, but he was smiling.

Blake's hand reached inside the car. His fingernails were rusted brown, crusty, and sharp. His sleeve was coated in some squalid amount of dirt, dressing his skin to look like the densely matted limb of a wild beast. He reached deep, grabbing Ben's neck and biting into it with his nails, crushing his larynx and breaking the skin. Quickly Ben felt every cavity struck wide with fear.

Ben awoke startled. Sweat dripped from his brows into his eyes and salted his lips. His chest palpitated without reason to ease as the vision of Blake posted lucidly in his mind. His look wandered frantically as anxiety podded out a deluded measure of perspiration that tingled from his face down his neck and chest. He tried to slow the pace of his breathing and take hold of those images to banish them. He put his fingers to his wrist and counted his pulse. Finally, he sat up over the disheveled covers. He ran his hand through his hair before dropping it to the back of his neck and letting it remain while he looked down at the wadded-up sheet in his lap. He reminded himself it was just a nightmare but could still feel the stabbing pain of Blake's fingernails below his hand on his neck.

Ben lifted his gaze and let the vision of his room start to clear and his sight adjust to the breaking color of the morning. The sun had risen just enough to paint the sky a shade becoming royal. The darkness had only thinned sufficiently to make out the windowsill and shadowy figures of trees swaying actively in front of a semicloudy atmosphere outside. However, the walls were painted in the absolute umbra of night, leaving the room with a sense of his belongings floating in infinite space.

Ben looked over to where his battery-operated clock blurred the dreadful time of 4:15. His body ached as one leg edged off the side of the bed, followed gradually by the other. He heard joints depressurizing and felt muscles straining in his back as he hoisted himself up. He yawned and, with a stifled moan, teetered toward the bathroom. His arm scaled up the somber inner wall of the bathroom, meeting the downward-facing nub of the switch with his wrist and pressing it up.

The halogen torches caused his eyes to sear; he ducked his face and covered his eyes. He then proceeded to go after the faucet and unleash a steady flow of cold water. With a series of deep chills, he splashed his face, slapping him numb and awake at the same time. He stood over the cold water, watching it rush between his fingers before bringing another full scoop to his face. It felt as if he was washing the encroaching crud out of his head within his imagination.

Ben turned off the faucet, lazily studying the last few trickles through blurred sight as they swirled down the hollow drain. He clutched the towel that hung loyally over the rack and pulled it straight to his face, pressing and patting away the moisture that still lingered. Gradually, the towel inched down his face—forehead to nose, nose to mouth, mouth to chin—pulling his face away from the sink to a position that forced his gaze on his reflection. The hand towel he held instantly dropped to the floor. His gut twisted into several contracting knots. What he saw was not a nightmare. It was not a dream. What he saw was worse—much worse.

EIGHT

Ben's eyes showed an advanced stage of jaundice in the sclera. His pupils were dilated, and his irises were an ashen gray. His hair fell thin and lifeless, translucent as a thick pile of spiderwebs wilting down his scalp. Skin dehydrated; it revealed a pasty somber tone. There was crusting around his mouth and over his pale white lips. Dark halos circled his eyes, shaded in deep purple, as if bruised, causing his eyes to sink beyond the bone with swallowing depth. His bone structure had become noticeably shaded, cut out from the thin, dry tissue that once boasted his youth, as if life had been sucked out of him while he slept.

What frightened him more was that he felt normal besides the typical achiness he experienced after a transfer. He briefly wondered if his exhaustion was performing a trick on his mind. He severely wanted to believe so, but he could see the skin thinning when he looked down at his hands and the loose flutter of his shirt, now three sizes too big for his frame. Boney claws lifted his shirt, revealing that his tight frame had withered, looking like he had a case of hypotonia. This wasn't normal.

Ben slipped out of his pants and boxers all at once, sheltering his eyes and refusing to look at the rest of his body. It all came off easily. He kicked the pile of clothes to the corner between the door and toilet and turned both shower knobs. It wasn't long before a cloud of steam formed around him. He stepped cautiously into the tub. The first bit of water took to his flesh like a swarm of bees, stinging his back before retreating down his thighs and draining into nonexistence. However, after a bit of time, the sting began to feel more like deep tissue therapy. He took a step back, letting the hot water trickle down his head and over his face. He lathered a soap bar and scaled up and down his body, disturbing the topsoil in foam as it raced down his skin. He then closed his eyes and scrubbed his face, drawing a long, soul-cleansing breath to let the steam whirl in the depths of his lungs until he was ready to let it back out. He then stood idle in the shower, under the faucet of rain, head down, eyes readily shut, as he waited for his mind to clear.

He finally allowed his eyes to creep open. Thin, fleshy sandpaper, grinding against burning corneas while still facing down to look directly at the tip of his feet. His toes bathed in the warmth of the water, thawing out and transitioning into a lively pink color. Muscles reswelled in his calves and thighs, sucking up the warmth from his feet up to his legs and into his abdomen. Ben's gut inflated and contracted. He could see that definition reforming in his abs as he bravely scanned his body with his hands, gradually returning to their normal, healthy state.

Just as he started to feel relief, something caught his eye that dripped down by his toes. He stared, unable to make it out when, suddenly, another one fell, and another. Something new, something he'd never seen before in all his years of doing the exchanges. Whatever it was loitered over the tile in a small tadpole shape. As more dark liquid dripped, it stretched between his feet, diluting into a thin brown stream in the middle of the shower's floor.

More droplets of the substance came, each one thicker than the last. They began to plop into the clean water with weight. Whatever this was leaked steadily, an unctuous liquid that appeared to hold the composition of an oily sort of tar. Ben raised his head to survey the ceiling, panning from side to side and front to back. It was dew soaked yet clean and as white as the tiles on the wall. He checked the showerhead, finding that it was clean as well. Again, he looked down, taken aback; he now could see a stream of it running down the center of his chest. With great caution, he touched the substance with the tip of his finger. It pulled away like a tacky rush of phlegm yet was just as greasy and as dense as oil. He brought his finger up to his nose to smell it. It had the scent of blood with the undertone of pepper.

In haste, Ben went to wash his chest under the showerhead, wiping his face with his hands. As he pulled his hands off his face, he noticed more on his finger than before. It glazed over a good half of his finger and ran down his knuckles. His heart jumped, and his breath stalled. Urgently, he wiped his nose along his forearm and pulled it away. His arm came back covered in a dark, sticky mess that quickly dispersed, washing diluted onto the floor. With speed, he lathered and scrubbed his arm and face. He then drenched himself under the showerhead, turned off the water, and jumped out of the tub. Urgently, Ben wrapped a towel around his waist and went gliding over the slick linoleum floor to face the mirror once more. His body was back to its usual pristine health, but his eyes were an intense black. His mouth struggled to draw open, locked shut by what felt like a trismus jaw. The mysterious substance continued to pour out from his eyes and nostrils. It scaled the inner part of his cheek down to the crevice of his lips, building at the slope of his chin.

* * *

Blat-blat-blat!

The gun sounded off in the early-morning air, spitting bullets into Travis's brother's old beer cans and sending them flying and twirling in the air. The sound echoed off the abandoned shed and ricocheted between the thicket-ridden hills. Curling a slight grin, Travis walked up to the rusted-out Chevy. Dirt stirred around his worn white and gray sneakers, bulldozing piles of sand and casting them in the air, giving his shoes the tinge of parched wheat. Again, he placed a row of cans and bottles over the bed and arranged them to be his next set of aluminum victims. He walked twenty paces, turned, aimed, and …

Blat-blat- blat!

Once again, Calvin flinched at the sound of each shot as Travis laid another round of cans out. They went down easier than the last. Every can, every bottle felt Travis's metal wrath in a way that developed more pleasure, more desirability as the morning went on.

After gutting the cans and exploding bottles, most of the bullets had been mitted into a thick sheet of rusted metal hanging on the garage wall. A few cut through the sheet entirely and pierced the rotted-out wood behind it. In contrast, a few of the earlier off-the-mark shots left a series of holes, the staggering imprints from less-skilled shots in the wood siding above or below.

Travis took another five paces back and held the pistol with both hands. His arms were slightly bent as he lined up his shot to the center of his body. One eye targeted the aluminum canister. His stance was wide, solid, making its mark in the dirt. Calvin stood back with his hands cupped over his ears as Travis fired off another three rounds …

Blat-blat-blat!

Glass bottles exploded, while the aluminum victims twirled and spun in the air before plunging to their shallow, dusty graves.

"Could you imagine if Gabe was here right now?" Travis said, scoping his next shot with a grin. "I bet he'd piss his pants right in front of us. Oh … what's that?" he said in a high-toned voice. "You wanted to say you're sorry?" His throat grunted out a chuckle. "Well, how's this for sorry …"

Blat-blat-blat!

Calvin clenched his eyes shut, tugging his ears into his shoulders. His eyes opened with strained tears to see Travis gibing the can as he walked up to one of them and pointed the barrel straight at its center. "Bet you're sorry now, you bag of—"

Blat!

Another shot went right through the can and wedged into the ground, executioner style, rising smoke and dust and pebbles in the air.

"You probably shouldn't say things like that," Calvin said, keeping a safe distance behind the shooter, just as his father had taught him.

"What if someone hears you? They might take you seriously. Call the cops on us or something."

"Who's gonna hear us all the way out here?" Travis said, looking up. Overhead, a hawk soared in loops high in the air, its feathers glowing auburn and orange like a scorching phoenix under the California sun. It circled above them as if the cans were rodents to be picked off as soon as the massacre occurred. Travis kept his sight on the bird, wondering if ancient gods fell to the salvo of a Glock. "Besides, I was only playing. You know that. And you think Gabe wouldn't say the same thing about us?" He dropped the gun and turned back at the can lying still on the ground. He boldly strutted up to it and placed the heel of his foot over the entire container. "He and those other shitheads would probably shoot us right in the middle of the schoolyard had they the chance," he uttered and brayed the can right into the earth.

Travis turned and walked back to Calvin. "Sometimes the best defense is a good offense," he said, reaching out the gun and placing it, handle out, in Calvin's hand. "And there doesn't get much better offense than this." He stepped around Calvin, placing his hands on his shoulders, and pushed Calvin to face the line of cans on the bed of the old Chevy. "Now," he said, "let's see what you got."

Calvin gripped the gun with both hands wrapped over the handle, one finger on the trigger, and raised it steady.

"He is right," that small voice said inside. *"They would shoot you right in the face if they had the chance. And the whole school would watch and cheer. But what can we do, Cal? What can we do?"*

Calvin closed one eye and targeted the can in his sight.

"Show me!"

Blat-blat-blat!

* * *

"Ugh ..."

The glow of afternoon light lanced from under the door and splayed over the top of Ben's head. He turned over to his side and sprawled over his bathroom floor in a crucifix manner, giving his lungs room to do their job. It took some time for his eyes to break open, looking toward the cupboards and door rising above him. The room spun blurrily in one direction and then the other. His head throbbed, and his eyes burned like they hadn't seen daylight in years.

With grunting force, Ben rolled to his knees. Immediately, he felt a feverish pain surging along the side of his body that took the brunt hit of a hard landing. Unconscious, it grew sorer lying in the same position for several hours. His body complained as he hoisted himself off the floor and up into a feeble stance. One hand remained stationed at the edge of the sink while the other pressed against the door. Once high enough, he looked in the mirror to see his face back to its everyday shade. His brown hair had thickened once more, with short strands hanging out in front.

He ran his fingers through his mane to comb it all back and squinted at the mirror, trying to get his eyes to behave normally. It wasn't long before he had a clear image of his face. The white in his eyes seemed brighter than before, enough to enhance his dark brown irises. He gulped while surveying his facial muscles. He had no black spots or bruises other than the one trailing the side of his face, which he studied only briefly.

His gaze drifted down toward the counter. Immediately he noticed that no signs of the dark, oily liquid remained. Gingerly, he wiped his fingers across the porcelain rim and rubbed them together. Even the hand towel was clean and folded neatly on the hook on the wall. There was nothing to prove that whatever had happened that morning did indeed happen, except that he still had a towel wrapped around his waist. There was still a pile of dirty clothes shoved in the corner between the door and the toilet.

Ben turned with befuddling speed to the shower and threw back the curtain. The tub was clean and moist, only with the perspiration of a hot shower. Confused, he brought the back of his hand up to his nose and pressed it just enough to get a trace of the substance and prove to himself he hadn't wholly lost his mind, but that too came back clean. He turned, head facing the door while his body slowly followed. He opened it suspiciously, glancing around the bathroom before flicking off the light and stepping out, perplexed and somewhat relieved that the ordeal was over.

There was no room in Ben's field of emotions to be surprised when he saw Jeremy sitting on the edge of his couch. His sausage-grade fingers hammered against a game controller as a militia of explosive sounds poured from the television. Jeremy's focus was rooted on the screen. His mouth twisted and scrunched over to one side of his face as he pounded his thumbs on the controller with intense determination. Ben made his way to the end of the hall and stopped, just shy of having the sunlight beam directly on his face. He watched as Jeremy took down one opponent after another with rapid-fire destruction.

"I wondered when you were going to get out," Jeremy said, twisting the controller and yanking it to the side like he was reeling in some monstrous fish. His stone glare never left the screen. "I hope you don't mind that I let myself in."

"Nah," Ben heard himself say.

"Long night, wasn't it?"

"Jeremy, buddy, you have no idea." Ben casually walked over to sit next to his friend.

Jeremy found a place to put the game on pause and turned to face Ben. In a flash, his eyes widened the way Ben's had when he saw himself in the mirror earlier that morning. "Hell!" Jeremy stood up, dropping the controller on the couch and giving an arresting glare. "You didn't look this bad when I dropped you off. Did you get jumped in the driveway or something?"

"I fell."

"Off a cliff?"

"No. I was in the bathroom, and it was … weird. I was taking a shower, right. When suddenly this dark goo started coming out of my nose."

"You mean like blood," Jeremy replied with a conclusive tone.

"Not really. It was more like tar." Ben squinted an awkward smile.

"Hmm." Jeremy shrugged with hardly any concern. "But it's gone now?"

"Obviously."

"Okay. Dude, that sounds like a nosebleed to me," Jeremy replied. "Probably high blood pressure from last night."

Ben raised a brow. For a moment, he thought maybe Jeremy was right. But if that was blood, it was practically coagulated, and wouldn't that mean he was a few steps away from being dead? How Ben wished he had paid more attention in his health class.

Ben asked, "Do people ever pass out from nosebleeds? It started while I was in the shower, and the next thing I knew, I was on the floor with a bruise across my face, and it was … wait … what time is it?"

Jeremy pulled out his cell phone and glanced at the screen. "It's about eleven thirty."

"I must have been on that floor for seven—no, eight—hours," Ben said. "That can't be."

"Yeah, 'cause that would mean you got up around four," Jeremy said. "When have you ever gotten up before the sun … or noon?"

Ben shrugged.

"Exactly. So, let's say you did get up that early and take a shower, which I'd be shocked if you did, there's no wonder you passed out. You must have been exhausted."

Ben nodded in agreement. To him, that made more sense than some unexplainable oil seeping through parts of his face. And he had hallucinated before a time or two—or thirty.

Jeremy reached for the controller and went back to destroying the digital world on the screen. "You know, the same thing happened to you last night at that junky's house," Jeremy said, as if Ben wouldn't have remembered. He didn't.

"Wait, what?" Ben exclaimed.

"Yeah, you remember. High blood pressure and exhaustion," Jeremy repeated. "That's what they said when they checked you out."

"When who checked me out?"

* * *

Why me, God?

It was the only thought Danica could hold onto, other than wanting to puke. Her decisions were now drowning her in self-hatred. She sat quietly in the cold hall, uncomfortably sitting on a flat bench, back against painted white cinder blocks as the officer stamped a round of forms. Each stamp hit the page as if he were trying to indent the desk. It made Danica think of all those old-timey movies where the criminals were linked together and hammering rock under a noonday sun, sweating away in black and white. Each hit, a rhythmic beat, like the heartbeat of their rotten lives. Now it was her turn.

Something churned in her, deeper than nerves. The bench only grew more uncomfortable as she shifted with discomfort and waited. The bench screeched as she leaned forward to peer down the hall. It was all stale, void, with white or gray walls and ceramic floor tiles that hadn't been adequately buffed since they were first laid there. A television hung in the corner, airing a muted repetition of the national news with quick ribbons of captions that scrolled too fast for anyone watching from her portion of the bench to read. Noise evaded her, other than what she had caused. Still, she hadn't uttered a peep since he planted her on that bench. Now her head rested on her hand as she sat staring straight at her.

Suddenly the pounding stopped. Danica looked back to see the officer shuffling and straightening out forms, neat and tidy as he stood. "Your parents should be arriving shortly," the officer muttered and stepped away from the desk.

As the officer went out, another came in with a shirtless Latino strutting in front of him like a human shield. The man's arms had been cuffed behind his back, giving him no choice but to let half his boxers expose themselves over a large, shiny belt buckle with something written in an old English font. A museum of tattoos vined up his arms and neck, portraying names and vulgarity, skulls and animals, Catholicism and nude women perfect in form, diluting around his ears before withering over his glossy bald head. His nose had been broken and healed like a seasoned boxer. His muscles were defined, tissue scarred from what could only be assumed as survival stab wounds. Wires of black hair sprouted from his chin and the side of his bleeding lips.

Danica stared, emotionless, as the man strutted by and flashed her a violating smile, exposing two rows of silver teeth. He said nothing, but she could hear his thoughts, the words of a thug portrayed in any hard-knock street movie. "Hey there, baby cakes," his Hispanic tongue would have called her as the officer pushed him forward. "How's 'bout I dip a piece of Mexican chocolate in that milky-white body of yours—see me if you can handle a real man, now that the boy had broken you in all good like."

Danica's attention sunk until her sight loomed over the floor. "Let's go, ese," the officer demanded as he nudged the cuffed man past her and down the hall. She tried her best not to react, but in her peripheral vision, she could see his tattooed face looking back at her the entire way, imagining him licking his lips, flexing scarred muscles for her to drool over. As if.

All this trouble for a forty-dollar blouse, Danica thought, her head cranked to the other side of the hall where the officer who had picked her up was now walking back.

"You know, I will never get why you kids do the stupidest things." The officer's arm swung firmly at his side. Each step had a committed intent to show his authority. "I think a night or two in lockup might do you some good if you ask me. Luckily for you, a forty-dollar piece of fabric doesn't permit such a punishment, so ..."

Danica heard a stream of concern under the steady current of his authoritative voice. It was too obvious to her that he was also a father. But it still didn't matter. She knew that controlling her own destiny was beyond her grasp by this point. The things that she knew to be moral didn't save her from tragedy, and the things that made her feel good led her to plunge into despair. All roads led to hopelessness. That was the lesson she now knew well, and not even an authoritative figure would change her mind.

As the officer freed Danica's wrists from his cuffs, her mother's frantic voice rang down the hall. "Danica Elizabeth Briggs!"

Both parents stormed down the hall; first, her mother, who was lit in rage, then her more reserved father. Danica didn't look at either of them. She simply stood up as if she had gone through these motions several times before. The shoplifting, the arrest, the dealing with parents—just another thing with which to be done.

"What the hell were you thinking, young lady?" Mrs. Briggs belted as she stormed down the hall, while Mr. Briggs focused more on keeping pace behind her. She cut her attention over to the officer standing over her daughter, raised her voice a respectful octave, and said, "Officer, I swear on my blessed mother's grave that she isn't normally like this."

The officer gave back nothing more than a raised brow and a nod offered to more parents' excuses than he could count.

"Jessica, take a breath," Mr. Briggs said, slightly winded. He took little time in laying his hands on his wife's shoulders and massaging them in a way that appeared to be keeping her from lunging at their daughter.

The officer, a sturdy man, crossed his arms and took a step between Danica and her parents. He towered over Mrs. Briggs with full use of his authority as he said, "Can I talk to you two alone, please? It will just take a minute of your time." From there, the officer beckoned her parents into another room. "You, young lady," he said, pointing at Danica, "take a seat and stay put. I don't want to find you moved an inch."

Danica mimicked his pose by crossing her arms, plodding back on the bench, and anchoring her head against the wall covered in old DARE posters and "Have you seen me" fliers. She rolled her head to glance over a few, reading birthdays, studying faces and digital reconstructions of how a few might look today. One or two caught her interest briefly. Most pictures looked old and had been missing for an uncomfortable amount of time. There was one she noticed to look unsettlingly similar to her, holding a reflected expression of what she might have looked like only months ago. Even in such despairing circumstances, the girl appeared to be happier than Danica, truly, like the worries of life had not yet affected this poor girl's beautiful ginger. Like nothing in life had disappointed her yet.

Danica repositioned her seat for a better view and read over the flier. She sat, half cross-legged with one foot settled on the floor and the other crookedly resting over the bench. She leaned over, allowing her eyes to transition from lazy to focus, branching into concern as she read over each descriptive line, word by unsettling word:

MISSING
HAVE YOU SEEN THIS WOMAN
DANICA BRIGGS
Last seen with Justin Thompson
attending a party at Anthony Harper's residence
Height: 5'5" Weight: 130 lbs.
PLEASE BRING DANICA BRIGGS HOME

"Ma'am."

Danica woke to the shop employee's lightly brass voice as it broke through her daydream. Her face was numb, frozen in the expression she had seen molded over her face in her dream. Her heart thudded against her chest so hard that she swore it flicked through her blouse and at her jacket. It surprised her to see the stolen blouse still in her hand and still on the hanger.

"Would you like to try that on?" the employee asked, probably for the second time according to her tone.

Breakfast erupted from her stomach and climbed her throat. With a fist to her mouth, she held onto the wretched meal and choked it back down. "Umm …" Her voice crackled as she squirmed at the sour flavor and slipped the blouse between two exact replicas back on the rack. She stepped away, hands surrendering. "I gotta go," Danica said and, with her face magnetized to her feet, darted out of the store, oathing to never return there again.

* * *

Calvin walked through the front door just as the sun and moon began to switch shifts and when the streetlights had flickered their caramel glow over the sidewalks and streets. The door was unlocked, as always, which always seemed weird to him, being that his father was a cop and hardly anyone was ever home. His dad's answer to that always seemed to be leaving the TV on, making it at least sound like somebody was home. Calvin and his mom thought that was stupid, a gamble they couldn't afford to lose, but went along with it by holding their tongues. A couple of lights were still on—the usual suspects, being the kitchen and entry hall. At that point, Calvin was convinced his parents had forgotten where both switches were.

Calvin made his way to the kitchen to carelessly rustle a sandwich, forsaking cleanliness or the sound of whatever tragedy the evening news found worthy of capitalizing on that day. He stood over the mess on the kitchen counter, eating his quick-fix meal, sprinkling crumbs without regard while listening to what had now become the weather report, which was at least tolerable.

One thing Calvin could appreciate about the news was the meteorologist. She was a hot little number with a forgettable Latina name who only wore attire to promote her best features. With a deep bite and rip of bread, he watched her petite figure turn to the side to point at whatever she was talking about, seducing his hormones while pointing at numbers placed over the usual map. Calvin's eyes were tranced. He focused heavily on her dress, attempting to notice the clasp of her bra or the line of her panties, something to dwell on for a few hours while gaping up at his ceiling and waiting for somnolence to retrieve him from the day.

"Where have you been all day?" Calvin's dad croaked out, hidden from view by the backside of his recliner, not standing or turning. Being unseen put a haunting presence to his voice, leaving Calvin dumbstruck as he briefly choked on his bread. Something about it made him scurry to clean up the mess he had lazily made over the counter. That feeling of being caught red-handed when oblivious to who was watching him the entire time put Calvin to work, though he was sure his dad hadn't seen a thing.

Calvin coughed, hacking tiny fragments of bread out along the counter while trying to net most of them with his hands. "What the—" He raced to catch his breath, holding back a word that seemed to flow more easily from his mouth these days. Straightaway, he went to work, sweeping the crumbs off the counter and into the cusp of his hand. "I didn't see you there."

Calvin's dad stood and rolled his starched back the way only a middle-aged man would. His eyes were fire, bloodshot by another twelve-hour shift and the rays of the screen. "Apparently not. You've seen your mom around?"

Calvin huffed out a brief chuckle. He dumped the small collection of crumbs into the trash. "You kidding me? I hadn't seen that woman since she bolted out of the house this morning. Though she did say something about working a double before she left."

Calvin's dad slowly rolled his eyes into the back of his head and crushed them tightly under their lids. Using his thumb and a finger, he pressed the burn out of them for several seconds. "Again," he rasped. "When is she not working a double?"

The silence that followed sparked a desire in Calvin to spill the beans about Tom. He wondered if his dad knew anything about the pudgy man in a cheap brown tie and uniform slacks who was seducing his wife. Instead, he chomped down on his sandwich and filled his mouth with an overwhelming chunk of meat and bread, as if it were some sort of ultimatum. To tell his dad everything, that his mom had been playing him for a fool, would be a load off his back but a much heavier one on his dad's. He couldn't risk the impact that would follow. Instead, he meagerly shrugged and then turned and opened the refrigerator door.

"Oh well. Guess it's just you and me tonight. So whaddya say? Movie? Pizza?"

Calvin lifted the last bit of his sandwich in the air.

"Okay. Just a movie then. Anything you want. Hey, I heard the one with all of those superheroes came out this week. I bet we could download that on that movie site?"

"Stream it, Dad," Calvin corrected as he picked out a can of root beer and let the door naturally close. "Damn, man, how old are you? A hundred and five?"

"Cute, but watch your language," Calvin's dad muttered with a comically authoritative nod. "Well ... are we streaming tonight or not?"

Calvin tried to smile. "Sure, Dad," Calvin said with an unmeaning notch in his voice. "That sounds fine."

Calvin's dad nodded again, standing in a second round of silence for a bit. He looked at one side of the room, then to the ceiling and over to the other side. At last, his dad broke. "So, what did you do today?"

Calvin shrugged. "I dunno," came out the typical adolescent response. "Hung out with Travis and goofed off around town. You know, whatever, I guess."

"How's, uh, how's Travis's mom doing these days?" he inquired, oddly curious.

Now Calvin could smile. He even chuckled a little. He wiped the cool sweat off his can of root beer to evade eye contact with his old man. "Fat … lazy."

"Hey, hey, c'mon, Cal," he said. "That's disrespectful. You know darn well she hasn't had the easiest time, what with all that's happened with her husband and then Travis's brother. That takes a toll on someone, you know. I've seen it time and again."

Her husband was a lazy piece of crap drunk too, but at least he did his family a service, something inside Calvin said, though he held his tongue. Never had he ever had such a dark perspective on … anyone before. *At least Travis's brother brought money home, even if it was drug money*, he thought. However, "Yep," was all that slipped from his tongue.

"Well …" Calvin's dad clapped his thick, workman-clad hands together and began rubbing them. "I am going to take a quick shower. Then we will get our movie streaming going."

Calvin forged a grin, eyes widened with fraudulent excitement as his dad hustled his way down the hall and into his room. Once alone, Calvin returned to his pensive self and went on chugging his root beer, imagining it was the real thing.

* * *

Dinner at the Briggs residence was gravied in awkward silence. A few words were shared over the table, none specifically for her, which suited her just fine, being that she probably wouldn't have responded.

A display of distant glares occupied the room. The rims of her mother's eyes were crimson. Her father glared stoically at nothing across the table. Danica had only been picking and stabbing at her grilled cedar-plank salmon and seared greens. Her lips were pale, thin, and locked shut. Her eyes stayed focused on the beautifully cooked piece of fish as a bloated feeling overtook her appetite. Everything she saw, everything she smelled at the table bittered her stomach. She disassembled it flake by exquisite flake, freeing steam from each layer, realizing how easy it was to take something so delicate and well made and break it apart into several unrecognizable slivers and pieces. It was a meal she would have graciously devoured on any other occasion, one deserving of praise to the chef.

After dinner, she grabbed a book and sprawled out over the living room couch, hoping a light read on a comfortable couch in a soft-lit room would do her some good. Danica scooped a pillow from one side of the couch and stacked it on top of its twin on the other side. The center of the couch plied to her weight as she sat and swiveled to the side. Danica's head drifted back as her legs floated up and over the other side, toes stretching and curling, legs clomping down with enough slack to allow her feet to trampoline off the cushion. With a deep stretch and a long breath, she slid her finger between two masses of pages and pried open the hardbound book. Her eyes focused, then blurred, then focused again, each line weaving into the ones on either side of it.

Without notice, time snuck by her. Drowsiness quickly settled in. The next thing she knew, sunlight drenched her face, and it was morning. Only now she was more nauseous, and her nausea brought with it a crowd of pain she hadn't recalled inviting. Things hurt in ways she never felt before. Decades attached themselves to her joints and bones, waking up to the sensation of middle age. Her back felt the struggle of a day's worth of hauling bags of sand, not that her velvet hands had ever endured such labor. Not a single page had been turned from the book that roofed over her chest. However, now the pages had a few horizontal creases that seemed to have appeared overnight, and the words shone to be printed a little bit crisper.

Danica flipped over to face the ceiling. Her chest fought against every breath she took as she began rubbing her torso. She poked at her stomach, almost expecting to be poked back, but all she found was that her stomach had sunk in a little deeper than usual. She was sure it had. The skin settled a bit looser as well. *And … are those stretch marks*? she thought, peering down her chest and over her exposed torso. Even now, it felt like something was missing. A part of her that she wasn't sure she wanted now felt like the only part of her that mattered. And it was gone. And she did it. Not Justin. Not her friends. Not her parents. She did it—alone.

What else was she supposed to do? It wasn't like she had a job or the ability to raise a child. Justin turned out to be an abhorrent bastard who threatened her, so a dad was out of the picture. His parents would not want the family name botched by such controversy once they found out—if they found out. Yes, they were loving, but they were also a staple in the community, especially since everything else had been going so well for them. The best she could've hoped for from them was a shred of emotional support and help finding the kiddo a good home, preferably far from her, had it been their way. As far as any church help went, she hadn't shown her face there for weeks, and it was doubtful they missed her much—or at all.

One by one, she shut them out, giving reasons to keep this whole thing a secret. Emotional walls were built and fortified with isolation. Morose demeanors were not. She thought the termination would have ended this all. She was sure putting a stopper on the pregnancy would shed the bitter lies and disgusting façade and would restore her back to her former glory. But all it did was birth a new, more complicated pregnancy. A new thing was growing inside her, a grotesque monster, feeding off her emotions and livelihood, this little bundle of guilt.

It would grow healthy over the days and weeks as it kicked and punched at her insides until all that was left was the ebbed remains of a battered old house. She would forever be remembered as someone who was once beautiful, now shambled by abuse and beat to hell, down to its brittle planks. And the monster would love every minute of it.

I have to tell someone, she thought. Her stomach gurgled from hunger, regretting the tasty salmon she had decided to rend into pieces instead of eating. She tried to push it down and fight it from eating her alive. She tried the positive thinking crap many others had suggested online. She tried meditating. She tried self-forgiveness. Nothing worked. And now, the shame was so intense that there was no other way to escape her turmoil. There was supposed to be a relief. At least that's what she said to herself as hands jittered and eyes billowed with tears that she also felt guilt for.

Why me, God? I was always a good girl. It was one damn mistake, she thought. *And for that, you put in me a …* She couldn't get herself to even consider it.

Danica's legs plummeted to the meadow of cool carpet as she sat up and wiped the pale streaks of concealer and gray mascara over her face. Her head lingered heavy, throbbing as a result of a crooked neck. Her eyes burned and felt as if they had in some way managed to pry loose from their sockets. They cooled with her hands, smearing the last of the mascara over her fingers before raising herself up.

In less than a minute, Justin, the abhorrent bastard who had attacked and threatened her, instantly came to mind, only now he wasn't so much of a person as he was a feeling, a creature of being she had evolved into. This grotesque monster had overtaken every sense of who she was, causing her to flirt with dark possibilities and take advantage of her lack of guilt. What was worse, she knew that in time, after she'd been thoroughly abused and beaten to hell by this inner creature, it would have to be destroyed by any means necessary.

NINE

Summer tended to bring a dry spell for dark episodes and exchanges. Something about a brighter sun, or warmer days, or a surplus of vitamin D seemed to do the world some good. For Ben, it was the silence. He didn't miss the fathomless episodes filled with the lamenting sounds of children and alarm bells in the least. And that worried him, especially since school was not done for the year. Not yet. It was like two tectonic plates grinding over each other, creating a mass amount of friction underground while it all seemed dormant on the surface. He knew, though, in time, something was sure to quake. After the past couple of seasons of awkward visions and meeting that kid in the creepy old house, Ben could use the extra rest. This and Jeremy's move gave him more time to do things for himself. He took strides to visit his mom regularly, keeping the flowers on her grave fresh and beautiful, laying out only the ones he knew she liked best. Talking to her eased some of his loneliness.

He'd tried to live each day not worrying about that, and for the most part, it had been ... nice. Occasionally, he'd catch a glimpse of some less severe exchange needed. A kiddo, lost at the end of his rope, finding his way into his parents' medicine cabinet or something of the sort. Most were in town. Some would be a day trip. Only one so far had required using Mr. Nelson's gifted buddy passes.

He had learned some time ago that there were expected levels of side effects associated with how and why someone was attempting to end their lives. In time, he came to see it like one of those pain charts that doctors show patients in the hospital—one with a yellow happy face or ten with a sobbing blue face. Only his chart had no happy faces. And the sobbing blue face was pretty much where it began.

The OD'ers had the most negligible consequences on him. Fortunately (for him), they were the most common. The exchange would hit him like the twenty-four-hour flu. He'd spend a day in bed, puking up whatever he ate the day before, chills shivering him to the bone, spending the night asleep on his porcelain pillow. It wasn't painless, that's for sure, but comparatively, it came and went relatively quickly.

Those who took the path of drowning or hanging themselves made the next unpleasant face on his pain chart—more than unpleasant. They carried a weight of drama to their methods. It was as if they felt they deserved to suffer their demise. It was their final reasonability to lavish their death in the form of some version of purgatory—and he felt that, the worst of a broken heart. Whenever his neck tightened or water flooded his lungs, the hot constriction of an unforgiving noose, or the cold belly of the wet abyss, it was a hell beyond words.

The CO_2 inhalers played a bitch on him. It lasted for days, charred everything from his lungs to the alkaline-flavored tip of his tongue. Recovering was like dealing with a three-day asthma attack. There was no nebulizer to subside its strangulating grip. They were just as menacing to recover from as the jumpers. Equally as long, only the jumpers left him with bruises and fractured bones, and it felt like an icepick lodged into his forehead, pressing deeper into his skull each day.

Of course, the worst were self-inflicted blasts to the head. Ben only had to deal with that once. Barely had he recovered, and since then, he thanked the stars in heaven for each day he hadn't had to go through that again.

But for Ben, it wasn't the physical effects that made it so hard to recover. It was all the memories of how it felt just before it was over. Those final gasps as he struggled to draw a morsel out of the withheld air. Swallow upon swallow of dark, murky water as his body plunged deeper, his body getting hotter, getting colder, tightening up while at the same time becoming numb. The pressure crushing him from the outside in. The blood pumping into his head, inflating until his eyes bulged from their sockets. His flesh swelling until it was about to pop, watching the hue of his skin change into a foreign color by the second while his vision blurred away into complete blindness. The longsuffering swish of a wilting heartbeat being felt only moments before slipping away into the darkness. And deciding this death was better than life.

He was thankful for his visit to Colorado to witness his friend begin his new adult life. The time they spent together had a therapeutic quality to it. Ben didn't think the transition from California to Colorado would be easy, but Jeremy proved him wrong. Settling right in and immediately getting to work to hunt down the most needed spots for a giving hand were top priorities. He quickly accumulated ideas and means for various outdoor activities. With all the excitement and business of the trip, Ben found a good reason not to tell Jeremy about the dark episodes and exchanges. At least a reason that was good enough.

* * *

It came down to the last week before school ended. Cal would spend his summer the way most kids his age did, where warm, bright summer days were spent confined to his room, blasting his way through soldiers and war-driven monsters that managed to crawl their way out of the center of the Earth. His parents (or, at least his dad) stopped in occasionally, if only to make sure he was still alive. He'd inform Cal about all the fun they had growing up, being outside on days like that, which would turn into a lecture about everything wrong with this current generation. And he might possibly have been right. Maybe kids today did need to go outside more, swim for a bit, ride their bikes, and get involved in some sort of innocent hijinks, like the ones their parents claimed made it "the best time of my life." But then, who would be ready to save the planet from the underground monster if ever—whenever—they attacked? The world's fate could rely on that sort of experience.

For Calvin, it would be like waiting to take that final walk down death row before being reluctantly pressed down and strapped into a metal bed from which no one had ever returned. Instead of a walkway, there were halls, and instead of a metal bed, there were lockers. Instead of venomous needles, creeps were dying to pick on the runts like himself. What was worse was that instead of being a prison, it would be Green Valley Junior High.

He imagined his parents watching from the living room window, safe behind a thick plate of glass as they witnessed the needle intricately inserted into his arms. Final words, "Please homeschool me, Mom!" Only his mother wasn't around to hear his plea. She stopped being there years ago when the little extra income turned into overtime hours. Then her overtime turned into additional overtime, which turned into, "I'm leaving so that I can find myself again."

Calvin's dad, who had miraculously kept himself from returning to the bottle, was all but certain that he was going to break. A good percentage of recovering alcoholics would've gone back for far less. Of course, he'd seen no hard statistics, but it would only make sense. Calvin was more surprised when it seemed he didn't even care she was gone some days. Then again, she made it easy for the two to feel that way by weening herself away. Instead, the man occupied himself with work, long hours that Cal couldn't help but take personally.

His mother's quick and regretless exit also made it a little easier for him to pull the trigger on Travis's brother's Glock. The rejection stewed with all the other emotions, brewing the perfect drive for his finger to act so willingly. Two days a week of shooting cans and bottles made his aim impressively accurate. The cans and bottles were no longer emptied before the shooting began. Travis found it much more pleasing to see the amber brew burst out in the air and splatter against the garage wall. Oh, how the cans flung and tumbled, chugging out what remained inside over the dirt soil like blood gushing out of the heart. It was as if the life of the cans was seeping into the hot, sandy earth.

There was tranquility for Calvin as he grew to uncage those emotions, a simplicity in an otherwise catastrophic life. All he had to do was allow the feelings to take what they wanted of him, aim, and pull back one meager little trigger.

The expression on mommy's facile face as she spat out that garbage, expecting him to cherish the words as her brave farewell. "I'm leaving so that I can find myself again."

Blat!

One can down. Sorry, Mommy.

And what about Tom and his cheap, home-wrecking suit? *You think you're gonna be my new daddy?* Cal thought as he closed one eye.

Blat!

Doesn't look so good for you, now does it, sport?

Then there was Gabe and his slimeball, pimple-wearing thugs.

Blat! Blat! Blat!

"Say adieu to you, you piece of degenerate shit." Calvin smiled as cans lay flat and eviscerated, and bottles became a shattered massacre all over the dirt.

By the end of their last session, starting a new school year for Cal didn't seem so bad. After holding the cold handle of judgment in his right hand, feeling the crescent of its trigger curving around his finger, the more he thought about it, the more he started to believe a new year could be fun.

Travis agreed.

* * *

Once again, he found himself in the darkness. Not since the lasagna incident had he experienced its cold, lonely blackness. His ears burst with that similar high-pitched mechanical scream, unending and torturing, echoing a loud blur deep into the center of his brain. The moment he recalled from what it stemmed it became clear—a bell. Not just any bell but a school fire alarm bell. However, this time there were no children to scream with it. Odd for a vision to change in such a way. *If this is to become the new norm*, he thought, trying to find the tip of his own fingers, *count me out.* The visions were terrible enough, but at least he still felt alive before he died, knew where he stood, even if it wasn't in the best of circumstances. This, he could only feel the nothingness from the beginning—thick, pressing against his skin like a lead quilt. The bitter taste of its void siphoned into his mouth and down his throat, drowning him inside bereaving darkness. These, he didn't know if he was standing at all. Ben expanded his lungs and gave out a cross-grained sigh. At least he could hear his breath, which meant he was still alive. And there were no shattered bones as far as he could tell. Now he had to figure out if that was a good thing or a bad thing.

Ben picked up the thrum of something profound starting to form out in the darkness. It came into play while the bell chime began to fade, as if he were walking away from one and toward another. It was an unorganized thumping, like a cupboard door slammed in a distant room, or more like a well-sized door left open to endure the tyrant gale of the Santa Anna winds banging against a wall over and again at its own crooked tempo.

Again, Ben expanded his lungs and breathed. Not only could he feel his breath, but now he could see it, steaming, crystalizing like ice vapor just before it was ciphered into more of the dense blackness. It was the only thing that let him know he was alive, though he still felt dead. With his breath, the thrumming got louder and closer. Was someone searching for something? Were these several doors? Perhaps ... yes.

Tiny voices began to come into play. These two distinct, high-pitched moans, like the squeal of trapped mice. They were alone, secretly revealing themselves in lurking puffs of indecipherable words, the steam of hot breaths in the dark, arctic air. One dawned an umber glow, indecisively changing between yellow and orange like a broken sunset. At the same time, the other held its firm redness at every puff. They would crescendo and dim, brighten and dim, sway in and out as the thrumming sound of a door transcended into a heavier type of thud. It went in and out of rooms no less, strengthening as the thuds maintained like they were being carried by the tailwind of a developing gale. They touched his ears like the voices of young children. Like they were friends, possibly siblings, moaning together, deepening in cold agony as they swayed in and out repeatedly with similar feelings of not belonging. Like they, too, were lost in this blackened hell, trying to find the way out.

There was a cry for help in one of the voices. To Ben, that was all too clear. It wasn't in words but the tone, a familiar quivering morose he'd heard so many times before when someone had lost all hope. He could have picked it out from a crowd of thousands. But the other—strange—came about as a sullen, pettish, and aggressive timbre, red and driven in anger so much he could almost see it. It was more of a snarl than a cry, troubled and defensive. It was as if the two were twins, derived from the same womb, only to branch out over different sides of the spectrum. The yin and yang of human emotions when put in a hostage position, the darkness being the abductor in this situation.

Ben reached out, fingers unseen yet splayed as he called to them, "It's okay. I'm a friend, here to help you."

There was a silence that followed ... a slam, louder than any so far, and then a long, heavy creak, close enough to touch Ben's nose.

"It's okay. You can trust me. I can help," Ben said. "Please. I'm your friend. Let me see you. I can get you out of here."

"What are you doing here?" the red voice questioned him. "You shouldn't be here. You're not one of them."

"Please let me help you. This is no place for a child. I can get you out. You only need to trust me."

The red voice growled, his impatience for Ben becoming evident. "You don't belong here. You have no business here."

"I do," Ben said. "You are my business. That's why I'm here—for you. You must believe I want to help you. I am your friend," he reiterated.

"You think us as fools? We have no friends," the other voice sounded off—now sinister, now orange—spreading its hostility like a web of toxic emotions. Ben couldn't read the thoughts of whoever's voice this was. He wasn't sure if it was speaking out like this as a defense or if it was indeed as cynical as the other. Either way, he had to try.

"Please," Ben cried. "I'm only here to help. I can make this better for you. It's what I do. You just gotta to trust me."

"What makes you think we want your help?" the red, heated voice snarled. A deep, wicked tone surfaced out of the steam with a billow of its intentions, while the other voice went back to yellow and mute.

"Is that for the both of you, or just the one?" Ben asked, trying to draw out a species of hope from the other voice. There was a short pause, then a reply that came back. It was small and timid but primarily contrived. To Ben, that too was clear. "Okay then. Tell me, what do you want? What do you need me to do if you don't want my help?"

With an explosion of magmatic smoke, a roar trembled across the darkness, sending a violent squall to athwart Ben's face, singeing his eyes to the point of blindness. There was light, and it came with a fury, unlike anything he had felt before. It burned like Hades, searing his face. It stung like revenge, the worst kind of revenge imaginable, an abolishing retribution. With one long voice, Ben's eardrums exploded, bringing him to his knees in a ghostly mist of blood as it cried, "Leave us alone!"

* * *

It was amazing what a single blue line could do. Such a small, no more than half an inch long, inanimate blue line. Just one could stop a young girl's heart for better or worse. It could bring joy or pain. Bring on excitement or fear. Stir in one's life a bit of hope or despair. It could feel like life had begun or ended, all by this simple blue line, especially when someone was never expecting to see one.

For her, the first blue line sparked shock. The second one gave birth to denial. The third and fourth turned that denial into fear and panic. And by the time that she and a hundred and fifty other students walked the stage to receive their diplomas, the consequence of spring break left her with enough blue lines to fill the pencil box stashed in her bottom dresser drawer. Now it was starting to reveal itself under her clothes. There were rumors and snickering but nothing that made it to the Briggs' dinner table. As far as her parents were concerned, it was depression weight. To some, it was a mistake. To others, the physical manifestation of a relationship that had gone wrong. Still, others found it as retribution for the prissy-perfect life she had flaunted around town. Then there were the silent few who called it as she saw it to be, a child. Only it was a baby formed out of cruel tragedy, a dilemma of sorts, one that who she had been and who she was now could not seem to agree on as to its fate.

As a graduation present to herself, Danica made one more effort to burn down what had become of her life. The clock moved a quarter minute slower that night as she sat in bed and waited, buffing her stomach with her hand in a slow, circular motion. A single desk lamp did its best to light her room as she waited, alone and quiet, running through the names that popped into her head. *I could name him Lucas if he's a boy or Violet if she's a girl. I always loved that name—Violet*, she thought, eyes deep into the plastered ceiling. *Mom loved that name too.*

What am I thinking? Her head jerked lucid. *I can't keep this thing. I'm a kid, for Christ's sake.* With little effort, Danica buried such thoughts to heed the instructions of the monster that lurked inside her. *It's time to go—now.*

With drive, she popped from her bed, throwing back the sheets to reveal a sleek black dress that cut off inches above her knees and even farther from her neck. The slightest bulge formed over her stomach, one that would easily be masked by the cut form and dark lighting. She kept the door cracked open to keep quiet when she snuck out of her room, tiptoeing down the hall and stairs with a black vinyl satchel over her shoulder and at her side and shoes hooked in her fingers. From there, she slipped ever so greasily across the entryway and out the front door. It was all cake.

Outside, she slipped on her shoes and breathed in the night. The air was free of clouds or expectations, as dark as her dress—a trend she could only hope would influence the rest of her night. She didn't know where she was going exactly, but she knew which bus to take to get there. She didn't know what would happen but banked on the chance that something would, one way or another.

The bus was empty, spare a seat or two. Black marker and carved graffiti scrolled along the walls over expired ads and off-white panels. Walking down the aisle between rows of empty benches, Danica soon realized that most people who were out that time of night were either running from trouble or heading toward it. From the looks of the other passengers, she was on the bus for the latter. A homeless-looking man with a zipperless backpack and three overpacked grocery bags watched with curiosity as Danica searched for her place among the fast food, diesel, and urine-scented seats that lined the walls of the bus. As if he had a shot, the man scooped his bags off the seat next to him and placed them down at his grungy, tattered shoes, opening up the spot next to him for a beautiful young woman in a black dress to sit. Danica gave no thought to his gesture as she proceeded to the back.

The bus shook and jolted and rolled from the curb, taking to the street well before Danica found her seat in the farthest spot from any of the few hitching a ride that night. It wasn't long before the familiarity of the neighborhood faded behind her. The bus shifted and growled as it used every amount of torque it could summon to climb the on-ramp onto an endless stretch of damp, glossy asphalt. The moonlight highlighted features of her face through the glass as they made their way toward the distant city lights that ascended under a dark sky.

"Hey, lady," the homeless-looking man hollered from across the bus. Danica refused to fuel any of his desire toward her as he slid a bit closer, then closer again. "Come here. Sit next to me. I have something I wanna show you," he said. Danica gave no reply in sight or words. "I'm rich, you know," he then said, as if he believed such a blatant lie.

"Hey," the driver hollered, catching Danica's and the man's full attention. The driver's face reflected off the oversized mirror and laced directly at the man. "Leave that poor girl alone, Murray. Or this will be that last time I give you a free ride into Denver."

The homeless-looking man turned and shrugged an apology to Danica. He then slid back in his bags and original seat, leaving only the unsavory scent of his lifestyle for her to endure. Danica said nothing. She looped her arms over her chest and held them tightly against her body. Her legs twitched. Her foot repeatedly tapped against the metal floor as she looked back out the window and watched as freeway lights gradually became overrun by even grander city lights.

The bus rumbled and squealed to a halt. Danica stood, securing her satchel and taking a fast-paced stride past the other few occupants and out of the bus. Heals tapped and slid over the metal steps as she rushed onto the main street of the depot district, holding onto the rail a hair second longer than needed. Music and chatter took no time in dusting her ears. Thuds of bass began compressions on her chest. Stumbling herds of intoxicated bodies overran the streets and sidewalks, fumbling into traffic, grazing along walls, and bumping into various objects as they moved from one scene to another, showcasing a whole other pedigree of heedlessness foreign to Danica's more conservative lifestyle.

As the bus pulled away, her shoulders relaxed a little, unmasking neon fluorescence that loomed over her. The lights called to her. The sound of clamoring young adults ready and willing to throw caution to the wind intrigued her. More bodies stumbled around street corners every second, chattering obnoxiously, laughing profusely, nudging her closer and closer toward the door like a gravitational pull she could not withstand.

Without warning, someone decided to throw her arm around Danica. She wore a similar cut dress but with an explosive amount of makeup and blonde, frizzy hair that made her look the part of a backup singer at a Billy Idol concert. A surplus of Channel perfume announced her presence as she held tightly, as if they had been friends their entire lives. Danica's head curved as the girl unleashed a whispering belch and belted a line of nonsense in Danica's ear. "Oh my God," she said. "We could so be twins! I mean, am I right?" The lady then called to a group of her friends a few steps closer to the door than her. "Hey, guys," she hollered, reaching a school of eyes, none sober. "Could we not so be twins?" she asked, to which all responded with overwhelming agreement.

Before she knew it, Danica was lost in a sea of people a few years older than her. She was suctioned to a bar with a crowded line of people, most too intimidated to take a chance on the dance floor. A few of her newfound friends stayed close by her, asking questions about her life but not once asking about the slight bulge pushing from her abdomen. It relieved her that they never cared to ask. In a handful of instances, she felt terrible about giving vague answers, despite the likeliness that they wouldn't remember a thing she said by the time the next round was served. She didn't mind.

Danica found one guy above the rest to be rather cute and polite, despite her repetitious refusal toward his advancements or allowing him to buy her a drink. He was a tall, thin man, perhaps a runner or basketball player. His nose was the shape of an arrow, brows rich florets of brown hair, which she found surprising, being that there wasn't a hint of hair on his sculpted chin or on the crevice of the chest that V'd above his shirt. Long legs bridged from his stool diagonally toward her feet. His eyes were pure, like arctic ice, when he looked at her. And if his eyes drifted, he hid it well.

"You know," he said, smiling, "there is something I find interesting about you."

"Really?" Danica poised a dubious glare and insecurely robed her arms around her stomach. "What's that?" she asked with an immediate weight of regret.

He crooked his head, exposing only one side of his face to the burning lights that tracked over the bar. "I dunno. But there is something."

"Uh-huh. And does that line work often for you?" Danica asked.

"Well, I was going to ask if it hurt when you fell from heaven, but that line seemed to be worked to death," he replied.

Danica's arms loosened a tad. "You know, demons were those angels that fell from heaven, don't you?"

He picked up his cup and saluted Danica. "Yet another reason to retire that line," he said, then helped himself to the rest of his beer and nailed the cup into the bar. Foam slunk gradually from the rim to the bottom as he wiped the dribble from his bottom lip. "You know, I never got your name." He offered a damp hand. "My name is Daniel."

"I'm Danica." She reluctantly grasped his hand, using her other hand to secure the bulge under her dress.

"Danica? Nice. Our names kind of go together. Wonder what that means." He grinned.

"I'd say nothing." Danica shook her head while forming a polite smile. "Odds are there are maybe half a dozen Daniels in this bar and about another fifty or so out there." She nudged toward the street just beyond the front doors. "So, if I may be more specific, I'd say it doesn't mean a damn thing."

"Marry me," Daniel said.

Danica offered a screwy glare. "Probably not. But thank you for the offer."

"Then let me at least buy you a drink." Daniel turned to the bar and caught the eyes of the bartender.

Danica nodded. This time, she didn't want to say no. She knew she should. She knew what it could do. But this time, her decision would be all about her. After all, this was why she was here. Consequences be damned.

Daniel casually leaned over and gave the bartender a wave. She was a piece of work. The most popular attraction in the establishment. Her shirt was tight, a second layer of white flesh that fastened in a knot just above her abdomen. Her hair was black as night, shimmering in a tight ponytail that swayed as she moved along the bar. She leaned over to give Daniel her undivided attention. She rested her elbows on the surface of the bar while using her hands to brush a maverick strand of hair back over her ears. "What can I get you, cutie?" she asked.

"Two beers. Odell, in bottles please," Daniel requested.

The bartender peered over at Danica and gave her a questionable look. Danica responded by avoiding eye contact and turned her head abruptly to observe couples dancing on the floor. The last thing she wanted was to look her age or suspicious. Even more so, she didn't want to look pregnant. In her mind, she was free to do what she wanted, when she wanted.

"Here." Daniel slid her over a glass. Danica took it and stared at it for a moment. "You look like you could use it."

Danica's hand hesitated around the sweaty glass. "What do you mean by that?"

Daniel put the glass to his lower lip and then took two grand chugs, letting his head tilt farther and farther back. He placed the glass next to hers and aired a belch from the corner of his mouth. "You look like you got a lot on your mind. Like something is troubling you."

Danica embraced the glass. "You have no idea." Her voice came out husky and broken.

"I could," Daniel replied.

Danica took a drink. "Trust me, you don't want to know. And even if you did, there is nothing you can do to help."

"Know about what?" The frizzy blonde appeared from nowhere, cutting across the space between the two to ask for a drink.

"Our poor friend Danica here has a problem," Daniel replied. "But she doesn't think we can help her."

"No," the frizzy blonde girl objected. "She said she doesn't think you can help. That's because guys your age only think with their lower brains." Daniel grinned but didn't object. A shot of something strong and clear appeared on the bar, which the frizzy blonde took, threw back, and swallowed, all in one smooth motion. She then threw a hand around Danica, just as she had outside, breathing over her with enough alcohol on her breath to keep them both drunk for the rest of the night. "Listen good. I am going to give you the best advice anyone has given me." Danica felt the weight of the girl's body pushing against her shoulder. "You are young and pretty and have a whole life ahead of you, so let go and let someone else deal with your problems. 'Cause you don't need 'em." The girl fell back, releasing Danica and giving her weight to the bar. "Now let's go get our dance on."

Music and motion took control of the rest of the night, pouring into the dark part of the morning. Dancing led to drinking, which led to more dancing. The lights blurred, as did the faces. Soon enough, Danica had danced with most of the guys but none more than Daniel. He knew how to hold her, how to sway her hips just so. He was gentle yet firm, twisting and turning her. Soon enough, that creature inside her wasn't even a thought in the back of her mind, so long as she was on that dance floor. She didn't have to think when she was moving out there. Her body was alive. Her mind was gone. A few drinks in, and soon enough, that shroud of disappointment darkening her mind was nothing more than a distant bad dream. She began to forget about everything. It was exactly as planned.

Last call came too soon, and, unfortunately, the dancing couldn't last forever. The night dwindled. So did the crowd. Lights were brought up, disillusioning the wonderment of the room to reveal a sticky, tattered floor, trashed booths, and splotches of food and Lord-knows-what splashed over the walls and tables. Trash cans flooded over with bottles, cheap eats, and plastic cups. The floodgates opened to the outside world, back to the land of problems and disappointment. Only now there was enough alcohol in the stream to forget what they were.

The signs of many other establishments had long gone dark, exposing the brilliance of a city being so close to the heavens. Litter gathered in gutters and crawled over the sidewalk as Danica stepped out with her one-night crowd. She stumbled toward the bus stop, alone. In contrast, others gathered in clumps of Uber and Lyft passengers, causing her to collect a handful of concerned looks.

"What are you doing over there, darling?" the frizzy blonde girl called, with one hand on the back door to a white Honda Accord, letting two of her posse slide in before her.

Danica combed her sweaty hand through the back of her head. "Oh, yeah, I'm waiting for the bus. Didn't call an Uber, so …"

"At this ungodly hour? Good luck. Where are you heading?"

"Greeley," Danica said with a hint of uncertainty.

"Oh, sweety. You won't get a bus to Greeley there. Trust me, I used to ride one in from Windsor a few nights a week. There's another stop, two blocks that way. You just make a left at the Loaf'N Jug, and you can't miss it. You should be safe."

Danica turned her attention in that direction and nodded back to the girl. "Thank you."

"Have a good night," the frizzy blonde girl sang as she descended into the Honda and vanished behind a tinted-out window.

Danica strolled the street, feeling the tackiness of the dance floor stick and pop under her shoes. Her satchel rested securely at her side. The quietness brought sobriety to her thoughts, which brought regret. The bulge was still there. No amount of dancing or drinking could take that away. Not without consequences. And she wasn't ready to make that decision. Walking alone on that warm summer night, she wasn't sure if she'd ever be prepared to make that decision. Like the frizzy blonde girl said, she was young and pretty and had her whole life ahead of her. Even so, the problem still existed, only now it was more of a dilemma—keep Lucas or don't.

Her hand gravitated toward her belly, fingers strumming over the soft fabric and tightening flesh. *Lucas.* The name swirled in her head. Somehow, she had this feeling. "His name is Lucas—will be Lucas." Something about saying the name out loud brought a peace that matched the tranquility of the night. She wasn't sure if it was the walk or the booze filtering through her bloodstream, but something brought a new sense of clarity to her dilemma. It was as if she had almost made her decision—almost.

The sign was still lit as she came to the bus stop. It was glowing blue, crying out from across the street, demanding attention. The building sat apart, a structure more like a church than a clinic, and like a church, Danica could see it bringing comfort to some. For her, it was a different feeling. Something she hadn't had the chance to feel. Why should she have to make this decision alone? Why couldn't she have someone else handle the dilemma, the problem—like the blonde frizzy girl said?

* * *

Ben had been lying in his bed, facing up, body sore, nose dripping with a thick, tar-like substance. He was swimming in the vast designs of his cottage cheese ceiling when another dark episode hit. As soon as it finished, he struggled to get his muscles and joints to pry him off the bed, panting with the overburdened fatigue of what had come and gone so vividly in his head. He rushed and slid to his knees to dig into the darkest crevice of his closet, scouring deep under bags and boxes until he could wedge out his duffel bag.

He got up before his head could reignite his balance, heart galloping over his chest like a thoroughbred racehorse, shambling across his room as if the floor had been made of rubber. He clutched his phone off the dresser and pressed on the screen. Its rectangular face brightened to life as he rushed to the far wall of the main room. There, a speaker system sat, one that Mr. Nelson had connected between the guesthouse and the main house. It had been put in place shortly after Ben's little blackout at the kitchen table. Ben flicked the two-way switch and called to see if anyone was awake. Mr. Nelson responded just as Ben had pulled up his weather app and typed in the little search bar, "Greeley, Colorado."

"What's going on, man?" Mr. Nelson's speaker voice called back.

"I need a buddy pass," he said, knowing that Mr. Nelson knew what he meant.

There was silence at first. Suddenly the speaker cracked to life. "When?" he asked.

Ben tapped the five-day forecast option at the bottom of the screen. "A week from today. To Denver. Anything you can get me on." The search wheel reappeared and was once more spinning, only a bit slower this time, or so it seemed.

Mr. Nelson went silent again, but this time Ben could hear the crackling noise of typing. "It looks like I can get you on a flight that leaves out of LAX next Tuesday at nine in the morning if that'll work."

Ben chewed on the corner of his lip. "I think that should be fine," he said, looking down at the forecast that popped up on the screen. Ben studied it, looking at it as if he were attempting to translate hieroglyphics:

Thursday 68° Clear skies
Friday 79° Sunny with a few scattered clouds

He scrolled down.

Tuesday 79° Rainy in the evening with storms overnight

"Actually, that would be perfect," Ben replied.

TEN

Why me, God? What have I done to deserve this? she thought, drowning in self-hatred, wallowing in turmoil, doubting her decision while the last girl before her was called to the back.

The chair was uncomfortable. Industrial cloth seating with metal and wooden armrests and a seat back straight enough to lay flush against the wall, far from the comfort of the pews in her church. There was also the thick wad of cash she had borrowed from her mom's purse, pressed into her hand like she was attempting to make a shoddy drug deal. It pushed its disgusting girth against her cheek from inside her back pocket. Loose clothes chosen to help her feel more comfortable failed to do so, as she could hardly swallow the whereabouts from where the money came. *Probably suckered it out of his father*, she toyed over as his most likely source. And he probably concocted some grand story of a charitable deed he wanted to provide for a down-and-out kid who needed that one kick start toward a better life. Or some crap like that. Anything to get what he wanted and be highly praised while he got it.

The room, stale and void, lacked any personality—gray walls, white floor, white counters, and couches and chairs of a retro brand. Greens and tans and grays in circles and cubism patterns. It was enough to make her puke 1970s all over the ceramic floor. Only a few watercolor paintings hung on the walls, all with the style of a similar artist. There were posters too, and a television set with one of those trashy late-afternoon talk shows on mute, but all that seemed uniform for any waiting room.

She'd never been to one of those clinics before. She never needed to. Pamphlets were crumpled in her hands, two of three, clenched tight in her fingers and rolled up into one tight cylinder. Not once had she considered opening one of them. She was afraid of what she might see and that she might change her mind—or vice versa.

There were a handful of girls other than her—no two the same. Some were her age, some were older, some younger. And about a third of them looked the way she felt, while the others at least appeared to be more poised. Most were alone, except the younger ones, who for the most part were in the company of guardians, or so Danica believed. They were of different races, different social statuses, and different backgrounds. Despite it all, there was one thing that brought them all together. One reason for all of them to be there in that waiting room. And she believed that was what kept them all so silent.

Peering around the room, her eyes fell on one of the younger girls crying in the embrace of what was clearly her older sister. She was young, fourteen at the most, and at the stage of having any equally slight bulge forcing her T-shirt to sit extra tight around her stomach. Straight dark hair veiled the pain in her face. Short gasps of breath pulsed through her back while bare feet in sandals hopped nervously on the floor. Her tears saturated the gray shoulder of her sister's shirt. A sister's comforting arm draped around her neck as she rubbed her arm. Her eyes were slightly closed as she whispered soft-spoken words in her pinkish ear like a mother's lullaby wooing her child to sleep.

Everyone in that room had a situation, a story, a reason for giving up their afternoon to sit and wait in those uncomfortable chairs—whether they wanted to or not. But that girl, for some reason, caught Danica's attention more than the others. She wanted to talk to her, break the silence between the chairs, stir a bit of sympathy in the stagnant air. She wanted to comfort her, place her hands on the young cringing fingers that quaked in the girl's lap as they cried and prayed, the way Danica had wanted to over the last cloistering weeks. She wanted to tell her to be strong, hang on. She wanted to say to that young girl that God doesn't make babies by mistake, that there is a reason for the life in her belly. But if she really believed that then she wouldn't have been there.

"Miss Briggs," a female voice said, stealing her attention, "we're ready to see you now." A lady dressed in casual work attire was behind the desk, waiting for her, apathetic in a way that came off as almost robotic. In her hand, she held a clipboard with a single sheet of paper, the future of Danica Briggs, summarized by a few checked boxes and a line or two of standard information.

Danica stood, tightening the pamphlets into a marker-sized tube, and made her way to the front desk. A bright-eyed, smiling woman was waiting to bring her into her office. "Are you Miss Briggs?" the woman asked sternly. She was beautifully pudgy, filled in in a way that fit her better than if she were of any less weight. Her hair shined and flowed as if she had just come from the salon, framing a bright, almost flawless complexion, if not for a half dozen moles scattered across her face. A bit of silver highlighted around her forehead in a way that seemed out of sorts compared to her youthful skin.

"Yes, ma'am," Danica replied, giving out a timid hand to shake the lady's, unsure if it was appropriate. However, it felt inappropriate not to.

The woman took a glimpse at Danica's hand, shaken and tense, and gave it a petite shake, if only to ease her nerves. It did not. "I'm Doctor Farrell, the counselor here. I see that this is your first time visiting us—correct?"

Danica nodded.

Doctor Farrell grinned. "Wonderful. Well, if you'd follow me, please, we'll head back to my office and discuss your condition."

The door to her office shut heavily, like most hospital doors, with that secure, almost permanent thud. The doctor offered Danica a seat. Danica took it.

By the time she walked out the door to the clinic and toward the bus stop, Danica's mind had only become more scrambled than when she first walked in. The doctor was friendly, almost motherly. Perhaps someone she could see as a close friend of her mother's. It was the opposite of what she'd expected to find there. She had been expecting … well … she wasn't sure what she had been expecting—just not that. But now, as she sat on that concrete bench, waiting on the next bus heading into town, all she knew for certain was that that small eight-by-ten picture she had crushing in her pocket thoroughly compromised her decision.

All she remembered was sitting in a room, some her age, some younger, some older. Her mind played games with her. She could feel the heartbeat in her stomach, playful movements stirring from under her own flesh. She remembered her name being called, muffled by her heartbeat rushing into her ears. She remembered the cold hallway and going into a windowless room where a table had been dressed just for her. She remembered refusing to look at the ultrasound but asking for the picture. She remembered taking a mixed batch of IVs and pain meds. She remembered the wait, the two narrow eyes of a masked doctor, the slight pinch in her stomach, and—done.

What Danica couldn't recall was when she got home or even when she got on the bus. She didn't remember getting dressed, signing paperwork, or walking to the bus stop for the second time in the last eight days, though somehow or another, she managed. Danica couldn't remember talking to a nurse about aftercare instructions. Yet the parade of paperwork and pamphlets laid out on her bed suggested she had. Apparently, there were to be cramps and bleeding that would follow, the side effects of what now felt might have been another one of the biggest mistakes of her life. Only, for this one, she swore she'd never forgive herself.

* * *

She lay there on a floor surrounded by a life she felt she had thrown away, in a room filled with memories no longer familiar, crying plaintively. She no longer thought she deserved to live. What had been dead inside had finally spread its disease to take the only innocent thing he had felt was left inside her. And she let it.

Now she was sitting in someone else's room, surrounded by the clutter of someone's beautiful life, all spread out in pictures and clothes and other pieces of memories. And none of it felt any more hers than a stranger's dream. And it was her job to sort through them and pack what she needed so she could lug them off to Northwestern before the fall semester. There were duffel bags left for her on her bed—none filled—waiting to be crammed with only what she felt was most necessary to take with her. Had it her way, she'd burn the whole room to the ground and sit cross-legged in the middle to ensure no scrap of wallpaper escaped the blaze. It all meant nothing to her, every last bit of it. College meant nothing to her. All the packing, prepping, scheduling, and signing meant nothing—a complete waste of time. So why was she doing it? Why had she tortured herself with the task of finding what she, in some past life, found valuable enough to shove inside a duffel bag and drag across four states? In the end, it all was no more valuable than a scrap piece of paper she'd use to peel gum off the bottom of her shoe and toss in the trash. Sitting in the center of that room—that hell-spawned room—treading a vat of sewage recollections and pointless waste while taking in gallons upon gallons of detritus self-loathing, she couldn't see herself trying to find her way out. Not to sort, not to pack, not to go. She couldn't see herself anywhere anymore.

Danica purged herself from the room, no longer able to spend another second surrounding herself with foreign memories. How she hated that tramp, her obliviousness, her gullibility. She took off down the stairs in bitter haste, each step more repulsed by herself than the last. Reaching the entryway, she looked toward the dining room, then shifted with a one-eighty glare to the living room. The whole house disgusted her—every picture, every window, every piece of furniture, home decor her parents had hand-selected. Everything was tied to a memory. Every memory was connected to that tramp.

A ball of disdain formed in her throat as her stomach tightened and wrenched. She moved toward the front door, sweaty palms shaking at her side, reached out for the deadbolt, and turned it. She hated the deadbolt too. With a click, the door unlocked. She pressed down on the door handle, her thumb slipping off just a smidge, and pried the door open.

"Where are you going, honey? Dinner's almost ready, you know." Her mother's smile was bitterly pleasing, standing under the arch of the dining room entrance but also concerned. She was holding a small, loomed dish towel in her hands, wiping them with it as if something needed to be wiped off.

How her mother ended up standing there without her knowing brought a jolt of a mystery that lapsed a few breaths. She was astonished that she hadn't heard her mother traipsing in from the kitchen, especially wearing those clogs of hers, though Danica had her theories. She crooked a smile (she hated smiling). "I promised Trisha I'd have dinner with her family tonight. She wanted to spend more time with me, so I thought it might be good."

Danica's mother rolled up the towel into an oblong ball. "You know, I am thrilled you two decided to be friends again," her mother replied. She tried to keep a level of delight despite her daughter's recent changes in behavior. "I think she is the sweetest girl. It's been so nice to see her around. And I think more time with her has helped you get out of this funk you've been in too. I do."

Danica gave an "all's well" shrug. *That's right; it's just a funk*, she thought as she stepped out the door and into the evening air. To her mother, it was always just a funk, a spell, a bad attitude that a girl like her should and will get over soon enough. It will pass, brush along like the rest of the curbside trash, scooped up in dirty rainwater and tossed down the gutter, never to be remembered again. *That's what happens to funks and spells, isn't it? There's only one problem. I won't forget this. I will never forget it, not until I make things right. And the only way to do that is to give a life for a life. That's what I deserve … life for life.*

Alone, she wandered the streets for what seemed like hours, despite the conflicting opinion of a still purplish sky, trying to search out a place, any place that was free of old memories. Unfortunately, Greeley was considered a small town, and there weren't many nooks in a small town that natives like her hadn't already uncovered. Somehow or another, she found her feet treading along a sidewalk she would have preferred not to be walking, but she was there nonetheless. She took her eyes off the ground for the first time in the last three or four blocks and looked up at a sign she hadn't seen in days.

Greeley High School
Home of the Cougars

A new year would begin in a handful of weeks, which she reasoned was the only reason it had kept the thing lit. She walked past the sign, gazing at it, glaring at it, threatening it with her eyes until her neck was too strained to look any longer.

She lost track of the sidewalk, trudging through a stretch of damp grass with a few trees posted around the lot. By the end, she found herself standing in front of a large chain-link fence with barbed wire threaded over the top. The security of the barbed wire always posed as a joke for the students of Greeley High, knowing that they never locked the gate for some reason or another. Even now, as school had not quite started for the year, she could see the gate wide open and the thick chain with a padlock dangling listlessly through one of the links nearest the entry pole. Danica followed the fence to the gate and walked through, grabbing the chain to pull it back and let it swing freely. It banged against the pole, ringing like a cathedral bell in the quiet field, fading slowly as its momentum dwindled.

Danica was on the other side of the gate, looking at the old concession stand boarded up with a hand-painted *Closed* sign brushed out in the school's colors. A stack of unused white plastic buckets they typically used to carry supplies for the upkeep of the feed—fertilizers and seed and all that—were stacked on top of each other like oversized Dixie cups. She walked past them, wondering for a brief minute if there might still be any snacks inside, then imagining how gross it would be if there were. It had been a hot summer. She cringed to think how much hotter it would have been in there, all wood and closed in with the scorch of a long afternoon sun beating down on it—like a solar-powered broiler.

She looked out at the field and up at the scoreboard. An oversized cougar was lurching out of the top with its teeth ferociously exposed. The cat's eyes settled with predatory intent out at the opposing team's side of the field, as if to turn the school's opponents into its prey. One claw, painted to look as if it were reaching out, scratched down the far side of the scoreboard. She's seen that board hundreds of times. She'd cheered for it. She'd hollered at it. She'd riled crowds up at the flickering change of the numbers on it. Now it was just an unlit piece of wood with a crappy painted cat on top.

Forgoing the field, she went straight for the bleachers. They, too, were painted in school colors—tan and green—a wardrobe nightmare on school T-shirt Day. She climbed the aluminum steps to their highest peak, turned, and sat. She could see the outline of the Rockies from there—just the peaks—and part of the next town over. As she sat, saturating herself in the quiet evening, she thought about those mountains and that town, then other mountains and towns and everything beyond that. There was once a whole lot of world she wanted to see. There were places she wanted to go far beyond the borders of the people who knew her. She felt a hunger to explore, to learn. She thought she could change lives and make the world a better place. Not anymore. Looking out on those snow-ridged peaks and the lights of her town and the next town over, all she felt was confining hopelessness.

Danica sat there for a few more moments crying, then sobbing, until every tear in her body had been expelled. She stood, her legs momentarily unstable, and grabbed the railing to escort her down the aluminum steps. Once at the bottom, she rounded the lowest row of seats opposite the way she came, took a few more steps down, and cut around under the stands. Below each row of seats was a spider web of aluminum bars crossing over each other, most of them too high to touch. There were a few, however, Danica felt she could almost touch when up on her toes.

An old urban legend about those beams under those stands came to mind. It was tragic, had it been real, of a former vice principal's son. He was destined to be a pro football player. All the colleges wanted him, offering him money and cars and all the crap a kid that age found enticing. However, during one of the season's final games, he got hit—hard. No one had seen a leg twist that way on the field or heard one snap so loudly. They said he was lying facedown on the ground, spasms twitching his body as he wailed out in pain. They said his knee had bent the opposite way it should, that his toes were pressed between the turf and his lower abdomen. By the time they carried him off the field, he was practically in shock.

Needless to say, a football career ended right there on that field. Unfortunately, he felt that a football career was all he had; without that, there was nothing left to live for. So, one night, the night of one of the senior dances, he went under the stands with a school chair and an extension cord he stole from the janitor's closet. He rapped the line—a bright orange one, Danica pictured, like those her dad sold in his hardware store—over and around one of the beams, then around his neck, and kicked the chair out from beneath him. It was only fitting that one of the janitors found the stolen cord while making his rounds, still wrapped around the neck the following day. The body was a dew-soaked, pasty white with crap and urine stains running down his pants. The boy's father was said to have suffered a mental breakdown. He was admitted to psychiatric care in Denver, and that was the last anyone had heard from him. His mom, no one knew what happened to her.

"It was tragic," Danica said to herself, "if it was true." She could imagine how a boy like that might have felt. No, not imagine—relate. "He probably felt useless to his school, worthless to his parents, and of nothing to himself. In the end, he was only a tragic reminder of all he had lost and what he could never be. People will never forget that young man so long as the school stands here. But then, what if it wasn't true? What if it was all made up, a swindle of a story that a new batch of students fell for every year because it was so intense and was placed right here where they now stood? That's unfair. They deserve better. This hellhole of a school deserves better. They all need a real story to talk about, those gossiping devils. And perhaps a person they know to go with it."

Just then, Danica figured out how she could give them that story and end her suffering at the same time.

* * *

Danica strolled in through her front door—late. There was a smile on her face, sincere and sinister. She leaped up the stairs to her room, with the overwhelming satisfaction that soon she would never have to climb those loathsome steps again. She barged into her room, kicked off her shoes, and began scooping up pictures, makeup, and clothes and ramming them into her deskside trash can. At first, she pushed it all down with the palm of her hand, which felt good. But it wasn't enough to do the job. She progressed to using her fist, punching down on it blow after blow, crushing the clutter until it looked like a tin ice-cream cone with one heaping scoop of adolescent paraphernalia. That made her feel great. She stepped back and looked at the waste basket of destruction resting by her desk. It pleased her.

Down the hall, she heard the muffled call of her mother asking if she was home, to which a cheerful reply said that she was. *At least for now*, she thought to add but kept it to herself. Inside, she felt a satisfaction she hadn't felt in a while. The burden dragging her feet through the past year was suddenly gone. She had a purpose. She had a new reason for life, just like that football player in the school legend. She was efficiently going to end it, just as he had and where he had.

Only one thing confounded her now, one itsy bitsy blip that was confusing her. If she felt this good and happy about her decision, then why couldn't she stop crying?

* * *

It was raining by the time Ben's head popped off his pillow. One of those obscure summer storms that had lost its way back in the springtime now grumbled in frustration over the Santa Clarita Valley with subtle thunder rolls. His body was still cold from the feeling of another place's downpour at another time. Naturally, his hand went for his neck to feel if the rope was still noosed around it.

No.

Not a rope.

An extension cord.

Thankfully, it was not. He was back in his bed, safe and sound—out of breath and sore, but safe and sound. It was always harder to tell when they came while he slept. He was vulnerable then, blending his dream with visions and scrambling them up in his head. Luckily for him, he didn't sleep all that much.

The lack of sleep allowed events to roll over in Ben's head as thick as storm clouds. Jeremy was still getting acquainted with his new life, his new career. There was a good chance his only friend wouldn't be available to pick him up or drive him around some unfamiliar town to find this school with those awful green and tan colors. As heartless as it sounded, how many people would be able to abandon whatever plans they had scheduled to go and pick someone up at the airport? And with that in mind, how was he even going to explain his little expedition, let alone his sudden visit to the mile-high city? Maybe betting on the art of surprise and Jeremy's unquestioning cooperation wasn't worth rolling the dice. Perhaps this was a gamble too risky to take. After all, a rental car would at least secure a means of getting around, let alone out of the airport.

Just then, Ben heard his mother's voice floating up in the back of his head. It was calm, floating soothingly like a bubble of air rising from the ocean's depths. "It's time, Ben," she said. He could almost feel her warm cotton hand cupping the side of his face. "It's time you let someone in. Show him what you can do. He's been waiting."

"It's time," Ben said. He was committed. No turning back. This was his decision. The dice had been tossed from his hands.

He wiped the sweat from his face and dragged his hand over his pounding chest. "Just a few more days." He gasped and swallowed. Every drop of saliva ran like flames down his throat. "I just hope she can make it."

ELEVEN

Mr. Nelson dropped Ben off at the curb of departures sometime around seven thirty that morning. He dressed in a worn-out T-shirt and a pair of khaki shorts he usually sported only on yardwork days, his thinning, light hair peeking out over his ears from under an old air force cap and his weary eyes covered in aviator sunglasses. They pulled next to one of those *No Parking, No Waiting* signs that appeared invisible to every car that rolled into the airport.

Ben came with only a backpack and a small duffel bag—no baggage check needed. He bypassed one line only to get held up in another lengthier one. He made it through security, no sweat, embracing a printed slip of paper that sucked up the moisture from his clammy hand. He dashed to his terminal, stopping only once to pick up a share-size bag of M&Ms and something to read on the flight.

There were two ladies stationed behind the counter at his terminal. One was a beautiful middle-aged woman with a name tag that simply read "Jackie." She had chestnut-colored hair that layered just below her shoulders and gave volume to her lightly petite face. Her eyes were framed under purplish rimmed glasses, a style that could only suit a face like hers. She wore a pink shade of lipstick that would typically color the lips of a teenager, but she pulled that style off as well. Her chest was slightly busty, just enough to funnel her form down into a size zero skirt without looking like a uniformed pole.

The other lady—younger probably but not by much—stood in contrast to Jackie. She had a familiar name on her tag, Kimberly, and was well formed in the chest, thin around the torso, and broad at the hips. Her hair looked damp and curly, a sandy blonde that she wore just out of the shower. Her face was not bad looking but not exactly an eye catcher either, just so-so. However, whatever she lacked in beauty was more than compensated by the arctic blue tinge of her eyes.

At first blush, Ben found Kimberly's eyes distracting and Jackie's smile alluring. His eyes shifted from one to the other as he walked up to the counter and informed them of his arrival. One smelled like vanilla, but they were too close together to tell which. He pictured it to be Jackie. Having that vanilla tint to her skin would only be fitting.

Good news came following two bright smiles. He had already been assigned a seat, seeing that there were already a few cancellations on the flight. Ben hoped for first class. He'd never been. Unfortunately, as they gave him his assigned seating, it looked like that trend would continue for now. He took the news with a grin, plucked the ticket from the woman's hand, and found a seat.

Ben sat still for a moment, then leaned down and unzipped the front pouch of his backpack to pull out his phone. The bars were full. The charge was full. He punched the little green phone on the bottom corner and scrolled down a few days' worth of phone calls until he found what he was looking for. He hit the name, then dialed. It rang.

Unlike Ben, Jeremy was prompt in answering his phone. It was like a tick of his. Letting it ring more than twice was unacceptable—or, as he saw it, rude. That night as he packed, Ben conjured up a story that he felt was simple enough to be authentic and exciting enough—for Jeremy—to be effective. He'd tell Jeremy he had a job opportunity in one of the local suburbs, working at one of the schools. It was entry-level, a janitor position, but still a job. Was it a lie? Most certainly but a necessary one for the time being. The only problem was, so the lie went, he put Jeremy's Denver address on his résumé. Now they were expecting him to be there for an interview on Thursday. Luckily (as if luck had anything to do with it), he had been able to secure a place on standby for a nine o'clock flight out but would need a ride and a place to stay.

Ben laid out the story as concocted, and just like that, Jeremy took the news like candy. It was perfect. It was more than perfect. As it turned out, Jeremy's company was doing some sort of family carnival that very afternoon, encouraged but not mandatory to attend. Jeremy was digging for a good excuse not to have to show. Seeing all those happy families wearing their bright and sunny faces, parents walking hand in hand, fingers laced together. At the same time, their kids scampered about, awing at this, oohing for that, getting high on cotton candy and cheap prizes, celebrating the feat of their ability to throw a dart at a balloon. It only made that itch for him wanting to start his own family break out into a full-blown rash.

Everything seemed to be going swimmingly. Ben would've chalked it all off to luck, but as his mother used to say, there's no such thing as luck in this world, only little miracles that God blesses us with. That had proven to be even more accurate over the years.

Nine o'clock on the dot, and they began boarding the plane. However, Ben still had a wait. One downside to catching a free ride was that he was most likely last to board. He waited, opening the slip of paper he had carried with him to study as group A, then group B, then group C made their way onto the plane. Finally, Ben folded up the paper, hiked up his backpack over his shoulder, grabbed his duffel bag, and made his way to the platform. On his way, he gave Jackie and Kimberly their own "nice to meet you" grin before plunging down the jet bridge and into the belly of the plane.

He found his seat across the aisle from a heavyset man in a loosened business suit who appeared to already have been asleep. The man's head tilted back. His mouth potted open and purred the deep breaths of slumber. The trifold skin of his neck rolled down to a relaxed, unbuttoned collar and loose tie. The man's hair was thin at his forehead, teetering over the edge of baldness and gradually thickening toward the back. It was just enough to splatter his dark, greased hair over the top of his seat. Ben made every ounce of effort to not wake the man as he heaved his duffel bag up to his shoulder and pushed it into the overhead compartment. At one point, the man gave a disrupted snort and turned his head, slightly miffed at the sound of plastic grinding against the base of Ben's bag, but not enough to crack an eye.

He took his seat, noticing that the one next to him and the two in were all empty. "It must have been a family," he said to himself, "that didn't make the flight for one reason or another. It could have been a change of plans, a trip that was no longer necessary. A sickly kid, possibly." He wondered whose seat he might have been able to take. Which family member was willing to sacrifice so that he wouldn't have to sit on the aisle seat next to the fat man who was now snoring his way straight to dreamland? He shrugged at the thought.

The flight attendants made their final rounds, checking seats and shutting the overhead compartments. Ben reached into his backpack and pulled out the book he had purchased from the airport newsstand—Stephen King, *The Outsider*. He liked some of King's stuff, though he could do without the gore and all that. There was enough in his life to make gore something he found entertaining. However, the stories were quite creative. And there was something about the characters he connected with. How they found themselves scalding in the boiling pot of abnormal situations, and all they had to endure—and did—to find that peace at the end of their dilemma. It made his life feel normal.

The engines sounded. The air and overhead signs came on. Ben flipped over a small batch of pages straight to chapter 1 as an attendant's voice came over the PA.

* * *

The plane landed at Denver International Airport fifteen minutes early. Good time for a smooth flight, other than the small bout of turbulence Jeremy had warned him about when getting over Denver's airspace. Ben had hardly made a crack in the book during the flight. His attention was constantly drawn to the vision and the slip of paper he kept pulling from his pocket and reviewing repeatedly. The fat man snorted to life as the captain announced his typical welcome to Denver spiel, eyes bloodshot and spooked at the sudden interruption as the plane rolled up the tarmac.

Ben made his way across the crowded airport, cutting and pushing against the ever-bustling crowd of Denver International toward the baggage claim exit. He figured if Jeremy was already there, he would be waiting by one of the carousels. He scanned the infinite room littered with friends greeting friends, family hugging family, and all sorts of people droning over the rotating luggage—like they had one shot at picking up their bag, or it was lost forever. Seeing them there, like mindless, robotic drones, made him glad he had only brought a carry-on. He proceeded to cut and push through a more stationary cluster of travelers out the sliding doors and into the thin mountain air of the mile-high city.

The street out front bustled with the noise of cars, busses, and taxis echoing off metal and pavement. Uber and Lyft tagged vehicles waited in no-parking zones for strangers. Exhaust fumes cluttered the air in gray, lingering smoke that billowed over the street and onto the sidewalk, choking out the clean mountain air he had expected to find. For the most part, it was like landing at LAX—same noise, same pollution, the same outbreak of gum on the walkway and streets. Only a few signs had changed, and those were few and far between.

He took a seat on one of the concrete benches that lined the inner part of the sideway and waited. Scoping down the road, he was eager to see if he could spot a squealing black Honda Civic or if he'd be surprised to find Jeremy pulling up in something a little more modern. Cars passed by, honking their horns at a teeth-grinding decibel. Drivers waved at pedestrians as they came to a screeching halt in the middle of the road, instigating more teeth-grinding honks. Finally, he heard a familiar voice call out his name in no particular direction. He looked down the road, turned, and peered the other way. Again, he called for Ben, this time rising out of a brand-spanking-new Ford Escape two vehicles out from the curb.

Jeremy towered over the small SUV enough for Ben to spot him instantly out of the corner of his eye, wielding a Jeremy-sized smile. Ben smiled back, scooping up the bag at his side and nipping between two tightly parked cars to get to Jeremy's new ride.

"Nice ride," Ben said, opening the rear door and launching his bags into the back seat.

"You like? It's an Escape. Got it in white plat-in-um," Jeremy said, putting a twist of a Spanish accent at the end. "This little baby's got a turbo-charged engine—could probably outrun the devil. Bluetooth, GPS, a sunroof the size of the entire ceiling—oh and an automatic four-wheel drive too. The guy in charge of our fleet said I'd need it once the weather turns to crap for the winter. I'm just glad I can fit in this thing without banging my head against the ceiling."

"Somehow, it suits you," Ben commented as he climbed in the passenger seat and watched Jeremy slip effortlessly into the driver's seat. The car had already been running, which Ben couldn't tell due to his inexperience with vehicles post '05. Jeremy shifted back into drive and pressed on the gas. The engine revved, unleashing his turbo-charged SUV into the rapid flow of airport traffic and the busy streets of Denver.

Jeremy's apartment wasn't too far from the airport. However, with the few detours he took to show Ben around and a quick stop for a bite to eat at his newfound taco stop, they didn't make it to his complex until sometime in the early evening. By then, Ben was hungry again and was sure Jeremy was but didn't want to pose much of an inconvenience on his first day there. Besides, he'd be doing plenty of inconveniencing tomorrow. His old pal was about to chauffeur him for a good hour or two north for what he still believed was a job interview. Ben still felt bad about lying, but there was no other way at this point. Besides, he'd know everything in twenty-four hours and witness it firsthand.

Jeremy's apartment was grander than any Ben had been in; over the years, he'd been in plenty. Most were rodent-ridden trash heaps occupied by the tenants of those who had given up on life, who didn't care what sort of diseases they might be breading in there. Jeremy's was clean and brilliant, with vaulted ceilings, white stoned floors, and walls of windows to let every drip of sunlight in at any hour of the day. For a one-bedroom, the place was huge. Most of his belongings had already been arranged, though a few marked boxes still rested against the wall by the gas-fed fireplace. The couch was new, brown suede, thick, and cozy—a three-seater that would be perfect for Ben to sprawl out over for the much-needed shut-eye. Ben dropped his bags at the door and began perusing the apartment. He peeked out the sliding doors of the balcony. In the distance, Mile-high Stadium rested like a nest in the midst of its chicks, ready for the next time she called them home. He reviewed old photos of summer trips and graduation ceremonies while appraising the amount of pottery and artwork he never knew Jeremy had a taste for. Ben could tell right off the bat that his friend's new job had perks indeed, and Jeremy took advantage of every one of them.

"You want something to drink?" Jeremy asked.

Ben turned his attention to see Jeremy's head already deep in the latest-model fridge. "Sure. What do you have?"

Jeremy pulled his head out, holding two cans of Mr. Pibb in his hands. He didn't need to say, and Ben didn't need to ask. Placing them on the counter, he reached into a high cupboard and pulled out a container of nacho cheese Pringles.

"It's as if you read my mind." Ben casually scurried to the bar that separated the kitchen from the living room and took a seat on one of Jeremy's never used leather barstools. He took a can, a handful of Pringles, and began munching—two and three at a time.

Jeremy bent against the counter and crossed his arms, appearing as a bouncer for the kitchen. "So, are you excited? Nervous?" he asked.

Ben looked at him with a flash of surprise and confusion. Chips crushed and ground in his mouth as he snacked the salty, dry serving and swallowed. "Hmm," he replied, his lips still smacking the cheesy baked goodness that lingered.

"The job interview," Jeremy clarified. "Are you excited or what? Nervous, I bet. Man, I hope you get it. It would be so awesome to have you here, you know."

Ben had already thrown a handful of chips in his mouth but quickly swallowed and cleared his throat. "Oh, yeah—excited." He nodded. "Definitely. Not too nervous though." He lied. His bones ached with nervousness.

Jeremy reached for his soda, pulled back the tab, and cracked the freshness out of it. He took a heavy chug out of his can before letting out a satisfying belch. "Okay, what is it again that you'd be doing at the school?"

Ben smirked as he continued to nod. His eyes were stoic and focused. It was a game as old as their friendship, though some might have considered it to be more of a trap. Jeremy knew exactly what Ben said he'd be doing. He just didn't fully believe him. Maybe there was a reason for that. A good reason.

"Janitor's assistant," Ben replied.

"Janitor's assistant? I didn't know they had assistants."

Ben was still nodding. "Oh yeah," he replied, nonchalantly. "They do the simpler things, you know, like picking up trash, scraping gum off tables and chairs, putting away tools and mopping up things—all that sort of stuff. Everything a janitor does but without the fixing stuff part."

"And it pays good, this janitor's assistant position?"

Ben's eyes squinted narrowly as he puckered a frown. "Hmm, no. The pay is crap," he said, based on what he thought an honest janitor might make. "But it's a job. And it's here, so …"

Jeremy picked up his can and raised it to salute. "Well, all right then. Let's get you a job that pays crap."

Ben raised his can and gave it a tap against Jeremy's. *Mission one—accomplished*, he thought.

* * *

She wasn't going to write a letter for two reasons. She found it might take away from the mystery and drama of the venture she was about to embark on, first of all. And secondly, she didn't want anyone to know how twisted her life ended up becoming at its grievous end. As if paper and ink could even begin to hold a spell of what had been fermenting inside her. As if her fingers could somehow expel the depths of her soul and scribe it all within the eleven inches of notebook paper by the prick of a ballpoint pen. To even try would be all for naught.

Danica snuck an extension cord out of the garage that morning. It was a bright orange one she found buried deep in an old plastic container her dad hardly cracked open as far as she could tell. It was smuggled from the garage to her room after her parents left for the store, then harbored in the bowels of one of the smaller bags packed to keep up all appearances—that being that she was still going to start her college life at Northwestern. It was long and thick, perfectly fitting what she had envisioned. She made plans to carry out her valediction the next night, despite the predicted unseemly weather. If anything, the foul weather would only make it more dramatic. To her parents, they'd only assume that she would be going to some mixer or farewell party. Just a couple of classmates spending one last night together before hugging out the opposite affections of sad goodbyes. What they didn't know wouldn't hurt them—at least not immediately. Not until some poor soul stumbled across her cold, damp body slung lifelessly pallid under the bleachers by a bright orange cord.

Danica reconsidered writing a note, taking a seat at the bare remains of her one cluttered desk and writing a few lines down on a girly, pastel-colored line paper out of her high-dollar journal. She jotted and scribbled, jotted and scribbled—finally scrunching her face into a disapproving mess. Finally, she ripped the page from the journal and balled it up to toss it disconcertingly at her wastebasket. It pinged and bounced off the basket's rim, rolling disarranged over the floor and stopping at the base of the wall. She stood from her chair, only to make the short journey to her bed and do a backward plunge onto the mattress.

She lay there, body splayed out, watching the fan blades spin in a hypnoidal flow over the ceiling, cooling the vascular numbness under her oversized Cougars jersey. Each blade's rotation interrupted the lighting on her ceiling. It pulsated steadily, this faint strobe of shadows and light, flickering between brilliance and somber. Her heart slowed to its pattern. She took in the air slowly and exhaled even slower.

"Just one more day," she said to herself. "Don't lose your cool. You can do this. You know you can."

* * *

"Just one more day," Ben said to himself while lying on Jeremy's couch, leg anchored off the side, watching the high ceiling fan spin with ease. "You can do this. You know you can. It's like all the others, only with a spectator this time."

A lead ball started to form in his chest, thinking about the exchange. *What will Jeremy think? What will he do? Will I even be able to concentrate and focus all my attention on this girl with Jeremy on the sidelines? He will most likely be befuddled at first. Maybe even feel driven to interfere that way this over caring giant always wants to do.*

Maybe this is wrong, he thought. *Maybe it was a bad idea to take advice from the voice of my dead mom this time. Or anytime, for that matter.*

"Hey, man, you still awake?" Jeremy said as he strolled into the room, speaking as if it were midnight and not two in the afternoon. "You are nervous about tomorrow, aren't ya?"

You have no idea, Ben thought. He pushed out a grin and uttered, "Nah," as he slid upright to let his friend crash down at the other end of the couch.

"Don't sweat it," Jeremy replied. "Confidence is key. When you walk in there, act as if you're doing them a favor. You know, like you're interviewing them to see if you want to bless them with your skill. Employers eat that crap up. You smile a bit, chat a bit, tell them why'd they be lucky to have you, and you're in. I'm telling you, bro, it's all about that confidence."

Jeremy leaned back and gave Ben a once-over. "Some new threads might not hurt your chances either. I'll tell you what. Take a few minutes to gather yourself, take a shower if you'd like, and get dressed. 'Cause I'm going to buy you something swank to wear tomorrow."

"Oh, dude, no. I-I don't—"

Jeremy shushed Ben with a grizzly-sized growl. "Bro, please," Jeremy said. He outstretched his arms and laid out his hands to exemplify his ritzy apartment. "My guest, my friend, my treat. Besides, if you're blessed, why not spread it around." He was truly blessed, Ben thought. "Now get ready. I know exactly where to go."

As Jeremy popped off the couch and returned to his room, Ben's feelings went from nervous to downright awful. He couldn't let his friend blow money on clothes for an interview that didn't truly exist. On the flip side, he couldn't let the cat out of the bag either. At that moment, he felt a bit like the prodigal son who, after mistreating his old man and squandering his inheritance, came home broke and ashamed, garbed in mucky, labor-worn rags, desperately in need, not worthy of spittle of help from his father. And yet in the end, his old man embraced him. He furnished the bratty kid with the nicest clothes in the house, made him the grandest meal, and celebrated his homecoming as if the boy had merely been lost. It fit the bill, didn't it? Ben never treated their friendship as well as he should. He was a flake on more occasions than not. Took whatever Jeremy offered for granted. He was never there when Jeremy needed him. Only when Jeremy was gone had he seen how much that friendship really meant to him. And now he was in Jeremy's house, in rags, unworthy of any help from his friend. And yet he fed him, took him in, and now wanted to buy him clothes.

"One more day," Ben said again as he stood from the couch and went to his bags to pull out a fresh shirt. "In twenty-four hours or so, Jeremy will know everything. And yes, he might accept it. Or he might freak and run. But either way, at least there will be no more secrets."

* * *

Danica spent the rest of the day sorting through her things, packing as if she were going somewhere she could take her belongings. She listened to her favorite songs one last time as a self-imposed in memoriam played out in her head of all the fond memories she had across the span of her life. After that, she had dinner with her parents. They were cheery. She was quiet. But she ate. That was a stride above the last several meals they had together. After, the three sat around the TV and watched an hour and a half of laugh-out-loud sitcoms. Her parents watched the TV. She watched her parents.

At last, she stood and paced soberly toward her mother, wrapped lovingly in her father's embrace on the couch, and gave her a kiss on the cheek. Danica's only thought was that after all these years, her mother's cheek was still as soft and vibrant as it had been when she was her age. The scent of Escada flavored her mother's skin fittingly, almost naturally. In the middle of her kiss, Danica felt the burly hand of her father run fingers over the top of her head, down the side, and brush her cheeks. Years of labor and hard work to give his family a better life had dried the skin into a permanent leather glove that somehow still touched his little girl's face like a string of rose petals.

At that moment, Danica knew they had done everything they could to protect her and give her a good and sheltered life. But there was only so much protection you could give somebody. There was only so much life. The rest was up to fate, and she blamed that fate for failing her.

Danica crept up the stairs, turning once to whisper one last good night, and made her way to her room. There would be no crying. The time for that had passed. There was no more memoriam. There was no more packing or music or attempted letters. There was only the night, and it was pure and dark, silent and alone. There was no tinkling of starlight outside. No sounds of a motorist. No lively breeze rustling the branches of pine trees outside her window. The fan above her bed gave no light to flicker on her ceiling and no steady spinning motion for her heart to sync with. Everything was dark. Everything was already dead.

A clock in the kitchen hung above the entryway, one of those sundial types, painted to look like ancient stone with Roman numerals on it. The kind one might find at a Ross or Kirkland's. Most days, Danica had ignored its faint ticking as she ate her breakfast at the kitchen counter. But that morning, each tick and every tock took to her ears like a chisel being hammered into stone. Her eyes burned, fighting the sunlight that lanced in through the window. Her head throbbed with swelling pain that would make a person beg for somebody to drill a hole in their temple. She hadn't felt this hungover since the morning after that party. And to top that, she hadn't even been drinking this time.

Danica's mother strolled in with a bright, smiling good morning that met Danica's ears about as welcoming as the sound of a seagull catching its wing in a blender. Her freshly washed complexion and damp hair brightened the room with a glittering joy that burned Danica's eyes worse than natural sunlight. Soon after, as Danica's mom began to pour herself a steaming cup of coffee, her dad strutted in, singing one of his favorite country songs—poorly. He sashayed over to his wife and scooped her up in his arms, leaving the coffee deserted on the counter with one hand around her waist. The other engulfed her petite little hand in the air and two-stepped her across the kitchen, singing and dancing until her face turned a rosy pink. Danica's face turned flush as a bit of adolescent hanky-panky pursued, leading into a dip and an overly passionate kiss, followed by a slap on her father's rear. Then it was back to the coffee for Mrs. Briggs and a heavy peck on the head from Danica's father as he sat beside her and waited to be served a cup of piping-hot joe.

"Big day, big day," her father's voice thundered. "One last night with you and your posse." He had tried to be hip and failed. "Bet you can't wait. You and the girls spending one last night getting into all sorts of mischief, doing each other's nails, talking about who's hot and who's not, twerking to Lady Googoo."

"It's Gaga, Dad," Danica said with her face down, buried in her hands. "And do you even know what twerking is?"

Mrs. Briggs's eyes asked the same question as her husband's sight went back and forth between her and Danica. "It's like a style of dance. Like the Macarena, right?" Danica and her mother looked away, shaking their heads and saying nothing. "Okay, okay. So I'm not as hip as I appear to be. But I'm still a pretty awesome dad with a heart that ..." He stumbled his way back into a country song, this one having the bitterly unrhythmic flavor of something he was making up off the cuff. He swayed his way up from the counter and waltzed back to his wife, half singing, half humming, and all out of key—to give her one more kiss before heading off to start his day.

"Well then, what do you girls have planned tonight?" her mother questioned, but she was immediately called to her phone at the chime of a new message. She pulled her phone out of her pocket and swiped open the screen, her fingers tap-dancing over message after message.

Danica shrugged. Her head crooked slightly to the side. "Nothing really." She paused for a minute, finding the lack of her mother's attention distracting. "I think we're just going to play the night by ear, maybe grab some dinner or see a movie or something like that. I know that that new Mediterranean place opened off Birch and Main, so we might check that out." Danica played it cool. Disturbingly calm, even for her. Seeing her mom's head buried in whatever had taken importance on her phone made her wonder if it even mattered.

Her mom nodded, eyebrows raised, tasting her coffee's first scorching sip. Her eyes twitched at whatever she was looking at. Danica knew she was listening but wasn't paying attention.

"Then we'll probably head to that strip club in Denver and see if they'll let us dance for some quick cash—or maybe drugs. I heard cocaine can give you one heck of a night," Danica continued. Her mother gave her nothing. Not even a concerning peek.

"Well, that all sounds great, hon," her mother said, clicking away some message to whoever. "You girls, just be safe and don't get into too much trouble."

"Oh, heavens no, my pimp wouldn't allow that," Danica replied at an ostentatious decibel.

"Uh-huh." Her mom finally looked up. She held her phone on display. "Look, I have to reply to a few of these messages and get ready to open the store. But I'm excited for you girls. And I think you will all have a good time tonight!" her mom exclaimed, striding backward out of the kitchen, facing Danica, eyes stapled to her phone. "I'll want to be the first to hear about it tomorrow morning, okay?"

"Yeah, sure," Danica murmured. Further words died in her throat as she stirred her cereal into mush cornmeal and watched her mother continue messaging her way out of the kitchen. It looked as if the woman's lack of awareness was heading her straight for the entryway wall, which Danica had to admit would have been hysterical. However, she cut sharp at the last minute to lightly graze her shoulder across the inside doorpost.

"So that was it," Danica said to herself. "That was the last conversation I'll be having with my parents. Not too memorable, was it? I guess it's better to cut ties with no emotional chains or any of that lovey-dovey stuff that makes a kid and her parents feel connected. Just shake hands and walk away like professional adults. Clean and easy."

But it wasn't clean.

It certainly wasn't easy.

* * *

Ben's new clothes hung off the front doorknob, still buttoned and draped over the store hangers. Jeremy had persuaded the cashier to let them keep the reusable ones, though it wasn't so much convincing as it was flirting. A nicely pressed auburn dress shirt with a checkered tie and a clean pair of slacks. Had the shirt been white, he could see himself passing as a missionary or one of those old door-to-door salesmen who tried to persuade folks that their vacuum was better than their competitors. No matter. Soon it would all be mucked up in the rain and mud of a deluged exchange. It wouldn't be the first time he'd gotten dirty from an exchange. However, it would be the first where he was dressed so professionally.

Ben's head levitated off the pillow to the warm smell of crackling bacon and fried eggs. The aroma carried from the kitchen to his perceptive nostrils. It was a far cry from the orthodox dry cereal and nonfat milk he had been accustomed to back home. As he arose, his body didn't ache as he expected it to. Jeremy's was relatively comfortable, unlike his austere couch—short and unyielding as a cylinder brick. No wooden planks lodged in his back, separating the top half of his spine from the bottom. No prickly, worn corners, sharp-edged armrests, or pockets of missed stuffing for any part of his body to get wedged into. His sleep had been as good as if he had been in his own bed—maybe better.

Jeremy came in, already showered and dressed for another day of managing. He strolled into the dining area in a big-and-tall navy suit, custom tailored by all appearances, with two hot plates of bacon and eggs in his hand. He placed them on the table, one where Ben was about to sit, the other where he could sit and eat beside his friend. Without a pulse of hesitation, Ben took to the plate and began to pick at the meal, hunched over and nibbling in a squirrel-like manner. Jeremy watched as his friend incinerated the plate as if he hadn't had a morsel of food in weeks. A man in such a suit was much more leveled in his table etiquette, shifting through his eggs with the fork before impaling a tiny stack and sliding it into his mouth.

Ben paused to chew and watched as Jeremy nibbled elegantly, then swallowed, shifted, and poked at another tiny stack of eggs. *Man, some things really do change*, he thought, thinking back to all those lunches.

Jeremy ate half his meal before they reached the table, and what was left had been practically inhaled.

"So, I rearranged my schedule to make it a half day today," Jeremy said, facing Ben with an empty mouth while preparing his next serving of eggs. "I thought it might be good to roleplay a little interview before heading out, and I wanted to give us plenty of time to get there as well." Jeremy reached out to grab something before realizing what was not on the table. "Oh crap. I forgot the orange juice. Give me a minute." He set his fork across the center of the plate, creating a wall that divided the small mound of eggs from the neat row of bacon. It was art; how neat and orderly it appeared to Ben. From the kitchen, Jeremy went on. "I'll tell you. I still don't get why they wanted to interview you so late in the day. It strikes me as rather odd; you know?" He plucked two glasses from the cupboard and sat them on the counter.

Ben, still mesmerized by the neatness of Jeremy's plate, called out, "It wasn't them. It was me. I told them I was staying with a friend in Denver and that he was my only ride up there. I said that I probably wouldn't be able to meet with anyone 'til after you got off work, and if that was a problem, I'd understand."

"And they said it wasn't?" Jeremy asked, returning with two half-filled glasses of orange juice.

"They said they'd work with my schedule," Ben replied, imitating the flurry of disbelief Jeremy portrayed.

Jeremy set one glass down for himself, then one for Ben. "Man, they must've dug you on the phone to accommodate that arrangement. Good for you," he said, taking his seat and reaching for a slice of bacon. "Makes me think I might have wasted a good half day to help you prepare."

Jeremy looked up at the clock he had mounted over his television set. "Good word, it's that late already," he said, scooping up the rest of his bacon while one stuck out the side of his mouth like a flattened cigar. "I gotta go. Can't be late if I'm leaving early. Ugh, you gonna be okay hanging out here by yourself?"

"You have Netflix, don't you?" Ben said, making it clear that was all he needed.

"That I do, and a fridge stuffed with food in case you get hungry. I should be back around three. Call me if you need anything."

"I'll be all right. You have yourself a good day, hon," Ben teased, jesting all prissy, getting a smirk and a roll of the eyes as Jeremy walked out the front door and locked it.

* * *

She was alone in the house to make her final arrangements. She took a shower, got dressed, and put on her makeup the way she always did. She tidied her room quickly, hauled the bags she packed down the stairs, and stacked them neatly by the door, leaving only one bag left to carry down—the bag with the orange extension cord. One last time, she contemplated writing a few words of farewell. But any sentiment grew legs, and why waste the energy chasing them down when no one who would read them would truly understand. At least that was what she accepted.

Danica took the time to glance out the window to the backyard, memorizing the old swing set her father put up for her when she was about five years of age. Seeing it there, with a verdigris coat and all weather beaten, deprived of attention through the ages from no fault of its own, she began to feel a rebirth of connection to it. As old memories pressed upon her, she remembered they both had good years, happy years, years when they felt important and wanted. She remembered the summers when her dad would spend hours pushing her on that swing, back when "making do" was a blessing. Back when her parents would rather close the doors on the shop than miss one of their daughter's many events. Back when she felt like she could tell them anything. And they'd be there for her. Because they were a family.

Time changes things. Priorities get rearranged. Small bits of joy evolve into a chore we no longer have time for. And an old swing set once cherished by a little girl and her family now sat withering of deprivation as a relic of more blessed days.

Danica proceeded out the back door. The metal beams creaked and bent as she sat on the dry plastic seat, chains clinging, fighting against its age to accommodate an old friend once more. She kicked off her shoes to let her toes comb through the blades of grass. They tickled under her feet. Her fingers wrapped around the cold chains that pigtailed down each side of the seat. They were thinner than she remembered as she gripped them tightly and took a few steps back until only her toes could reach the ground. Then her feet let go of the earth, and she took off. She was free. In time, she was smiling.

After some time in the backyard, Danica returned, shoes dangling by the hooks of her fingers, and rested on the couch, dropping the shoes where they may. She reached and grabbed the remote for the TV and powered it on. Whatever was on at that time didn't matter to her. She wanted noise, that was all. She wanted the sound of voices to drown out every second thought she had that might deter her mission. She desired to stay as committed as she had been before stepping outside and revisiting her younger years. She wanted to have a clear, decisive mind for once. She wanted to leave this world without a seedling of doubt that she was doing what was necessary.

She placed the remote on the floor, propped up her legs, and lay back on the couch, resting her head on the armrest. Her hands splayed lazily over her stomach, feeling nothing but thin cotton and flaccid skin. She closed her eyes to think about how it would have felt had it still been there, Lucas. Would it have felt as tight as an overinflated ball? Would she have felt movement, a kick, or a turn? Maybe. Or maybe she would have felt nothing. But she never gave herself the chance to know. Keeping that in mind was enough for her to rest easy on what she had decided to do.

* * *

The first roll of thunder came in around two o'clock, as Ben was on his ninth episode of season three of some Tim Allen show. Thin clouds shrouded the sky, coloring more of a damper gray than white. A wabbled breeze had turned the air only gently cool, as if to apologize for the hot summer days. The sliding glass door had gathered only a spritz of rain, too meager to roll down. However, despite no sun, the sky was still bright, and the thunder sounded distant. Ben knew that would soon change. He was certain the weather would become torrential, even dangerous. The worst was yet to come.

Despite Jeremy's grand array of food, he forwent lunch for two small bowls of Froot Loops and one and a half Pop-Tarts dispersed throughout the day. Old habits die hard. One can of Mr. Pibb now rested in the trash, while another sat flattening on the coffee table in front of him. A mess was accumulating without trying, and he knew he had to clean it up before Jeremy got back, which would be any time now. Not only that but he still hadn't gotten dressed. He didn't know why, but looking at the new threads, knowing his friend forked out a reasonable sum of money for them, made it seem wrong to wear them during an exchange. It made it all feel … business, not personal, like he was out to do what he was hired to do, nothing more. He had three seasons to get over it, but looking at them hanging there, so neat and proper, made it hard to digest.

At two forty-five, Ben shut off the TV, scooped up the bowl, the Mr. Pibb, and the foil wrapper still containing half a Pop-Tart, and walked them into the kitchen. He washed out his bowl, poured the dark, flat beverage into the sink before tossing the can in the trash, and took one final bite of his strawberry pastry. He then returned to sweep the crumbs off the coffee table with the corner of his palm and carried them cupped in his hands to the trash. Next, and most difficult, he took the clothes hanging on the door and walked them to the bathroom, where he gave himself a quick shower before getting dressed. It all seemed pointless.

Jeremy came through the door at fifteen past four, filling the air with the scent of rainwater and apologies. Ben didn't mind. It allowed him to clean a little better and adjust to his crisp attire. Jeremy shook the rain off his umbrella, swearing he could just kick himself for not giving enough time to roleplay an interview. The only thing that concerned Ben was that the rain had intensified, as predicted, but that would mean more time on the road than he had estimated when he arranged it. He should have known better; for that, he would have kicked himself. But there was no time, and the two were in and out in a flash.

* * *

Danica awoke to one triumphant crash of thunder. The sky was dark. The rain hammered violently on the roof to make a muzzled drumming noise. She hadn't meant to fall asleep, only to clear her mind. She wiped her eyes, dragging a skid of mascara off with her hands, and sat up and put on her shoes. As she stood, she stretched and yawned, then made her way upstairs to grab her bag.

The hallway was dark, and so was her room, brooding in a stillness that brought the residuum of memories and decisions that had cost her dearly. It fed her morose demeanor, thinking in absolutes as to what she now must do. She stepped in just long enough to scoop her bag off the ground, reach for her phone, and shoot a quick glance as a final adieu to a room that had served her so well. She descended the stairs at speed, dialing voice mail to hear the one missed call that came in while she slept.

"Hey, honey, it's Mom. Listen, your dad and I have been super busy at the store—yes, even with all this rain—so I think I'm going to stay a while longer to help him out. I didn't know if you wanted to see if you could catch a ride wi—"

Danica hung up the phone and placed it on a small, round-topped pedestal at the edge of the stairwell, leaving it behind next to her mother's prized antique Ming vase. She unhooked her jacket from the coat rack and flung it over her shoulder as she reached for the deadbolt with her bag in hand. The door's lock seemed weighty to her touch in a way she had never noticed. Regardless, she made her way out of the house and into the wild torrent of summer rain.

The streetlights were already on but didn't do much good against the blinding downpour. Rain spattered against the concrete and stone walls of the house in gallon-sized proportions. The thunder muttered high and grumbled ferociously in the distance. Danica slipped her hands into the sleeves of her jacket and zipped it up tight. She flipped the hood over her damp hair, hoisted the bag over her shoulders, making it snug, and marched out into the downpour, bowing her head to fight against the biting rain.

* * *

Traffic wasn't so much a mess as the rain was. Water rushed down the road with the persona of an asphalt river, sending small waves to the side as cars disrupted its flow. Jeremy's wiper blades were on full throttle and barely made a dent in his visibility.

"Maybe you should call and reschedule," he suggested.

Ben grinned without warmth, crushing his eyes to see through the rain clearer. He knew that wasn't possible. "We can make it. I know we can," he said.

"All right," Jeremy replied with a sudden boost of confidence as he leaned closer to the windshield, squinted his eyes, and pressed harder on the gas. The speedometer went up another five miles, not a lot, but for Ben, hopefully enough to make it on time.

* * *

Danica could see the Greeley High School sign lit up deep behind a curtain of rain. It blurred in the school colors, illegible no matter how close she got. Her body was soaked and chilled to the bone, shivering and grinding her perfectly aligned teeth. "It isn't much farther," she said to herself, teeth chattering as she pressed on down the flooded sidewalk. Soon she'd have to trudge through the muddy grass and somehow find the entrance through the gate. It would be difficult, she knew, but not impossible. And she was determined.

* * *

The Escape successfully voyaged along the freeway and was now cutting through the only town before Greeley. Their speed had been unaltered, even after merging onto city streets. They prayed they didn't get pulled over but for two completely different reasons. Luckily, the power went out all over town at some point, and most of the lights had been left to flash yellow. All but one in their favor.

"God is doing something special for you," Jeremy said, cruising through an intersection with cautious haste.

"He's doing something special for someone," Ben said to himself. "I only hope it's not too little too late."

Soon enough, the town faded into the watery backdrop, and they were out on an unlit road. Two lanes were left, surrounded by what looked to be fields, undulated and painted by a gothic Vincent Van Gogh. They rolled up and down the hilled street, the vehicle's four-wheel drive activating at the tiniest slip of a tire. Mile markers flashed as they passed one after another. Suddenly a green sign appeared. Ben wasn't quite sure, but he believed it read,

You Are Now Entering
Greeley

They rounded a few bulging hills past a modified speed limit sign and a transformer lot. Lights and buildings began to reappear in the distance with more flashing traffic lights, the first one being red. However, as they came to the intersection, it became abundantly clear that no one in their right mind would be out on the road other than themselves. Anyone who dared take on such weather was either crazy or going to save a life. Ben and Jeremy were both.

Jeremy eased a left turn through the intersection with little pause.

Ben looked down at the map on his phone. It was practically a straight shot from there. One, possibly two side streets if they missed the first turn. He was going to make sure they wouldn't.

* * *

Danica took a few minutes to rest under the lighted sign, watching as passing car lights zoomed by without ever slowing to ask the girl in the rain if she was all right. Most likely, they couldn't even see her. If they had, she was sure someone would. It didn't matter now.

She leaned against the thick metal pole under the sign to give her face a break. The rain felt like God had joined in on teasing her, splattering her face with bitter rainwater on the day she thought he'd be there the most. But to her, there was no God that day. Not in Greeley. Not anymore.

A few more cars went by. Halogen and xenon lights flashed over her, none acknowledging the girl alone in the rain. She wiped her face of bitter water and makeup only to replace it with more bitterness that saturated the sleeve of her jacket. Her eyes burned with the blend of hairspray and cosmetics and atmosphere. But she had to move on. She was so close she could hear the faint sound of that loose chain banging against a pole. After one more car, Danica gripped the straps of her bag and clenched them, lowering her head to shake off the water, and continued toward the gate.

* * *

Ben timed the road perfectly with his Google map, calling for Jeremy to turn just as a small, one-and-a-half-lane side street appeared out of nowhere. They headed down the rough path of asphalt. Deserted cars lined the road in front of lit houses but were only visible by the few strands of streetlamps glittering in the rain. Surprisingly enough, the red taillights of another car had turned onto the road in front of them and given them something to trail. Lord willing, it would illuminate the school before they got there and risked missing it.

While Jeremy's side of the road continued to be lined with houses, Ben's became a vacant lot, veering out (from what he could see) into a suspiciously well-groomed field. With straining effort, he could just make out the cube-like structure of a freestanding fence outlining the field. The ends had been lined with banners that cracked fiercely in the torrent.

"Hey, Jeremy," Ben said, "does that look like a baseball field to you?"

Jeremy turned, maintaining his sharp squint. "Where?"

"Out there." He pointed into the nearing distance.

Jeremy studied it for a second. "Yeah, it does," he said as he lightened his foot off the gas. "And that looks an awful lot like a school sign." He pointed to a small, rectangular, lit sign that undulated in the rain.

"Slow down," Ben requested, as if Jeremy hadn't already.

Just then, a *Teacher Parking Only* sign appeared by the sidewalk. Only by the grace of God and Jeremy's acute eyes had they caught it.

Bodies lunged forward, hands pressing against the dashboard as the brakes engaged and made a sharp turn. Like that, they were in an ocean of downpours, drifting in a sea over a parking lot, with no lit buildings to direct them where to go.

"It looks like no one's here," Jeremy said, pulling into one of the many free spots and shutting off the car. "Are you sure they didn't call to reschedule your interview?"

Ben made quick time unbuckling his seat belt. "Yeah, I'm sure," he said, shutting down his phone and burying it deep in his pocket.

Jeremy sent him a cross-examined look. "This doesn't make sense to me. These people set an appointment to meet with you at the oddest hour of the day, on a day that is gushing down rain, and at no point called to see if you wanted to reschedule. Something's not right, bro. I'm telling you, there is no one here."

Ben fought against a squall to open the door. A blast of water came spraying in, instantly soaking the side facing out the car. "Jeremy," he said, looking at him with deeply stoned eyes, "you must trust me. There is someone here. It is not an employee though." Jeremy responded with no reply and a worried glare. "It's a girl. She needs our help. She is about to do something bad, something you can't come back from if we don't stop her."

Jeremy's mouth opened to give an addled look. Though at first nothing came out, he managed to say, "I don't get it," at a snail's pace. "How do you know about this girl?"

"I saw her about a week ago. And then again, the night before I left."

"Uh-huh," Jeremy said. "But you weren't here a few days ago. You hadn't even planned on coming, as far as I know. So how can that be?"

Ben began chewing the side of his lip. He knew there wasn't the time to dive into the complex logistics of how it all worked right now, as if it wasn't hard enough to explain something so indefinable during the most lax times. "I saw her in a vision. I've seen many people in visions. Every time they need my help. That's what I do, Jer. I help people."

"Okay. Hold up a minute. Explain these visions for me 'cause this is getting a little too *Sixth Sense* for my taste. How long have you been seeing things? I mean, have you consulted a doctor? Do the Nelsons know about these visions of yours?"

Ben looked away for a second, biting his lip before returning with a solidly honest glare. "Look, man, it's all complicated. And I promise I will answer anything I can when this is over. But you wanted to know why I was always such a flake, right?" he said. "Well, this is it."

Jeremy's expression turned from addled to that of a scorned child. "Yeah," he said, difficultly, almost shamefully.

"That's why I wanted you to come with me. I need you to see what it is I do. If you don't, fine. You can wait in the car. But I must go right now, or a dead girl will be found hanging under the bleachers tomorrow."

"Wait, what?" Jeremy exclaimed, succumbing to Ben's artless persistency and opening his door to follow him. "Hang on. I'm coming. But I swear to you, Ben, if this is your warped idea of a prank, there is nothing in heaven or earth that will save you from the beatdown I will unleash upon you."

Ben was well on his way, yelling back and letting the gale carry his words. "No joke. We gotta go. We need to find a way into the football stands."

TWELVE

Ben had searched through mud and rain, fighting his way through the belly of the storm. His fingers were drenched to the point of wrinkling. His eyes were tormented by the unforgiving shower. His feet had no traction, gliding over the mud of the morass field as he strummed along the fence until he felt his fingers numbed. All he needed was to find a break in the barrier significant enough for him to fit through. At a time, he slipped, feet skating away from underneath him, feeling the slack of weightlessness as the upper half of his body crashed to the ground. Caked in mud, he clawed the ground, pulling in fistfuls of mud and grass to get back to his feet.

"You all right?" Jeremy howled.

"Fine," he hollered back. "Just keep looking." Ben cleared the mud from his face and let a shower of rain wash out his eyes.

"I found it!" Jeremy cried. "Over here." Ben rushed toward Jeremy's stout cry without waiting for his eyes to catch up. "Look." Jeremy pointed. "See?"

Ben focused. He could only make out the lower few rows of the bleachers in the distance, as the top part appeared to vanish into the sky like a phantom arena. "That's great. But we still need to get to it."

"No, you need to get to it," Jeremy corrected. "I need to make sure you do." Suddenly, Ben heard the cracking of thin braided metal bending to the force of a strong pair of hands. He turned to see Jeremy prying up the lower part of the fence and pulling it back like a human can opener. "Climb under. I'll catch up later."

Ben dropped and shuffled under the gate, ignoring the bite of metal teeth grading along his back. Once cleared, he sprung to his feet and slid into a sprint, running against the torrential stream that pelted his face with a slew of liquid pellets. He negotiated his way past the track, picking up the sharp, hollow sound of the rain pinging off the aluminum. It sounded like coins being jingled in an old coffee can. He slowed as he approached the part of the bleachers shielding the light and curtailed the next corner.

In front of him, about twenty yards out, was the gate to the fence, pried open, with Jeremy charging toward him. "Stop!" Ben yelled. As expected, Jeremy was too far to catch his words but was approaching fast. Ben knew he wouldn't have time to save the girl and protect Jeremy or explain why he needed protection. Ben thought a prayer, turned back toward the bleachers, and ducked under them.

The rain was less violent under the protection of the noisy aluminum seating. He ducked along the cavernous underbelly of the lower stands, making his way until it was high enough for him to safely stand erect. The steady thrumming matched his pace.

"Ben!" Jeremy called out against the clamor, not completely drowned out by the ruckus from above.

Ben turned. Jeremy had his head poking in under the shelter of one of the rows. "Jeremy," Ben said boldly and slowly. "Stay there. I need you to wait and watch. But whatever happens, do not touch me."

Jeremy nodded.

Ben turned and crept deeper under the bleachers as Jeremy followed him with his eyes, watching and listening for any sign of movement in the darkness. After a few more strides, he proceeded to inchworm through the gathering pool below him. There was a sudden freeze as he shot his gaze to the other side of the stands and held it there. There was movement in the form of what looked to be a hooded figure.

"Ben," Jeremy howled from behind, "I think I see someone. Out there."

Ben shushed and left his friend for the shadowy crevice under a row of higher seating. He could sense Jeremy watching. A classic look of befuddlement was written on his face, peeking into the shadows as Ben stalked toward the hooded figure.

* * *

She stopped under one of the beams. It was high enough yet low enough for her to swing the cord over and construct her gallows. She reached over, grabbed a bucket she had snatched next to the concession stand, then turned it over onto the flooded sod and unbraced her bag. Its weight allowed it to naturally slip down with a bursting splash at her side. She knelt and ripped the zipper open, tossing clothes into the murky black soil before pulling out the orange extension cord she had harbored at the bottom. Her fingers, cold and damp, shivered to work at laying out the cable and creating a tightly formed noose at the end.

Danica stood back and brushed her hair into a dank mess of tangles that looped and draped along her face and nestled against the nape of her neck. Thick beads of water dripped from the strands, laying rain tracks down her forehead and trailing her petite jawline.

She looked up and evaluated the height of the beam to determine how much effort was needed to throw the cord over. She swung it back and forth until she was ready to launch the line freely into the air, the small noose leading the way. It soared over the beam, across the other side, and descended only a foot above Danica's head. She reached up and pulled it down. She then picked up the other end of the cord and threaded it through the noose, sliding it and watching as her a means to an end rose higher and closer to the beam. Finally, Danica gave the cord a sturdy tug. She began to wrap the line around the shaft, throwing it up and over repeatedly until there was a good amount of cable tightly secured to hold her weight.

Danica stood back to survey her work as tears began to form and well up under her eyes. Part of her didn't want to do this. But the more significant part, the darkness that had taken over, convinced her that this was all she had left. She had allowed herself to become cheap and ruined and had taken a life to conceal it. This was her justice.

Danica took up the bucket and aligned it under the hanging cord. Sobs now heaved out of her as she placed one foot on the bucket and struggled to follow it with the other. Her legs quivered. "Oh God, I am s-so, s-so, s-s-sorry," she repeated through gasping breaths as she reached for the cord with a frigid hand. She closed her eyes. "Forgive me."

"Lucas," she heard a voice say—a concerned, warm voice. Had it been in her head? Danica opened her eyes and saw no one.

"H-hello?" she said. Her knees buckled with nervous fear as she cast her sight into the darkness.

A foot stepped forward, and then a form, dark and stoic, exposing open hands and splayed fingers. A set of eyes reflected fragments of light in small, fractured pieces as he looked at her. "If it was a boy, you wanted to name him Lucas. You always liked that name. So does your mom."

Danica's brows furrowed as she squinted to see a young man cautiously moving toward her. She attempted to speak, to tell him to stay away, but her words had already abandoned her. Regardless, his hands shot up in anticipation of it. His fingers remained upturned and casually splayed. There was his face, the childlike countenance of innocence and empathy. But he was a man.

He continued, "I always liked that name too."

Jeremy had only peeked his way out of the shadows, more lost than Danica as to what was happening. "You were hoping it would be a boy, weren't you?" Danica nodded just a hair, as if bewitched. "And he took that from you—Justin—didn't he?" Again, she nodded. Ben continued to reach out. "I can't imagine how you feel right now," he said, lying. He knew exactly how she felt, but that was not what she needed to hear.

Danica found only a few words. "Who are you?" she asked, struggling to keep her balance on the slick bucket.

"My name is Ben Weaver. I'm here because I know what you're going through and what you feel is the only way out," he said with passive ease.

"It is," Danica replied. Her eyes were dull with plaintive abstractions. She sniffled in her sullen grief. "It is all that is left for me."

Ben shook his head. He took a rolling step closer to avoid disturbing the water beneath him. "No, it's not," he replied with certainty. "You have people who love you. People who care for you. You just need to trust them and let them in."

"I did trust people. And this is where it led me."

Ben chewed down on the corner of his lip. "I know." He sighed. "And they were bad to you. But just as there are bad people in this world, there are good people as well. People who will take care of you, motivate you, build you up, and be there when you feel like you are falling."

"And I suppose you're a good one?"

"I believe I am. That's why I need you to trust me and step down from there."

Danica pulled her head back as if to keep the spread. "I-I don't even know you. And you sure as hell don't know me. So why—why should I trust you? How could I trust you?" Her eyes sank to the muddy surface of the ground. "I can't even trust myself anymore." She sniffled. She wiped her nose and the rain from her face. From Ben's view, the rain sparkled off her nose as it dripped from her bridge, off the tip, forever lost somewhere around the bucket under her feet.

"It's too late for me. The damage has already been done; I have failed at everything I was supposed to be, and not you or anyone else can change that. I have nothing left in this world but pain and hatred and, and shame." Danica's mouth began to tremble once more, hearing what she believed to be her truth.

In some way, almost supernaturally, Ben's eyes drew her back to him, glistening like a polished diamond and growing brighter. She began to feel as if he could actually see into her and through her in a way no one possibly could. He stepped closer, radiating a warmth she found comforting, even now as she stood at the precipice of her planned farewell.

"You're wrong, Danica. You have so much to offer this world, so much to give. What's worse than failing is giving up. It isn't life that gave up on you. Don't give up on life. It doesn't end here. This is where it begins."

Her arms grew heavy and relaxed by his words. Danica's hand slid off the cord and swayed hypnotically at her side. He was doing something to her. She knew this much. But it felt good. In a way, she didn't want to let it go. Without any effort on her part, her knees loosened. Her feet practically begged her to step down.

"How?" she asked. "How could you know all this? How can you be certain that things won't get worse or that I'll make a bigger mistake than before?"

Once again, Ben offered his hand to catch the rain that had breached the awning of bleachers. This time, it was at an arm's length from her. "I can show you," he said.

Jeremy had strayed from his place, his Kodiak form lurching under the stands, taking one curious step at a time until he found himself peeking out of the shadows a mere ten yards back. Only small fragments of Ben and Danica's conversation were picked up among the steady thrumming of rain. Still, it was enough for him to understand what was going on and naturally be intrigued.

Danica eyed his hand. Her fingers started to fidget, mutable on whether to take it or not. Her eyes moved to his. He was seeing in her. He knew things, things he had no way of possibly knowing. She reached out, stepped down, and slid her fingers over his and into his damp palm.

Jeremy continued moving forward, ducking furtively in the shadows and dangerously close to being exposed. Ben had told him to not get involved but didn't say why. And Jeremy developed a qualm about Ben's ability to handle this pedigree of situation as time passed.

Ben's fingers softly closed around Danica's. He stared at her as she stared back and raised a smile. "It's going to be okay," he said. With that, he pulled her in and embraced her.

Danica shook. Her arms gripped Ben's back. She squeezed him with every ounce of strength in her. Steam arose from their bodies, building on the warmth Ben had already generated. She gasped for air, taking every bit of oxygen her lungs could handle and drinking down rain. Her toes curled inside her shoes while at the same time lifting her heels off the ground and arching her back to have her face meet the showering sky.

It was all there, from the invitation to the party to the chair by the pool. The school and bathroom, the clinic and club and the bleachers, even the intricate happenings inside her house—it all flashed by like a montage of bad memories. She watched every face that hurt her come and go in slideshow formation. Every thought and idea she had about herself bubbled to the surface of her brain. They exploded into nothing, leaving room for only a future. It was as if Ben had opened the doors to her soul, thrown back the curtains, and evicted who she had been to let in the light of what she was predestined to become.

Danica felt the empty space in her stomach once again filled. A tiny pulse was beating, thrumming rapidly, swirling around into a tightly formed ball, and rapidly growing. She could feel the skin around her torso tighten and bulge, his comforting presence growing bigger and stronger. She could feel his tiny hands pushing against her insides. She could feel his feet kick and twist and roll around as he swam in her accommodating belly, the activity of months passing in mere seconds. She felt the pleasure of carrying him, the nurturing glow of his development. It was the magnificent cycle of life being formed within her womb. But this wasn't a hello. No. It was a goodbye. The goodbye she never allowed herself a chance to give, and in a way, she never had a chance to feel. And as he grew, so he dissolved. His presence dissipated into the form of his soul—a warm, vapor-like essence that surged up into her throat. Danica's mouth broke wide as his infant soul wisped out of her mouth and into the protective hand of God with silent tranquility. It was the assurance. For the first time, sitting in this stranger's embrace, feeling her, knowing her better than anyone, she was able to grieve over the loss of her son.

Jeremy was now in the audible range of Ben and Danica, his eyes widened, mouth opened with dreadful awe and wonder. A charged silence overtook him as he watched a billow of steam aura around their connected bodies as their faces remained lifted toward the web of rain-seeping beams above their heads. Their eyes sheened a steady marvel of whiteness that bled over the wet surface of their faces. While one person displayed miraculous healing, the other portrayed something more disturbing than anything he had seen before. He continued to watch as Danica breathed deep into the vapor that surrounded them. At the same time, Ben gasped to catch a breath. Her skin glistened, polished into a new layer of flesh as Ben's neck grew flush. She was beautiful, spotless, an image of all things lovely. His body turned purple and then crimson as veins bulged from his throat all the way to the peak of his face. All

Jeremy could make out was that whatever kind of phenomenon this lovely girl had been swimming in, Ben was the catalyst from which it had flowed.

As quickly as they came, they vanished, like shadows overtaken by the light. All the pain, suffering, and abuse were being sucked out of her down to the marrow of her soul. Her body became a weightless burden. She could no longer feel the assaulting rain or the ground. There was no storm where he had taken her. There was no underbelly of aluminum bleachers. No orange extension cord tied gravely to a beam. Instead, she found an audience. Thousands of people dressed in suits and sitting in what seemed to be an auditorium. She wasn't dressed in street clothes and a damp jacket. No, she was in a lustrous evening gown. Not a hood but a gorgeous silk and wool, white-flowered shawl draped over her shoulders.

Danica found her attention locked on to a beautiful young lady who could not have been any older than her early twenties. She stood gracefully behind a podium, dead center on the stage between the two sides of a fixated room. Her dress sparkled and shimmered brilliantly under the lights. Her airbrushed skin was like fine-cut marble with hair that nested artistically atop her head.

"Today we celebrate the life's work of an extraordinary lady," the woman announced. Her high-spirited voice resonated over the vast ocean of spectators. "She is someone who has, in one way or another, impacted all our lives, whether through her music, her charity, or simply her kind words and perspective on the value of life." The lady gently laid her hand over her chest. She continued, "I myself wouldn't have been here today if it weren't for the Lucas Briggs Foundation and all they did to find the people I am grateful to call my parents. But I am just one of the thousands of lives spared," the young woman emphasized. "Ladies and gentlemen, I give you a great woman, an amazing artist, and the founder of the Lucas Briggs Foundation, Miss Danica Turner."

The crowds arose in thunderous applause as she stood from her seat and walked, train in hand, up the steps to the podium. The young lady offered a hand to escort her up the last step onto the stage, which Danica accepted, noticing the age that had thinned and bleached the skin of her own hand. Veins protruded in a lavender trail that ran under her crepe-paper skin. The young woman held it gently, leading with grace as she strode up the steps to the stage. The audience cheered with admiration as she continued up the stage, only stopping at the place where the young lady had stood. Danica took in the crowd, tears welling in her eyes as each of their faces bloomed with life as they looked at her. Never had she felt such admiration, such accomplishment.

Danica laid her arms over the podium. She saw the island of liver spots chain from her hands and up her arms. A speck of fidgetiness wobbled the years of her hands on either side of the microphone. More than that, she noticed a trifecta of beautifully cut diamonds wrapped in white gold around her ring finger on her left hand. She looked not far from where she sat and saw a handsome young man sitting next to his wife. He had a poof of rich, curly hair that sprouted from the top of his head and had been tied back behind his ears. His skin was a caramel mocha shade, a refined complexion, with some attributes she could see had been inherited from her and others that had been inherited from—

There he sat. The large mountain of a man she had spent the last thirty or so years calling her husband. His hair was now grayed and wool, yet he still held the brightest smile she had ever seen, shining even more brilliant within his dark complexion. It was a beacon of love and respect that towered above the rest of the crowd, front and center, the way he had been from the moment they first met. He had been the kindest soul of any man she'd ever met, and it showed down to the finest crook in his unending smile.

Ben choked for air. He felt the pop of his spine separate from the back of his skull, lashing back like the breaking of a stretched rubber band. He became warm, then hot. A pulsating rush of moisture pushed his face, swollen from the inside until his skin was about to burst. He tried to breathe and swallow, but his every effort only found the stopple of a tightening cord around his neck. He held fast to Danica as the final exchanges were made. Finally, he dropped his hands and keeled over. Then Ben collapsed into the muddy sod, away from Danica, and lay at her feet, lifeless.

Jeremy rushed in as Danica fell to her knees and began to weep. Her hands coddled her face, blocking her sight from Jeremy's staggering reveal. Despite the overwhelming sobs, Jeremy couldn't help but feel a profound degree of relief overpowering her. He collapsed to his knees at Ben's side, his sight resting on Danica a moment longer before locking his attention on his friend. There was a thin line of a burn that noosed around Ben's neck like a raspberry tattooed collar. His skin was gray, waxy, and swollen. His fingers were cold and white. His face had already become a greenish blue, burying his eyes deep in a livid pit of flesh. There was no puffing of his chest—no inhales or exhales. There was no rolling of eyes, no flicks, no swallows. Nothing.

Jeremy's heart pulsated like a rickety old generator. His first instinct was to try to bring him back to consciousness. His second was to call for an ambulance, though everything he saw suggested it was far too late for both of those.

"Ben … Ben!" he cried out, every muscle in his body aching to begin compressions on Ben's lifeless body.

Danica's head sprouted out of her hands. She was startled to see the young man who had changed her now lying in the mud as a strangulated corpse, void of the warm life with which he had first appeared. But even more, she was alarmed at the giant black fellow who had come out of nowhere. She pulled back, her voice resonating in a grinding whisper. "Wh-who are you?"

Jeremy was silent as he towered there, this dark, shadowy giant casting a concerned glare over his friend. There was nothing on his face other than concentration and purpose. He was unheeded to her interest in his presence. Jeremy remembered what Ben had told him. *Don't try to help. Don't say a word. And for goodness' sake, don't touch me no matter what you see.* Even so, he had already failed at the first two, one most definitely. Jeremy fought against his better judgment. He ransacked the front of his brain and buried his hands deep into his pockets, looming over Ben's body with an uncomfortably safe gap between them.

"Shouldn't we call nine-one-one or something?" Danica asked, becoming reasonably frantic at the lifeless body. She had never seen a dead body before. She didn't know that this was how they would have found her. Her face went sallow. Her stomach craved to unleash itself as she looked at him. She felt dizzy and nauseous. It wasn't eloquent or theatrically tragic. It was unsettling, disgusting, and traumatizing.

"No," Jeremy said decisively. Despite everything inside him telling him to scream yes, he risked trusting the command of his friend. "I believe he has done this before." He craned his head over Ben's body, trying to numb his emotions to the sight underneath him. "Ben ... Ben. I need you to wake up, buddy," he continued.

Danica slid her knees across the muddy floor toward Ben. Her first instinct was to reach out to touch his hand. Jeremy hastily intercepted and held hers, unintentionally pulling her back and up to her feet. Danica fell into Jeremy's chest. He, too, was warm but in a different way. She had never felt that sense of warmth before but liked it.

"Don't touch him," Jeremy said. His voice was low, his chest vibrating against Danica's cheek as he held her close to him. "We can't touch him. He said so himself. We must let him be."

Danica slowly slipped her hand out of Jeremy's and rested it over Jeremy's chest. She liked his touch. It was firm and protective. "You're big," she said rather bluntly, cracking the awkward meet of two strangers.

"Yeah, I get that a lot," he said, giving an artificial grin as if an uncommon shyness had befallen him.

Over time, the two sat opposite Ben's body, watching and waiting, praying. Jeremy began noticing a species of prettiness in her. Not a word had been spoken for the longest while. Everything that came to mind just felt petty and inappropriate for the time. Jeremy had no intention of letting her pick at his interest, driven purely by the fact that his friend could very well be dead. He was sitting, knees in the mud like a mischievous little boy, doing nothing about it, just as instructed. However, the occasional glance snuck from him from time to time, becoming more frequent and evident as the storm passed and the night wore on.

The storm passed by in symmetry to the exchange. There was new visibility under the bleachers. They were graced by the lights that only heaven could produce—and adequately so. Danica had become enamored by this enormous man in a short time. She felt comfortable around Jeremy, a stranger radiating the company of an old friend that made her feel at ease. He held a certain degree of a well-known soul. He was a spirit she had possibly met in a dream not too long ago or a vision that had now somehow developed in front of her very eyes. How else could he have found her in this place?

Jeremy was taken aback by her delicate features. She fared under the rich silver glow of new moonlight as it cascaded over her face and fragile body. Never would he have believed that someone as interesting as her would be found in such a situation. He had found pleasure in memorizing minute details of her face. How her nose sparked up just a tad at the end, how her chin paralleled the natural drooping of her bottom lip flawlessly. He dieted each look, giving her enough of a glance to put together the features of this young woman in his mind piece by exquisite piece. He had discovered not a one to be lackluster. In some way, it felt inappropriate, the timing of their meeting. In other ways, it was almost providential, and between the two, they both found themselves walking a fine line.

All that stopped when color began to mount back on Ben's cheeks and over his face, running down his neck and drifting under his rumpled shirt. Jeremy and Danica looked on with stoned interest as his fingers twitched with convulsions. Jeremy could make out his eyes rolling under their lids, as a child's would if they were walking through a dream. At last, his chest raised. His lungs held it and let out a soundless breath of air, putting a break between his lips.

Jeremy leaned in close to Ben's ear, not touching a hair on his body. "Ben," he whispered. "Buddy. I need you to wake up for me."

Startled, Danica jumped and pointed to Ben's feet. "Look, look," she said as her finger drew chaotically in the air.

Jeremy peered down to see a pair of legs retracting. One knee mounted up. On the other end, a long grunting hum drifted from Ben's lips, leaving his mouth even more ajar. His head rolled over his shoulder, escalating into a dazed wobble. Finally, his eyes broke open as the final remains of the exchange fogged his iris with a seafoam gray.

Ben first noticed the lack of space between him and Jeremy. He shoveled his hands into the ground, taking no time to scoot his rear. Spasmodically, he used an inclined backstroke across a fresh layer of mud to swim away from Jeremy, only to be startled by the blindsiding presence of Danica peering down on the other side. Breathing became deep and rapid as his heart pounded against his chest. Each thump was louder than the final trickles of rain that had lingered off the edges of the bleachers.

"I-you-what—" Ben tried to collect his thoughts, fearful of the worst, eyes serving about like an out-of-control driver. His hands went straight to his chest. *Thump-thump … thump-thump*. He was still alive.

Jeremy addressed the question Ben failed to ask. "I didn't touch you," he said, giving a solemn oath, one hand perched, surrendering in the air, while the other fastened to his chest. "Neither of us did."

Ben found it challenging to steady his head. He cast a comprehensive glance from Jeremy to Danica and back to Jeremy before falling back again. Arms flung over his face and rested over him like a sleep mask, with no concern for the pool of mud that bedded his sore flesh. His head. His poor, throbbing head. An electric sting ran from his skull, down his crooked neck, and branched to his fingers and toes. But he was alive, and so was Danica. For that, he sighed a painful relief.

"You weren't … s'pose … to come out," Ben huffed, his voice taut from abuse. He sucked down a heavy stream of oxygen into his lungs that burned like hot fragments of shard copper and pushed against his ribs. "I told you … to stay … hidden."

Jeremy shrugged, glancing at Danica with an impish frown, to which she gave back a discrete chuckle. "You seriously thought I'd just stay back and watch my friend do … whatever that was?"

"Yeah, I guess not," Ben replied, shifting his body as the birth pains of joints and muscles returned to normal. "Still, I had to try."

"What was that all about anyway?" Jeremy probed, taking Danica's interest with it. "I mean, I think I understand what happened. But how?"

Ben wanted to explain. He knew he had to. He promised he would. But he found it more productive at that time to rest than give a lecture on what he called an exchange.

"Your friend said we couldn't touch you. Why? What would have happened if we did?" Danica asked.

Again, far too complicated to explain.

"His name is Jeremy," Ben said. "Jeremy, this is Danica."

With the abrupt introduction, Jeremy offered his hand, again treating her to a handshake. This time willingly. Danica peered down at another opportunity to touch it and took advantage, savoring every cell of his palm.

Butterflies she hadn't felt since her first crush in grade school fluttered about in her stomach. "Danica Briggs," she said, presenting a luminous smile between a pair of feverish cheeks.

"Pleasure to meet you, ma'am," Jeremy replied, sporting a slightly bashful grin. Holding her hand and looking at her face for more than a moment, he realized she wasn't pretty. She was arrestingly beautiful. "I'm Jeremy Turner."

Danica froze, leveling her smile to a stupefied slack of revelation. She refused to let go of Jeremy's hand, as if he were attempting to pull away. "Turner?" she said.

"That's right. Just moved here from California," he explained. "Well, to Denver. I guess that's not really here. But it's close—or close enough."

Danica's stomach tightened. Butterflies suddenly turned into hornets, stopping her heart with their real sting as she looked down at Ben. He was now peeking back at her under the sleeve of his mud-stained shirt with a revealing glare. "No. That's not possible."

Jeremy looked perplexed. "Oh yes. And what's funny about it is that the only reason we are here is that my good buddy over here"—an oversized hand thudded down on Ben's shoulder, instigating an agonizing squeal— "said he had a job interview for the school."

"At this time of night?" Danica replied. "And you believed him?"

Jeremy's hand found a spot on the back of his head to scratch, hoping it would flake away his gullibility. "Yeah, I kinda thought the same thing. But then he did fly in from California and let me buy him these expensive new clothes."

"So how is that funny?" Danica asked.

Jeremy paused, watching Ben cover his face again before the guilt trip radiating from Jeremy's eyes melted his face. "That's a good point, Danica," he said with a monotone timbre. "I guess it's a funny later kinda thing. What do you think, Ben?"

Danica considered Ben as he lay there and pretended to be dead once again, then hopped back to Jeremy, studying the similarities of his face to the one she saw looking up from the seat in the auditorium. "If you are both from California, how did you know I would be here?" Jeremy displayed an equal amount of silent confusion. "And not only that, but how is it that you were the man in my dream?" She again turned to Ben with certainty that he had some answer for her.

Ben's hand fell to his side and leveraged himself up gradually until he could sit. He crept out a nod and again tried to swallow. "Because it wasn't a dream," he said with a steady grit.

Danica followed up. "What was it then?"

Ben looked deep into her and filled her eyes, leaving no room for misconstrued fallacies. "It was a glimpse of your future."

THIRTEEN

"Holy crap, my parents!" she exclaimed. Another realization. "They've probably seen my phone on the table and are freaking out by now. What am I going to tell them? I mean, how could I even begin to explain this to them?"

"You could start with the truth," Ben replied. His voice was still a little bit husky from wear and abuse. He had now been sitting with his legs outstretched in front of him, hunched over, nursing a sore neck. The fog in his eyes had passed, leaving a rejuvenated chocolatey brown and hazel on his iris. "Tell them all of it. Everything that happened. All those feelings of guilt and pain. You need to let them know."

"And what about you? How am I supposed to explain that to them?"

"You don't. It would be better if you said that God intervened and that you had a change of heart. Say you realized there were still things in this life worth living for."

"Or you could say I saved you," Jeremy suggested, standing closer to Danica than his recovering friend. The outside of their hands tapped flirtatiously against each other as Danica looked at Ben. His brows sat high with a possibility in the suggestion.

"I don't know," said Ben.

"Aw, come on," Jeremy said. "It could be like my Lois Lane and Clark Kent moment. Me swooping in to save the day and all that."

"What's up with you and all the Superman analogies?" Ben questioned.

"Ben, please. I know I can make this work."

"And how exactly are you going to do that?" Ben asked but received no answer. "I thought so. Don't worry, my friend. This will all work out."

Jeremy stepped forward and took a knee at Ben's side. He brought his voice down to a whisper. "Look, she could say …" Jeremy fumbled in his head. "Well, what if I say that I saw her when driving down the street and pulled over to see if she was okay. It's simple and believable."

Ben cocked his head sideways and gave a doubtful expression. "You saw her … while driving … in a torrential rainstorm that gave zero visibility. You'd have to be Superman. Because that is not too likely, bro." With a finger, he lured Jeremy down to whisper in his ear. "Seriously. Jeremy, this is all how it's supposed to be. You don't need to try so hard."

Danica's thoughts moved behind her eyes like bits of glass. She was lost, wandering among her own transient ideas. She began to think of how much easier it would be to tell her parents if she never acted on ending her life. How much simpler it would be if she never walked through the gate, tied that orange cord around that beam, and stood on that bucket. If none of that had happened, somehow. If they had run into her prior, then …

"He would if he almost hit me." Danica's voice broke into the conversation.

Ben questioned her with his face. "Excuse me?"

"Think about it. What if I went out for a walk, which I did, intending to … you know, but they don't have to know all the details about that. But then, like any distraught girl in my shoes, I wandered into the street just as a cautious and slow-driving civilian in a …"

"Escape," Jeremy filled in the blank.

"Right. Escape was passing by. He slams on his horn and grinds his brakes to a halt—so close that I realized I was inches away from getting run over by this man and possibly dying. And then it hit me. I don't want to die. There's still so much I want to do. So many things I have yet to accomplish.

"So, Jeremy." She took his hand and clutched it, feeling as cozy in her hand as a down comforter. "This kind giant of an angel hops out of his car to make sure I'm okay. He sits me down on the sidewalk as the rain washes my senses clear and talks with me for a while, asking me questions, making sure I'm in my right mind, which for once, I am. Finally, after a long, soul-searching conversation, he persuades me to go back home and talk it through with my parents, which I will certainly do. You're out of the story, and no one is wiser."

Ben looked blankly at her. "You've done this before," he said as if it were a matter of fact.

"Only one thing," Danica said, then turned and cast her sight at Jeremy. "I think it might be best if you come with me. It only makes sense if you drive me home."

Jeremy's brows furrowed, connecting dead center on his crooked face. "I'm sorry, what's that?"

"What kind of stranger would take the time to sit with a troubled young girl and talk through her problems yet fail to give her a ride home and make sure she made it back okay?"

The grin on Ben's face came from pure amusement. He watched as every blush of shyness enveloped the big guy's face. "She has a point," he said, feeding the flame to Jeremy's uncomfortable predicament.

Jeremy whipped an icy glare back, intending to be scolding. However, it only made Ben more amused. There was nothing more fun than seeing the big guy squirm uncomfortably.

"Sure," Jeremy replied, trying his best to be calm while nettled. "I'll go. But ..." In a blink, he turned conspicuously dramatic, using every feature of his face and limbs to sell it. "Oh no. I've got to give Ben a ride back to my place. Darn it all. I don't think this is going to work."

Ben's grin broadened. "It's all good. I'll call an Uber," he fired back, his words cackling at the end. He knew one was coming and had prepared to shoot it right out of the sky.

"Great," Jeremy said at length. Danica's arm had made its way constricting around his, quite possibly to keep him from finally tearing Ben to pieces. "Well then, I guess we should just wait for Uber to arrive then."

"No need." Another shot from Ben. "I got this. You two take off, and I'll see you back at the apartment."

Jeremy's eyes were stone. His lips were tight. His neck bulged one python of a vein. "Are you sure?"

Ben held his grin. "Certainly. I've done this several times." In fact, he hadn't. Ben always drove himself home after an exchange. The way he saw it, the fewer people involved, the better, even though it had temporarily cost him his license and the appearance of his neighbor's poor tree.

"Fantastic. Taking Danica home. Meeting her parents. Within the first two hours of meeting her." Jeremy could feel the blood leaving his face and turning his stomach into a quarter ton of bricks. "This will be great. Great."

* * *

It was somewhat alarming to see Jeremy cast his massive shadow at their front door behind their daughter. So was seeing her phone left stranded on the table at the base of the stairwell. But neither of those brought Danica's mother to sob unrestrainedly on the bottom steps, cloaked in the compassionate embrace of Danica's father. It was not knowing what condition they'd see their daughter in, if they ever saw her again.

The doorknob shimmied from the outside, provoking Mrs. Briggs to call out to her. "Danica … Danica." She rushed to the door, leaving Mr. Briggs where he was on the steps as he stood anxiously.

Mrs. Briggs's fingers took to the deadbolt like two negative ends of a magnet, struggling against the grip of errant emotions to steady her lavishly groomed fingers.

"Mom," she heard from the other side of the door. More tears flooded down. Tears of relief. Tears of joy. She wanted to call back, but her tongue had coiled to the back of her throat, refusing to let her speak. She grabbed the lock and turned it with enough force to propel a turbine plane. The door flung open.

"Oh God, thank you!" Mrs. Briggs broke down at the sight of her very sopping, very alive daughter, showcasing a whole other pedigree of sobs.

Before Danica could take her first step across the doorsill, she succumbed to her mother's grief-stricken enfold. Tears poured over her as her mother hugged and kissed her strenuously. She was squeezed and swayed, squeezed and swayed, makeup and perfume and tears rubbing off her cheeks, head, and clothes. Danica couldn't remember when she started crying, but it felt good—the final casting off of all her guilt and shame.

Mr. Briggs overtook the steps with a leap. He dashed to embrace his family, not considering the massive stranger who looked at them from under the porch's light. Finally, the sobbing started to trickle. An embrace loosened to a gingery hug. Mrs. Briggs viewed the body of mass that stood muddy and courteously receptive to her family's moment outside the door.

"My sweet heaven." She gasped.

Danica's head perked, turning back to Jeremy and then to her parents. "It's okay," she said, offering her hands to calm them. "He's a friend of mine—a very dear friend."

Jeremy smiled at the suspicious pairs of eyes that leered over him. A bow of white brilliance was stranded in a sea of dark skin. As Danica escorted him inside, making proper introductions, her parents were uncharacteristically reserved about this man and his evident fondness for their daughter—and hers for him. At first, they'd be ashamed to say, they were downright frightened, especially when he reached out his Jimmy Dean fingers and offered his best and most sincere "Pleasure to meet you."

Danica's father gave a befuddled once-over the big guy and took it, nonetheless. Her mother followed suit, surprised to feel his hand gently engulf hers and shake it with a touch of caress. Seeing the two, they looked as if they had swum the rapids of the Colorado River and were equally exhausted. She offered Jeremy a towel and Danica a chance to rush upstairs for a quick dry-down and change of clothes. They both graciously accepted. Danica and her mother trotted upstairs, and Mrs. Briggs expediently returned with their most oversized beach towel.

* * *

Danica opened the door to her room slowly, not knowing what to expect or how to feel, like seeing an old boyfriend years after a bad breakup. She flipped on the light and crept in, taking one step at a time. It was all as she had left it, a honey glow sweetening the room, with black windows reflecting a calm atmosphere. Her bed, her dresser, her clutter of trash jammed into the waste basket by her nightstand—it was all the same. And yet, for some reason, it all felt odd.

She slid and skated her fingers over her belongings, dresser, and bed, then turned and took a seat at the edge of her bed. Looking out, she saw a face in the mirror that she hadn't seen in a long time—a lifetime ago, so it seemed. Danica saw herself reformed and rebirthed. There were the summer green eyes that saw so much beauty in the world, the ears that heard sweet music in the voice of the breeze. There were the lips from which encouragement and hope and expectations flowed. It was all there again, as if it had never left.

Her eyes veered down to the desk she had spent so many hours running through homework and scribbling down lyrics for her latest masterpiece. She saw something she hadn't recalled leaving there. It was a slip of lined paper from her diary, once balled up, now pressed flat and evidently read. She stood and moved toward the desk, craning her neck to eye its inked contents at a safe distance. She saw the words. She read the ones she had failed to cross out before wadding them up and throwing them at the waste basket.

> I have given up.
> I find no need to carry on this life.
> God has left me empty inside.
> I am sorry.

The words she felt were not strong enough to depict her ineffable anguish now spoke volumes to her.

She stood a while longer and looked down on the wrinkled slip of paper, thinking of how all it took was one moment, one person, one chance of trusting someone for all that to change.

* * *

Jeremy ran the towel over his head and across his arms, picking up the water and mud he had collected over the evening. He fought valiantly against hypothermia and tried his best to rouse small talk with Danica's parents. Each subject came with a peppering of inquisitions only concerned parents would find appropriate. What was her father's line of work turned to where he saw himself in ten years and what he was doing to ensure he was financially stable. Commenting on the house's elegance turned to where he was from, where he lived, and how was his family life. Even a chirping comment about the size of their TV set went into the field of how Jeremy spent his time and whether it was wasted in front of a similar set or not.

He stood there for what felt like a lifetime, unwieldy stiff as he took on the seasoning of questions. One hand eventually attached itself to the post at the base of the stairs. His feet had become planted firmly on the floor. He stood there nodding and replying like an ageless tree moving against a swift and steady breeze—all trunk, with only two branches and no leaves. And in the end, he was still undecided as to which of Danica's parents took most of his attention.

His stature had at first taken them aback; now it was his replies. His passion for fulfilling the needs of the homeless and the vast selection of books he'd read, especially those involving American classics and theology, shocked them slack. His plans to settle down and raise a family of his own, just like the solid home life he had grown up with, unraveled all the assumptions a lesser person would have presumed. He spoke of life like it was one extended blessing, abdicating any mention of Ben to keep from exposing the truth about his friend. Now, if only Danica could pull off the same.

That night, the four sat around an unseasonable fire, with its warming molten glow dancing over the walls and furniture of the room. Moving shadows loomed over them from the walls. A soft honey lamp stood glowing by the curtains, making a dark-pitched mirror out of the window. Jeremy couldn't help but stare at his reflection and see how out of place he appeared to be in that room with those people. But seeing Danica sitting casually beside him, as if she had done so for years, dressed in all the things that made her beautiful, made him feel he was precisely where he was supposed to be.

Out on the coffee table lay the paper left on Danica's desk, the one her mother found balled up on the floor of her room next to the waste basket. It was the same one her mother had opened at her daughter's desk and read with terrified eyes, the same one that had caused her mother to break down in tears over the bottom steps of the stairs. With that paper came the start of a long-awaited conversation. They talked, or at least Danica did. The rest listened. When she spoke, she cried. When she cried, her mother cried. And when it felt like her words became an avalanche of emotions to her parents—or herself—and she found it hard to go on, Jeremy took her hand and coddled it in his own. She liked him. She liked his warmth and support, no matter that this man was virtually a stranger. Her heart had beat for him as if she had loved him for years. Maybe the quality of the vision left a distinctive picture of their lives together in her head. Or perhaps it was that this man could say everything she had needed and wanted in a man without saying a word. Or maybe it was that she felt that connection she longed for out in the park that night, watching the elderly couple stroll by, hand in hand as if they had no desire to let go.

Jeremy's phone began to chime as another round of tissues passed from Danica to her mother. He quickly fished it out of his pocket and noticed Ben's name pulsating on the screen. He sent it to voice mail. Danica went on. She talked about the pregnancy, about her conflict with Justin, about her—

It chimed again. Again, it was Ben. Jeremy apologized to the family for the interruption in a deep, soft-spoken tone and sent it to voice mail again, plunging the volume into silent mode and laying it facedown at his side. As Danica continued, a strange vibrating fart noise started a long on-and-off session over the couch, only to take a short break and start up again. Jeremy flipped the phone over. It was Ben.

Jeremy stood, taking a squeeze at Danica's hand before letting it go and excusing himself from the conversation. He dashed out of the living room, past the stairs, and into the unlit dining room. The phone continued to vibrate almost as loud as his ringtone. He accepted the call and placed the phone against his ear.

"Ben, we're kind of in the middle of some—"

"Is this Jeremy Turner?" a strange, boyish voice panted from the other end.

"Yeah, this is. Who is this?" He didn't mean to sound brash, but he did.

"I'm Clyde Novarro, your friend Ben's Uber driver. I'm sorry for interrupting you, but he told me to call Jeremy, and your name is the only one on his phone, so I figured you were the guy." The boyish voice seemed flustered—close to frightened.

"Okay," Jeremy replied. "What seems to be the matter?" Judging by the voice, a matter was all but inevitable.

"Well, that's just it. I don't know. I picked him up outside the school, and everything seemed fine then. Better than fine actually. Normally at this time of night, I'm practically scooping drunk corpses off the curb and hauling them across town. But your friend didn't seem drunk at all—or high. He was in rather good spirits."

"Okay."

"Well, then we started talking about family a-and our dads. I asked him what his father was like—or something like that. We were just chatting, you know?"

"Ben never knew his dad," Jeremy replied.

"Right. That's what he said. Said he died when he was practically a baby. Anyways, sorry. After that, his nose started to bleed, or at least it looked like blood at first. Then it started to come out of his eyes. I asked if he was okay, but all he could do was give out this zombielike moan and then told me to call Jeremy. Then he fell over in his seat and was completely gone. I-I thought he might be dead."

All the blood drained from Jeremy's face as both sides of the phone sat quietly. "Well?" Jeremy inquired.

"Oh-oh no, he's not dead. Frankly, I don't know what kinda shape he's in. All I know is that it wasn't good when they rolled him into the ER."

"Where is he now?"

"He's at a hospital off Thirty-four and Centerra, just before you hit Interstate Twenty-five. I'm still here too. They wanted me to stay in case they had any questions that might need answering, though I don't know what good I'm gonna be, seeing that—"

"I got it," Jeremy said over the nerve-stricken driver. "I'll be there as fast as I can. Thank you."

"Yeah, so it's—"

Jeremy hung up the phone and rushed back into the living room, where Danica's mother had now taken possession of his seat. She was hunched over with Danica tight in her embrace, holding tissues under their eyes to look like floating snowcapped peaks. Danica looked up and saw a shade of pale gray over Jeremy's face as he froze at the entryway, his phone still clutched in his hand.

"Is everything okay?" Danica asked, causing her mother to turn at look back at Jeremy.

Jeremy peered down at the phone in his hand. "No. I've gotta go."

"What is it?" Danica's mother asked. Her father stood.

Jeremy gave an eye at one of them and then the other. "I've got to go. I'm sorry, but I've got to go," he said again before turning and heading out the door.

* * *

Ben waited at the curb by the teachers' parking lot for his Uber to arrive. The clouds thinned into a fine silvery weave that occasionally broke apart to unveil large clusters of stars. Even under the crippling flow, they shined brighter and more significantly than he had ever witnessed back home. All that was left of the storm was its exhausted whisper that wafted a truce within the silky air. The moon's silver glow blazed its bloated presence in a fresh sheet of darkness. Its scintillating heavenly shine crystalized the raindrops over the earth. He sucked the damp night into his lungs, letting it flush out the stains left in exchange for a crisp, sweet, wet, piney air. More cars than before had now made their appearance driving down the street.

It felt strange being picked up in a stranger's vehicle after an exchange, despite all the good things he'd heard about their drivers. Unorthodox indeed. It struck him that he was posing as an undercover cop working the beat out in the ghettos of Westwood. He was there waiting for his perp on some sort of drug sting, his man unaware that tonight was the night that Detective Ben Weaver was going to catch him red-handed.

A sleek black Toyota sedan studded in raindrops slowed to a stop in front of Ben, cutting over the line that separated the two-lane road to park passenger door to curb. It had all the appeal of a budget rental car—nice and clean and bland and probably with more miles on it than it looked.

The passenger window scrolled down for Ben to view a kid who looked one year past his learner's permit. "You Ben?" he called out in a high boyish tone.

Ben nodded. "For as long as I can remember."

"Heading to the Southfield Apartment towers in Denver?" he asked to confirm.

"That'd be correct," he answered.

"Well then, hop on in. Let's get you home."

Ben reached for the front passenger door but stopped when he heard the driver call out, "Woah. Back seat only, guy. No front seats in an Uber."

Ben felt the urge to apologize as he moved to the rear door and slipped in. He had forgotten how soaked he was until sitting in the back seat. An immediate feeling of awfulness weighed over him, thinking about what mud-crust stain would probably be left in his wake. All he could think about for the longest while was how much of a tip would be needed to cover the cleaning as streetlights became bare.

Soon, the lights went nonexistent as they drove down that same two-lane road Jeremy had struggled to tread down at the peak of the storm. Even at such an hour, it was more visible, reflecting its wet brush off the moonlight. Beautiful rolling hills of wheat and corn and wild grass had been left to angle from the passing gale.

"So, you from Denver?" the driver asked. "Out visiting family or what?"

"A friend," Ben answered. "He moved recently."

"Really? Where from?"

"California."

"Hmm." The kid paused. "Northern or Southern?"

"Southern. Around the Los Angeles area."

"Oh really? Sweet. I have an aunt who lives a bit more south in a place called Mission Villejo," he said.

"You mean Mission Viejo," Ben corrected.

The kid propped a finger over the rearview mirror and flicked it, curling an eyebrow. "That's it. Nice place. Awesome weather. Not like all the crap we get out here." He spoke specifically to the storm that had passed a few hours ago. "Bet you don't get storms like that out in So-Cal." Ben's mind was on too many other things to reply. The kid went on regardless. "So, I guess you grew up out there then. Surfer dude being raised by surfer dude parents and what-not."

"Not so much."

"No? What, they moved?" he inquired of Ben.

"They died," Ben replied.

The driver slouched in his seat and sat quietly for a time. More hills rolled by. "I'm sorry, sir," he eventually said.

"No biggie. It happened a long time ago. Sadly, I don't surf either. I have a thing about the ocean."

"You don't like the water?" he inquired.

Ben peered out the window as flashes of all the times he had drowned by someone trying to cast themselves in the ocean flicked in his head. If he never saw the ocean again, it would be too soon. "More or less," he replied.

"I had a grandpa that passed away a few years back. It was awful. I cried for months. I couldn't imagine losing my parents—mom or dad. But my dad especially. We're as tight as shit, if you know what I mean."

Ben didn't. He never knew his father—not directly anyway. All he had were bits and pieces of him, fed by his mom in small doses when he was younger, stories of how he was and what he did. She always said he had his father's eyes and chin and build, enough to create a spitting image of the man he never met but always looked up to. He used to chew on his lip as well whenever nervous or thinking. Ben always wondered if it was a trait or something he did simply because he heard his father did it.

He was alive when Ben was born, stuck around for a few years, but had his fatherhood tragically stolen from him a few days before his fifth birthday. Ben's mom always said he had a big heart. The biggest of any heart she had ever met. Their love affair started in high school, blossoming over the years. It drifted through his four hard years of service to Uncle Sam, including a year spent as a temporary resident of Camp Lester Marine Corps Base in Chatan Town, Japan. No sooner did he get out than he married his girl in a quaint little ceremony with only a dozen or so friends and family in attendance. Ben's mother used to say she would have been fine going to the justice of the peace, but he'd hear nothing of it.

After that, he wrapped up two years of classes to become a certified first responder and took a job with the Los Angeles County Fire Department. It was no surprise that he worked the EMT beat. They gave him the name "The Defibrillator" for what some said were his darn near-supernatural ability to keep people from walking into the bright light of death.

Benjamin James Weaver was born shortly after, at seven pounds nine ounces. And four short years after that, his father was gone. Among all the stories and rumors, Ben never got a straight answer on what exactly happened on that tragic day. It was hard for his mother to speak of it. Hard for her to relive it. He could feel the deep space in his brain's earliest development, remembering the two uniformed men knocking as his mother laid him over his soft pale blue blanket on the floor. How she must have regretted opening their door to the tragic news. He could still see her collapsing in the arms of one of the men who had spent time in that house joking and chatting up a storm with his father over a barbeque grill or football game. His face, always bulging with excitement, was now thinned and grimly. Ben remembered it too well. Even after all these years, it turned his stomach.

From all he gathered (which wasn't much), a domestic disturbance call led to a standoff between a drunken down-and-out wife beater and the LAPD. Two girls were hiding somewhere in the house while their mother, all black and blue and salivating blood, stood with a gun pressed to bruise against her temple. Two shots were fired in that house before SWAT broke down the door. EMT units followed shortly behind. In the end, the wife lived, and so did the two little girls and the abusive husband, though fifty to life in federal prison was hardly what someone might consider living. However, one person did give up their lives that day, Charles "The Defibrillator" Weaver.

"Yep," Ben said as his stomach began to turn from the back seat of the Toyota. "Unfortunately, my dad died before I was born."

The car once again succumbed to a rich silence. Ben's sight blurred a little as he saw the driver's reflection trying to pull another subject out of his head. Like a fog rolling over his eyes, everything past nose length became hazy and swishing. He felt more like he was in a boat fighting against the swells of an angry sea than in a smoothly cruising sedan. He tried to speak, but his words came out stillborn, leaving a slurry of sounds that gripped the driver's attention.

"Hey, you all right back there?" said the driver. "Your nose is bleeding pretty badly."

Ben reached up to feel under his nose. His arms were the weight of steel. He tapped his fingers under his nose and pulled them away to see that it wasn't blood gushing from his nostrils. Blood wasn't that black and tacky.

"Oh my God! What is that?" The driver gasped as more liquid gushed from Ben's nose and trailed down his chin and neck. Ben's head began to spool and wabble with a swirl of lightheadedness. "Sir, your eyes! It's coming from them too!"

Ben couldn't feel it, but he could tell, as the world around him had been suddenly submerged in a rusty hue. His jaw dropped and hung lazily to the side. His head struggled to maintain its balance. His eyes spit the dark liquid as they closed and opened tiredly, rushing down his cheeks and trailing his neck.

Ben spoke two long, distinguishable words. "Call … Jeremy," he said before collapsing facedown into his own lap. He was gone.

* * *

Jeremy made it to the emergency room center within twenty minutes, revving at every red light that cussed him out with its unconcerned glow. The doors swished open too slowly, scraping against his stout shoulders as he hurried into the waiting area. It was a quiet night, medically speaking. Only a handful of people were in the waiting room, making it easy for him to spot the young man pacing back and forth in front of the check-in counter. Clutched in his hand was a familiar-looking phone that looked half beaten to hell and probably was. Jeremy trudged toward him.

The young driver braced his back to the wall when he saw Jeremy's size stampeding from the entryway with such velocity. His face flinched against his shoulder, expecting the charge to ram him through the white cinder wall and clear into an operating room. However, it speedily changed the moment he heard Jeremy call out, "You Uber?"

The driver expelled relief. "Oh my God. You are Jeremy, right."

Jeremy's gaze fluttered around the room without rest. His fingers twitched. His legs teetered, feet hopping from side to side. "Where is he?" he asked impatiently.

"He's not here anymore," the driver said, forgoing any introductions and handing Jeremy Ben's phone. "I tried to call you, but you didn't answer." Of course not. Jeremy was busy screaming words on the edge of profanity at red lights. "They rushed him outta here. More of that stuff was coming out of his nose and eyes. I mean, it was like pouring out of him. I ain't seen shit like that in my entire life. What's wrong with him?"

"I don't know. Where is Ben now?" Jeremy asked, taking the phone and pushing it into his pocket.

"They said they were taking him to a hospital in Denver. A nurse said something about needing a specialist or something like that." The kid gulped a breath. "Sir, I swear to you, I had nothing to do with this. I-I—"

Jeremy thudded one of his hands on the kid's lurching shoulder as his face sank toward the floor. "I know. Thank you for taking care of him."

The young man looked up, face flushed, eyes glossed in a well of tears at the brink of flowing over. "The nurse has the address of where they took him for you. I am so sorry. I hope he'll be okay."

FOURTEEN

Calvin was three days into school and familiarizing himself with homeroom, classrooms, and daily schedules. Already, out of the vast array of losers, he had become the loser. Only Travis parred his level of social status—no big shocker there. Something written on that boy's face or back told people to keep away. It didn't matter if they were at school, in a grocery aisle, or getting a meal at some run-down fast-food joint. The kid was treated like a walking plague.

How they missed the simplicity of elementary school. Back then, they had one teacher, possibly two, and one classroom. Now there were six classrooms and six teachers, none of whom were aware of exactly how many hours were in a day for a kid to do homework after school. One hour of studying per class, six classes, which equaled six hours of homework. Calvin did the math. Question number one was this: if Calvin got home at four, took an hour for dinner, and had six hours of homework, at what time could Cal be in bed to cry his overly strained eyes to sleep and wish he were dead?

There was one good side to the beginning of their first year at Green Valley Junior High. Gabe was not there. The bastard and his family had moved over the summer—to where, Calvin couldn't have cared less. Getting rid of him was like ridding his house of a giant, dead rodent festering somewhere within his attic. He didn't care what they did with the foul thing. He was just glad it was gone. Gabe was Calvin's dead rodent. And now that rodent had been found and removed, and that was what mattered.

On the other hand, Travis regretted not having his crack at being the exterminator. He vowed one day he would meet Gabe again on the street, whether nineteen or ninety. One way or another, he would beat the living hell out of him for years of undeserved punishment. Calvin didn't doubt he would.

What Calvin didn't realize (despite Travis's constant warnings) was that with the loss of one giant rodent, several tiny ones wanted to take his place. And there were plenty of rodents at Green Valley. It was a conglomerate of merging schools, a stirring pot of messed-up, mixed-up, hormone-driven preteens with nothing to care about but themselves. Kids yell profanity in the open air, cursing at teachers, overdramatizing their disapproval while undermining authority. All of them were unaware that one day they'd be on the receiving side of such tantrums. You reap what you sow. That was what the Good Book said, and that was how it would be.

Gabe's goons were also there, battling over who would take their lost king's throne. On day one, they displayed a barrage of tormenting antics aimed at Calvin and Travis. There were more stalls to get pushed in for a quick beating, more fields for them to be picked on, and more unwatched crevices to be crammed in, spit on, pantsed, or flat-out pummeled. And each goon was willing to do what they felt necessary to show the others they were worthy of being called the head of the group.

It didn't help that Calvin's mom ran out on him and his old man. A cop lost his missus to a fast-food manager (Tom was indeed a restaurant's regional manager, but gossip and miscommunication went hand in hand). That dish was passed around more than a bag of weed at a Grateful Dead concert. And wasn't it just like a bully to make things personal? "She couldn't stand you either," and all that. And worse.

* * *

He was engulfed in a vast ocean of complete blackness. There wasn't a sound or glimmer of light or life or anything other than his thoughts and the thick cloud of darkness he could feel pressing over him. He was afraid to move, reluctant to breathe. In such a shadow, he couldn't feel the movements of his body, if he was standing or floating, if he was paralyzed or attempting to look around. The darkness took everything. It controlled everything.

Ben began to feel a hard surface under his feet. It was cold and smooth as polished stone. He dared to take a step. Then another. And another. Every bold step came with the noise of clanging under his feet, like a pen dropping over the tile of an empty hall. It echoed and echoed for what sounded like miles. He took more steps, and more clanging echoed. His arms reached full length in front of him, tickling the environment the way a blind man would without a cane. He stepped—another clang—reaching and scanning with the tips of his fingers. There was nothing.

Finally, he felt something. It was long, thin, and plastically smooth, running loose and horizontal at a fraction over waist high. Ben grabbed at it and closed his fist. It folded like paper, two inches long, an eternity in width. He found it pliable enough to pull up and duck under with little resistance and proceeded to move. He stepped-clang, stepped-clang.

With a few more steps, there was something else his fingers ran into—a wall, built of thin, hollowed-out metal in a series of rectangular plates. They sat two plates high then cut to an ascending grade at the top. At first, he believed them to be stacks of cages. As he continued to study them with his hands, he noticed that each hollowed plate had a small, four-gap ventilation dead center at the top.

"Lockers," he said to himself, recalling them quite well.

He felt around and found the handles. No locks. A few he opened and scurried the insides with his hands. All empty. Ben continued to do so with several other lockers at random, rounding a corner and moving to another two-stacked row.

One, in particular, was difficult to budge. It had become twerked somehow in a way that someone hammered it to offset its aligned door. He felt around, clutching what felt like a combination lock within his hands. With a hefty tug, the lock broke apart in his hands, leaving the locker vulnerable to be wrenched open. The door swung across his face with more force than Ben could control and banged against another locker. Resounding echoes cried loud enough that it made him freeze and wait to see what might have heard an end to the darkness. No such luck.

Gradually, he slipped his hand into the opened locker and reached around. There was something there, several things in fact, all about the same, laid out in pairs. Two were longer than the others, propped up in the back of the locker, while the four smaller ones rested two on top of each other along the base. They all were made of metal and had holes the size of pinky fingers on one end. They all had handles. They all had triggers.

The high-pitched ring of an alarm bell shattered the silence with it ear-bleeding scream. Ben grimaced and flinched and covered his ears as a sudden stampede of feet and voices could be heard under the cloak of the bell. For the first time in these visions, he could see them not as people but as mystically brilliant orbs, stirring around like balls of smoke, lit up in a pulsating sunset. Some were brighter than others. Some pulsated faster, some slower. Some held more clarity to their glow. However, each of them brightened, dimmed, brightened, and then dimmed. They bounced over the darkness with frenzied celerity, hundreds of them, fireflies pulsating like translucent hearts moving together in the pitch of the night.

In the distance, he heard a scream. Then a few more. Then several more. The faint popping of fireworks brought more and more screams. The bell continued to sound as the many bloodcurdling wails of children rushed into Ben's ears. He watched the flow of orbs turn erratic and disoriented as the popping turned into a pulsating repetition of high-sounding *blats*.

Ben reached back into the locker. There was no longer anything there. It had been emptied right in front of him, without a sound or a hint of someone's presence, as if time lapsed while he clenched his ears.

Blat-blat-blat! Blat-blat!

With each shot fired, an orb would burst into a fiery red puff of smoke. The vapor spilled from the light, diminishing until it had fully splayed under the darkness in a settled pool over the unseen ground. More shots were fired, with more of these orbs and more puffs of red smoke. More were taken. More smoke bled, creating an eerie mist that trailed the ground, a stream of ghostly red fog that reached closer to his feet by the minute.

It was all getting louder. Closer. One came so close he could feel the wisp of a bullet cut through the air. The aroma of gunpowder left trailing behind as a charge of students rushed past him. One of the lights he felt dropped at his feet, convulsing and gargling liters of blood smoke as they crawled and pulsated slower and slower, until no life was left in them to move.

Blat-blat-blat!

More salvo of gunfire ascended the halls, herding the students like sheep among a pack of wolves.

"Oh, Miss Hawthorne. Miss Hawthorne. You're needed in homeroom, Miss Hawthorne."

Ben heard them chuckling, stalking toward him, the two familiar voices of umber and red devilishly calling out the name of a fleeing ball of light down the hall. He could smell the womanly perfume of the one they called so abhorrently Miss Hawthorne. A distinct fragrance that had expired back in the eighties. Ben recalled the smell. It wasn't the first time he'd crossed paths with such a fragrance.

The scent of Miss Hawthorne stirred in with the copper taste of blood, the burning aroma of spent gunpowder, and the perspiration of several frightened students. She howled in pain as one slug lanced her calf, causing her to tumble onto the red-fogged floor of the hall. Her redness seeped into the mix as Ben listened to her beg God, beg her assailants to spare her life.

"Now, Miss Hawthorne, why on earth would you run from us? We have our homework to give to you. You want it, don't you … Come on, Patty. Don't you!"

With a smattering of chuckles, one resounding bullet answered her plea as the rest of her light burst into a still pool of red. Ben listened as her head cracked against the concrete floor and rolled over its bloody essence. Even to a blind man, the kid who took the shot emitted a species of satisfaction in the kill.

Ben held still, refusing to give in to his unsettled stomach. Every muscle in his abdomen urged him to puke, but he kept his mouth closed and his breath paced. He would have closed his eyes had he been sure they were open.

"You!" The red voice sounded so violently familiar that every vertebra in Ben's feigned body chilled. It had that same bark, that same baneful snarl as before. "I told you to stay away. You don't belong here. This is none of your concern." Ben remained frozen in silence and held his reply. "It looks like I'm going to have to send you away permanently," it said.

Ben could hear the gun cock even against the undying scream of the alarm bell.

"No," the other assailant of an umber color called out. He was now on the brink of his companion's red hue and had become more of a burnt orange than the last time. "You can't. He's not one of them. He's done nothing to us."

Flares lashed out of the red, snapping whiplike in the air. "It's what he could do, idiot, not what he has done. He could ruin this all for us."

"But what if he doesn't?" the umber light asked.

Ben felt the barrel of one of the larger guns press against the space between his eyebrows as the red voice pulsated its gnarly glow less than an arm's length from his face. He could feel its hot, stank breath breathing over his face. It wanted to shoot him at point-blank range. A sudden kill without a gap of hesitation. Ben remained still. He could only wonder if when the shot was fired, he too would blend into the stream of red fog—or would he simply wake up?

"Can't risk it," the red voice said. "Sorry, cowboy, but it's your time to go."

Blat!

One fire.
One bullet.

One crack of pointed metal streamed fatally in the air with no space to miss its target. And yet Ben felt nothing. He still stood.

He could hear the gun fall to the floor, followed by crushing knees as the red voice fell under Ben. A tail of its own light gushed from behind it, spreading into a wide, circular sheet of powdery crimson.

"Why, Cal?" The red voice choked for a moment, then coughed, gargling out again, "Why?"

The rest of him fell after that and was lost in the blend of the fog.

"I'm sorry. I didn't mean to," the umber voice said. There was a trembling rising in his tone. It was his sadness—his regret. "I … it wasn't supposed to go this far. You weren't supposed to be here. They weren't all supposed to get hurt. This was all my fault. If I hadn't … If I just … I'm sorry."

Blat!

One last ball of smoke fell into the red stream of fog and left Ben alone, surrounded by the still odious flavor of a battlefield after the war. It came abruptly and passed even more so. He didn't need to see to measure the number of victims left in the two boys' wake. Their blood cried out in the air. Too many for an exchange, even if they had all died on their own accord. It wasn't in him to be able to save that many.

The crimson mist ran over his feet, its stench with it. It gagged him far worse than anything he had taken in in his short yet active life. "This cannot happen," he said to no one. "I can't let it. I must find these kids, find this school. Somehow, I must stop them. Somehow."

* * *

Ben awoke to a throbbing headache and that godawful sound he prayed he'd never have to hear again, so long as there was a whisper of breath in his body. It was the mechanical sound of his own heart this time. The sound of his pulse translated into rhythmic beeps along a digital scale that went up and down … beep … up and down … beep. How he hated that sound. Still, it was better than not hearing it at all.

Each beep grounded the tips of his teeth down into a fine powder. The only thing worse was that iodoform odor that wreaked havoc on the senses after a freshly mopped room.

Outside his window, dull shades of pink and gold filled the horizon and leaked into his room. It had been a different day from the one he had last seen riding in the back seat of that kid's sedan, at least twenty-four hours from the looks of it. A line of colorful flowers lined the windowsill. Exhausted, metallic balloons with obnoxious ways of saying "Get Well" made their last stand, floating with desperation at half the height they were leashed to float. Underneath the window, slivers of a tan plastic couch could be seen under the sprawled-out body of a big, worried friend. Jeremy was left resting like a tuckered-out vampire in an open coffin. His arms crossed over his chest. His head hung over one armrest like a guillotine, while his legs dangled off the other just beyond his knees.

Ben raised the back of his bed as if there was something to see other than the everyday appeal of any other hospital room. Across from his perspective was a darkened x-ray screen with one of those happy-to-sad-face charts they used to measure a patient's pain. Looking at it, he considered the side effects of his most recent exchange. "Let's see. A twenty-four-hour blackout leading to a horrible vision of a mass shooting at a school and a head-splitting migraine. I'm definitely ranking this one on the side of a sad crying face."

His attention shifted gradually toward the door, where he saw a dry-erase board. On it, two things were written by hand: the name Nurse Chatman and a date weeks after his encounter with Danica. Both were penned in a broad red marker. His eyes exploded. His hands brushed down his face to wipe the tiredness off him. His face felt wilted and prickly along his cheeks and chin.

Before he could wake up Jeremy, the door began to open. He watched as an elderly redhead with her lush amount of hair pinned up tight and neatly walked in. She wore standard-issued nurse sneakers and scrubs that did nothing for her figure. Her makeup was clean in a way that he could tell her shift had just begun for the day. Ben found it amusing, watching her stroll from one end of the room to the other, with her head too deep into her clipboard to notice a fully conscious patient watching her. At one point, she turned and walked back to the dry-erase board and began to write something down.

"Excuse me, miss," Ben rasped. His mouth was as dry as the Sahara, leaving his words withered. The nurse turned, clipboard pressed firmly against her chest, with a look of startle running over her face. "Can I get an aspirin if it's not too much to ask? I've got a horrible headache."

The nurse rushed out the door, paler than when she came in. *Huh. Maybe I'm supposed to be dead*, Ben thought as he shrugged, then twisted out his joints and turned to fix his blankets.

There was a long yawn and a grunt as Jeremy's body stretched to life. His eyelids battered a few times, catching flickers of Ben upright and fully alert.

"Oh my—Ben? Ben!" Jeremy sprung off the couch faster than anyone would think a man his size could. He rushed to the side of the bed and fell into a Jeremy-size hug over Ben's body. "I can't believe you are awake. The doctors, they thought … they said … Screw what they said. You are awake!"

Ben turned rigid under Jeremy's embrace. "How long was I out?" Ben rasped.

Jeremy pulled his head back, face gaping at Ben. "Three weeks," he said. "About to go on week four."

Ben found himself dumbstruck. "But how? I have never, ever been out this long."

Jeremy nodded. "I'm telling you, it was touch and go for a while there. Mrs. Nelson flew in for a week and a half. She would have stayed longer, but the kids, you know? They had school coming up. At one point, there was even talk about pulling the plug."

"On what?" Ben replied.

"Oh, dude. You were on a respiratory device for like the first two weeks. You've only been off since Thursday. Ever since then, they've been monitoring you around the clock. You must be some sort of a medical anomaly because they won't tell me anything. They say it's because I'm not family. But the truth is I don't think they have a clue about what they are dealing with."

"Why do you say that?"

Jeremy chuckled. "Because I have never seen so many doctors on one case for so many days. You've got this entire hospital scratching their heads, bro."

As Ben succumbed to that tidbit of shock, he asked about Danica.

"She's fine, bro. More than fine." He meant it in more ways than one. Ben could tell by the waggling grin Jeremy was fighting back he had some deeply rooted emotions. "She was here yesterday to see you. Comes by a few days a week. She wanted to thank you personally for what you did. I told her you probably couldn't hear her, but you know, chicks, man. Nothing will persuade them otherwise if they have something set in their mind. She brought you those flowers and a card though." Jeremy pointed to a wilting set of flowers full of dried colors. "They actually smelled pretty good when they were fresh."

Ben could smell nothing other than the poisonous toxins they mopped the room with.

"What was it like?" Jeremy asked. "Being out for so long, did you feel anything or-or see anything?"

Before Ben could answer, the door opened again. A well-dressed doctor in a white coat and spring-colored tie immediately grabbed their attention as he whisked into the room most unprofessionally. The doctor's clipboard was three times as thick as the nurse's, with enough sheets of paper attached that they might have mistaken him for a playwright.

"Hello, Mr. Weaver. Welcome back," the doctor said. His voice was as low and husky as the bags that hung under his eyes. "I'm Doctor Wells." Ben found his name ironically funny, being that he was a doctor. "This here is Nurse Chatman. We have been monitoring you for a few weeks now." He paused to let the shock roll over Ben but was baffled to see no change in Ben's demeanor. Unfortunately, Jeremy had already stolen that moment. He cleared his throat as if mistakenly sucking down a lozenge and continued. "Mr. Weaver, we need to discuss something with you, and I'm not sure if you'd like your friend to hear what I have to say."

Ben glanced up at Jeremy, who was already glancing back, and then at the nurse, then the doctor. "It's fine. He already knows everything about me. Might as well be here to listen to this gem of news."

"Very good," the doctor said before turning around and flipping on the x-ray screen. Out of the vast number of papers, he pulled out a translucent sheet and slid it into the sleeves over the screen. "Mr. Weaver, this is a scan of a normal human brain." He used his finger as a pointer. "As you can see, a healthy brain structure is quite wrinkled. The gyri, that's these ridges you see here, is separated by wide sulci. You may also note that the surface has a healthy amount of gray and white matter, and there is no swelling of any brain area. There are no signs of aneurism or dementia. No tumors—nothing but a neat, clean, healthy brain." He took down the scan, placed it at the top of his pile, and pulled out another one. "This is your brain, Mr. Weaver." He slipped the scan over the screen.

Whatever amount of shock the doctor missed out on telling him how long he'd been out was more than made up for by what Ben was looking at. There was very little gray and no white whatsoever. There were no wrinkles, no ridges, no ... whatever else the doctor said. There was a whole lot of blackness though. And it was splattered against that thin transparent sheet of plastic that resembled his brain.

"I don't know where to begin, Mr. Weaver," the doctor said, looking at the scan as if it were his first time. "In part, it's because we truly have no idea what we are witnessing here. We know that roughly ninety percent of your brain is covered in this substance. Unfortunately, whatever it is is more foreign to us than anything I have seen in my thirty-seven years of practice. On top of that, this substance has consumed most of your brain tissue. So much that we are in awe of how you are even alive, let alone functioning at any normal level."

Jeremy said, "Do you think it could be some sort of a tumor?"

"Doubtful yet possible," the doctor replied as he scratched the top of his balding scalp. "In so many ways, it appears to be so. But look." He took down the scan, handing it off to the nurse, and pulled out his final scan. Three shots appeared on this one. They were very similar brains in one sense but very different in another. "This one here we took the night you arrived, when that …" He rolled his fingers, taking time to find an appropriate word. "When that substance was still coming out of your eyes and nose. This one was a scan we took last week. Notice how much more the mass has spread over the brain tissue. This one we had taken this morning before you surprised the entire ward with your awakening. You see, Mr. Weaver and Mr. …"

"Turner, sir. Jeremy Turner," Jeremy responded in his best James Bond impersonation.

"Turner. Yes. From the appearance, it could be seen as a tumor. But the way it acts? The way it moves and consumes?" he said as a question but not quite. "I mean, my word. This stuff is almost behaving like a parasite."

"So, what do you suggest we do?" Jeremy asked.

Doctor Wells flipped off the screen. "That is the question, isn't it. My advice—and I sincerely hope you take it—is that we officially admit you and keep monitoring the thing until we find out what it is and what exactly it is doing to you. I would also like to get some sample tissue to study and examine it. If this thing is transferable or contagious, I can only fear we will see many more cases coming through those doors."

Ben leaned over and whispered in Jeremy's ear, "I can't stay here." He then repeated it out loud. "I can't stay here. I must get home. I'm needed there."

"I understand your hesitation, Mr. Weaver. This is a fearful situation for all of us. But—"

Ben edged himself up a bit higher. "It's not that. Trust me. There is an important issue back home that I must resolve."

"More important than this?" Doctor Wells choked. "Mr. Weaver, I implore you. It is in everyone's best interest for you to stay here. Think about it. What if this thing spreads, and we don't know how to treat it? You could very well go back under on your flight back home. Then what? And that's not even mentioning the risk of this being contagious."

"It's not contagious, Doctor," Ben replied, then turned to Jeremy, who had a mixture of concern scrolling over his eyes. "It's not contagious. You have to trust me on that."

Jeremy nodded.

"Mr. Weaver, I salute the optimism you have toward your condition. But to be frank, neither you nor I nor the entire medical community can know what we are dealing with here."

"I know you don't. But trust me when I say I have a better understanding than you."

Ben turned and slid his feet out of bed, rising to a wobbled stance that three weeks of lying in bed might churn out. Jeremy rushed to grip him by the arm and help him stabilize.

The nurse scurried past the doctor, as he stood somewhat miffed, brow line furrowed with displeasure. "Mr. Weaver, please, you must stay in your bed," the nurse pleaded.

Ben reached down, grabbed hold of the catheter, and began pulling. His face became squinty, agonizing for one long pull. Jeremy turned away halfway past the point of losing his lunch. The nurse gasped as the long tube slid out from under Ben's hospital gown and flapped like a dead fish on the ground, trickling urine down around His feet. The nurse leaped back.

Doctor Wells strode out of the room in haste as Ben worked on disconnecting the monitors and IVs. "Where are my clothes?" he asked no one in particular.

Jeremy made his way around the pool of urine to a thin blond cabinet and pulled out a large white bag stuffed with Ben's belongings. "Danica washed your clothes for you. She said it was the least she could do," he said, handing them off to Ben.

With a huff, Ben poured his belongings out over the bed. "Nice girl. I like her." He turned and saw that look in Jeremy's eye. "Not like that, you turd. Calm down, Romeo."

The nurse had waved the white flag on settling her patient and flipped the switch into dressing the puncture holes left by the IVs. Out of compulsion, she lectured him on treating the wounds, when to take the bandages off, and so on.

Ben slipped on his boxers under the gown and did the same with his pants. He fell into his shoes, abdicating his socks for the time being to untie the gown and throw on his button-up shirt. "Wow, she did a good job," Ben called to Jeremy.

The nurse's face perked. At first, she believed he had been referring to her, only to find disappointment as to whom he was referring. She slouched back down and concentrated on the final IV, her expression as sterile as the gauze she used to dress him.

Doctor Wells reappeared right as Ben scooped the rest of his belongings back into the bag. "Mr. Weaver," he said, recollected and passive.

"I'm not staying, Doc," Ben replied without a glance at the doctor.

"I understand. However, a doctor in Los Angeles might be able to help you. I have met her once or twice. She is a remarkable neurologist specializing in more challenging situations like yours. I beg you to at least see her." He reached out a folded piece of paper he had torn off his prescription pad.

Ben gazed at it for a time, then took it and opened it up. "Doctor Veronica Dupree. She's good?"

"One of the best, Mr. Weaver," the doctor said, flapping his pad shut. He reached out again, this time offering an empty hand. "Good luck to you, young man."

Ben shook it. "Thank you, sir. And I want you to know I will set an appointment with Doctor Dupree. Definitely," he said, then patted Jeremy on the back. The two headed out of the room, followed by the doctor, nurse, and an entire staff's worth of fixated glares.

Jeremy led Ben to the Ford Escape waiting and running out in the parking lot. They both hopped in simultaneously, both doors slamming with a unison thud.

"So, are you going to tell me what this is all about, or are you going to leave me in the dark like you did with everything else?" Jeremy said. He shifted the Escape into reverse.

Ben worked to click on his seat belt, finding it difficult to get his body to comply with his brain's demands. "You remember that kid back in Westwood, the one we found in that old shack?"

"*You* found," Jeremy corrected. "And yes. What about him?"

"Well, he was dying, way past saving by any medical means. And I wasn't sure if I could save him. I never tried, not on someone like that."

"Save him like in the way you saved Danica, you mean," Jeremy clarified.

"Yes, only he wasn't trying to end his own life. And like I said, I've never helped someone like that before. I had to try, though, right? So, I got into his memories, looking for this thing that was killing him. And then I saw it."

"You saw what?"

"Well, I don't know. Not exactly. But whatever it had attacked me. At first, I thought I had been able to fight it off. I was pretty sure I did—that is, until now."

"Are you saying that whatever was killing that boy is still alive?" Jeremy asked.

Ben looked at Jeremy and then nodded. "Not only alive, but I believe it has made a home in me—in my brain."

"Okay, so what is it?" Jeremy asked. "Maybe we can find a way to kill the damn thing."

"I don't know for sure, but the last two times it got the better of me, I've had these visions of these two kids. They are attacking a school."

"And you've only had these ones after the kid in Westwood?"

"No. Actually, the first vision came sometime prior. But this thing has seemed to magnify my presence in the visions. The kids. These attackers. They can see me somehow."

"What do you mean?" Jeremy said with his sight focused on the road.

"I mean, they speak to me. One has even threatened me. Normally, I see things from a first-person perspective. I am looking through their eyes. I am the one who is about to commit suicide. But in these, I am a spectator, and they see me there somehow. They even seemed threatened by my presence, like I can stop them from doing whatever they are about to do."

"Well, can you?" Jeremy asked.

"I hope so," Ben replied. "I just have to find them first."

"All right. So, what do these kids look like? If you could identify them, I'm sure kids like that would probably have track records, right? Something we could look up, like a heat sheet or a juvenile detention list of some sort?"

Ben sighed. "That's the thing. I don't know what they look like. Everything is always black. I see nothing but hear and feel everything."

"Okay, okay." Jeremy rolled the information, or lack of it, over in his head. "So how are we going to find them then?"

"In this last vision, they used names. One called the other Cal."

"Cal, huh." Jeremy played with the name, mumbling it a few more times as if there was a secret code in the syllable arrangement. "Not much to go on there. Anything else?"

Ben concentrated. He ran over the vision like a confession tape in his mind, realizing he skirted over another name spoken. This one struck him as oddly familiar when heard it from the mouths of one of the boys. A name that was most likely traceable. His eyes brightened, and he snapped his fingers. "They called out a teacher's name. Miss ... Hawthorne. Patty Hawthorne, I believe it was."

Jeremy's eyebrows waggled. "Patty Hawthorne," Jeremy reiterated with a temperament of unbelief.

"Yeah," Ben replied. "I swear I know that name from somewhere, like a bad taste that haunts your mouth, you know? I don't know. Maybe it's that kind of name that rings familiar when you hear it."

Jeremy's eyes frowned with a similar taste to the name. He mouthed the name once and whispered it again, scratching the wheels that started to turn in his head. "Miss Hawthorne," he said. "Miss Patty Hawthorne." He held back his voice as the wheels kept turning. Ben, too, was mulling the name over within his memory. "Hey, didn't we have a psychotic homeroom teacher back in junior high named Patty Hawthorne?"

Ben's eyes burst open to the size of grapefruit. His jaw became slack with the actualization that he did—they did. Jeremy slammed on the brakes, causing a ruckus of skidding tires and horns blaring behind him as he pulled off to the side of the road. He turned to Ben. "We did have a Miss Hawthorne, didn't we," he said, not as a question but as a statement.

Ben looked back. Both sets of eyes marbled over in realization. "Yes, we did," he said. "Patty Hawthorne."

* * *

What was said about Cal's mom wasted no time in brimming over into social media. Every rumor was permanently available, never erased, and eternally ready to be pulled from the cloud at the simplest of whims for anyone who might find the information entertaining. It was one more notch for them to add to the collar of that beast some would call "a bit of childish fun." The victims, however, had a different name for it—cyberbullying.

The beasts that lived uncaged within the wilds of several computers were dying to sink their salivating teeth into the meatiest parts of Calvin. They found recent events more delectable than the simplicity of the boney, insecure youngling Calvin used to be. The beasts had studied their prey over the years. They toyed with him. They nipped at the heels to see if they would kick back or not. A few taps with the paw, a nip, waiting and listening to it bellowing cries to see if big momma or papa would come out of the bushes to protect their young. Finally, they'd chomped down, gotten a taste of his blood. And they liked it. They all thirsted for it.

Calvin's only escape came from the hours he spent shooting down the bad guys with elaborate weapons of destruction from the controller of his Xbox. Travis was often by his side, escaping his own somber life at home with his mother and her exhausting drunken tirades. His house had transformed from the house that time forgot to a waste heap of booze, cigarette butts, and unkempt rooms. Every inch of the place was ridden in the yellow scent of cigarettes. Rotten food and trash decorated every countertop, with nothing to eat except for stale bags of potato chips, which his mom had more of an attachment to than her son's well-being.

"Let's clean house," Travis hollered as their avatars were dropped back into the war zone. He wore a bruise under one eye and another matching one on his arm. Calvin couldn't help but gravitate his attention to it every now and again, to which Traves would grunt and shift and tell Cal to get his head in the game.

Calvin had no qualms using each shot fired as one mental cheap shot to the punks who littered their lives at school.

"S'up, loser," Cal spouted as he blasted another gamer from behind.

"I wonder if this is just as fun in real life," Travis said, sparking a quick glance from Cal. Before Calvin's mom left, these comments were a bit concerning, but since then, they didn't bother him as much. "I'm just saying it would be interesting to find out."

Calvin threw his headset down after their final loss. "Dammit!" He slouched back in the chair. "You want a Coke?"

Travis turned to him. "Hell yeah, I want coke! Oh, you mean *a* Coke. Sure!"

Calvin lifted himself up and strolled pathetically to the kitchen. After reaching in for a couple drinks, he turned around, surprised to see Travis taking a spot on a stool behind the counter.

"I guess I'm your bartender now." He slid the can to Travis.

"Let's reverse the roles. How about I be yours." Calvin leaned forward. "Tell me about that girl you've been checking out in history."

Cal choked on the liquid. "Wait, what?"

"The one who asked if you were okay after your latest beatdown." Travis took a swig. "Sorry to break it to you, homie, but you looked pathetic."

"Last time I offer you a Coke, turd bag."

Travis grinned and then burped. "I don't want to tear you down, but I also don't want you going soft on me. The chick is hot, but you're only gaining sympathy points while her popularity is rising."

Calvin didn't want to respond but simply said, "I don't know ..."

* * *

Back at school, Travis and Calvin would sit, hiding in a secluded grotto of lockers masked with caution tape due to structural damage from an earthquake a few years back. The entire building had been locked up, boarded over, and masked off with strips of caution tape, finding it too structurally unsound to hold classes or let students wander about. Cal and Travis found it as a sanctuary. It was their only blessing from a merciful God, Travis would say after sneaking under the bright yellow tape and into a three-walled cavern of unused lockers. It was their sanctuary, a grotto that no one else seemed to wonder about. It had also quickly become their lunch spot. Rushing from a classroom, undeterred, their focus was dead set on getting there before one of the school goons picked up their scent.

As Cal are, sharing what he could with his wilting friend, Travis would scour old lockers to see what, if anything, the last group of students left behind of value. Who knew? "Maybe in the clutter of old papers, a student stashed a wad of cash inside one of them and completely forgot about it," he'd fantasize. A few were still locked up, protected from Travis's interest with a combination lock, which only fueled his desire to want to get inside.

No one ever went beyond the bright yellow tape except for one janitor who would sweep the collected dust, vagrant leaves, and debris of careless students to clear the walkway. But that was only the first two Mondays. Every now and again, the janitor would see them, tag sowed on his janitor uniform with a Hispanic name they couldn't begin to pronounce. They simply called him "Pablo." He didn't seem to mind. When he passed, he gave the boys a smirk and a shake of the head. Cal would sit knees to chest in the flank of towering lockers as Travis went on excavating whichever ones he could.

"Es a good place to hide tings," Pablo would say from time to time, catching Travis red-handed with his arm scouring the inside of a locker. "But no drugs or beer, okay? Dat's no bueno."

Travis would nod, flashing a sideways grin as Pablo continued his way with a broom down the walkway and onto another part of the condemned building.

"Hey, you ever wonder how Miss Hawthorne keeps her job, treating kids like that?" Travis asked, elbow deep into a jackpot locker. Cal peered up. "She makes the Wicked Witch of the West look like friggin' Mother Teresa some days, you know? And she's been here for like—what, a hundred years? People like that shouldn't be able to work with children."

Calvin bit into the sandwich he had made himself that very morning. "She has her good side," he protested.

"Yeah." Travis chuckled. "And what side is that? 'Cause I've checked out every side of her from ass to face, and I can't tell no difference."

Calvin posed a grin and took another bite of his sandwich. "I think you're being too hard on her. She's like old and stuff."

"Dude, she's like forty. Fifty at best."

Calvin shrugged. "I dunno. I just think it must be hard at her age with no husband or kids or nothing."

Travis pulled his arm from the locker. He slammed it shut and flung the dust off in the air. "That's because she's probably a lesbo," he said before plopping down by Calvin and reaching for a handful of generic potato chips. "Lesbos don't need stuff like that. They're weird and mean and have cats."

"What are you talking about?" Calvin said. "She's not a lesbian, stupid. And cats—really?"

"You ever meet someone with cats that isn't?" Travis asked, spitting shards of chips from his mouth.

"Um, yeah—a lot of people. Hell, we used to have a cat."

Travis shook his head. "Nope. Nah, Captain Scuttles was not a cat. He was a goddamn tiger. Remember when he used to terrorize your neighbor's dogs? How they'd howl and whimper like little bitches?"

Calvin grinned at the reflection. "They were Dobermans too," he said.

"Whatever happened to Captain Scuttles?"

Calvin peered deep into his lunch sack. "I dunno. He ran off and never came back. He wasn't that old, so I don't think he died," he said, fishing out something from the bag that looked like a gelatinized blend of sugar.

"Yeah, and strong enough to take on a Mac truck," Travis said and reached for a few more chips. The two ate. "Hey, maybe we should find Captain Scuttles and unleash him on Miss Hawthorne. See if there's anything left of her bitching after that."

Calvin tore open the pack. "Travis, let me ask you, have you ever had a teacher you did like?"

Travis exaggerated his thinking, tapping a greasy, crumb-encrusted finger against the corner of his mouth. "Mmm, nope. None I can think of. Why do you ask?"

"I'm just wondering if there might be a common denominator here," Calvin replied.

"Really," Travis said, taking offense. "I'm not the one that said your handwriting looks like first-grade scribble," Travis fired back. "Or the homework was so easy that someone like you could do it. That wasn't me. I'm telling you, that lady is a monster and needs to be fired."

Calvin reached under his shirt and pulled the cross necklace up from his chest and fumbled with it in his hand. "Yeah, well, they ain't gonna fire her for two complaints by students like us. So, we're gonna have to live with her until next semester or a year or whenever they move us to a different homeroom."

Something about the necklace tormented a part of Travis, like a splinter too small to pull from the flesh. He watched, enduring Calvin's tick of rolling and flipping the summer camp cross in his hands until it finally struck his nerves like a sudden jolt of electricity. "Dude, why do you still have that thing?" Calvin shrugged, keeping his face low. "Nothing in your life has ever proven that stupid … whatever you wanna call it as lucky or blessed or, or anything. Blankets don't keep the monsters away. They never have, and they never will. That necklace," Travis said, making every effort to make sure Calvin knew he was pointing at the one in his hand, "is your blanket."

The bell chimed over the school grounds, heralding students to their next class. Travis stood and slapped his hands clean over his pants, while Calvin buried his necklace back under his shirt and gathered the trash into his paper bag and rolled it into a brown wrinkled ball.

"I don't think I can deal with her that long," Travis said. "This whole school is f'd up. I never thought I'd wish to be back in grade school."

Calvin stood and shot the brown paper into one of the abandoned lockers. "Well, it can't get much worse," he said as if they were at a midpoint to something hopeful.

Soon the time would say otherwise.

* * *

Jeremy had driven Ben to the airport two days after the hospital visit, taking a midday flight (for once) back to LAX in executive class, provided by his dear friend. He was back in a set of his old clothes. Still, he kept the new ones neatly folded at the top of his bag out of respect for Jeremy's generosity, rushing down a long line of terminals to catch his flight. He felt that no matter when he arrived, he always ran late. There was a time paradox when he stepped into an airport, the moment he passed security. It stole valuable minutes off his schedule as he scuffled with his shoelaces that never seemed tied right on those metal benches.

The flight was easy: first in line, complimentary drinks, arm room, leg room, breathing room. Plus, there was still Stephen King and the gruesome adventures of Detective Jack Hoskins from the flight into Denver. Ben figured he could knock out four to five more chapters before the plane started to descend.

By the time he was back into the smoggy breeze of a late Los Angeles summer, Mr. Nelson had already wedged his SUV at an angle between an old taxicab and a minivan overtaken by grumpy kids and flustered parents. "So," Mr. Nelson said, preparing for a long, traffic-cluttered ride home, "how was your trip? Eventful from what I've heard."

"I wouldn't say that," Ben replied. Eventful didn't even begin to describe it. Ben would say it was leaning more on the side of an out-of-control circus between Danica's exchange, the blackout, the vision, and the three-week hospital stay.

"No?"

"No, I would say it was nuts."

Mr. Nelson gave a laugh. "Son, when isn't it nuts in your life?"

Ben looked out the window to the wall of traffic they were coming to, thinking how true that was. "Did Mrs. Nelson get a chance to set my appointment?" he asked.

Mr. Nelson laid pressure on the brakes, almost coming to a complete stop. "Oh yeah, she's got you scheduled for Friday afternoon. Did her homework too, the way only she can do it." Mr. Nelson leaned over the gear shifter to Ben. "You know she did a full-on background check of that doctor? She Googled her, Yelped her, Fantangled her or whatever else you can do to find the dirt in someone's nails."

"And?"

"And she was impressed. Can you believe it? My wife was impressed." He sounded shocked. "She can find the discoloration in a rainbow but not a thing on this Doctor Dupree. In fact, she said she'd never seen such a young neurologist with so many accomplishments or, more importantly," he said, "so many great reviews. And to think she's a local practitioner. As far as doctors go, you hit pay dirt with this one."

"Let's hope so," Ben replied.

Two hours later, Ben was back in his small, walled-in corner of the earth. His bag was tossed haphazardly over his couch to tumble and fall where it may as he headed off to drain the dragon after five hours of traveling, before getting a few long winks of shut-eye. It was all but certain that tomorrow would be a long day. He'd visit the school he hadn't seen in over half a decade and see if he could find these two faceless boys and stop them before any of what had haunted his brain came to pass. Tonight, he'd need the rest. A good, long, undeterred rest.

* * *

It happened Wednesday when the sun smacked the schoolyard with its blinding effulgence. All the bullying had gone too far. Way too far. There was no Miss Hawthorne that morning to muddy the homeroom with her sludge of chastening insults, making them feel like the day might actually go in their favor, lowering their defenses to a morning dressed as a prank can of salted nuts. Only this can wasn't holding in something as bemusing as a few spring-loaded snakes. No, this one had a real serpent with plated scales, coiled fangs, and venom, building up its wild desire to bite the first unfortunate soul that pulled back the lid. And that regrettable soul could only be Calvin.

The bell that ended the second period was still fresh in the air. Calvin dashed from the room. He had a mere three minutes, three ticktocking minutes, to finagle his way across the school to the farthest building on campus. Most Wednesdays, he'd cut across the open field where the delinquents loitered about, hiding behind walls to suck on cigarettes and who knew what. His first mistake was changing his routine journey. His second was having the audacity to think he could use the restroom in that building before his next class.

As he entered, they waited, a band of greasy-haired cretins dressed in grunge, death metal fanatics, two boasting the subtle shade of an early pubescent beard. Two went in after Calvin, a tall, stringy fellow with hair as black and glossy as spray paint and a much shorter skinheaded kid. The other two made sure there'd be no interruptions from the outside.

Calvin had barely made it to the stalls before he felt his gut being pushed in by a firm quartet of knuckles. Air expelled from his mouth with a pig-like squeal as he felt two arms slip under his own and hold him up. His head's declivity gave access to a clean knock across his temple, sending his head back and charge into the tiled wall. His ears rang. His flesh became warm, then hot. He felt nothing other than the pressure of his skull burning under his scalp. Black and purple spots detracted his view of anything around him. While dazed, they pulled Calvin away from the wall. They hit him with another windblown thrust to his gut and a blast across his face. This time, his jaw cracked as he fell to the sticky cold floor, knocked senseless. Words were spoken, undistinguishable under the current of blood rushing through his ears. His face was on fire. His stomach had fled into his chest and was scaling his throat. He could taste the copper flavor of his blood as the indecipherable words grew louder and more aggressive. Calvin tried to get to his knees but had been met with a foot to his tailbone. A sharp boney knee collided with his back.

When the fun was over, and they were good and ready, they rolled him over and took to his pockets, raiding them for anything of value he might have on him. Unsatisfied, they did the same to his backpack, pouring all his belongings over the floor and kicking them around.

"Little shitstain's got nothing," one said as he'd slap-shot a book across the floor to crush in Calvin's nose.

A thread of sunlight appeared from the door. "You guys, let's go," an outside voice called in a hurried whisper.

If he decided to have the balls to tell anyone what happened, they swore to Calvin a gruesome death. Then they were gone, leaving his belongings in as bad a state as they left him, torn to pieces and scattered all over the bathroom floor. Pages of books and paper soaked up stale urine and grime left by thousands of feet trotting in and out throughout the day. Electronic were crushed, and pencils and pens snapped like autumn twigs. Calvin coddled his gut, balled on the floor, necklace swaying like a pendulum half at work, taunting him as he cried relentless tears brought on by the unbearable pain.

The bell rang. It meant nothing to Calvin as tears and phlegm bubbled over his mouth and out of his nose, cursing and crying, crying and cursing. He didn't want to get up. He wanted to die there, right there, just as he was.

In a short time, a yard monitor stumbled in and saw him kneeling over the floor, chocked, red-faced, and bleeding from his mouth and nose, dangling over the edge of consciousness. After the nurse dressed him, they called his parents.

Mom didn't answer. She never did anymore.

Dad took the call, promised he'd be there in a beat, and didn't disappoint. By the time he had arrived, a bruised head and swollen jaw had developed from his injuries, making it hard to chalk it off as a careless accident. In the surrounding of charts and bandages, posters of body parts and bone structure, while the eyes of a nurse, a principal, and a blue-blooded father looked worriedly at him, Calvin was interrogated over and again about what exactly had happened in that bathroom and who was involved. Words boggled in his mouth like foam. He couldn't tell. He wouldn't tell.

A visit to the emergency room was the first stop on Officer Gardner's list. Cal expected a lengthy patrol car ride lecture along the way. In some ways, he wanted it. His dad's nostrils worked overtime, trying to make up for his tightly clenched lips. His chin protruded over the steering wheel, eyes beady, brows so sharply pointed that they could cut metal. Calvin could see the temperament of his father throbbing out of his forehead. His neck tightened with stress. His knuckles drained white with pressure. It had worsened since his mom walked out the door and never returned. It had become an unspoken rule: never talk about Mom. If only erasing her helped. Calvin felt it; the stress and anxiety had become overwhelming. Neither of them found complacency in this new way of life. But still, all Cal wanted was the lecture. Some bold, ferocious words to let him know that his dad still cared about him. Nothing was said.

Officer Gardner silently dropped Calvin off at the house. Calvin scooted out and then turned to tug on his backpack and grab the bottle of pain meds from the cup holder.

"I'll be home late," his dad said nonchalantly, shifting the car into reverse. Calvin's toes were no more than an inch from the tires as the squad car zipped out of the driveway, rocking like a boat out at sea as it straightened out on the road. Cal's dad sped away without the simplest of glances, leaving his battered son to tend to himself for the rest of the day, possibly longer.

Calvin teetered up the driveway, rocking his sore, tuckered stride. He dropped his bag at the doorway and gave it a few kicked nudges into the house. He took a moment to digest the room. His head still throbbed, but it was nothing that a few milligrams of naproxen couldn't drown out.

Cal took down a glass, filled it with tap water, and moved to the living room to park himself on the couch. He popped two pills in his mouth, chugged the glass, and lay back, glaring at his reflection in the blackness of a dead television screen. The world seemed to make more sense in that particular shade to him, not a whole lot of color coated in a grayish brown gloom. Calvin shut his eyes and succumbed to the effects of medicine, taking in the silence and exhaling the errant emotions that crossed his mind: anger, pain, abandonment, loneliness, shame.

Anger.

It felt like only a blink before he could hear the phone ringing from his room. Two stolen cell phones taught him it was best to leave them home. His eyes struggled to open, finding a much darker hue of tan in the living room than how he had remembered it. Time had passed without him knowing. Hours were lost in a matter of what only felt like a minute.

He sat on the couch and weightily pulled his body into the air. His feet didn't want to move but did so with much reluctance. Calvin sloshed down the hall to his room and used his entire body to open the door. The phone stopped for a break, then started back up again. He continued to trudge the terrain of a messy room. He grabbed the phone. It read, Travis Cell.

"Hey, Travis," Calvin answered, each syllable slurring.

"Dude, are you okay? People said they saw you dragged out of school in handcuffs by a cop this afternoon and that you drove off in the back of a squad car."

He took a deep breath. "It was my dad. He came and picked me up."

"Oh. So, then what was the deal with the cuffs then?"

"There were no cuffs. People were just making crap up. I got hurt, and he had to come and get me and take me to the ER to have it looked at."

"So that's why I didn't see you at lunch. What happened?"

"Nothing. I had an accident in one of the bathrooms, that's all." Calvin forgot who he was talking to.

"Oh yeah, and exactly how many accidents were in that bathroom when you got hurt?"

Calvin was silent.

"Cal? How many?"

Cal rested his hand over his forehead before dragging it down the less sore side of his face and over his swollen lip. "Two," he said, with shame seeping off his lips. "And probably two more keeping watch outside."

"Dammit! Did you let the principal know who they were?" Travis asked.

"Not really. They said they'd kill me if I ratted."

"And you believed them?"

Calvin again was silent. Hot tears began to well up under his eyes. "Yes," he muttered.

Cal could hear the rage in Travis's breathing. "They can't get away with this. We can't let them. You know that, right?"

Calvin sniffled. "Yeah," he said.

"We need to take control of this, show these assholes we are done being their victims. The teachers can't do it for us, and you know it's only the two of us that have each other's back, and alone we're not strong enough to take them on."

"What are you suggesting we do?"

"What I'm suggesting is we bring firepower to the school. Make an example of these turds. Show the school what happens when you pick on the wrong kid on the wrong day. Show everyone. All it will take is a few, just the few that deserve it, and I mean really deserve it. This is friggin' survival of the fittest. It's time we up our place on the food chain."

Cal rubbed his head. "Someone else could get hurt by mistake."

"And how's that, Cal? No one else will have what we have. I've been noticing how much better you've gotten at your aim. You're good, man. We both are. We can do this."

Calvin couldn't pretend to be that certain. "Okay, Travis, let's say I go along with this. Say I think it is the only way to rid us of these guys. How are you gonna get the guns into school? They have security guards and metal detectors at all the entrances and sniff the lockers. There is no way we wouldn't be caught before the first bell rang."

"Don't you worry your sweet little heart 'bout that, man. I've got it covered."

FIFTEEN

Ben's beat-up green Ranger smoked out the school's parking lot bright and early the following day. It rattled and puttered gray billows of exhaust until he finally put it out of its misery. He sat in his truck, thinking and waiting, still galvanized over the idea that this whole thing was about to play out in his backyard. He watched as kids from all walks of life funneled from the street and behind car doors into the school, bright and smiling, still holding onto that burst of morning optimism that seven hours of schoolwork would gradually chip away for the benefit of elevating their knowledge. They all looked so young, like … children. He found it hard to believe that any of these would be capable of executing such an event. But visions never lied—never.

Ben waited for that last student to run across the well-kept grass of the front yard. After, he stepped out of his truck and walked over to the guard posted out front. "Excuse me, sir," he called out, waving, stopping the uniformed man dead in his tracks. The guard waited, hand resting instinctively over his taser holster as Ben jogged to the gate's entrance with a waving hand.

"Can I help you, son?" The guard's voice came out a little too authoritative.

"Yes, I believe you can," Ben replied, trying to catch the part of his breath that got away from him. "You see, I used to go to school here." The guard gave him a once-over. Ben addressed the guard's negating glare. "I know, I know. It's been a while. Anyhow, a teacher had a tremendous influence on me here, and I was in town, so I thought it might be cool to surprise her with a little blast from the past. The only thing is I don't know if she still teaches here. Honestly, I don't know if she is still alive."

"Well, you would have to talk to the principal about that," the guard replied, adding a no-duh look to his face.

"Oh, okay. Well, is there any way I can talk with the principal then?"

The guard gave him a look once more to evaluate Ben. "Yeah, sure. Follow me."

The guard led Ben down through the doors and halls of long-forgotten memories. He surveyed the walls and ceiling, noticing how much they had shrunk over the years. Some things had changed completely. Some had a fresh coat of paint. Some looked worse than when he had left it. It awed him that even though most things had changed, it all struck him as so familiar.

"Man. Everything looks much smaller than I remember it," he said.

The guard chose not to reply.

"Are you guys here all day?" Ben asked him.

Not being one for small talk, the guard made his comments brief. "We come in in the morning, stay for a while, and then leave. Come back around lunch for an hour or so, leave again, then are back at the end of the day."

The guard led him right up to the doors of the administration office and opened the door for him. "This is where I leave you," he said, holding the door for Ben as he thanked the man and proceeded inside.

Ben made his way to the front counter. A familiar silvery-haired lady in a pale pink cardigan appeared behind a tall counter. She wielded an excessive coat of makeup, a wandering trail of lipstick, and a cheery expression that formed valleys in her foundation. Gingerly, she intertwined her loose-fleshed fingers over the counter and asked if she could help him.

"Can you tell me if the principal is in?" he asked, smiling back at her.

"Can I get your name, young man?" she requested in a delightfully professional manner.

"Ben Weaver," he replied.

The silvery-haired lady reached for an outdated landline with one of those long spiraling cords and a 1980s-style switchboard. As she paged over the system, the loud flash of a rectangular red light bleeped on the panel, as if using a morse code to reach the other room. "Yes, Principal Holder," she said, as if unprepared for the principal to actually answer the page. "There is a Mr. Weaver here to see you … O-okay … Yes, ma'am. I'll let him know." She hung up the phone, the cord twisting and looping tightly.

"The principal will be with you shortly, if you would like to have a seat," she said, holding an upturned hand over the counter to present a row of chairs that faced Ben's back.

As he pondered which seat to take, he realized that each one looked decades past retirement. Ben nodded a thank you as he took a seat. He only sat briefly until a milky glass-paneled door opened and a sternly attractive woman in a sport coat and form-fitting skirt walked out. Her hair was pulled back tight and looped into a bun, boasting the lack of age on her face. Her eyes held an ice blue tint as clean as the arctic sky. Her skin was as delicate as silk, her lips plump and vibrant with color. Her natural youth hid it well if she had been anywhere north of her late thirties. However, she also appeared stern, as if it might hurt her to crack a smile.

Ben stood from his chair.

"Mr. Weaver, I'm Principal Holder." The principal held out a rigid arm attached to an even more rigid hand. "How may I help you today?"

"I am sorry to interrupt your busy day," Ben said. She nodded once, as if to acknowledge that he indeed had. "You see, I went to school here at one time. During that time, I lost my mother to cancer, and there were a couple ladies on staff who had a tremendous influence over me."

The silver-haired receptionist's ears perked up at his story. Ben noticed her head peeking over the counter, eyeing him as if he'd suddenly become recognizable.

"And so, you came back to thank them for all they meant to you." Principal Holder cut to the chase. "Yes, I believe one of our security guards made me aware of your intentions."

Ben was taken aback. "Well … yeah. So, I was wondering, if it's not too much trouble, if I might stop by their classroom and just say thank you? If not all, then at least one, if she's still here? She, above all, did so much for me in that dark hour."

Principal Holder laced her arms across her chest and took a noticeable step to the side, thrusting her hips in the other direction. "Mmm-hmm. And what is that teacher's name?"

"I believe it was Miss Hawthorne," Ben replied, biting down and chewing his lip.

Principal Holder's eyebrows crooked with suspicion. "Miss Hawthorne?" she said, as more of a question. "Patricia Hawthorne?"

Ben replied, "That's right. So, she's still here then?"

"Oh, she's still here all right. But to hear of her being spoken of so fondly by a student, Mr. Weaver, I must say in confidence this rings contrary to decades of frightened children and parental complaints." She leaned in close. "They call her the boogieman's grandma for goodness' sake."

Ben grinned at her slight lack of professionalism. This lady was fast growing on him. "Really? Wow. Maybe she changed over the years." He made every attempt to sound believable. "Do you think it might be all right if I visited her for a few minutes?"

"I would love to say yes, Mr. Weaver, but unfortunately she will be out until Tuesday of next week."

"I see." Ben began to panic a little. "May I ask? Do you have a couple of students who tend to be more trouble than the others around here?"

The principal leaned back. "Mr. Weaver, this is junior high. Every child tends to find themselves in trouble more often than not. Is there anything else I might be able to help you with?"

How about a date? Say around eight o'clock tonight. Dinner, maybe some dancing or a few games of pool, he wanted to say. "Yes, actually. I was wondering if there's any chance I can stroll by her classroom and maybe take a quick peek inside, if only for nostalgic reasons."

"Well, homeroom is about to end, so I don't see it being too much of a bother. You could sign in with Maddie over here. I'm sure she can print you off a thirty-minute pass. Anything else, sir?"

"No, ma'am." Ben made a slight bow. "You have been more than helpful to me. I really do appreciate it."

The halls of the school were empty of foot traffic, leaving only Ben's shoes to step-clack, step-clack. He walked to the far end of the school, turning left at the last T-shaped divide, and made it to the door just as the first bell rang overhead. His heart jumped into his throat at the familiar grisly sound of the chime, like a phobia causing his body to lock up as the floodgates of students rushed into the open halls and streamed heavily around him. A few kids stood out of the many who drained from Miss Hawthorne's classroom. He profiled a few as troubled, possibly violent, narrowing his search down to those who walked out in pairs. Most seemed like average teenagers. A few walked the path of skaters in their overly tight jeans that looked a size too short, or emos, or the silent, dorky type. That's when one with a smashed-up face walked out protectively close to his friend. Ben scanned around, keeping one eye on the pair as the herd thinned. They rounded a corner, vanishing with the rest of the crowd. In less than a handful of minutes, Ben found himself standing alone.

He walked to the tinted window and made a quick glance inside, only to find rows of empty desks and a tall male substitute reorganizing the assignments at his desk. Pulling away, he sighed out of frustration, biting his lip. He hadn't known what he was expecting to find. He just anticipated there would have been something. He returned to the office, turning right at the fork in the hall, and proceeded down the long path. His mind wandered off for a spell. While formulating new strategies and reevaluating the students who wandered out of Miss Hawthorne's class from the images in his head, Ben realized he had passed the administration office. In fact, he was now coming to the other end of the school.

As he began to turn back around, he caught the tail end of something fluttering along the corner of a boarded-up classroom, thin and long. He continued to walk, seeing it grow longer and longer until he saw both ends of the strand tied off and the tape flapping right about waist high to him.

He strolled up to touch it. Closing his eyes, he slid his fingers along its unstable path from one end of the wall to the other. It felt plastic and paper thin, pliable enough to duck under, which he did, filling in the pictures to the vision in his head. Beyond the caution tape was a cavern walled with a lineup of lockers all vented at the top. It was just as he had felt them deep in his coma. He walked up to one and tapped it. Thin, empty metal. He took a few steps back. His eyes circled over the concrete floor. The pictures of lifeless bodies appeared like ghosts in his view. He saw blood pooling around his feet like a mist. He could hear the echoing banshee of screams wailing faintly in the distance. The bell for the second period rang brutally in his ears, completing the medium he had envisioned. There was something there, and no matter what he was expecting to find, this would surely help.

SIXTEEN

Ben spent the next few days masterminding his approach and researching any student he found familiar on the school's web page. He knew the day, the place, and the time, and that should have been enough, but something irked him about not being able to put a tracker on the assailants. For the first time, he couldn't pinpoint them, couldn't spot them out or feel what they had been feeling. He knew he was still going into this blindly, which frightened him more than anything.

* * *

Calvin and Travis met after school every day by the old shed. They were still firing pistols but graduated to a pair of modified hunting rifles Travis had found when breaking into a pathetically locked safe under his brother's bed. With those came a bounty of ammunition. Cans and bottles were no longer the targets. Now they had melons, cantaloupes and watermelons, pineapples as well. Travis had rigged a clothesline of galvanized cable reel over the shed's dual sliding doors to hang them. He used old screws and braided fishing lines for them to swing from as moving targets roughly the size of a person's head.

Calvin struggled to keep an accurate shot. Even when he held out the pistol and fired, his mind was distracted, leaving one good shot to every three misses. Travis was still good but had become a fan of the modified brands. He found glee in how the shot ignited the melons into a firework explosion that splattered and thudded over the ground in a fruit salad mess. He'd call out names, aiming with intent, letting each fire crack in the air, smoking shells popping off to the side as another good piece of fruit exploded into shard fragments.

"And you are certain this is the best way to stop them?" Calvin asked as Travis reloaded for another round.

"This is the only way. You want to reach the masses. You gotta make an extreme example out of the few."

"And then what? They're not going to just let us walk away, you know. There'll be cops and SWAT teams. There'll be a lockdown."

"Dude, your mom abandoned you. Your dad is a freaking workaholic. My dad offed himself, my brother's in jail, and my mom's a drunk. We have both been bullied our entire lives. There's not a warm-blooded jury out there who would see what we've been through and find it our fault. We are poster children for the consequences of bullying and poor upbringing. No one's going to do a thing to us. Hell, we'll probably get free therapy and a few talk shows outta this. Just not before we get the punks on my list," Travis said, pressing in the last shell.

"What list?" Calvin asked.

Travis reached deep into his back pocket, fished out a folded piece of notebook paper, and slapped it into Calvin's hand. "Read it," he said.

Calvin opened it up. The corners of the paper flapped in the wind. His eyes became squinty as he read over the names. "Dude, this is a pretty long list," he said.

"There's a lot of people who have done us wrong." Travis aimed.

Calvin read down the list. "Miss Hawthorne? You have a teacher on the list?"

Travis fired, exterminating a delicious cantaloupe. "Boogieman's grandma needs to go. We will be doing all future students a favor." He chambered the next round and aimed. "Dude, you gotta try this thing."

Calvin folded the paper closed. "I'm not sure about this. I was thinking like two or three of the nastiest guys. You have, like, twenty almost."

"Seriously, you are worrying too much. Look, it will be easy. We'll skip homeroom by hiding out by the old lockers, right? Once the rent-a-cops bolt, we'll make our way to the other end of the school and wait for the bell to ring. Then I'll go after the people on my list, and you go after the bastards on yours. It will be quick."

"I still don't see how you're going to get the guns onto school grounds," Calvin said.

"I told you I have that part covered," Travis answered and fired, blasting a pineapple into chunks of yellow confetti.

"But we'll be locked up in the school? We won't be able to get in or out. Hell, we couldn't escape if we wanted to."

"So, you wait by the front gate and surrender as soon as the fuzz arrives."

"And then we go to jail for the rest of our lives?"

"Cal, think about it. We are already in prison. All you would do is swap one cell for another and take down a few pieces of trash in the process. Seriously, dude, don't be such a coward." He chambered and aimed.

That's right, Cal, you hear that? Even your friend thinks you're a coward. Pathetic and a coward, the old voice called as it came back, crawling out of the sewer of the back of his head. *You won't pull the trigger on yourself, don't have the guts to do it on those you let push you around. You really are pathetic. At least your boy has the* cajones *to do what must be done. What do you have—a busted jaw and a broken family? Good for you.*

Think about it, Cal. Don't you want to stand up for yourself? Don't you want to give your old man the satisfaction of knowing that his boy finally said, "Enough with the crap! I'm not going to take it anymore!" Sure, he might be troubled at first, but he'd be proud to call you son in the end.

"What if I don't want to surrender?" Calvin asked, seriously grim.

Travis took his sight off the target. He turned back and gave Cal a devilishly appeased look. "I'm not planning to," he said.

Thatta boy, Cal.

* * *

The waiting room was packed that Friday with a rather healthy-looking bunch. Ben sat patiently and quietly, hands clasped over his knees as Mrs. Nelson thumbed over an old gossip rag in the seat next to him. She was persistent in coming along to ask the question he might have not thought to ask, or be too out of sorts to remember, or just not care.

After forty-five minutes of glaring over a muted CNN program, Ben finally heard his name called from an open door. He stood, Mrs. Nelson, dropping the magazine on the tabletop following suit, and walked past the onlookers of patients, back with the nurse into a secluded room. All the usual things were checked—height, weight, blood pressure. One nurse came in and drained him of a few vials of blood, which made him queasy for a spell but subsided once left bandaged up.

Time passed, and a knock at the door was immediately followed by a heavyset doctor with shoulder-length hair, no bangs, and a gentle smile. She held a laptop and clipboard in her arms, just like Dr. Wells had but thinned out, covering the embroidered name on her jacket until it was placed on the half table, half sink. In ways, she looked no different from how he remembered her last. In other ways, she had an age of accomplishment marking her face and highlighting strands of hair with just a touch of gray.

"Mr. Weaver." Her voice was bubbly. "It is so nice to meet you. I am Dr. Dupree." She offered a handshake to Ben, which he took, then another to Mrs. Nelson. "And you are?"

"Peggy Nelson. It is a privilege to meet you, Dr. Dupree," Mrs. Nelson said as she shook her hand.

Dr. Dupree gave a heartfelt look bordering what might be seen as a playful frown. "Aww, well, aren't you sweet. Thank you." The doctor sat, surveying Ben with an intense glare. "You have a familiar look to you. Very handsome, you know that?"

"I get that from time to time," Ben acknowledged as she finished her brief assessment of him with a clearing of her throat.

The doctor stepped back and had a seat on her stool. "Where to begin, where-to-be-gin," she started saying, leading into a single-breath hum. "Mr. Weaver—"

"Call me Ben, please," he said.

"Okay, Ben. Ben, I received your records from Dr. Wells on Tuesday, and I've got to say you are a medical anomaly. Parts of your brain are functioning in ways I have never seen in all my years of practice or in any medical journal. This … mass you have shows signs of some hybrid tumor or parasite that doesn't only seem to be feeding off you. Instead, it's enhancing certain brain functions, which makes absolutely no sense to me. But here's where I scratch my head most …"

The doctor reached out for her laptop and opened a file titled Weaver Case, popping up a clip of something on pause.

"Ben, this was recorded from your scans in Denver." She hit play. "The mass in your brain is expanding but not growing. It's like it's not there one minute, and then it's there the next. Do you understand what I'm saying?"

Ben said nothing as he watched blotches of black mass pop up over his brain on the screen.

"No," Mrs. Nelson said. "I'm sorry, you'll have to explain it to me."

"Let me see if I can put it a different way," the doctor said, shutting down her laptop as Ben's eyes blinked away from the screen. "When dealing with a tumor, we can tell if it's benign or aggressive based on how it's progressing. How it grows. We can measure that progress, track its direction, where it's spreading to, and that will give us a pretty good understanding of how to treat it and the risk of its progression. In Ben's case, we get none of that. It's almost as if the mass is simply willing it to be bigger and," she snapped her finger, "suddenly it is. It gives no sign of direction and no distinct functionality. I'd almost like to say it is more becoming you than living off you."

"Until it, what—takes over his whole brain?" Mrs. Nelson asked.

"We don't know. It might stop there. It might move down the spine, over into his bones, and into his muscles' fibers. Whatever it's doing, Mr. Weaver, Ben, I will tell you this. I believe it is not trying to kill you. What I believe it is doing is trying to possess you, making your body its own."

"So, what do you need from me?" Ben asked.

"I would like some tissue samples to study, get a fresh MRI and see what has changed over the last several days."

Ben didn't refuse. "Okay."

"Very good." Dr. Dupree opened her clipboard, withdrew a pen, and started to write something down. She stopped abruptly. "Mr. Weaver—Ben …" She paused as if uncertain about speaking what she wanted to say. "Sorry. Do you have any idea as to how you may have obtained this mass in your head?"

Without hesitation, Ben answered, "Yes. I do."

Mrs. Nelson's face shot over to Ben. Her eyes became wide and crazed white with apprehension.

Dr. Dupree dropped her pen and looked sluggishly up from her clipboard. "Really? And how was that?"

"I got it from a boy in a house in Westwood. He was sick and dying, and I took it from him."

The doctor's face messed up, blotched in confusion as she placed the clipboard back on the table.

"Don't." Mrs. Nelson gasped at Ben. She placed a hand over his and gripped it as a mother would to an overly blunt child.

Ben turned to Mrs. Nelson. "It's okay," he said.

"I'm sorry, but you will have to be more specific than that. If this child was ill, how were you able to take it from him?"

Ben looked at the doctor and said, "Pretty much the same way I took it from you."

Dupree froze. She saw it. It was in his eyes, the way they saw through her, into her. It was in that look he gave. The look of hope. The look of affection. The look of possibility. The look of love. It had been there the whole time—sitting in front of her. It was like he wore a mask and suddenly pulled it off with a jarring surprise.

"You …" She pointed. She paused. She gulped. "You're that boy I ran into all those years ago. Striped shirt and overalls and that ball." Her breathing grew wispy and thick. "You wanted to play."

"That's right, Veronica Dupree."

Ben looked up at her, not as the man he was but as the child he had been all those years ago. And she saw him as that. Just as young. Just as full of spirit and gentleness. It ached to see that as she blossomed into becoming the woman she now was. And now, this beautiful person who saved her had been filled with the vile possession of a sickening mass. She wanted to cry. She desired to hug him, to hug him as he did for her, and take it all away. But that was not her gift or her curse. It was his.

She bolstered herself and choked back her tears. "Well, Ben Weaver, it has been a pleasure seeing you again. Let's get a sample and an MRI, and we will go from there." And with that, she walked out the door.

Dr. Dupree unlocked the door to her office and took a seat behind her desk, dropping Ben's file over the blanket of papers already set out for the day. She reclined back, wiping her face with both hands, from nose to temples, trying to fight the tears that welled up from her soul. Each breath drawn escaped her before she could fill her lungs. She couldn't hold them back, not anymore. Suddenly, she dropped her head forward and wept.

* * *

It was a good Saturday—a lazy day spent with the Nelson family, swimming and barbequing in the backyard. And it was the perfect day for that—the temperature in the eighties, sunny with a subtle breeze. The pool was perfectly chilled to the degree of refreshing and no colder. Between swim races and diving competitions, the family organized a two-on-three water volleyball match, with Ben and the kids on one side and the parents on the other. Not a word was spoken of the doctor's visit. Nothing was said of the mass in Ben's head. And no mention was made of what would come about on Tuesday of the following week. It was a Saturday of no worries and all pleasure.

During a brief intermission between grilled hamburgers and swimming, Ben gave Jeremy a call to see how things were up there. Jeremy sounded cheerful. He spoke of his job, Danica starting her year at Northwestern, and a surprise visit he had planned to see her up there for an extended weekend. He missed his best friend but was grateful that Ben had finally opened up to him and allowed him to be involved in that part of his life.

The call ended abruptly, with Danica calling on Jeremy's other line, giving a short talk-to-you-later and then a tone. Ben was okay with it. More than okay. Jeremy knew his secret and was still alive. Not only that, but he was in love with a wonderful girl who deserved someone like him.

Ben left his phone in his room and went back outside, just as the ice cream was being served in waffle cones, their daughter's favorite tunes blaring out the living room window. It was a good Saturday.

Early the next morning, Ben dressed himself in the clothes Jeremy had bought him and attended the service at a church he hadn't been to in a while. He felt it was about time for him to straighten things up with the big man and settle his tab, in a manner of speaking.

Two Dapper Dans were waiting to greet him at the door, black suits and dark ties, giving him the sense that he was attending a wake, if not for their sustained grins. He went inside only to find the men's doppelgangers doing the same thing, in the same fashion and wearing identical suits. The only difference was they were passing out leaflets into the hands of everyone who had made their way inside. Ben plucked one the way a rooster would a seed. He could smell the fresh warmth of printed ink, the scent of old-timey perfume and parchment, while elderly women used their leaflets as fans. There was chatter in the air, none of which he could make out.

It was as if nothing had changed over the last many years. Except for the faces—some looked familiar, but most did not. The pastor had a few more grays than he remembered. A few more wrinkles as well. His tone now had a rasp, portraying years of gathering experience and knowledge. His voice made use of all its range, high and low, brightened then dimmed, raged to calm. Ben watched with hungry interest as he gave every steady eye his stern honesty before moving on to the next passage. He was a tempest of theological passion. His fist was a hammer on the podium. It was a brush in the air, painting a picture every three or four minutes as he paced back and forth to make good use of the stage.

About half an hour in, Ben felt a desire to pray. And so he prayed, just as the pastor's voice tickled his ears with a snippet of divine truth, not his own words but from a man named Paul, who also suffered in his mission. "*But God, being rich in mercy, because of the great love with which he loved us, even when we were dead in our trespasses, made us alive together with Christ—by grace you have been saved.*"

He chewed on those words for a while.

* * *

Calvin and Travis spent half of Sunday playing video games and the other half vegging on whatever they could scrounge up in Calvin's kitchen. They vomited up grievances over a countertop littered with chips, leftover pizza, and their spittle-flecked screeds of those who had caused it all. Travis decided it would be best to save the remaining ammo for when it would be most needed. He had a new list, ranking his soon-to-be victims from "most in need of a bullet to the head" to "at least they pissed their pants" on a scale of one to ten. Calvin agreed and added that he should probably let his hand rest a while before the big day.

Any second thought Calvin had was quickly extinguished by that voice in the back of his head: *You're pathetic … You're a coward.* Calvin dared to prove the voice wrong. His only regret was that his mom wouldn't be there to see the man her abandoned son had become.

With bellies full, they went back to Calvin's room and finished the day with more games, stopping once to talk to his dad and tell him that Travis would be crashing on the floor of his room for the night. Travis's mom was in no mood to have him around; he was unsure as to what that meant but damned certain it had something to do with a fresh bottle of Jack Daniels.

* * *

When Calvin got up, Travis was already gone—shoes and bag missing as well. Calvin shimmied out of bed, foot landing first in a crusty, old bowl of fruity cereal, and scurried to his closet to get dressed. He left the house with his belt unbuckled and a pastry in hand, rushing down the street for his long expedition to school.

Calvin walked into homeroom looking like dreck and was greeted by the frightful splendor of Travis's smile. It was the same one he gave when he had bested Calvin and was waiting tranquilly at his desk. As he walked to his seat, his eyes were stapled to his mischievous friend. "Thanks for letting me know you were bolting," he said, flippantly agitated. Then he turned and faced the front, dropping his backpack under his chair and digging for a pencil and notebook.

Travis leaned over his desk and whispered in Calvin's ear. "I'm sorry, but I had to take care of something this morning. But I have a surprise for you at lunch," he said and then sat back in his seat.

Calvin turned and looked back right as the substitute made his opening address to the class. Travis maintained his bested smile.

Hours, teachers, and schoolwork passed by as Calvin felt the sting of nervous anticipation poking at his insides. It swelled, puncturing every organ inside his trepid body. He could only fathom what his friend might consider a surprise at this point, riffling over gifts the mafia might send to someone they found pleasure in. It could be the hand of an enemy, maybe? Or perhaps a complete set of teeth and matching tongue from someone who called him names? The grotesque possibilities were endless.

Calvin shot out of class like a bottle rocket, impatient to meet Travis by the abandoned lockers. He practically ripped the caution tape from its ends as he haphazardly skated under the taped line and cut around the flanking wall of bricks and metal. Somehow, Travis was already there. His smile settled into an arced grin that mimicked the subtle curve of his chin. He had been waiting, leaning coolly against the inner corner of lockers. His arms crossed over his chest, legs crossed at the ankles, head veering downward, resembling one of those old cowboys pictured in a Marlboro ad.

"Dude, you couldn't have waited, like, five seconds?" Calvin said, huffing with a much more leisurely stride toward his friend.

"Don't be so slow," Travis said, head tilted. Before Calvin could take another step, Travis held up his hand, palm facing out, to stop Calvin from coming farther.

"What?" Calvin questioned.

"I did it," Travis boasted. "This morning before anyone got here, just to see what would happen. Nothing, just as I thought."

"What the hell are you talking about?" Calvin asked.

"I'm talking about this." Travis reached to the side of him and pulled up the handle to one of the lockers, one that looked as if one side had been beaten to death by a hammer. Giving it a firm pull, he got the door to swing open. It pounced off the one next to it with a resounding clank, loud enough to make even Travis shudder. He then stepped in closer, enough to see the inner wall that now held a small black bag with two of his brother's guns.

"Are you flipping crazy!" Calvin gasped. His eyes were whitened in various shades of shock and dread. "Do you know what will happen if someone finds these?"

"That's just it," Travis answered, raising his voice to the level of excitement. "They didn't. It was exactly like I knew it would be. They sniff out the lockers in use but not the ones over here. Heck, they didn't even come close. Besides, who would they pin it on if they did find them? They're stolen guns, unregistered, in lockers no one has used in years. It's only a shame that there wasn't enough room for the rifles," he added.

Hearing this gave Calvin a chance to breathe. He hated those things. They made him feel like he would be game-hunting people. Only the air was slightly thinner than he hoped for. "So, what do we do now? I mean, if we are going to go through with the plan, when are we thinking?"

"Tomorrow."

"Tomorrow?"

"That's right. Tomorrow," Travis confirmed. "Rumor going around is that Miss Hawthorne will be back then. We'll skip out on first period, wait for Johnny Law to leave, and then take the guns to the other side of the school while the principal makes her morning announcements. That way, she won't catch us cutting across the yard. From there, we will make our way to the far gate, where no one will see us when they open the doors after the bell rings. We'll have to make sure to keep low. That way, no one spots us outside the windows. Once that happens, and the halls are crowded with people …" Travis turned his fingers into a gun and closed an eye. His finger quickly notched up just as he made a *puchooing* sound. "Fish in a barrel, my friend."

"And if someone decides to raid the lockers in the meantime? Like, say, a janitor perhaps? And then, when we get here, we find the boys in blue waiting for us?"

Travis smirked. "I got that covered too." Calvin watched as Travis reached deep into the front pouch of his backpack and fished out a shiny new combination lock. It was heavy-duty, the kind they used at construction sites to keep the heavy equipment safe. He pierced it through the hole in the bottom of the handle and clicked it shut. "Now, all we have to do is make it through one more day," Travis said.

"Oh, and one other thing." Calvin held his sight on the lock as Travis asked, "You wouldn't mind if I stayed the night at your house again, would you? My mom hasn't been feeling well, and it's getting kinda creepy being in the house with her."

He turned to Travis. "How would you know that? You haven't been home in days."

"Just let me stay, will ya? I'll run home, take care of a few last-minute things, grab a pair of my brother's hoodies, and head right over. It'll be quick. Hell, I could even sneak through your window. Your dad will never know. For real, think about it. This could be the last night we get to hang out together," Travis said with a fisting nudge into Cal's chest.

Calvin agreed.

* * *

Ben's phone rang louder on that call than any other he'd had before. It was as if the phone knew who it was and the importance of the call. He rushed into his room, silencing the TV, and cast the remote onto the couch. He answered.

"Hello, Ben," the light yet downtrodden voice said. "This is Veronica, er … Dr. Dupree. Do you have a minute to spare?" He did for her. "I have been going over your scans and … well … I am sorry, but I found no way to get a tissue sample from you. Whatever this is has since threaded itself past the lobes and has barbed every piece of itself deep into the thalamus in such a way that any attempt to separate a section from your brain would most likely cause catastrophic damage. I don't know. It's as if it has become, in a way, defensive.

"Unfortunately, we also found that it has made similar progress on its way past your cerebellum, consuming the pons, and has taken over your medulla. This probably doesn't mean much to you, but it causes me to believe what I feared most. That it will soon be tracing down your spinal cord. Do you understand what I am telling you, Ben? This thing is not stopping within your brain. At its current measure of progress, I can estimate that within days it will have reached the end of your spine and have started to make its way into your limbs, possibly your organs. It is simply moving too fast for us to try and stop it."

"I understand" was Ben's only reply.

"I am sorry. I wish there was something more we could do. Something more I can do. I know I owe you—"

"Nothing," he interrupted. "You owe me nothing. Thank you for all you've done, Dr. Dupree. You have become a wonderful person. Keep up the good work, okay?"

"Yeah," she said. Ben could hear her heart breaking in her feeble response. He only wished he could be there to give her one last hug. To let her know it was okay. That he'd be okay.

As the phone call ended, another verse popped into Ben's mind. It was one most people would never have the unfortunate chance to put into practice. *"Greater love has no man than this, that he lay down his life for his friends."* He didn't know why, but it gave him peace. He couldn't help but think about the man who said those words before reaching out his hands and willfully taking all the pain, hopelessness, and sin of the world on his shoulders. Praying to his father as he drew his last suffocating breath alone on a meager piece of wood. It made Ben not feel so alone on his journey, no matter where this road led him.

* * *

Ben went out that night, noticing that the stars were a notch dimmer than he remembered them, even for Los Angeles standards. He made a quick stop by the local Walmart. He picked up a long, black duffel bag, a Maglite and batteries, and a pair of bolt cutters. He then headed to Green Valley Junior High. Ben parked along the far side of the school, out along the gate where all he could see were conjoined baseball fields and the sliver of portable buildings arising from the knolls.

The houses surrounding the other end of the street had all gone to bed under the night lights of streetlamps. Ben took a minute to pray in the confines of his truck. He asked for strength. He asked for a chance to let this pass him. But most of all, he asked for God's will to be done, just as the man before him had probably done on a night similar to the one he found himself currently in.

He proceeded to step out of the truck, duffel bag in hand, and made his way to the gate, where he took a knee and unzipped the bag. One hand pulled out a pair of bolt cutters and used them to bite the lowest strand of the gate. One after the other, he made its way up, snipping the strands apart, popping each diamond link until there was a break high enough and long enough for him to slip between.

In the distant night, the chirping of crickets called out their persistent warning of his intrusion from the weald of grass, falling silent only at the cusp of being trampled on. A dog's aggressive bark had sent rippling its sharp, punishing bite in the settled air to stir its own brand of agitation at nothing in particular. However, that soon went.

Ben scudded across the black hairs of grass, frosted in sprinkler water and the moon's glow. The bolt cutter swung with violence back and forth from within the long black duffel bag. It flounced at his side with the occasional caning to the back and side of his leg, connecting iron to bone with brutal force. "First things first," he said, sprinting across the field in a limping stride. "Got to find the guns and get rid of them. Eliminate the cause of the threat. Then tomorrow, I can deal with the boys."

He continued to dash until the grass cut to the firm pavement, then took a few minutes to catch his breath and address his throbbing leg. He flipped the bag to the other side and continued, cutting between buildings and turning down the long main hall that would lead him straight to the cavern of lockers. He moved briskly, listening to the step-clicking echo that had arisen from his feet. Step-click, step-click, the night adding to its unsettling familiarity.

Finally, Ben reached the complex that had been masked off and boarded. It had been abandoned for so long even the moon kept away from its haunting presence. He dropped the bag, unzipped it again, and pulled out the Maglite. He proceeded under the caution tape, this time giving no care to its feel, and turned into the cavern of lockers. Two up, ten across on each side—double that along the inner wall—led to eighty lockers in all. Ben clicked off the light. He closed his eyes and reached out to the lockers. Hollowed out metal. Small vent slits at the top. It all came back as if he were still in the vision. He felt around, looking for something familiar, a sticker or a chip of a—.

He opened his eyes. One locker with a slanted door, looking as if hammered in on one side, and a shiny new combination lock sat in front of him. He put back the light and drew out the bolt cutters. Its sharp jaw bit down on the u bend of the lock, sinking iron into metal, teeth into bone. Ben squeezed and shuddered to break the arching bolt. Suddenly, the bolt snapped with a heavy satisfactory clank, and the rest dangled limply. Ben pulled it out of the handle most hastily and lifted the handle. With a firm tug, the door blasted open, yet this time he kept hold of it to prevent it from smashing against another locker. He dropped the lock in his bag, did the same with the bolt cutter, and one last time brought out the Maglite.

There was no need to feel around this time. They were all there, as vivid to his eyes as if being seen in the bright afternoon sun. Two laid out in unison, snuggled in a thin plastic bag with the barrels eyeing him dead-on. Ben felt it was safe to assume both were fully loaded and ready for a busy Tuesday morning. He took the pistols out, one at a time, handling them with care as he assiduously placed them in the long black bag, then zipped it up.

The walk back to his truck felt twice as long, gliding his feet over the concrete like he had been walking on thin ice, fearful that one might discharge at any awkward motion. By the time he reached his truck, he had found his assiduous care well worth it. He even took heed to ensure that the guns never faced a house. He shimmied between the split strands of the gate first, then dragged the bag through. He placed them in the passenger seat of his truck. The barrels faced toward the rear.

He seat-belted the bag in and took a long, long drive to find a police station where he could drop them off at the front door, quickly and discretely, no questions asked. From there, he swung into a drive-through to take a small victory meal home. A hamburger, fries, and a large Mr. Pibb were the least he deserved for a job well done.

Less than half of his meal made it unscathed across his front door. He puttered out on the couch, dropping keys and his wallet and cell phone over the floor before flipping on the tube and finding something funny to zone out and eat in front of. He reached into the brown paper bag, dug out a handful of fries, and shoved them barbarically into his mouth. He chewed slowly, eyes weighing heavy with something more than just tiredness. He never expected to crash out there. He had every intention of getting a good night's rest in his bed. But some things happen, nonetheless. And as he chewed slower and slower, his eyes grew heavier and heavier until his head rolled back over the couch, leaving a pocket of half-consumed fries in the corner of his mouth and a small stream of black, oily goop trickling out of his nose and down his face.

* * *

The bell sounded off. The doors opened, unleashing a current of footsteps and clamoring voices.

Blat!

The first one cracked in the air. There was screaming.

Blat, blat!

Another two were fired. Then came the stampede of frightened students. Then came the harsh bellows and bloodcurdling shrieks of the hunted, trying to escape the one place they should have felt safe.

Blat, blat!

Victims had already found their place on the ground. Their bodies grew cold. Their blood gushing warm until that last breath dwindled from their lips out in the air.

Ben could see it, all of it. There was no more ominous darkness to navigate. No more obscure balls of light wrapped in smoke. No mist or fog or unseen materials to be celebrated over and interpreted. There was flesh and blood, lockers and hallways, concrete and bricks, and sunlight.

Ben went for the locker and threw it open. Empty, just as he had left it. He looked back as the stampede of children started to run across his hall corridor. He saw the tears and sallow faces blotched in splatters of foreign blood, pale in horror, running for their lives. He walked out among them, watching as they scaled the fence that—built to protect—now became an obstruction to their survival.

More gunfire caught Ben's attention as he turned and ran against the exfiltration of the tide. Cutting through the sharp cry of the alarm bell and the many faces of students fleeing for safety in any possible direction, he was like a ghost, undeterred by the elemental differences between the vision and him. As he reached a closed-in section, he witnessed a clog of teenagers pushing and shoving at those in front, forcing the slower out of the way, struggling to keep a potent flow in the funneling hall.

Ben brushed past them with as much resistance as a gust of wind, just in time to see an elderly teacher ambling toward him. Her ankles bent unstably over her pumps as she wheezed thin, senescent gasps down the open hall in terrified haste. She had already appeared to be moments away from natural death, a moldy, pruned face spritzed in beads of terrified perspiration. Her skeletal figure hardly showed any form under her attire, even with her chest pumping adrenaline to keep her moving.

"Oh, Miss Hawthorne," he called out to her with the voice of the one previously lit in red. He knew the name now. Travis.

Blat!

Before she could turn the corner and head out into the open yard, her left leg burst open in a splatter of red. She let out a broken squeal as the agony of a bullet pierced the rigid, twiggy hew of her calf and sent her tumbling to the ground. She went into a slither, trying to escape their line of sight by cutting in front of a building. Every second came with a plea for God to save her. Every movement forward left a trail of blood streaming out of her leg.

Two boys. One bearing the undaunted face of a devil, while the other appeared angry yet held a fright not too far off from the rest of his peers. Both strolled the open hall behind her, allowing Ben to finally put a face to the voices in the clarity of morning light. He studied them as they came in closer, memorizing the details of their faces and distinguishable markings. It was safe to assume that the frightened one was Cal. They treated the bodies left in their murderous wake as if they were everyday pieces of litter to be kicked at or ignored. Ben saw the guns being swung nonchalantly at their side as the devilish one practically skipped up behind Miss Hawthorne. They were different from the ones he had taken from the locker. Much different.

As Miss Hawthorne made a futile effort to escape their tirade, they mocked and toyed with her like a cat would to its mousey little victim. Ben had come to the gut-bombed epiphany that nothing had changed. He realized that what he was seeing was that his late-night break-in at the school hadn't altered the outcome in the least. Even by stealing their arsenal from the locker, they could still accomplish what they set out to do. His effort hadn't even seemed to recess the time of their actions or make them have a second thought—despite knowing that someone found out they had stashed guns in that locker.

One barrel rested at the back of her silver head. Smoking metal pushed down into her skull, hard enough to force her nose to bend to the pavement. The sound of a pulsating heartbeat started to rise out of obscurity. The atmosphere felt chilly and hot at the same time. Ben could feel his actual body collapsing into a panic attack as she cried. She begged. She pleaded. Then suddenly—

Blat!

That was it. Miss Hawthorne was no more.

SEVENTEEN

Travis snuck through the window, as he had planned, and hung back in Calvin's room as Cal walked into the living room to meet his dad at the door. The old man was determined to get off his black work sneakers, working on unknotting a pair of laces. Calvin could see the exhaustion in the pink circling his beady eyes. Calvin waited patiently as his dad uttered curses under his breath at the puzzle of undoing a double knot. It wasn't long before he was barefoot, walking into the room and giving his son a light pat on the shoulder, asking about his day.

"All right," Calvin replied, following the weary man into the kitchen as he unbuckled his pants and began pulling sections of his shirt out for some air. Cal watched him duck his head into the fridge, searching for whatever leftovers might still be edible. "I was wondering if we could talk for a little bit."

His dad returned from the fridge with a can of soda and a Tupperware container holding something that looked like brains. Last week's lasagna was all Cal could assume. His old man's eye contact didn't make it to his son as he curtailed around his son to the other side of the kitchen.

"Augh, kiddo, can we do it later?" He moaned as he slid the Tupperware into the microwave and pressed a few overly used buttons. "It has been one hell of a day and … I don't," he cracked open the can of soda and chugged its first sharp drink, then continued, "I don't have the brain power to hold a conversation right now. Why don't you go play with your game thing in your room or give Travis a call or something? I'm sure he'd love to chat with you."

Calvin nodded with the bitter flavor of disappointment, one he'd tasted far too many times, more frequently since his mom left. Cal turned and returned to his room, where Travis was.

* * *

The black, oily substance had smeared all over his face and arms. His head beat like a bad hangover after a long night of barhopping. The world held a blur in Ben's sight as he opened and closed his eyes several times to wipe them clean. The morning was still early and had only broken into a magenta sea of clouds over a dull powder sky. He rolled off the couch, catching himself with his feet and hands. Once on his feet, he shook clarity into his head and began scanning the carpet for his shoes, wallet, and keys.

Ben gathered his belongings and shoved them all into his pockets. He then crossed the room to his desk. He pulled out a pen and a small yellow Post-it, jotting down fourteen words over three lines for whatever member of the Nelson family would stumble across it:

Call police.
Shooting at Green Valley Jr. High
And if anything happens, wear white.

He dropped the pen and tore the Post-it from the top of the stack. Ben darted out of the guesthouse, slapping the note outside his door on his way to his truck.

* * *

Calvin and Travis walked to school together this time, uttering hardly a word on the long walk there. Cal couldn't help thinking that they were only hours away from either being locked up for the rest of their merciless lives or shot dead in a salvo of gunfire.

They had come dressed to match, unobtrusive, in black hooded sweatshirts that held the unique aroma of whiskey and weed, layered on top of each other and even more potent from over a year of basting in

Travis's brother's closet. It was an attire that would be too warm for the forecasted afternoon but acceptable for such a cool morning. They also had on crisp pairs of dark, loose jeans. They carried their backpacks as a disguise, knowing there wasn't a chance in hell that a single book they were carrying would be cracked open even for a second.

Calvin's hands knuckled in the front pockets of his sweatshirt as the two walked side by side down that neighborhood sidewalk they had grown accustomed to so quickly. It was always peaceful that way, always alone. They only needed to endure the occasional nipping bark of some overly frisky dog tromping up and down a linked fence around a nearby yard and the growling of a few distance lawn mowers. It was a small price to pay for minor traffic and even fewer pedestrians.

Calvin's mind aired an endless loop of how this would all play out. He saw his mother, a jaw-dropped mess, slopping coffee from an industrial pot over her customers. The guilt would overflow her insides and spill out in tears as she watched the son she had abandoned return fire on the SWAT team sent in to stop him. Maybe she'd wish she was there to stop him. It would be like her to still think she could control him with her shallow motherly love. She would fall on her knees, staring down the barrel at the face of his last two rounds, begging, pleading for him to stop, and finally tell him she loved him. But it would be too late for such a pitiful effort.

He then wondered if his dad would be called to the scene. Would he be one of the officers waiting with his gun drawn behind the shield of his cruiser, as line after line of students was rushed out of the school? Would he be ushering the survivors, dressed in military-grade armor? Suddenly, there would be a slew of gunfire. Like most other officers waiting outside the school grounds, he would flinch and shudder for a hiccup of a second before rushing in. And, of course, he would be too late, finding the perps lying dead on the ground, blood soaked and netted with bullet wounds. "Holier than a saint, redder than the devil," an officer might say as his dad walked up and saw the lifeless face of his son looking smudgy and bloated back at him. *Too late for that conversation now, Dad*, his last expression would say, face up off the floor, resting in a pool of the crimson answer.

As the two came along the back side of the school, Travis hopped into a jog, moving briskly ahead of Calvin.

"Dude, we totally lucked out," Travis said, pulling a loose portion of the fence surrounding a field. "You remember seeing a hole in the gate here?" he asked. Calvin nodded. "Looks like someone's looking out for us," he said and widened the hole until it made a small, triangular shape big enough for a body to fit through.

Cal handed his bag off to Travis, squatted, and inched his way through the newly discovered opening. He reached back to pull his backpack through, then did the same with Travis's. Trave went through next, side-sliding one leg, ducking under, and then pulling in his other leg. It was easy.

They walked toward the portable buildings rising out of the knolls. Behind them sat the boarded-up complex and, behind that, the abandoned lockers. Within one of those lockers sat two fully loaded solutions to all their problems, waiting for their opportunity to finally collect their dues.

* * *

Ben pulled into one of the parking spots with a teeth-grinding squeal, praying that one of the Nelsons had already found his note and called the authorities. He jumped out of the truck, paying no attention to the cold glares of students and parents whose ears were recovering from his truck's lack of noise etiquette. He managed his way between the accumulating students currently funneling into the school. Two guards stood on each side of the entryway, one outside and the other just beyond the threshold. He picked the closest one to plead his case to let him inside or, at least, take caution and search for Travis and Calvin before it was too late.

The guard eyed him suspiciously. From a distance, he looked like the one on duty the last time he was there. Up close, however, this man was a weight class too thin and close to a decade older. The guard's hand rested on his stun gun, just as the other one had done before. Only this one seemed to have an itch to use it.

"Can I help you, sir?" the guard said over the heads of a dozen or so kids walking past him and into the school.

"Yes, you can. I need to speak with you about a situation."

The guard's thumb dug under the button of his holster. His eyes thinned into narrow slivers of black, blue, and white. "What kind of situation are we talking about exactly?"

"Do you mind if we talk away from the students?" Ben's sight kept a firm attachment to the stun gun. At first, he hoped he'd spot Calvin or Travis to confront them before they entered the school. But now, seeing that a sporting goods store stun gun was all they had as a line of defense, he was worried that the school's line of defense was well outgunned.

The guard peered through the metal detector at his partner. "Hey, Dekker," he called. The other guard looked back. "Give me a sec to chat with this guy, will ya." The other guard nodded and then stepped aside as Ben requested. "All right, guy. Follow me." Ben followed the guard to a corner of the school wall where huge blocks of A/C units hummed loudly enough to keep a guy from hearing his own thoughts. The guard held his hand floating over his stun gun as he turned to face Ben. "All right then, what seems to be the problem?"

Ben's eyes circled around with a taste of paranoia. "There are two students here that are planning to do something really, really bad today. They intend to hurt people, and if they're not stopped, I'm afraid some might die."

"Uh-huh." The guard breathed long. "And how would you know this?"

"I saw them," Ben said, omitting the part about it being in a vision. He also found it unnecessary to reveal that he cut a hole in the gate around the back and snuck into the school to try to prevent it. "They have guns. I don't know how many. But I know they have every intention to use them."

"Well, that would be quite a feat, seeing as how the only way to get into the school is by walking past two armed guards and a metal detector." Ben fell silent, weighing how he wanted to respond. The guard continued, "Do you know the names of these suspects you are claiming have these plans?"

Ben looked dazed and glassy-eyed. For some reason, he struggled to collect himself. "One's name is Cal. I don't know the last name, but I believe Cal will look banged up pretty well."

The guard reached out to his partner over his radio. "Hey, Dekker, you, uh, see two kids walking in together that might look to be wanting to hurt some people? One of them will probably have a black eye or some shit like that. Over."

"You got names? Over."

"Yeah, we got one. The kid goes by the name of Cal. Over."

"Cal? I know a Calvin. He has a friend that calls him Cal. He's Gardner's kid, the one that was farting around in the bathroom and got himself beat up something fierce. You thinking it's him?"

The guard's eyes questioned Ben. Ben nodded. "Sounds like it. Keep an eye out, will ya? For him and his compadre. I think they might try to sneak around us today. Over."

"I certainly haven't seen him today. The kid's face is pretty hard to miss these days. But I'll be looking. Over."

"Thanks, boss. Oh, and if you do see 'em, send them my way. I need to ask them a couple of questions. That's all. Over."

"Ten-four."

The guard focused on Ben. "Until the kid shows up, there isn't much more we can do. We'll keep an eye out."

Ben thanked the guard and walked back over to his truck. He leaned against the passenger door for a spell, then longer, causing a few disdainful glares from worried parents. But he couldn't walk away. Not yet. He waited. And while he waited, he watched, all the way until the last kid scurried into the school. Then he watched as the guards locked the gate behind them and headed off to do their other work for the day, whatever that might be.

Ben walked around the truck and crawled inside. He took the wheel, twisting and tightening his grip until his insecurity banged out with his hand smacking the wheel. Frustrated, he turned the key. The shifter ground it into reverse and backed out onto the street until it squealed to a dramatic stop. Ben shifted into drive. His stomach bulged with a nauseating dose of uncertainty. His throat swelled with the ingredients of a regretful decision as he decided to take the back way home this time, giving him a few extra stops to reconsider the situation. He made a left, then another left, heading to the street he had parked along the night before. His peripheral eyes hooked to the school from the moment he left the parking lot to the time he coasted along the far-end field.

Ben yanked the wheel, cutting across the other lane before his foot smashed down on the brakes. One tire popped the curb, taking a fraction of air before bucking in the thin patch of grass that separated the walkway from the curb. He saw it. The thing he had created. His way into the school. That cut in the chain-link fence he had made, still holding its wound, had been opened wide.

* * *

They took to the hall. Travis and Calvin rounded the back corner toward the lockers, blending in with the crowd. They looked at the backs of a thousand student bodies as they moved in front of them, ants traipsing toward their sole purpose in life. At the bell's ring, as the rest of the students scampered to get to their homerooms, Calvin and Travis ducked into the restroom and only reemerged when everything became utterly silent. They rushed hastily to the cavern of abandoned lockers, glancing in every direction and stopping at every turn in the hall. When they identified the two guards rounding a corner, they began to sprint, hunched over, ducking behind trash cans and poles and anything else that might conceal them.

Travis froze first, and Cal stopped a hair shy of colliding with his backpack. It was the beat-up locker, the one he had safely locked up. It wasn't locked up anymore. In fact, there was no combination lock in sight. Travis rushed to grab the handle and pry the locker open.

Panic leapt to Travis's elongated face. "Shit, shit, shit …" He began to curse unendingly.

Calvin looked in and saw an empty locker. "We're dead." He ran his hands down his face and began pacing. "We are so freaking dead. Somebody knows. They've told. And now we are dead and going to prison with nothing to show for it."

Travis slammed the locker shut, exercising his right to curse at the world. He dropped his bag on the floor, ripped apart the zipper, and drove both of his hands in together. "That's it! They all need to go," he said. "Every stinking one of them. We are in a school overtaken by rats, and we alone are the exterminators." He pulled a pair of sleek matte-gray guns, locked and loaded with fresh magazines, ready to go.

"What are those?" Calvin asked, eyes protruding from his worried face.

"They are Berettas. Badass, right?"

"Where did you get them?" Calvin asked.

"What does it matter?" Travis replied.

"It matters because they look like my dad's. The ones he keeps in his nightstand drawer."

Travis didn't respond.

"Travis! Those are registered, you ass wipe!"

Travis charged at Cal and then stopped abruptly, nose to nose. Both guns lay in the crevice of their chests, facing up, crossing the sides of their jaw. "You think it's going to make any difference once the bullets go flying? It doesn't matter how we get the job done or by what means. What matters is we do it."

Calvin's lips bit down thin. He stared his friend down, eyes beady and as sharp as knives, gripping one of the guns, and taking it as his own.

"That's my boy," Travis said. "Now let's get this done."

* * *

Ben launched out of the vehicle and dove under the gate. The first bell became damp as it sailed across the field and under the gate to whisper in his ears. He scurried under the gate, leaped to his feet, and went off sprinting, crossing an open field to a school that looked deserted. As he drew closer, he noticed that there was not a student in sight. The first period had already begun.

As he came to the condemned building, he thought hard about how he would get to them without being seen and hopefully catch them by surprise. He moved quickly but with a sidestepped prowl, not wanting to be heard or seen. He passed the first cavern of lockers, then the second, swallowing his breath and holding it tightly within his gut. He bit down on his lip, said a brief and honest prayer, and stepped around the wall of lockers.

They weren't there.

* * *

They were approaching the last row of classrooms at the end of the main hall. Soon they would make their final turn and duck across the broad strand of windows, just as they had planned. The morning announcements had ended, meaning Principal Holder would soon be making her rounds. Even armed, they had a respectful fear of her, so much that if she said, "Drop the guns," Calvin was confident that he would do it.

They took to the corner of the building and began to squat-walk past the first classroom. No problem. They passed the second with ease as well. By the end of the third room, their legs began to feel the discomfort of holding a sustained flexion, yet they still had one more to go. Halfway across the fourth room, two sets of legs began to quiver. The tops of their heads started to poke dangerously close to the window. Easy-peasy was exchanged for who might break first and blow the operation.

Travis crossed first and wasted no time stretching the tightening pain out of his legs. Calvin soon followed and did more or less the same. Both sets of eyes circled around with the taste of paranoia, taking in oxygen as if they had just finished a 5K, all the while keeping the guns concealed behind their backs, hand over hand, military style. They waited, chests pulsating, blood racing, heartbeats elevating higher and higher as they did their best to keep some degree of composure.

* * *

Ben had been practically skating down the hall at Mach speed. He knew (approximately) where the shooting would begin and had to make it there with plenty of time to try to talk them down before the next bell rang. Suddenly, the face and body of Principal Holder graced his view in close range. Never had he seen such a deer in the headlights sort of look.

He made a sudden side leap around her as she called out his name with a flustered and startled tone. Without looking back, he hollered something in the vicinity of telling her to call 911, holding onto his momentum without a trip in his step.

* * *

They waited with their backs against the wall and guns held behind them in twisted anticipation. Their eyes focused on the small square box bolted high on the wall outside one of the classrooms. They knew it was preparing to do its timely duty of sounding the end of the first period. An insuperable boost of confidence came over the two. Under a layer of nervousness, they felt godlike. It was their time to look down on a world and let it beg for their vengeful hand to show a level of mercy. They would receive none. For Cal and Travis, it was time to unleash all the power of their fury, and now there was nothing to stop that vengeance from raining down.

It feels good, doesn't it, Cal? The voice tickled inside of him. There was a pride to its timbre, one he hadn't heard before, whether inside or outside his head. *You finally have your man balls. All the power and all the choices are in your hands. You alone can give or deny mercy, spare or take a life. Now it's their turn to suffer, and they will. Oh, they will beg and cower. They will plead and snivel. Cheap tears will fall from the eyes that once looked down on you, or not at all.*

Well, let them. Let them tremble as your fingers wrap around the throat of their destiny. Let them squirm like the flee-ridden varmints they are while trying to escape the consequences of their reckless deeds. Let them feel your anger boiling over their pathetically asinine faces as you look down on them this time, casting your judgment from the snout of a cold, hard barrel. And then, as you sentence them, you drop that hammer right between their beady little eyes. Only after will they rest respect you. Only when they are good and dead will the whole world see you as a man not to be trifled with.

Calvin liked the sound of that.

* * *

Ben was only a few agonizing strides away from the last turn the main hall had to offer. His legs burned, but he hadn't slowed, only altered his poise as he came to the last cavern of lockers. Then he would tip around the corner. Then he would face them. Then …

* * *

There had to have been at least five minutes left before the next bell rang, so why were they seeing one of the doors pushing outward into the hall? It was too soon. Calvin turned to Travis. Travis looked back. Then they both watched, as still as stone, as the door was pushed fully out into the hall. It slowed, stopped, and started on its return when they found the back side of a girl with a bathroom pass standing diagonally three doors in front of them.

Calvin knew her, even without seeing her face. Her face flashed in front of him out of memory, and he saw the concerned look in her eyes. Ever since the day she asked him if he was okay after he took a thorough beating, she sat a little more closely to him in third-period geography. Occasionally, she would even slip him a note when she could tell he wasn't mentally able to comprehend that day's lesson. He didn't have the guts to talk to her much, but he grasped that her humor was puckish and subtly dry, and he liked that. He was also fond of her calling him by his full name, not Cal but Calvin, and she put her own perky twist to the sound of it.

Do not turn around. Please do not turn around, Calvin chanted in his head.

She started to walk away from them, looking down at the pass in her hands. Then she stopped. The blood drained from Calvin's face as he watched her legs turn first, the balls of her heels never leaving the ground. Her hips soon followed, then her arms and chest. And then finally, her bewildered face.

"Calvin?" The spunky flavor had dulled into a perplexed bitterness.

Travis unclasped his hand and raised his gun. Calvin froze.

The gun clicked.

"Stop!" Ben's voice shouted from down the hall.

Travis held his pose as the man simmered to a dilatory walk, quickly catching his breath. The girl turned to face him as well. Ben first noticed a couple of tears trickling down her cheeks. Travis curled his lips with rage as this man percolated into his thinning eyes and aimed again.

"Please, you don't have to do this," Ben said, taking a step forward. He did what he could to keep the attention on himself as the girl slipped swiftly back into the classroom.

"Who the hell are you?" Travis sneered.

Ben offered his hands well in the air above his head. "It doesn't matter who I am. All that matters right now is that you put the guns down."

Travis's hand followed Ben's incremental stride. "And why would we do that?"

"Because this isn't going to give you what you want."

Travis angled his gun down, angling at Ben's abdomen. "Oh really?" he cackled. "And what is it that you think we want?"

"Respect," Ben started, "and an amount of value in a shitty world. Maybe a chance to see someone act like they actually care about you. That is what you want, isn't it?"

Travis turned to Calvin, who was still resting frozen, and nudged his shoulder for him to raise his gun. He did so nervously. Finding the palms of his hands caked in sweat made it harder to keep his aim.

Travis mocked Ben's assessment. "To be respected and valued. To feel like someone cares. Blah-blah-blah. What kind of wusses do you think we are? You don't know a damn thing about us or what we want."

Calvin's eyes became squinty as he cast them out in the distance.

"I disagree. When it comes down to it, I would say, above anything, you just want to be loved. Am I right, Travis?" Ben asked. Travis didn't respond. "So does your friend Cal—or Calvin. Sorry. You prefer Calvin, don't you?"

Calvin's mouth hardly broke open before Travis said, "Don't you dare try to get into his head! I know what you're doing. You're trying to stall us until the cops arrive, but let me let you in on something. We aren't here to talk or negotiate. We are here to right the wrongs these assholes have done to us, and we're not going to let this rogue guidance counselor persuade us otherwise."

"Travis," Calvin whispered.

"You're clever, Travis, but this isn't going to go the way you expect it to," Ben said.

"Hey, Travis," Cal whispered again.

Ben continued, "I know what it's like to be a loner, trying to survive in this messed-up world, full of messed-up people doing messed-up things."

"Oh, I see. So, you want to join our little club then?" Travis spat.

"No. I want to show you that you have a choice. You're at a crossroads here, boys. And there is only one road—a different road—that will truly place you on top."

"Travis," Calvin said again.

"What, dude?" Travis replied, clearly agitated. He turned to his friend, who was pointing his gun past Ben.

"Look."

Travis looked out to see Principal Holder peeking out the side of the building with a cell phone glued to her ear. Her mouth had been rambling with urgency, as she'd hide for a spell and then reappear.

Travis flexed every muscle in his body. "You son of a—" he started to say but bit out the last word. "Look what you did now," he said to Ben.

Calvin looked at Ben, then at Travis, then back to Ben. "Travis, we don't even know this guy," he protested. "He wasn't part of the plan."

"Plans change, Cal," said Travis as he took aim and stepped closer to his target. Ben raised his hands.

"Travis, no," Calvin said. "This isn't right. None of this is right. This guy's done nothing to us."

Travis kept focus. "He ruined our plan."

"The girl ruined our plan. He showed up later," Calvin said.

Travis's eyes made a dramatic roll as he sighed. "Okay, so we shoot him first, then the girl."

"Wait!" Calvin said.

Ben pushed his sight onto Calvin. He initially seemed impenetrable, but now there was a glint of instability. "Calvin," Ben said. "And then the principal, huh, Calvin. And then Miss Hawthorne. And then some punk kids that jumped you. And then, and then … and then what? And then what, Calvin? All these people are dead. Cops outside, ready to charge in and return fire. Then you will be dead too. Parents will mourn. Flowers and candles will be spread down this hallway. Vigils with be held, but none of it will be for you. You're the ones who took the lives. So you sacrificed your own for what? A lifetime of people not remembering you but all those people you believe have done you wrong. And what do you get out of it?"

Don't listen to him, Cal. He doesn't belong here. This man doesn't know you. I know you. Travis knows you. But this man only wants to hurt you like all the rest. He's pinned you as a fool. Don't play into it, Cal. Be a man.

Stunned, Ben quickly looked about as he heard the voice that spoke to Calvin, the red voice. It was a demon, posing as Travis, as his mom, his dad, drunk and disappointed. It had become all of them. All those who mattered most to him, whom he felt he had disappointed; it had used them all to persuade Calvin this whole time. This boy had been harassed by his peers and family but primarily by his own demon. It was clear that breaking his link with Travis would be difficult at best. Ben had no upper hand on the armed boy. However, demons were his forte. They fed off the anger and despair of their victims—strong when their hosts were weak and weak when their hosts were strong.

"He's wrong, Calvin," Ben started his work, finding the slits in this boy's wall to grab hold of and climb. Calvin looked confused. "The voice inside you is wrong."

"How do you—"

"I can hear it too. I've been hearing it for some time now. But that … thing doesn't know you either. Nor does it care to. It's a parasite who only wants power over you and to turn you into a monster. That, or it would have you die."

Travis's head flung between the two, back and forth. "What the hell is he talking about, Cal?"

Ben reached out his hand. "I can show you what he doesn't want you to see. All your potential, all your future is right here in my hand."

"Guy, you're friggin' out of your mind," Travis said as he refocused the gun to Ben's head. "I think it's time you say good night."

"No, wait," Calvin said. He placed his bandaged hand on Travis's shoulder and pulled him away. "I want to see."

Ben stretched out a hand slightly farther. Calvin knelt and laid the gun on the floor. He stood, took a few heavy steps, and took the stranger's hand, shivering, feeling the abrupt pull of Ben reeling him into a full embrace.

The voice wailed in bellowing anguish as it became snared in a vortex of exchanges. Strands of hope, mercy, and purpose tethered around its cruel form as it was pulled from the dark hollows of his brain, pleading with Calvin. It tried to barter with him, spiraling, sucking, and then being dragged out of his head as the nooks left empty were filled with the irresistible peace of his worth. More than the nickels and dimes of what value others had appraised him for. More than that dark voice, his classmates or his parents, his friend. More than he had put on himself.

With that last howling plea of the voice came the toppling of his malice for the past. The monarch that once ruled all his ideas, emotions, and actions had been dethroned. Its harrowing presence had been cast into the same exile where it had bound Calvin's true self. Never again would it rule over his life. He wouldn't feel the iron fist of its shaming, the burdening of its tax of his inadequacy. He was his own self, a new self, and whatever he had left of the past became just that—his past. Not forgotten but forgiven and let go.

Ben felt the first shot puncture his gut. Smoldering metal tore through his flesh and muscle, forcing the air out of him with a ferocious blow. The second one hit his right shoulder and came with an explosion of bones that made it feel like every nerve that ran down his arm was on fire. Another one struck. And another one. He tried to keep awake. Tried to fight back the need to go dark. After all, he had taken a bullet before in an exchange and was able to keep out of the darkness. But this wasn't one bullet. This was six—no, seven. Each one, he felt, gunning for his chest, looking for that kill shot that would still make a kid presentable in an open casket. Metal filled his body, leaving no room for him to draw a breath. He affirmed his grip on Calvin, coughing and spitting blood, and braced his eyes open. Ben was determined. He was going to get through this. They both were.

Calvin's heart grew aflutter. His arms trembled, unrestrained, as the rest continued to funnel into Ben. A firework display of suppressed emotions and foreseen visions burst open with spectacular clarity. He felt that one thing he had been searching for his entire life. All the fishing trips, ball games, movies, backpacking, and late nights of endless gaggles in front of the television screen. Everything with his father began to play out in his head. He felt it when, in a transition, the girl popped up. She was beautifully dressed in an emerald gown, a tiara, and a corsage. Every part of her was perfect. Her hair was pinned to look like a rose blossoming from the back of her head, and she looked up at him with an endless smile. He could feel the sway of her body as her arms draped over his shoulders.

One vision flowed after another before everything was exchanged, and Calvin was left feeling only relief and happiness. Ben let go and toppled to the floor. He was down but lucid as he took a moment to digest the exchange. Calvin slumped to the floor and tucked his head between his knees, crying and smiling simultaneously.

Travis stood back, trying to assess what had just happened before him. The display perplexed Travis to the point that he hadn't picked up on the faint sounds of sirens that could be heard screaming from around the block, closing in with every howling loop. He watched as Ben delicately took to his feet, gun held on him, shaking.

Ben rose to the point of slouched over. His fingers dug into his knees as blood continued to spit from his mouth. His face was the tone of death as his spine arched toward the sky, fluctuating in small, urgent palpitations. He cast his sight up to Travis, staring down the barrel of his unstable gun and reached out his hand.

"Take it, Travis," Calvin said. He was now looking at Travis with a solid, earnest expression. "It's what he's here for."

Travis backstepped away from them both. He refocused his aim, poised it for the barrel to spit clean at the side of Ben's head, jittered in panic. "What the hell did he do to you?" he asked Calvin.

"He helped me," Calvin replied. "Trust me, Travis. Just take his hand."

Travis shook his head. "No. No way. No friggin' way, man." He thrust the gun at Ben, both hands on the handle, one fidgety finger over the trigger. "He did some sort of hypnotist crap on you. Your eyes were white, man. I mean really white. For heaven's sake, you looked like you were being abducted by aliens."

The sirens grew louder, and Ben could hear the door beside him opening. Principal Holder hadn't moved from the space at the edge of the building.

"I'm fine, Travis. No, I'm good, totally good."

"You're not fine, and you're not good. This guy is toying with your brain. He's trying to make you think you're okay, so you give up, turn a coward, surrender. He's probably one of those cops that make you feel warm and cozy so they can persuade you to confess to a crime you never committed." He stepped closer to Ben to put the tip of the barrel right next to his temple. "Are you a cop, man? Are you a stinkin' cop?"

Travis flung the gun in a rage, hitting Ben with the edge of the handle directly at the side of the head. The blow was sudden and sharp, sending Ben to the ground.

"Sweet Lord, Travis, the guy ain't a cop!" Calvin said. "You need to put the gun down and listen to me."

"I can't do that. You're my friend, and I am going to take care of you whether you think you need me to or not," Travis replied. "This guy is dangerous. He's not right, and people who aren't right can't be trusted."

Calvin pleaded, "Travis, please don't do this, if not for your own sake, then for mine. I see what he sees. He's right. This will not turn out how we hoped it would at all."

Squad cars screeched to a halt outside the school. Jackpot lights flashed red and blue. Units of cops surrounded the building. "Drop the gun!" Travis didn't know where the demand came from but wasn't ready to cave. He looked glassy-eyed and soullessly down at Ben.

"It's already begun," Travis announced. "We have to see this through."

Calvin protested, "Nothing has begun. No one has been hurt. We haven't killed anybody."

"You haven't," Travis replied, cold.

"What do you mean? Travis? Who have you killed?"

Travis kept his arresting glare on Ben. "It was a long time coming, Cal. She deserved it; you know she did. Always screaming and cursing. She'd hit me. Did you know that? And I'm not talking 'bout that spanking kind of hit either. I'm talking about fists in the gut, hammer in the back, plate throwing, skin breaking kind of shit."

"Travis, I … I'm—"

"Don't say you're sorry, Cal. No one is sorry for what she's done. Especially her." Travis wiped a single tear away and then gave out a clucked laugh, though he was hardly elated. "You know she still wouldn't apologize even after I shot her in the leg. She just cursed and cursed. She still called me worthless. I don't know." He lowered the gun for a moment. "Maybe I am? Maybe I was that one mistake God made."

"You're not a mistake," Ben huffed out.

"Shut up, you," Travis said and punted a sharp kick to Ben's stomach. "I wasn't talking to you. I was talking with my friend." As Ben fell back over, Travis straightened out his arm and held the gun just so.

"Please," Calvin said once more. "Don't do this."

"I must. It is all I have left in me."

"It's not. We can get through this. No one else needs to die. Come on, Travis, just put the gun down."

"I'm sorry, Cal …"

Blat!

"Shots fired! We have shots fired!"

EIGHTEEN

"Cal? … Calvin?"

Calvin was deaf to the world. His body shivered, arms tightly retracted to his chest, fingers contorted to the shapes of naked tree branches. He had tumbled down in front of Ben, his gut spewing out blood at every thin, gaping breath. His eyes were marbles, wide and already becoming dull of life. His flesh drained of color as blood spurt from under his shirt, pooling around him, taking his tone back to a canvas of white. He looked at the friend who shot him with a pleading glare, curled up in a bed of expanding blood, unable to say a word as each breath grew thinner … and slower … and …

Travis dropped the gun. He collapsed to his knees, his pants soaking up the blood he had stolen from his friend. His eyes were a blur of swelling tears, burning, blistering red as he dropped farther and dug his nose deep into the cold cheek of his friend. Travis's back expanded in short draws of putrid air, exhaling a long, shattered breath. "Calvin, I'm so sorry. Please don't die. Please don't die."

Lips thin and bloody, a single word found its way out of Calvin's mouth. "Mommy?"

Travis wept as a single tear trailed his friend's lifeless face, watching saliva and blood drool out of the corner of his mouth. Calvin's muscles began to relax. His chest sunk and didn't come back up. His head rolled to the side, eyes hollow and black as night.

The gate burst open. A fleet of cops rushed in, three yanking Travis away from his friend and cuffing him on the ground while the rest tended to Calvin and Ben. They immediately began securing the scene. One officer after another pounded on the classroom doors, gaining entrance and checking room after room to ensure everyone was safe. Principal Holder had made her way to the location as well. She walked speedily with one of the cops escorting her, giving her a statement. Her sight remained glued to the tragedy in her hallway.

Travis continued to plead his remorse, his mistake. He begged them to let him die instead as they pulled him to his feet and pressed him against the wall. One officer came in with a tarp and laid it over Calvin's body to sheath the gruesome sight from innocent eyes. One officer helped Ben to his feet, asking questions that went into his ears, only to muffle and blur and never be returned with a response.

Ben slid down a wall and took a seat at the base of one of the classrooms. He stared at the puffed-up tarp with one large blotch of red staining the middle section as officers moved in and out of the school. Medics arrived to examine the body. Multiple figures asked Ben if he was okay. Classroom by classroom had been evacuated in fire drill fashion. The students were told to shield their eyes. Most did; a few curious ones did not and regretted it.

Another two units showed up and went to work helping with the crime scene. One stopped at the entrance of the gate and hollered at Travis. The officer knelt by Travis and repeated his name. Travis refused to look in the officer's eyes as he kept chanting the same phrases, "I'm sorry. I didn't mean to. Please, just kill me. Let me die instead," displaying a whole other pedigree of despair.

Ben watched as the officer turned and shot his sight toward the body covered in a now primarily red tarp. His eyes were already pink, verging on red and building up moisture without restraint. Another officer came over to him, head sunk into his chest, and offered his condolences with an extended, rolling pat on the back.

Ben drew out his phone.

After several minutes, the officer stood and crept tearfully toward the body as another two lifted Travis off the ground and ushered him into the back of a squad car. The other officers and medics also took leave, giving a father his time to mourn in peace. Principal Holder kept an eye at a distance. Ben remained seated against the wall as he returned his phone to his pocket.

The officer knelt and pulled back the sticky tarp from his son's face. His heart palpitated violently. His face turned crimson in the shade of lament. His eyes drowned in a pool of saline and regret, seeing his son, all the things he could have been, all the things they could have done, gone in a thieving moment. His face bowed into his son's neck as he wept and tried to catch the fragrance of his boy one last time. All he could smell was his blood.

"He's not gone," Ben rasped. Officer Gardner's head jarred up, facing Ben, unaware that somebody was watching a broken man mourn for his son. Sympathy had ridden Ben's face. "Not completely anyway. Most of him is still in there." Ben's eyes pointed to the body. "I can bring him back to you, sir—if you'll let me. There's still time."

The officer struggled to speak. "I-I don't understand. The medics said there was no heartbeat. He had lost too much blood."

Ben looked at the officer, half-dazed. "A life is more than a heartbeat and blood," he replied. "There is a soul and a will, and both remain intact. I can feel them. They're still in there. Please, sir. Your son trusted me to help him, and I did. Do you think you could trust me as well?"

The officer looked down at his son, his heart breaking over and again at the sight of his boy, helpless and still. He then looked back at Ben. "What do you need me to do?" he asked.

Ben got to his feet. "Get rid of the tarp and his shirt," he instructed, and Ben began to remove his own shirt.

The officer pulled out his tactical knife, sawed his son's shirt in two, from the neck down to Calvin's waist, and flapped open the shirt like small, bloodied curtains. The wound was dark, just above the rib under his left breast. Some blood had already started to dry in color, starkly contrasting the pale death of his skin.

"Can you lay his hands at his side?" Ben asked. Officer Gardner responded.

Principal Holder looked on with great interest and suspense. She couldn't hear a word and was too far away to read lips. All she could tell was that Ben was directing the officer on what to do as if he were a doctor of sorts; to her, it was evident he was no such thing.

"Okay," Ben continued, "this part is going to get a bit tricky, but I need you to see if the bullet is still in there."

"I don't have the equipment for that on me."

"I know. You are going to have to use your fingers and feel around."

"But that might cause irreparable damage, puncture a lung or screw up something else. I don't think I can do that."

Ben promised, "There is nothing you can damage or screw up that I can't fix, but we need to make sure there is no bullet in there before I do that."

Officer Gardner wedged two of his fingers in the wound like a fleshy set of pliers. The swishing sound of Calvin's insides smacked and bubbled and gassed. "Wait," the officer said and then paused. "I got it." Slowly he pulled his fingers out, holding a small copper pebble in his stained fingers.

Ben said, "Now stand back and pray."

Ben took a stance over the body, feet to feet, like a shadow that had seen better days, and gradually made his way over Calvin's body. He rested across the boy in mimicking fashion, gripping around him and pulling him near until flesh pressed against flesh. He then tied his arms across Calvin's back body and locked his hands in a twisted fashion. Ben rolled over, putting Calvin on top and hiding his own figure, then breathed over Calvin's face.

Steam began to arise from Calvin's back as it swelled and settled. His flesh gradually turned gold and lit up like the beginning of a sunset. An undecipherable low, grinding moan soon dwindled in the air.

Calvin's back swelled and settled to Ben's heartbeat, *thump-thump … thump-thump …*

Lifeless fingers began to fidget. Cold toes started to warm and curl. Thicker steam broke out like a fog and rolled over them as Calvin's body went from gold to peach.

Calvin's back swelled and settled.

One of Calvin's hands reached out and posted firmly on the ground. His back swelled and settled. The other arm came up, stretching a splayed array of fingers in the air like a creature from a fogged lagoon, then settled out firmly on the ground and moaned with his own voice.

Calvin's back swelled and settled. He could feel Ben's heart knocking against his chest like a jump charge of transferred electricity, *thump-thump ... thump ... thump ...* His fingers, toes, and everything in between quivered statically, washed in a current of electric revival. His shoulders rotated once and then again before pushing his chest up and out. He raised his head and threw it back to let his face meet the sky. Life sucked deep into his lungs. His eyes became brilliantly mutable with every sort of color before settling back into his typical baby blues.

Calvin looked poised to howl. Instead, he opened his jaw and cried in the open air, "Dad!"

As Ben rolled over to the ground, Officer Gardner collapsed and embraced his son, weeping in delight. He flooded his son's face with kisses, pulling him off Ben and into his own chest.

Principal Holder stared in wide-eyed disbelief.

Officers and medics began spilling back in after hearing the cry of Calvin, none less in a state of shock than the rest. They studied Calvin and checked him out as best they could under the strenuous hold of his father.

Ben remained on the ground. His eyes were open, cast obscurely to the side, swimming in a black haze and lackluster of what once was a sweet shade of brown. He heard his heart, *thump ... thump ... thump ... thump ...* And then nothing. Inside, there was no reserved breath for him to hold onto, no thrum of a heartbeat, no warm flow within his veins. Outside, there was only a pasty, cold shell of skin dressed in a lethal red stain just below his chest, where Calvin's wound had once been. A black oily substance dripped from his nose, mouth, and eyes, pooling into a placid sheet of dark liquid glass that reflected his lifeless face. There was no motion, no means to return. It was all calmness. It was all peace.

* * *

The sun smacked the afternoon brighter that day and more than all the days that year had brought. It was almost as if God himself had used the sun to show his face to the world. Out over the rippling knolls, dressed in shades of green, stones were scattered that had, for centuries, carried the names, dates, and passages of loved ones. Some were adorned with flowers. Some had the belongings that held significance only to those who placed them there and those who were now forever resting. Yet others showed to be considered by no one except the groundkeepers.

Over the knolls, casting shade over stone benches and eloquently sculpted birdbaths, they all stood, dressed in white as Ben requested. The sparrows chirped their vivaciously complex song for those who mourned and those who slumbered. Willow trees hung their branches low to the ground. They dripped their sorrowful limbs, reaching down toward the soil, where those who would never leave resided.

It was on top of one of these knolls on this warm summer day that they all came to bid farewell to Benjamin Weaver. Those who had known him best. Those whose lives he had forever changed. Some came to simply pay their respects to a great man—a great friend. Others came to say a final thank you to the one who showed them the value of life, even when it felt most valueless. The Nelsons were all there dressed in white, as requested by Ben in his own spare-of-the-moment way. Jeremy had also made the trip with Danica, dressed in matching linen and solemn grief. Dr. Dupree had also heard the news, watching a somber reporter interview Principal Holder and several other witnesses of the tragedy on a television screen. Each one omitted only what they could never have explained, what happened in that open hall of the school. She knew though. They all knew.

Calvin and his father had made it as well, possibly grieving more than any others who had attended. They were the only two there who would never have the chance to thank him, to show what his sacrific had done for them. To them, Ben had not only spared a son's life b had also given a second chance to a father who had long neglecte relationship with his son. It made Ben's swan song that of one he never realize he had made.

In the end, it wasn't the magic or the miracles or whatever might call it. It was that basic human desire to care for and one care. Enough care to take a piece of darkness that wo troubled soul and exchange it for a little speck of light tha burn in one's heart and spread like a forest fire. That was Ben's true gift. He cared. If only for one man or woman, one girl or one boy, he cared enough to sacrifice his life and had done just that.

As they looked down on the polished box where their friend now slept, each holding onto that speck of light he had given them, the pastor spoke a heart-grieving sermon. He waxed eloquence over the hard truth of loss and the reassurance that one glorious day they would see him again in the peaceful house of the Lord. They stood side by side, hand in hand, taking little comfort in the pastor's words of the promise for this reaped soul. What he had gained from leaving this world behind had left a faded candle for those still living.

Benjamin Weaver was laid to rest between his father, Charles Weaver, and his mother, Tiffany Weaver. It was where he had always wanted to be. It was where he deserved to be, as he had dreamed of most of his life. And if not possible in life, then most certainly in death. If there was to be any content, it would be from knowing that he would forever slumber beside the parents he had loved and who had loved him in return.

One after another departed from the knoll, down to their families and lives. In the end, it was Mrs. Nelson who stayed. She sat on that stone bench alone. Over the stone, a necklace tapped at the cool gray tone. It had been made by a child, forged from three nails and spun her to form a cross. It was old and worn, rusted at the edges, stained d and grabbled to the point of frail by the hands of this child rs. But it was everything to him. To that boy, it was once Now it was Ben's.

tched the necklace teeter and sway by the rolling nlight as she reread those words that were mbstone. They were words she never got to hear them. What he did, he did she would read these words to n she loved him, telling him own the gravel path to her car something to her, as they had for own Benjamin Weaver:

Here lies
Benjamin Eugene Weaver,
a man who would
exchange your death for life;
barter your misery for pleasure;
trade your despair for hope.
Take your rest now in the presence of our Lord,
knowing you have done your job well,
our beloved suicide merchant.

CPSIA information can be obtained
at www.ICGtesting.com
Printed in the USA
BVHW071210210223
658921BV00001B/49